WHATEVER GODS MAY BE

by

Sophia Kell Hagin

2010

WHATEVER GODS MAY BE

ISBN 10: 1-60282-183-6
ISBN 13: 978-1-60282-183-5

This Trade Paperback Original Is Published By
Bold Strokes Books, Inc.
P.O. Box 249
Valley Falls, NY 12185

First Edition: October 2010

CREDITS
EDITORS: CINDY CRESAP AND STACIA SEAMAN
PRODUCTION DESIGN: STACIA SEAMAN
COVER DESIGN BY SHERI (GRAPHICARTIST2020@HOTMAIL.COM)

Acknowledgments

I want to thank Susan first, last, and always. You are my life. All my words, now and forever, are for you.

I also want to thank…

Bianca Cody Murphy, professor extraordinaire, for her encouragement and for persuading me to show my writing to strangers,

The ladies at the Lesbian Fiction Forum (www.lesbianfiction.org)—especially Baker, FranW, DeJay, Mindancer, BobiR, Proofrdr, and Alex D'Brassis—for their frank, incisive, but ever gentle writing advice,

Cindy Cresap, my editor, for showing me how to do it better,

Sheri, for developing such an excellent cover design, and

Len Barot, for deciding to publish this story—and for her vision, strength, and tenacity.

Dedication

For Susan

The Divine Ms. M
who has shown me what love is

The chief part of human happiness arises from the consciousness of being beloved.

—Adam Smith
The Theory of Moral Sentiments
1759

Chapter One

I cannot go back there

S wamp's got gators, y'know."

She didn't. Joe had never mentioned alligators. To her left, faraway small-town lights glinted off the vast expanse of black water, tempting her gaze away from the seatback in front of her. She'd heard about the swamp. A salt marsh, actually, now succumbing so fast to the Broad River tidal channel and Port Royal Sound that a few more storms would take what little was left of the island at the end of the causeway.

But alligators? *Sure as shit I woulda remembered about alligators.*

Flicking her eyes rightward, only her eyes, she glanced at the thick, blond, baby-faced boy-man next to her in the aisle seat who knew about the alligators. She noticed his nose first, how it heralded the fight that once broke it. His hands gripped his thighs and he stared straight ahead, still as a statue. Like he never whispered anything at all.

Somewhere on the bus in the seats behind them sat another blonde. Proud by the look of her. Strong. The only other woman on the bus, picked up at a stop in southern Virginia. Jamie had watched the woman come down the aisle, watched those dark eyes probe, assess, and then lock on to hers.

For just a second, her clit punched a double flip that reverberated into her belly. Maybe the woman would sit next to her and, once the drone of the bus engine resumed, murmur a name or a comment. Maybe they'd end up in line together, maybe go through the whole thing together.

But it was the boy-man who had taken the seat next to her, and the woman walked on.

Boy-man blinked. They had only seconds left now.

"I'm Arnoldt," he whispered.

"Gwynmorgan," she whispered. "Jamie Gwynmorgan."

Whereupon what remained of Parris Island pummeled them.

She couldn't quite believe her eyes or her ears as she hurried to disembark. Backlit by assaultive klieglights, a small herd of mostly men wearing Smokey the Bear hats and combat utilities charged toward the bus screeching pseudo obscenities at the people ahead of her. Drill instructors in full rut.

Oh christ. Her stomach spasmed at the sight of so many DIs. *This is what he meant.*

Joe had warned her. Now his warning reverberated in hyper fast-forward. The rules of normal behavior will be suspended, he said. Everything she was accustomed to would be ripped from her by the DIs.

"Ripped" was the word Joe had used more than once.

"Ripped" didn't scare her then.

"Ripped" sounded okay then because, hell, she needed to be ripped from the way she'd lived since Alby left. And Joe had gotten her ready, right?

"Move your ass, maggot!" one of the DIs roared at the guy who'd been sitting across the aisle from Arnoldt. Now just ahead of her in the bus doorway, the guy winced but didn't scamper, which provoked the DI to loom into his face, millimeters from his nose.

"You *deaf*, puke?" the DI shrieked.

"No, sir," Puke answered, his voice too quiet, like he dared consider himself a normal human being. Still wincing, he started to run. But too late. Way too late. The DI stayed with him, nose to nose, toe to toe.

"Wha-*at*? You talking to me, puke?"

Puke hesitated, afraid to speak, afraid to move.

"Did I tell you to *halt* your ugly butt, puke?"

Hey! Behind Puke, forehead suddenly humid with revolt, Jamie jumped off the bus. *Just wait one fucking minute! I didn't sign up for this!* All of Joe's fearsome tales notwithstanding, these guys in their perfect uniforms and arcane hats weren't at all what she expected. Her stomach wrenched its warning and she slit her eyes to see beyond the onslaught, to find its limit. *Thirteen weeks, that's all.*

She counted in her head as if a refuge could be made of counting. *Thirteen weeks—less than a quarter of the fifty-seven weeks since... Thirteen divided by fifty-seven...that's twenty-two point eight percent...*

Off to her left, another DI approached, his animal eyes glued to her.

Oh shit. An intense band of heat tightened around her head. *Just gotta make it to January twenty-eighth...*

She tried to ignore the *No!* rising from her gut and got ready to blindly obey. In her last second as a regular person, Jamie wondered why, why she didn't feel this *No!* before now and understood her doom. It couldn't be undone. She had signed her name on the papers, given up all rights to *No!* Now *No!* meant disobeying a lawful order. Insubordination. Now *No!* could be court-martialed and land her in a Marine Corps lockup.

"You eyeballing me, asswipe?"

"Sir-No-*Sir*!" This she shouted, just the way Joe taught her. Never look them in the eye, Joe had said more than once. She took a couple of steps, preparing to run. Certainly he wanted her to run.

"Who told you to move, suckface?"

"Sir!" She halted, riveted her eyes straight ahead, tried to remember what Joe had told her about assuming the position of attention. "I'm sorry, sir!"

Oh shit. Just one tiny word. How she wished she could grab it out of the air and squish it out of existence. *Shit shit shit shit shit...*

"I?" the DI bellowed, eyes bulging outrage off to her left. "You are a worthless buttbrain attempting to become a *United States Marine*! How *dare* you speak the word 'I'! You are less than human. You are less than maggot. You will get on your face and give me your pathetic excuse for pushups. *Right* now, *Recruit Suckface!*"

Jamie dropped like a stone and pumped as fast as she ever had in her life while he screamed at somebody else. When she was at twenty or so, she felt his hot breath on her face. Onion breath. The brim of his hat bumped against her temple.

"What're you doing down here, suckface? *Get! Up!*"

Bawling sir-yes-sir, she leapt to her feet and attempted to obey the DI's staccato of contradictory commands. Left suckface. Right suckface. About suckface. She messed up all of it. An eternity passed before she was ordered to join the other dazed recruits, each of them anchored to a pair of yellow footprints painted on the blacktop, all of them desperate not to be noticed.

"You are to stand at *attention* when you stand on my yellow footprints, fool!" The blare came from right behind her. "Shoulders back! Tuck that jiggly excuse for a chin!"

Twenty minutes ago, Jamie would never have believed anyone except a prison screw could legally behave this way. *Jailhouse rule number seven: Never attract a screw's attention.* She stopped breathing and zombied in on the tree trunk–sized neck of the man in front of her; the DI passed her by with merely a snarl. She dared a surreptitious inhalation—god knew what one of these monsters might do if they caught her in the act of consuming oxygen without permission.

Guess Joe left a few things out.

"Gonna be really tough, Jamie Blue Eyes," Joe had said when she boarded the recruiter's van back in Hyannis.

He'd never called her that, never once gave a hint that he'd done anything so gushy as register the color of her eyes. She had tried not to show her surprise, her discomfort, and forced herself to gaze back at him.

"But the training's a lot more righteous now than it used to be," he continued a little too quickly. His words, his tone had apology in them while his eyes drifted past her and he repeated the warning she'd heard so often, the warning that sounded so jarringly different this last time he'd have a chance to say it. "Better by the time I was a DI. They're not kind or anything, but…" He stopped to study his boots, his face in an almost-frown. No doubt about it—Joe never expected her to actually enlist. He was upset. Maybe even disappointed.

She almost asked him then, confronted him: *Why'd you help me?* He was just a guy from her part-time job, after all. This older guy who used stories from his days as a Marine Corps DI to get a smile out of her, to get her to talk some while they loaded packages onto trucks.

It had taken a lot of Joe's time, all that help. Before they ever worked out together, she told him about Alby, about getting arrested, and he convinced her not to do a runner, reminded her that if she kept her head down until October twelfth and showed up in court, the judge would expunge her record and then she could join up. "You're fucking smart," Joe had said. "The GED'll be a snap for you."

She'd scowled, of course, and early on she'd had her suspicions. Hell, nobody ever cared if she talked, except that high school librarian who left after her sophomore year. But she'd run out of options and Joe always behaved while he showed her all that Marine Corps stuff. He'd been a straight shooter the whole way, and if there'd been more to his motives, he never let on. Not once in six months.

She figured he needed the good-bye to be done with, needed time to settle back into thinking of her as a friend, just a friend. So, reaching out to brush his forearm, she said only, "Yeah, more righteous now."

She watched Joe nod, watched his eyes tense with what she didn't want to believe was regret. "You'll be the one I call when I get there, Joe." She offered him an it'll-be-okay smile.

It seemed to her that his face smiled back. A reluctant smile, almost involuntary. She hoped he understood what she didn't say aloud: *I cannot stay here.*

That was twenty-one hours and almost eleven hundred miles ago. Now, resisting an urge to flinch beneath the corrosive, caterwauling belligerence of the drill instructors, Jamie Gwynmorgan stood at attention on a pair of yellow footprints and reminded herself—*I cannot go back there.*

The memories fluttered before her, an inescapable gossamer over everything, each flutter carrying a different imprint to stamp on the moment. Meaty hands squeezed her throat, slammed fisted into her head. She yanked her mind away, but with another flutter, handcuffs compressed her wrists, sparked an inferno low in her gut, made her want to squirm and scream against the unyielding restraint.

I cannot go back there.

Jamie double-timed up the steps to the Recruit Receiving Center, chased by apparitional recollections spawned of the smell of ocean air, crisp now in South Carolina's November as it mingled in her mind with odors of charred grass and gasoline. They said her mother crashed the car, and the smell of ocean made her wonder again: Did Alby die there? Or had it really been the mother of all her mother's many pharma-induced debacles? Was Alby still out there somewhere, still lost in a fog fifty-seven weeks later?

Joining a crotch-to-butt line of recruits, Jamie shook off the haunts and waited for her turn to call "home." As fast as she'd be able, she'd recite the words she was supposed to, the minimal script informing Joe that she'd made it to—

To the jaws of hell on Planet Mindfuck, that's where. Just thirty seconds to tell him. *Tell him what? That Woody here cuddled up to my backside needs some saltpeter and a shower? That I'm shit-scared?*

Marine Corps landlink in hand, Jamie zoomed through the phrases on a placard tacked to the wall in front of her. "This-is-Recruit-Gwynmorgan-I've-arrived-safely-at-Parris-Island-in-a-few-days-I'll-textmail-you-thank-you-for-your-support."

She risked a furtive glance around. No DIs within fifteen feet, none of them looking her way. "Jeez, Joe," she whispered, "you didn't tell me they're all infected with frigging rabies. And hey, what the hell does 'fug' mean?"

Joe chuckled. *Yeah, good, he sounds okay.* And she heard his "Ooh-rah!" before a DI materialized next to her. She squirted out the approved "G'bye-for-now" just as the DI ripped the landlink from her hand and passed it along to Woody.

❖

Processing, they called it.

Examinations, questions, tests, more questions. "Have you ever been treated for an RNA virus?" "Were you or any members of your family quarantined during the pandemic?" "Have you ever resided in a nation other than the United States?"

Hours of being poked, pumped, berated, and quick-marched jumbled until Jamie found herself in a wide, glass-walled hallway.

An arm's length between her and anyone else—proper marching distance—provided some relief, since Woody stood behind her still. The line of recruits executed a ragged left-face, and for a moment before being ordered about-face, she saw through the glass a lanky, bald stranger wearing a combat utility uniform. Familiar eyes gazed back at her. She risked DI wrath and hiked one eyebrow. The bald stranger's own dark slash of an eyebrow anticipated her and moved, too. *Yep, it's a reflection. That's me!*

With the three inches of rowdy brown curls shaved away, her

forehead seemed enormous, her cheekbones seemed bolder, her jaw squarer. During last night's quickie medical exam, she measured seventy-three inches tall, a whole inch taller than fifty-seven weeks ago.

She'd been awake for more than twenty-four hours and had at least another twelve to go before she'd be allowed to sleep. But she stood a little straighter in her very own cammies, thinking she kind of looked like a marine.

The illusion didn't last long.

Although she passed the Initial Strength Test with ease, the cred she hoped this would give her backfired. How much it backfired became clear once she and sixty-four men were formed into Platoon 2128, Echo Company, Second Recruit Training Battalion, and ownership of them passed to the senior DI and his two assistants, the J hat and the kill hat.

Joe had called the DIs' technique good-cop, bad-cop, worse-cop, and at the time Jamie shrugged. *That's twenty-something recruits per DI. How nasty can it be?* But three days in, she already thought of the arrangement as dangerous-screw, demented-screw, diabolical-screw.

"Hey, Plah-*too*-oon! Looky, looky. We got us here a *special* sistah," the kill hat sneered an hour after first laying eyes upon her. "Tested better than half you shrinking dongs. C'mon, sistah, slide your sistah ass over here on my quarterdeck and show me how special you are."

Thus she devoted the evening's precious hour of free time to lunges, pushups, side-straddle hops, double-time running in place, more pushups. But never fast enough. Never with acceptable form. The kill hat gleefully declared Recruit Gwynmorgan a maggot sistah.

Every day after that, at least twice a day, the kill hat fried her. For Jamie, the recruits' daily hour of free time was theoretical only. And nearly every night, her name ended up on the firewatch list, ensuring she wouldn't sleep more than three hours at a time, nor more than five hours a night.

It didn't take long for Recruit Gwynmorgan to despise the DIs, especially the kill hat. Nor did it take long for her to notice that the only Echo Company platoon with but one female in it was hers. She'd hoped the dark-eyed blonde would show up in Platoon 2128, but the woman had disappeared among the hundreds of other bald would-be grunts, and none of the sixty-four guys around her inspired anything like a double flip.

She couldn't help but wonder if some higher power—a god, a sergeant, a perverse computer program—had done this on purpose.

A parade of rules maintained discipline in the co-ed squadbays and dictated with excruciating precision who could be where and when. No matter. Every morning in Platoon 2128's squadbay, sixty-four erect guys in their skivvies found ways to ape the roles their gravity-defying members would play in the care and feeding of a certain recruit's under-utilized female body parts.

"That's it? That's all you got?" Jamie scoffed back in those rare moments when the DIs weren't crawling all over them. "Jeez, look—it's starting to curl now. Like a itty-bitty pretzel."

No one she targeted could prevent himself from checking out the state of his equipment, as did any others within earshot. This diverted them—briefly—from her to each other. Often it even elicited a laugh. But the men around her refused to buddy up. Not even Arnoldt, who was in her squad but acted like he'd never seen her before.

Jamie remained on the far side of a great divide, on her own. Sixty-four to one. She told herself this was what she'd expected all along. She told herself every morning, in the pseudo privacy of the F-head, where she got to shit and shower alone while a bullyragging DI always stood next to the doorway, counting her down.

"Ten...nine...sixfive...four...two..." She learned damn fast to be standing in the doorway at meticulous attention by the time the count reached zero, ready to grab the bar some sadist had put across the top of the F-head door frame and pop off pullups until her arms and back melted.

Thus began each training day. Every other day brought a new mindfuck. Like with the sandpits, those soggy, flea-infested hells just outside the barracks where bouts of physical training weren't supposed to exceed five minutes. The DIs simply ordered recruits to scramble from one sandpit to the other twenty feet away for another five minutes of "incentivization."

Not even the kill hat's relentless demand for more pullups faster, faster galvanized Jamie's *No!* quite like doing pushups in the sandpit.

She, not he, would decide when her body hurt too much and when she stopped.

"Sir," she'd croak. "Can't." And she'd halt just shy of the unequivocal exhaustion the DIs demanded, flattening onto her belly. *I am not a convict. I am not a slave. That's all you get!*

Jamie tried to remember what she'd said to that damn recruiter back in Hyannis, because a couple of weeks in the platoon—during which she'd had maybe, just maybe three hours of free time and not one single night of uninterrupted sleep—had convinced her the DIs and the recruiters must be in cahoots.

She recalled telling the recruiter about how her buddy Josh would sneak off with one of his cop father's guns and they'd go shoot up the dunes in Bodfish Park, about how she always did better than Josh, who was older than her, bigger than her, who called her Fucking Annie Fucking Oakley. She had hoped it would help her get in, even though the Barnstable County Wheels of Justice had almost made roadkill of her, even though she had only a GED, even though she'd be enlisting just a day after turning seventeen.

Those conversations, all informal and friendly, had gone fuzzy in the sandpit, in the squadbay. Of course she'd mentioned being asked by the coach to join the high school gymnastics team all the way back in sixth grade. And she must have bragged about that iron cross on the rings, about being the only girl so far at Barnstable High School to do it.

Never attract a screw's attention. But she'd done twenty-six pullups during the Initial Strength Test—about twenty too many.

That had to be it. Plus maybe she wasn't so good at hiding the how-fucking-dare-you that burned through her chest whenever a DI voice called her maggot or fugger.

So, okay, she'd attracted the screws' attention. But she wasn't the only one. The guides, the squad leaders and scribes and other "special recruits" all got smoked plenty.

So, okay, it wasn't entirely personal either. She grasped, at least in principle, the idea that the whole squad or even the whole platoon would be pounded for the fuckup of just one person. It was supposed to encourage teamwork.

But Jamie didn't trust teams. Not the kind where your performance, your survival, depended on other people. Because other people couldn't be depended on. Certainly the guys in her squad couldn't be depended on.

Not even three weeks into training, and somebody had mucked up her weapon so it didn't pass inspection, swiped her boonie hat so she wasn't in proper uniform when it mattered to be in proper uniform. Both times the whole squad got slammed and she got the blame. *If this is frigging teamwork, give me alone every time.*

The DIs, however, were merciless—like sharks who smelled the possibility of blood in the water. Her blood.

Jamie came to Parris Island already too lean, too stressed to menstruate. She never even bothered with an ovu-suppress patch. Yet the DIs had other ways to make her bleed. Although even mild derogations like "pussy" and "bitch" had been banished from DI-speak, "bleed" remained acceptable, and it became the kill hat's favorite word.

"How come you're letting your squad bleed like this, Gwynmorgan? Whatsamatter, you got cramps? Need a lie-down, sistah?"

"Sir-No-*Sir*!"

"Squad, on your foul faces and gimme another bleeding thirty. 'Cept you, sistah. Recruit Gwynmorgan will rest her delicate little heinie right over here next to me and keep count for her squad. Sound off, sistah!"

CHAPTER TWO

NO HOLDS BARRED

N ow?"
The whisper was so soft Jamie almost didn't hear it. She could only guess at the time. Maybe 0100 hours, maybe later.

"Yeah." Sheet and blanket rustled. A nearby bunk creaked. "Let's go."

On her back in a bottom bunk, Jamie slivered an eye open just enough to see one of the guys in her squad get out of his rack and glance over at her. Then another squaddie got up. And another. And another. Arnoldt got up last.

Somehow Jamie just knew. They had decided to throw a blanket party.

Her blanket party, which likely explained the just-your-imagination sidelong glances coming her way for days.

Ha! Just your imagination.

Alby used to tell her that. But it had never been just her imagination. Oh no, it was a quite distinct phenomenon, and it always began with a peculiar, unnerving chill that skittered up her spine from the small of her back to the base of her neck.

Then something would happen.

That chill needled up Jamie's spine now as she pretended sleep and watched the four men assemble.

Fucking knew it.

Jamie had always been a light sleeper, too easily wakened by innocent sounds, since she couldn't ever be sure: Is it Alby stumbling home stratosphere-high with some creep? Or could one of Alby's degenerate junkie friends be coming around in the wee hours to demand charity?

Early on, her mother plucked her from the bed and hid her in the crawlspace under the cottage. In the beginning, she'd pull herself up and crack open the crawlspace hatch to watch, mutely begging the universe to keep her mother safe. Until the time one of those "friends" beat Alby senseless and she decided she couldn't depend on the universe for safety any more than she could depend on Alby for safety.

That's when she learned: If the timing was right, even a scrawny kid raging unexpectedly out of the shadows at an intruder could take a hit and get up again and again to fight some more. Fight not to win, for in fact she never won, but to survive.

And she survived for just one reason: She had something left after quailing in the dark. Something in reserve that made her tenacious enough that the asshole du jour would leave.

Who the hell's on firewatch? Some recruit should've been nearby, alert, walking the perimeter of the squadbay with a flashlight. Jamie listened, looked through slitted eyelids for the low sweep of light. Nothing. Nobody stomping out of the DI hut, either—even though her bunk was close by, even though the squadbay abounded with surveillance cameras.

Fucking knew it.

Diller, the biggest of the four, had begun to sneak up on her left holding wide the blanket they planned to wrap around her so she wouldn't be able to identify them or fight them off. Elias skulked toward her from the right, and George and Arnoldt approached her feet. Diller and Elias were so close she could smell their sour breath.

She thought she saw erections. Certainly, all four of them exuded their testosterone-fueled conceit. They would beat the crap out of her *and* show the dyke what men are for. She was on her own for this one and they knew it.

Linebacker large, they stifled self-confident sniggers and kept glancing at each other, which was why Jamie dared to hope. Maybe they wouldn't detect her feet inching to the edges of the mattress, positioning themselves just free of the covers. *At least I can try to do a little damage before they swab the deck with me.*

As Jamie scouted for the signal that would launch them, something happened to time. Quite suddenly, everyone, everything except her moved in slow motion.

It had happened before. She'd been maybe nine or ten the first time. But ever since the day that cop ratcheted handcuffs on to her wrists, this skill or gift or whatever it was had abandoned her. Now that it had returned, she couldn't risk trusting it.

Yet she continued to speed up while the rest of the world slowed down. The four men coming for her seemed almost at a standstill, and she had the time she needed to anticipate, to plan, to prepare.

Please, please let me be strong enough.

Before Diller and Elias finished exchanging a nod, Jamie pumped her legs upward and wide apart, arching her body off her elbows to invigorate the reach and force of her kicks.

She had aimed well. The heels of her feet pounded hard into the genitals of the two nearest men. They grunted and folded, gripping themselves as they ricocheted noisily off the neighboring bunks. A low rumble of murmurs rippled through the squadbay.

Jamie vaulted off her rack into the narrow space next to it and hopped over Diller even before he thumped to the deck. Pivoting on her right leg, she plowed her left heel into George's crotch.

Aw-right. One to go. Steeped in an otherworldly calm, she spun into one more long step to face off with Arnoldt. Up on her toes, she was eye to eye with him. He gaped at her, still as a tree stump. The squadbay went abruptly silent.

"Anything I can do for you, Arnoldt?" Jamie stood close enough to kiss him. Even though she kept her voice quiet, it seemed to have a will of its own. She noted how it reverberated, liked its glacial edge.

Arnoldt blinked once, twice, but he didn't seem to be breathing. Then, as if released from a trance, he blinked again, inhaled, and blurted, "Um, uh, no, I-I'm, uh, just, uh, y'know, goin' for an oh-dark-thirty dump."

Yeah. Sure.

Jamie squinted at the blob between his legs. "Whaddaya do in there with that stuff, anyway? Just let your balls hang down in the shitter and get splashed? Or do you hold on to 'em real tight?"

His mouth opened, but no sound came out.

"Don't work too hard, Arnoldt. That was a rhetorical question."

He had two inches and at least thirty pounds on her, but she trusted an atavistic impulse and turned her back on him before he began his retreat.

❖

In the light of day, none of Jamie's attackers could meet her relentless stare. She'd spent the remainder of the night listening for the retaliation that never came; at reveille, she understood—no one in the platoon would be fucking with her anymore. Because, no DIs stopping them, no holds barred, four guys failed to beat a girl.

No holds barred.

All day, those three words badgered her for attention she had no time to give. Not until hours later when she was getting bled yet again, out in the sandpit yet again sounding off a pushup count yet again while the kill hat bawled colorful descriptions of her innumerable inadequacies. Yet again.

This time the five-minute limit to sandpit incentivization passed unrecognized by the kill hat and his henchmen, the feasting sand fleas. This time something had changed. The kill hat was escalating. So tired she could taste her craving for sleep, Jamie girded.

Push—drop—tap tits. Push—drop—tap tits.

"Sir! Fif' three 'shups, sir!"

Push—drop—tap tits. Push—drop—tap tits.

"Sir! Fif' four 'shups, sir!"

At sixty-four, she was weakening past tolerance, past retrieval. If she didn't stop now, there would be nothing left, she would forfeit all ability to protect herself. *You prick, gimme a break!* This was how she'd always done it, how she'd been able to survive. *Like last night, dammit! Where the fuck were* you *last night?*

"Faster, Gwynmorgan! This ain't the freaking Magic Kingdom!" hollered the kill hat, shoving his boot under her nose. "And get your grody ass outta the ozone layer! *Now!*"

One more'll be sixty-five. One more's gotta be enough. Just one more's all you want and you'll back off, right? You owe me that after last night, okay?

"Sir!" Pushing, pushing, Jamie tried to shout, "Faster and getting this recruit's grody ass outta the ozone layer! Aye-aye, *sir!*"

Slowly, she made her harrowed arms straighten, got her shrieking lats and glutes and abdominals to pull her butt into line. Her arms quaked but they held, exacting only a groan from her before they managed to bend and halt just as her chest grazed the sand. Then, groaning anew, she repeated it all to achieve one more Marine Corps pushup, trying not to think about the fact that one Marine Corps pushup equaled two of anybody else's.

"Sir! Six' five 'shups, *sir!*"

She paused, her tits teasing the sand, waiting for the kill hat to keep the bargain she'd invented, waiting for his boot to depart. *I gave it to you, so say it. Say I can stop. Please.* But his boot, so close she could lick it, demanded more. She inched her head leftward, just the littlest bit leftward for relief from that evil boot.

And there at the periphery of her vision, perhaps fifty feet away, stood Platoon 2128's senior drill instructor. Cold and ferocious, he said nothing, but he communicated with the kill hat—Jamie could tell. She slid her eyes toward him and beheld a Look she hadn't seen before, a Look she could read like a neon sign: Now—take her down now. And then the senior DI turned about-face and walked away.

You let that happen last night. Watched them on the goddamn surveillance screens in the goddamn DI hut and let it goddamn happen!

He had abandoned her, just like everyone else.

Like Alby who never came back from a car crash and Josh who forgot her when his father shipped him off to Dublin so he wouldn't get busted and even Joe who'd never replied to any of her textmails. A yelp clawed at her throat and escaped into sound, filling her ears at the same instant the thought filled her mind.

Who am I kidding? Give it up and just let them NOB me. Noncombat-Oriented Basic Training. Cunt camp. For the duds, the washouts. The thought ruled her, coursed through her body, oozed into her jagged breathing.

"How stupid *are* you, Gwyn-moron?" The kill hat's tone kept her burning, doddering arms from surrender. "Only way you get outta here is through *me*. No NOB for you."

She squinched her eyes shut against the implacable noise of him, against the tears flooding her eyes. "Please," Jamie wheezed. *I…can't… do…this.*

"Oh yeah, sweet cheeks, we're keeping *you*," the kill hat crooned. "I'll be working you real good 'til you learn that. And if thirteen weeks ain't enough time for your pea brain to embrace your future, Gwyn-moron, we'll be real happy to cycle you through thirteen more."

She believed him so unreservedly that her arms held. But how could she push again?

Then, from right behind her, where her neck met the base of her skull, she heard a faint voice, a woman's voice, and she thought it said, "You *can* do it. Push!"

Her eyes snapped open, her clit pounded into high alert, like somebody had pinched it.

"No!" Jamie sobbed, pushing. "Holds!" She dropped. "Barred!" She stayed her enflamed arms so her tits tempted the fleas while her tears tumbled into the sand.

All of her hummed, a scorching vibration that demanded her scream. Resisting the scream felt like suicide, like she would disintegrate. She squeezed her eyes shut once more so she wouldn't have to hate the kill hat's boot, so her pushing would be for her, for her alone.

"*No!*" Pu-ush! "*Holds!*" Drop. "*Barred!*" Tap tits. "Sir! Six' six 'shups, *sir*!"

When she got to seventy-four, she opened her eyes. The kill hat's boot had disappeared. Her clit whirred wildly, pitching higher, faster. At eighty-three, she realized her aching arms and shoulders no longer threatened failure. She lilted—an invisible hand lifted her crotch, soothed her electrified clit, relieved her of caring about what happened next.

"Sir! Eigh' eigh' 'shups, *sir*!"

At one hundred, the kill hat interrupted his off-key improvisation of a new jody call that featured "No Holds Barred" to order her out of the sandpit.

As she double-timed into the squadbay, the senior drill instructor sent her to the F-head for a shower. And she heard him tell the scribe to remove Recruit Gwynmorgan's name from that night's firewatch list.

Training day thirty. Fifty-three training days to go.

"Jeez, stinks, huh?" Arnoldt scrunched his nose. "What's that smell?"

CS gas and eau de vomit, Jamie concluded, but said nothing.

"Fucking stinging my skin," said Diller. "And my eyes!"

"*So*, maggot!" Having snuck up behind Diller, the kill hat now trumpeted in his ear. "Guess you won't be needing that mask in my gas chamber."

Diller jumped. "Sir! No, sir! Uh, yes—No!" His face paled. "Sir! Please, sir, this recruit needs a gas mask, sir!"

The kill hat ordered them to don their masks and make sure the seal was unbroken—all except Diller, who was ordered to wait long enough before the kill hat yielded that Jamie forgot her own apprehension and actually felt sorry for him.

Once inside, instructors clad head to toe in chemical warfare suits taunted them as the doors slammed shut and the tear gas activated. The room quickly filled with a noxious fog. "Side-straddle hops, boys and girls," yelled one of the instructors, and they did jumping jacks until their sweat intensified the sting of the gas on their arms and necks.

"Now bend over like you like it, boys and girls, and shake your skulls. C'mon. Back and forth. Good and fast."

It was a surprise. The seals on their masks held.

"Heads up! Eyes shut!" Everyone had to break the seals, allow in gas. With the order to don and clear, they repositioned their masks to reseal them and then blew hard to force out the gas inside the masks. Not so bad since they'd been able to hold their breath the whole time.

But the real test was yet to come.

"Now you will remove your masks entirely and hold them at arm's length until instructed otherwise. And remember your knowledge."

They held their breath again, pulled off the masks, and waited for the order to don and clear. And waited.

Knowledge. He said knowledge. Jamie struggled for recall. Around her, recruits coughed and choked. A few whimpered. Somebody screamed. She heard more than a few throw up.

Finally, Jamie remembered. *Supposed to relax. Relax and inhale just a bit during a CS attack.* She tried it, got some air. It wasn't pleasant, but it worked. Eyes still closed, she signaled the instructor with a thumbs-up. Then somebody bumped into her.

Through stinging tears, she beheld Arnoldt. He hadn't yet taken a breath and had lost his balance. Several others were already on their knees. And the instructors' tactics had become obvious. None of the recruits would be allowed to don their masks again until all of them exhibited sufficient self-control and presence of mind. Teamwork would be the quickest way out of the gas chamber.

"Gotta breathe just a little, Arnoldt," Jamie panted.

Arnoldt peeked at her. "Fucking A. You *nuts*?"

"Just a little, like they told us." Jamie's lungs burned, her eyes burned, tears streamed down her face. But she inhaled again, then blew thick mucus out of her nose. "See?"

The fear in Arnoldt's eyes abated with his tentative breaths. Jamie grabbed the next squaddie's arm. "C'mon, man, breathe. Do it." Soon they followed her lead, straightened, and signaled the instructor.

All except Diller. The panicked leader of the blanket party made a dash for the door.

Jamie caught his arm as he stumbled by her and got dragged several feet before she could trip him, sending them both to their knees on the vomit-slimed concrete deck. She yanked on his cammie blouse and rasped into his ear, "Diller! You're okay. Just gotta take small breaths."

He looked at her like she was a lunatic, then tried to put on his mask. Jamie stopped him.

"You want to spend the rest of your life in here, man? *Small breaths!*" This time it was a command, and it sank in. But he couldn't obey. He stared at her, desperate, and she realized he was stuck, frozen.

"C'mon, shallow breaths—in—out. *C'mon, dammit!* In—out. In—out."

At last, Diller allowed his breathing to imitate hers. Soon he and Jamie stood together and Diller turned up his thumb.

"Don and clear!" ordered the instructor.

❖

"You know the drill, recruit."

Jamie had already practiced this for a week, but the patient coaching helped. "You'll load the ammo stack with your left hand and flip the safety switch with your left hand, too," the instructor said. "That way your right hand's always positioned at the trigger."

"Aye aye, sir." Jamie planted her feet shoulder wide, pointed her toes toward the target, and followed instructions. In seconds, she had the rifle snugged into her right shoulder and gazed through its smartscope.

"Lower your elbow some. Good. You'll ID your target and calc it by pushing the button at the top of the trigger. The laser in the scope will show you range first, followed by wind speeds and air density between you and your target. Then it'll automatically adjust for elevation and atmospherics. Remember, the scope only does the math and shows you where you want to aim—*you* do the aiming and the shooting. A miss is *your* bad, recruit—not the scope's, not the rifle's. To nail your target, you have to find that zone in your head while you're sighting."

The chance to shoot an E19X4 assault rifle would have seduced Jamie into enlisting even if the Marines *hadn't* abolished the female bucket-style hat so that everyone wore exactly the same uniform. Nevertheless, the prospect of popping off live rounds with it had her nerved up. All her Fucking Annie Fucking Oakley experience had been just guessing about how to hit a bunch of beer cans with an old nine-mil pistol and a nearly antique bolt-action twenty-two.

The instructor's voice became softly hypnotic. "You want to breathe slow, smooth, calm. You get into your zone and the rest is easy. Once you're in your zone, you want to keep the calc button depressed while you match up the crosshairs with the center of the concentric circles in your scope. Nice and steady. Soon as those crosshairs light up green, you'll squeeze the trigger."

The challenge, of course, came in lining up everything fast enough, smooth enough. Jiggle the weapon or wait too long and the calcs had to refresh, so the shot was lost.

Squinting through the smartscope, Jamie exhaled and let her breathing cease while she pushed the calc button. That's when she saw it: A phantasm that looked exactly like Bob Baines.

Bloated, brutish Bob Baines. That Fucker who was the reason she joined the Marine Corps in the first place. Because if she'd stayed there, he'd be dead now. She'd have killed him.

Before the crosshairs went green, her finger twitched hard on the trigger and she nailed him. She also bull's-eyed the target, which she figured had to be dumb luck since she couldn't remember moving her scope's crosshairs where they were supposed to go.

But when his image filled her scope the next time she took aim, she nailed him—and the target—again. She nailed him from every firing position—standing, kneeling, prone, sitting. She nailed him with slow fire, with rapid fire. She nailed him at every distance, known and unknown.

During Combat Firing, oblivious of the clumsy gas mask and outdated night-vision gear, she saw multiples of Bob Baines running and nailed him. *You're dead, you fucker! Dead!*

After that, the ghost of Bob Baines disappeared from her scope, but Jamie had already found her zone—a kind of bubble of effortless, instinct-driven acuity in which she knew exactly what to do, when to do it. She bull's-eyed again and again and again—and every time, she did it before her scope's crosshairs lit up green.

Jamie's scores earned her an expert marksman badge. And a nod from the senior drill instructor. "Getting there, girl."

Girl? Not maggot?

"Sir!" Jamie shouted. "This recruit is extremely grateful for the senior drill instructor's help, sir!"

He glared at her, ramrod straight just a centimeter from her nose, and Jamie prepared for yet another smoking, contemplating how many pushups she could do today before she crumpled into the Carolina mud.

Instead, the senior DI winked and walked away without another word.

She gaped into the space the man occupied only a second before, suddenly breathless and slightly dizzy. *Oh god, this is gonna be really bad. The Parris Island Mindfuck, Phase Nineteen.*

Later, the senior DI called her to the DI hut, where she stood at rigid attention three feet from the desk, her eyes fixed on the wall behind it.

"Know what it means to be impeccable, recruit?" the senior DI asked.

"Sir?" *Here it comes.*

"Being impeccable means you always do the very best you are capable of, every moment of your life, no matter how mundane the task, no matter how pointless your efforts may seem—even when no one's watching you. *Especially* when no one's watching you."

"Sir! Yes! Sir!" Jamie hoped her bewilderment didn't show.

"Recruiter signed you up for infantry, right?"

"Sir! Yes! Sir!"

"Your marksmanship scores are way up there, Gwynmorgan. Which is saying something, since we're now qualifying on mobility and speed of fire as well as much greater kill accuracy. Means you got a solid chance to go straight from here to Scout/Sniper School. But you will have to be impeccable."

"Sir?"

"Scout/Sniper School, recruit," the senior DI barked while Jamie repelled a powerful desire to look at him. "Just what part of that don't you understand?"

The man's grin showed. Jamie could see it hovering just above the tip of her nose. *What the hell is happening here?* She opened her mouth to speak, since she was supposed to say something, but how did one talk to a grinning senior DI?

Speak, dammit! "Sir! Th-this recruit—" Jamie sucked air as fast as she could. *He said Scout/Sniper School, right?* "This recruit understands and…and this recruit wants to go to Scout/Sniper School, *sir!*"

"Good." Grin extinguished, the senior DI shoved a piece of paper across the desk without another glance at her. "Here's what you're gonna need to do to get your ass in. Impeccably. Pick it up and go to work, recruit. Dismissed."

"Sir! Aye-aye, *sir!*" Jamie's heart slammed against her chest as she whisked the paper off the desk, whirled into a crisp about-face, and marched out of the DI hut. *Jeezus, he* did *say Scout/Sniper School!*

❖

"…And his leg's in a fugging cast, so it's your squad now, Gwynmorgan," said the kill hat.

Training day sixty-two, less than twenty-four hours before the Company Commander's Inspection, and now she had charge of fourteen men.

The squaddies called her "twat leader" and the DIs were seriously tensed out. The Company Commander's Inspection tested instructors as much as recruits, and the DIs made clear that they expected perfection.

"Any of you meatheads fugger this up and all of you will sleep in the pit for the duration," declared the kill hat. "In your fugging skivvies."

"They can't do that!" Arnoldt said when the kill hat was out of earshot. "Can they?"

No one wanted to find out. But after sixty-two days of training and several clandestine study nights in the M-head, neither Elias nor Arnoldt could yet recite all eleven general orders and the code of conduct.

On training day sixty-three, the captain who served as the company commander marched down the middle of Platoon 2128's squadbay. Too many recruits to stop and examine each one, but the captain made sure to poke at each squad. Jamie wanted him to pass her by, but she, like the rest, truly dreaded that he might decide to query Elias—or, worse, Arnoldt.

In front of Jamie, the captain halted and executed a neat left-face.

"Recruit Gwynmorgan, sir," said the J hat, who was scribing for the stern-faced captain.

"Ah yes." The captain examined every inch of her. "You're the one with those marksmanship scores. What do you know about the fifth general order, recruit?"

"Sir! The Fifth General Order of a Sentry is to quit my post only when properly relieved, sir!"

"And what does the second article of the United States Marine Corps Code of Conduct state?"

"Sir! When questioned, should I become a prisoner of war, I am required to give name, rank, service number, and date of birth. I will evade answering further questions to the utmost of my ability. I will make no oral or written statements disloyal to my country or its allies or harmful to their cause, sir!"

The captain right-faced and marched out of the squadbay. Behind him, Platoon 2128's three DIs didn't bother to contain their relieved smiles.

That night, Jamie couldn't get into her rack. It had been short-sheeted. "What the hell is this?" she protested in a high-pitched whisper.

Titters—soft, almost squealy, unequivocally male—spilled out on her right, then her left, then above her.

"Jeezus, guys." But she giggled and kicked her feet free. "I'm not used to this terrible ill treatment, y'know. And now I gotta frigging pee." Since nobody could leave their racks for fifteen minutes after lights-out, Jamie had to wait before scampering to the F-head. "I call first dibs, fellas."

When she returned, her rack had been remade. Perfectly. For the first time on Parris Island, Jamie felt camaraderie.

In the days that followed, the squad drilled snap-crackle-pop to the kill hat's new, improved "No Holds Barred" jody call. Just in time for Final Drill, after which the kill hat only scowled, sign of the squad's success.

Then they faced the culmination of Marine Corps Basic Training—the Crucible, recently intensified into an arduous 102-hour test of field skills, teamwork, and endurance that included 120 kilometers of full-pack marching on little rest or sustenance.

It started with a night march and quickly intensified into a chaos of exhausting live-ammunition combat events alternated with ever more complex problem-solving tasks. They did everything except sleep, eat, and hydrate. Sixty-odd courses in all, but everyone in the squad made it through. Because failure meant having to do boot camp again. And nobody wanted to endure boot camp—or the Crucible—twice.

She had done it. Hungry, thirsty, sore, and very tired, Jamie mustered to attention with her squad in a chilly morning drizzle.

"Congratulations, Marine," the senior DI said when he placed the coveted Eagle, Globe, and Anchor pin in Jamie's hand. "I've got a rep for picking out winners, Gwynmorgan. I picked you out when you jumped off the bus. You had me worried there for a while, so I'm real glad to welcome you to the Corps."

"Sir—"

"Call me Staff Sergeant, Marine."

"Thank you, Staff Sergeant."

Jamie's victory was short-lived, however.

A brief textmail waiting for her back at the squadbay told her Joe was dead—killed on a road, in a car, just like they said Alby was. Healthy and alive one instant, dead the next. It happened three days after she stepped on the bus to Parris Island and explained why Joe never answered any of her messages.

Jamie stared at the screen, absorbing the implications of this new reality. She'd thought of herself as pretty close to Joe, but she never was, not really. The textmail came from a son she didn't know Joe had, a son who wasn't aware of her until he got around to cleaning out his father's place and came across her unanswered messages in Joe's inbox.

Now she had no one at all.

The day before graduation, when almost everyone else spent the afternoon with family, Jamie sat at the squadbay comlink, remaking plans for her ten-day leave. Everyone else was going home, so she had pretended that she'd be going home, too. For a while early on, she'd hoped Joe would reply in some kind of okay way to one of those carefully constructed just-friends messages she sent him. And maybe he'd even decide to come down to Parris Island to see her graduate and hang out with some of his old DI buddies...

His unbroken silence suggested to her that he couldn't do just-friends, and that left her in a quandary—go back to Hyannis and at least say hi and thanks and look-I-did-it and hope he didn't try to grope her, or just—? Just what? She'd become accomplished at not thinking about it, at telling herself to just wait a little longer.

Others came through the squadbay with family members. She got introduced, she got congratulated. She smiled—heartily, she hoped, she tried—when they talked about how much they looked forward to going home, and she always said yes, it was a long way back to Massachusetts, ain't it always like that.

She gazed at a map of the eastern seaboard, trying to decide what to do, wondering if Joe would still have been her friend if only he had not ceased to exist. It felt black, this domain where everyone but her had someone who cared about them. She tried to light the blackness with memories of Alby. But Alby slid away from her, shrinking to a tiny pinprick of light that finally flickered out, leaving her with only the blackness.

Jamie graduated with honors. She had the highest marksmanship scores in the entire company and won a trophy for her platoon. This earned her a slot in Scout/Sniper School and the rank of Private First Class. But, unlike the other new marines around her, Jamie had no interest in celebrating.

CHAPTER THREE

THE MAVERICK HEART

It'll be all right. You're doing what you have to."

Jamie shot upright out of sleep and scanned the cheap motel room. *What the fuck?* The woman who murmured in her right ear couldn't have been more than an inch or two away, but had already disappeared. It'd been real, the voice, no question. And not merely real. *Why do I feel like I know that voice?*

She checked the closet. Behind the shower curtain. Under the bed. But she found only a wayward candy wrapper that had escaped the last vacuuming. The old-fashioned clock radio and television were both off. She listened for sounds from beyond the room but heard nothing more than the dull white noise of morning traffic on the busy street outside.

The clock radio's display changed from 5:38 to 5:39.

She'd slept a measly thirty-eight minutes past Parris Island reveille. Shaking her head, Jamie sat on the bed. And then she remembered the dream.

In the dream, she wore cammies. Carrying a couple of weapons, bags of ammunition stacks, the myriad stuff of surviving in a wilderness, she crouched in a forest clearing. Human bodies surrounded her, but she was the only one still alive. Though she had no recollection of it, she knew she had used her weapons to kill them all.

Jamie rubbed the dream from her eyes.

Yesterday's bus ride from Parris Island to Washington, DC, took almost ten hours. By the time she retrieved her seabag, walked to the motel, and checked in, the clock radio had showed eleven-something. She'd stripped down to her skivvies and crawled under the bed's covers into a sleep that had been deep, uninterrupted. But now her body weighed too much, like the dream had followed her into waking.

I locked the damn door, right? She pushed off the bed to make sure, to slough off the sluggishness that dogged her. For this first full day of her leave, she had a plan—by god, she would visit the Smithsonian no matter how shitty she felt.

Doesn't open 'til ten hundred hours, goober. Jamie swung her legs onto the mattress, lay back, and allowed her eyes to close. *I'll just hang here a while yet. To celebrate no DIs counting me down.*

Yet a moment later, she stood in front of the motel room's scruffy dresser and for the first time noticed the small round object on it. A fat, grinning four-inch buddha with, incongruously, great pendulous tits like the ones on those ancient headless Maltese statuettes. She couldn't help smiling back at its grin.

"Well, well. Where'd you come from?"

Picking it up, she discovered the lady buddha had two parts that connected at its rotund waist. And she wondered how she even knew about ancient headless Maltese statuettes with great pendulous tits. *Must've read it. Somewhere.* Yet the memory eluded her.

The longer she stared at the lady buddha, the more its vibrant reds, golds, and blues distracted her. As if her hands belonged to someone else, she watched her fingers explore its waist until the two sections detached, one piece in each hand. With caution she peeked inside the piece in her left hand, not sure what to expect.

It was empty. Lined with something cloudy, milky but just slightly gray-pink. *Mother-of-pearl maybe?* Transfixed, Jamie stared at its shifting depths and tones. *Curious how the light in here makes it look like it's actually moving…*

And then she found herself up in the mountains, in a high valley surrounded by snow-covered peaks under the bluest sky she'd ever seen.

She stood in a town center. Tibetan? Nepalese? Definitely not Western. A murmuring throng of people waited on folding chairs neatly arranged on either side of a wide center aisle that led to a rough stone platform. Conversation ceased when a huge, swollen figure in an ornate blue and silver military uniform drifted up from behind the platform and floated across it.

Ah. So this is why everyone's here. To Jamie, the figure resembled one of those big balloons at New York City's Thanksgiving Day Parade, but she sensed these people were supposed to be awed by it, fearful even.

Instead, they laughed while the figure slowly lifted away, lighter than the thin mountain air. Soon came a second balloonish character, this one wearing a uniform of red and gold. It, too, wafted off, provoking even more merriment from the people, now impatient and ready to depart. Jamie assumed the entertainment had ended.

Abruptly, however, an omnipotent rumble hushed the crowd.

As one, the gathering gasped at the source of this sound so deep it could only be felt, not heard. A colossal abstraction of a human face hewn out of granite rose from behind the platform. Then, as the infrasound intensified, a whole granite being of incomprehensible weight loomed over them, tall as a ten-story building. Adorned in a simple long robe, it glided across the platform and down the center aisle through the crowd. Although it moved sleekly, entirely without friction, its tenacious oscillations shook the ground.

Jamie stared up agape. Her chest, her head thrummed, claimed by an unfathomable seismic vibration that had begun to disperse every molecule in her body. Yet she had no fear, only awe.

And then the folding chairs were all askew; the crowd had left. Slowly, slowly, Jamie turned around in her chair toward a white-haired woman in a simple, oatmeal-colored robe who sat behind her, framed by a sky grown even more intensely blue than before. Jamie talked and talked to this woman who listened and understood everything, whose benevolent eyes never left her face, whose smile embraced her. And Jamie knew she was safe.

Then she was standing again before the motel room dresser, gazing at the mother-of-pearl interior of the little lady buddha. Closing the container, Jamie realized the woman and the immense granite being were one and the same. And she realized something else, too. *You're the one who whispered in my ear. You said it'd be all right.*

When Jamie woke up, the numbers on the clock radio had changed. 7:53. She found nothing when she searched the room for the lady buddha. Convinced for nearly an hour that it must have been there somewhere, she looked again and again.

By the time she gave up the search, she couldn't remember what she'd said to the white-haired woman or recall the details of the woman's face. But she couldn't forget what the woman's smile, the woman's eyes had given her. Jamie hunted for the word.

Bliss.

❖

Thirty-two hours after the senior DI boomed his final "Dis-missed!" Jamie still expected a banshee to blow right through the motel room door howling, "Pla-toon! Fall-*IN*!"

Every few minutes, an echo of DI thunder clattered in on some innocent noise, especially if she dared lie down on the motel room bed. Once she scrambled all the way to her feet and found herself pulling in her chin, adjusting her heels, and sending her thumbs in surreptitious search of her pants seams before she realized the sound was in her head, only in her head.

Shit. I gotta calm down.

Thirty-two hours after the last of Parris Island, Jamie faced eight days and nine nights of time to fill and nothing to fill it with. So she paced the room. After a few minutes, she recognized the cadence. *How many hours close-order drilling?* Once she got the moves down, she liked the autopilot relief of close-order drilling.

So she paced some more. In cadence, the kill hat's favorite jody call playing in her head. *Once you take the devil's card, hell will claim you no holds barred...*

It didn't help. She flopped onto the bed and turned on the TV, but five minutes later, she flicked it off again and wandered into the bathroom, to the mirror, where the face there stared back at her.

It's because you're alone, you know. Because you don't have a home to go to or anyone who gives a shit that you're a frigging marine.

During those thirteen weeks on Parris Island, she had wished there was someone to miss, wished Joe had been clingable to. Yet she knew the truth: Being cut loose from all the world made boot camp less wretched.

Now the person in the mirror demanded a conversation—just like the old days when the person in the mirror was the only person she could really trust, really talk to.

C'mon, admit it. They got a real slick racket going. Didn't take them long to have you living minute to minute, humiliation to humiliation, trying not to beg, not to cry—

"And then, after you're groveling, only then come the morsels of praise, those little cult rewards for surrendering your body, your mind.

They're meaningless to everyone else, but god, you wanted them, didn't you?"

There it was. Spoken.

The old Jamie Gwynmorgan took in a deep breath, forced it out again, and studied what the mirror showed her. The face there was leaner now, but yes, she could still see the skinny girl with the maverick heart who almost got out. Almost.

Jamie had to avert her eyes from the kid who'd gotten so, so close, the kid who always soothed the cramping in her stomach which she refused to think of as fear by telling herself it's okay, it's okay, she *would* find that safe place, that home she yearned for. It was out there somewhere on the path that began in the comlink screens at the Barnstable High School library. She just had to keep searching. Even got herself, with the librarian's help, into the school's Special Self-Directed Study Program so she didn't have to endure classrooms where she was scorned for being way too dyky, no comlink of her own, has to wear the same clothes more than once a week, and then there's that drugged-up whore of a mother of hers. Instead, she searched and learned at a pace fast enough, exhilarating enough to trade despair for a long shot at a college scholarship—until Alby crashed and burned. Until Bob Baines.

Ah hell. At least I get to play with a real nice rifle.

"So what the fuck is wrong with you?" she defiantly demanded of the mirror. "Buy a damn comlink!"

The store she needed was just four blocks away. She spent a hefty chunk of her pay on the best she could find—a high-performance, multi-powersource wrist/eyescreen model—so she could finally return to the Internet's many libraries and begin reading again.

While the store clerk generated a receipt, Jamie donned the comlink eyewear, activated its shadowscreen, and launched a dictionary search:

fug *(noun):* A heavy, stale, or ill-smelling atmosphere, especially the musty air of an overcrowded or poorly ventilated room.

That's it? That's *what it means?*

"They can't hit you," she informed the bewildered clerk. "Can't even swear. But they use that Look and that Frog Voice when they say 'fug,' and we're all frigging terrified. Wizard of Oz in a Smokey the Bear hat."

The clerk smiled polite wariness. When Jamie started giggling, he grinned, then couldn't keep himself from giggling too. The sound of his laughter pealed through the store and followed her out the door.

❖

For six days and seven nights, Jamie read, interrupted only by the time she took for food, workouts, sleep, and basic bodily functions. At first, she tried to pick up where she'd left off before Parris Island and finish reading the ten books of Vitruvius's *De Architectura*. But she couldn't get past "Classification of Temples" and began to poke around in *The Art of War* by Sun Tzu.

When she came upon "All warfare is based on deception," she was hooked. She consumed as much as she could. Machiavelli, Chanakya, von Clausewitz. Essays on asymmetric warfare, Fabian strategies, fourth-generation conflicts, network-centric operations, wicked problems, soft power. *At least Private First Class Cannon Fodder'll have a clue.*

Then, on the eighth evening of her leave, she couldn't keep her eyes on the screen anymore. Restless memories of Alby and Joe had finally made reading impossible.

Damn. If she thought about them, she'd have to think about them not existing, which wrecked the sensation that they were out there somewhere, too busy to deal with her, but out there somewhere, able to return when they were ready.

Maybe it would've been better for her to have seen them dead instead of finding out from someone else that they no longer existed. Jamie closed the comlink, then closed her eyes. She tried to imagine Joe's dead body, then Alby's.

Alby all burned up, sizzling like fried butter.

That would make it real, right? To see Alby all burned up and know for certain that Alby could no longer exist. *What does burning flesh look like, smell like?*

"I'm told it happened very, very quickly. Your mother didn't suffer."

One more time, Jamie sat on the scorched grass that stank of gasoline, staring at Provincetown in the distance from the bluff several miles away, attempting to feel something. Anything. One more time, the day was clear, bright, crisply suggesting autumn, and Provincetown shimmered, a smiling little town at the end of the world defying the rising sea. If it had been any other place, maybe the whole thing wouldn't have been so hard to believe. But here? Here on the very spot Alby made such a big deal of showing her, that favorite spot on the bluff?

Jamie remembered, a memory within a memory, how they had stood there, just the two of them, while Alby pointed to Provincetown in the distance. "Hey, look. It's Avalon," Alby had said to her in a tone so uncharacteristically wistful that later she looked it up. Avalon—mythic Isle of Apples, Isle of the Blessed, realm of the fay.

"No," Jamie growled at the empty motel room, on her feet now but keeping well away from the mirror so she couldn't see her own face. "Alby doesn't exist."

What does burning flesh look like, smell like?

Responding not so much to a decision as to an inarticulable, felt command, Jamie packed her stuff and checked out of the motel. Civilian-anonymous in faded jeans and her hand-me-down leather aviator jacket, she boarded a night train for Providence. Shortly after dawn, she settled in at the back of a bus bound for Cape Cod. By midmorning, she was walking.

From the dilapidated Hyannis Transport Center, Jamie walked a mile and a half to the even more bedraggled seasonal cottage where she and her mother had lived for years. Built a century ago for summer tourists on a budget but long since too crappy even for them, the leaky, uninsulated place had been "a good deal" because Alby could barter unspecified services to pay the rent.

Shoulders hunched against the bite of the winter wind, Jamie stood in the driveway and examined the cottage's raggedy cedar shingles, the familiar rip in its screen door, searching for— What? Nothing had changed in the seventy weeks since she and Alby had lived there. *Except it's empty now. Nobody lives here now. Alby doesn't exist.*

"Even the weariest river winds somewhere safe to sea," she said after a while. Alby's words, from some poem, always recited with a sigh. Jamie couldn't recall the rest of the verse, much less the whole poem. She snorted a small laugh, shook her head; her forgetting seemed appropriate. Alby's epitaph would always be no more than a fragment.

And yet, for the first time in her life, Jamie could follow the thin, tenuous thread all the way to who her mother might have been, wanted to be. *Safe. You wanted to be safe. Just like me.*

Able to smile back at the image in her mind's eye of her mother's soft, amiable face, now Jamie sighed. It helped to know—or believe anyway—that Alby didn't do a runner. Fucked up as Alby was by the pharma, Alby tried, always tried, right to the end, to find Safe. Alby's trying hovered, a diminutive, winking point of light.

After turning back toward the Transport Center, Jamie stopped a block later and changed direction. She had one more bit of unfinished business in Hyannis. *Won't take long.* Fifteen minutes later, she stood on the step of a run-down ranch house. With a tug, she pulled the storm door handle free from its feeble lock, positioned the door behind her, and rang the bell.

Before the door opened more than a few inches, Jamie struck, punching Bob Baines hard in his solar plexus. Just once in just the right place so he doubled up, straining fruitlessly for breath.

She kicked the door wide and grabbed a fistful of his sweatshirt right below his neck to keep him from sinking further. It would have been so easy. So easy to reach down and apply a guillotine choke with a nice, firm jolt. *To crunch his larynx so he'll never breathe again...*

On his knees, he looked up at her, cringing eyes rimmed in fear, body bent in pain, his fleshy hands clutching his fat gut.

"Remember me, you asshole fuck?" Jamie pulled him up another few inches and bent forward, lowering her head so they were nose to nose. A small whimper dribbled out of his mouth and he managed a nod.

"Good." She drawled the word into a threat and rammed her knee into his testicles, letting go of his sweatshirt at the same time.

Jamie watched him collapse and decided, *Yes. It's enough.* She pivoted and walked away, satisfied to leave Bob Baines lumped in his doorway.

CHAPTER FOUR

THIS IS JUST TRAINING

G reat. We're screwed now."
Nobody in the stuffy double field hooch responded, a signal for the private squatting beside Jamie to shut up. But he didn't. "We should be dispersed, not all bunched up like sitting fucking ducks! Why'd they make Fontana squad leader anyway? He's clueless."

"Keep it *down*, Arnoldt!" Jamie hissed at him. *Why, oh fucking why is this guy still in my life?* "It's just training. We're supposed to be screwed. But maybe we can screw with them some, too, y'know?"

The rules of engagement generally had plenty of wiggle room. Private First Class Gwynmorgan learned that well in boot camp, and she figured the Cock, as the grunts called this exercise, was no exception.

She didn't look up from the modified E19 she had disassembled and cleaned by flashlight. Her movements were careful and deliberate, but she was in a hurry. According to scuttlebutt, the longest any squad had ever avoided capture was three days. Most squads got caught during the first day. Or the first night.

"Screw with them?" Arnoldt asked. "Let's hear it."

"Really?" Surprised, Jamie glanced up from the weapon.

Mistake.

There's that smirk on his ugly puss again. Jamie thought about the dark-eyed blonde on the bus to Parris Island. *How the hell can it happen twice like that?* Twice she'd almost hooked up with that woman and twice it turned into a near miss. All she ended up with was a chance to learn the woman's name: Martina Rhys. *If we were in the same squad, odds are we'd end up in the same hooch. But no, oh no, I'm in a hooch with frigging Arnoldt. And now he's gonna give me shit again.*

Arnoldt snorted disdain, the nostrils of his broad, crooked nose flaring. "Oh, I get it," he said. "You'll *screw* your way out of it."

"Yep." With a snide grin, Jamie interrupted her work on the weapon, pulled a floppy funnel-like object from a cargo pocket, and twirled it so the rubbery tube at one end came within a centimeter of Arnoldt's crinkling nose. It was her FUD—female urinary device— issued by the Corps so females could pee without having to pull their pants down. "And I bet my six inches are way harder than yours."

"Oh, woman, that's definitely oversharing," said Moss, an outrageously handsome African American who was the third party in the crowded tent. Large and levelheaded, he seemed willing to once again keep the peace between Jamie and the lumbering Arnoldt, who now glared silently.

"Where the hell is Karpinsky, anyway?" Jamie asked Moss. The four of them made up the second squad's first fire team, which Karpinsky led.

"He agrees with Arnoldt. Said he was gonna go talk to Fontana—"

"We should have somebody of our own out there on watch," Jamie declared. As the only other private first class on the team, she was technically in charge whenever Karpinsky was absent. It was bullshit, of course, but she had to get out of that tent.

"Fontana's already posted a watch," said Moss.

"Oh yeah, that makes me feel *real* safe," said Arnoldt.

"I'll take the first four hours," Jamie said, her weapon reassembled and ready to fire paint-blanks.

She fingered the integrated multiwave surveillance binoculars around her neck—"IMS nocs" that combined through-wall radar and thermal imaging—then fished in her right chest pocket for the handheld detector while she reviewed every word every instructor had said about the devices.

Used properly, they could pick up a human form on the darkest night, sometimes even through concrete walls. Used properly with a little luck, maybe the squad could stretch the rules of engagement and defy the odds. At least it was worth a try. And at least the possibility, although dim unto ridiculous, helped keep Jamie's fear at bay.

Confidence my ass.

After thirty-seven uninterrupted days of fiercely physical infantry training and two days of survival-evasion-resistance-escape classroom work, everyone in Scout/Sniper Class 2801 now had to put it on the line during the Combat Opponent Confidence Exercise, brassword for the Cock.

The stated goal of the Cock was to evade a mock enemy force—actually instructors and students of the Marine Reconnaissance Field Interrogation Training Course—bent on capturing and interrogating members of Class 2801. Although the class's instructors offered up stories about those who had successfully evaded "the Pirates"—so called due to the red winking skull-and-crossbones insignia on their black bandanna armbands—no one believed any of it. After all, how do you train interrogators if the people they're supposed to interrogate get away? And how better to identify those unable to wrestle with that potential bad bear in a snipe's job—capture by an enemy—*before* the Corps invested in any scout/sniper training?

So no one proceeded to those final fifty-seven days of scout/sniper training without being "inoculated" against the techniques of enemy interrogation by means of the Cock, which was more than legendary. The deeply dreaded Cock was infamous. As were the Pirates, led by a maniacal gunnery sergeant whose name no one could ever quite be sure of.

For Scout/Sniper Class 2801, the Cock had begun with its members forming into three squads that marched out together at midnight into the vast woods on Camp Lejeune's 200,000 humid, sodden acres. Thirty hours, two twenty-klick full-pack humps, one five-klick paddle in rubber dinghies across a windy Stone Bay, a trio of stress-fire simulations, and four hours of sleep later, they were sufficiently beat.

Then a single briefing and they split up. Three squads, three missions to "capture" a piece of "enemy equipment"—a sixty-pound black box—at three different locations and bring the boxes back across Stone Bay to Class 2801's barracks. All of them knew where each squad was heading. All of them had intel the Pirates wanted, intel the Pirates would try damn hard to get.

And once they split up, they became fair game for capture.

Jamie's squad had moved unhindered for another long day toward their black box situated atop an abandoned water tower. They had traveled slowly to prevent detection by Pirate IMS gear. Sixteen kilometers, maybe eighteen, too much of it on their bellies under hot, heavy countersurveillance-material ponchos. Forty-six hours into the Cock simulation and they were on their asses. At least eight days, maybe as much as ten days to go.

Beneath a hazy sliver-moon, a thin fog hugged the ground. Of course, the fog obscured the warmth of Pirate breath, reducing the likelihood that anyone in the squad would detect them until it was too late.

Jamie felt somewhat consoled, however. The fog also hid her squad—as long as everyone stayed alert and careful. She checked the setting on her IMS detector again. Yep, all tuned up.

With their detectors tuned to an agreed setting, they could move around outside the tents within a ten-meter perimeter without triggering alerts on each other's devices. Jamie smeared another layer of cloaking cream on her face and hands before pulling her poncho over her head.

As she edged toward the tent opening, Arnoldt tugged on her sleeve. "You really got an idea about how to screw with them?"

"Yeah, I do. I think we should try to fight them off."

"Christ!"

"Why not? Once they're paint-blanked, rule is they can't be part of further capture attempts, right? So if they make their move with referees around and we zap 'em, we got solid odds to pick up the black box and get back to barracks with it."

Arnoldt slumped like a man facing execution.

"Got a better idea?"

Arnoldt frowned at his feet.

"Hey, man, take it easy." Jamie nudged him. "This is just training."

"What the fuck," sighed Moss. "I'm not gonna get any sleep anyway. I'll relieve you at zero-two-hundred."

Jamie nodded at Moss, then jabbed Arnoldt's arm. "Douse that goddamn moonbeam." When Arnoldt turned off his flashlight, she slipped out of the tent, careful to manipulate the tent flaps so anyone scanning the area wouldn't be able to detect the people and gear inside.

Ten minutes later, she had snugged into the rotting trunk of a large dead oak at the edge of the perimeter around the squad's three tents.

Just under ten meters southwest of the hooch, halfway between the two sentries, Jamie watched from behind her poncho's face screen, pleased that the returning Karpinsky kept stealth well enough to be undetectable on her IMS nocs. This boosted her spirits. So did knowing that Karpinsky would let her stay outside all night if she wanted.

She wanted. *Better out here where there's fresh air to breathe, even it means staying in this goddamn chainmail poncho.*

She assumed the Pirates would use recon techniques to get right on top of them. Careful, patient stealth. Skills she didn't have yet. *Bet they come tonight, probably from the south, maybe the higher terrain to the southwest. Right over the same ground we covered today.*

❖

"Hey, man, ace timing," Jamie whispered when Moss joined her shortly before 0200 hours. "I've been getting anomalies on my detector for about the last ten minutes. Real short blips, progressively closer. Then it reads False Positive. I don't like it."

"Direction?" he asked.

"South-southwest." She pointed to her right. "Exactly where you'd expect if they decided to come up behind us."

"Hmm." Moss didn't disguise his skepticism. "I figured them coming right at dawn from that scrub to the east. You know, with the sunrise behind them, the glare in our eyes."

"Diddle your detector." Jamie scanned from south to southwest through her binoculars. "Flip it into the really high frequencies, then back down to thermal, and hold it there for maybe three, four seconds. Now roll higher again, swing it low pretty quick, then back up *fast*."

He tried it repeatedly for about a minute. "Fuck!" he rasped in a high-pitched whisper. "It's popping, then flicking to FP like you said, but right before that it's showing activity between thirty and sixty meters!"

"That's the closest yet. Jeezus, I see zip in the nocs. Nothing. I'll probably get whacked for this in the morning, but I'm gonna ping the hooches. Keep tweaking that thing, okay?"

Jamie pushed a button on her detector, and from behind them came the scratchy, edgy sounds of the squad scrambling. Seconds later, Moss whispered tensely, "This says they're right on top of—"

Before he finished his sentence, they heard the quick, quiet steps of at least ten people moving fast. The closest came within a meter of them, swooping right over their position toward the tents.

Jamie rose from under her poncho and paint-blanked a black form no more than three meters away. Moss, she knew, was doing the same, and a couple of guys in the squad lit up, too. To the northwest of the tents, Jamie glimpsed the dim yellow swath of a referee's vest. *Yes!* With a referee watching, the rules remained in play.

She fired again at a red winking skull and crossbones visible in a flashlight beam thrashing through the dark. *That's two anyway. Two for sure.*

For one more nanosecond, she thought they might be able to fight off the Pirates. Then the vicious, fiery jolt of a knockout stungun on her neck threw her against the decayed tree trunk. She held on to consciousness long enough to understand: Captured.

When her awareness returned—*How long?*—she was face down, her hands tightly zip-strapped behind her back. She couldn't get her body to stop its violent involuntary jerking. Everything hurt.

"...And these two," a voice above her scolded, "took out four more." Someone kicked her hard enough to lift her torso off the ground, extracting an aggrieved grunt as the air exited her lungs. "That makes six. *Six that were counted,* goddammit! Nobody's *ever* fucking done that before!"

At his feet, Jamie grinned into the dirt.

The entire squad was transported together—hooded, hogtied, hollered at, and heaved roughly into the back of a single truck, then driven around for what seemed like hours. Since there was no point in trying to disorient them—everyone knew where the mock POW field camp was—she realized the Pirates did it to make them more uncomfortable, wear them out. Wear them down.

Finally, the truck stopped. One by one, they were pulled out and tossed into a sandpit where someone released their feet and forced them to their knees, hands still bound, heads still hooded. They were all lined up, Jamie sensed from the sounds, and she listened keenly for what would come next, trying to stay calm. *This is just training.* But she could remember nothing of what the classroom instructors told them about how to resist...nothing...

"Okay, that one and that one," said the same irritated voice she'd heard before. *Could this be him, the infamous gunnery sergeant?*

A fist grabbed her cammie blouse and yanked her up, impelling her forward before she could get her feet under her. She fell over some sort of soft edge and tumbled down an incline, followed shortly by a thud and a groan announcing the arrival of someone in the space next to her. *Just training, just training…*

"That you, Moss?" she whispered after a moment.

"Unnh," Moss's unhappy baritone answered.

Jamie knew they were about to pay for the six who'd been counted.

CHAPTER FIVE

CRAVING

Under the stinking black hood, Jamie tried to suck in air without gagging and hoped the Pirates wouldn't tape the damn thing tight around her neck.

She'd been stungunned again and hogtied again, too—this time with metal cuffs—and had lost any sense of how much time had passed or where they'd taken her. Shivering intermittently from cold in spite of the humidity under the hood, she listened for Moss but heard only a low-pitched, monotonous buzzing.

And then somebody unlocked the restraints on her hands and her now-bare feet. "Get up, asshole," a chilling male voice said, "and strip off those filthy fucking cammies."

She responded slowly, reluctantly, first moving a hand to pull off the hood. "*Leave* it!" Her hand was stilled by a solid kick too close to her kidney. The kick coerced a ragged, helpless grunt; she imagined they wanted to see that helplessness before—

Before what?

Several hands yanked Jamie to her feet, then ripped off her uniform, her T-shirt, her underwear. If the sound of her clothes shredding was meant to scare her, it succeeded.

Before upping the ante.

Just as she started worrying about what else was in store, the Pirates spread-eagled her against a cold, rough wall. *Concrete block, gotta be.* Her hands were pulled wide apart. Her feet, too, got shoved away from each other and kicked so far from the wall that she strained to stay upright.

But no stungunning. Which gave her a little time to think. *Inside, I'm inside somewhere.*

The intermission was brief. With slaps, shoves, and insults, they insisted she hold her position against the wall while they forced her to lift her weight onto her toes and the tips of her fingers. They made her keep her back, arms, and legs straight, her head held up. If she moved or tried to relax, she got smacked back into the same position.

And there she stayed, tense and freaked out that no one asked any questions. *Am I the only one in here?* She tried to hear beyond the buzzing for hints about who might be around her. *Was that a moan?*

"Moss?" Jamie whispered toward the apparent sound on her left and in return got a slap so hard against her backside that pinpricks of light whirled under the hood. Her body arched away from the blow, but she persevered against an instinct to cry out. *What the hell'd they use to do* that?

"Shut the fuck up, asshole. No talking."

Her hands cramped up first. Then her neck and shoulders. Then blades of fire sliced down her back, into her legs. When her hands began to go numb, she closed them into fists for relief. They were pounded until she opened them again, until the tips of her fingers held her weight again.

Unable to see, knowing only that her captors had complete sovereignty over her imploding world, Jamie began to hear something else in the incessant buzzing—a bass fiddle playing rumbly Irish reels.

Eventually—*How long?*—she could no longer hold up her trembling arms. She didn't realize she'd collapsed until kicks and slaps roused her and she was again forced into position against the wall.

Later—*How long?*—the hood over her head was pulled up slightly and a hand pushed a bit of bread into her mouth, then some more, then maybe half a cup of water. But she wasn't allowed to move.

Sometime after that, Alby showed up, naked, all strung out, whining and slobbering, *"Please, Jamie, I need to tell you something."* Behind Alby stood a naked man, laughing contemptuously.

Jamie wanted to help her mother, but all she could do was tremble. And vomit. She didn't know how she ended up on the floor. She could have sworn she'd been on her feet, trying to stave off dizziness, and… And now some asshole was whacking on her again.

A burst of white light preceded a soft, whooshing *pop!* of clarity and adrenaline. *Fucking asshole!* Jamie clawed the hood off her head and rose toward a subliminal sense of enemy to land a savage punch on one of the Pirates. "Fuck you!" she croaked and tried to hit him again. But she was drubbed to the floor, stungunned into stupor.

❖

Jamie discovered the hard way how her hands were bound behind her, how a rope tied them to a ceiling hook. Before she understood about the rope, it was pulled taut, angling her shoulders toward dislocation.

Moaning, she shivered and twitched to her feet. The hood had disappeared; she was alone in a buzzing, gloomy concrete chamber.

A cruel, unseen god had pulled the rope just so. If she bent forward, the balls of her feet reached the inclined ramp beneath them just enough to ease the pressure on her wrists and shoulders.

It was a balancing act. With the wrong move, she lost her footing and her shoulders suffered again, and each wrong move exacted more than the one before, became tougher to recover from. *That's the point*, she thought, and knew the Pirates intended to drag her past any capacity for thought, any ability to hold on to herself.

When she felt warm liquid running down the insides of her legs, she grasped that she was peeing and unable to stop it. Her body was their body now. Perhaps minutes, perhaps hours later, disembodied hands put the hood back on her head and she was hosed down with frigid water. The hood drenched and for a while, perhaps minutes, perhaps hours, she believed she was drowning.

Next they hit her with something hard—a strap? a paddle?—and each time her feet slipped, her clit trilled feverishly until she found the ramp once more. She found something else, too. *What's pain without fear? If you can get yourself not to be scared of what the pain means— if you don't care about the damage—then the pain is just another feeling.*

Just another feeling. She tried to say it aloud. But it didn't sound right. And then she was sinking to the bottom of an engulfing black whirlpool, getting smaller and smaller.

❖

"How'd you do it?"

The hood was still in place, but it was dry and more light showed at the bottom of it as Jamie roused back to consciousness.

Where? Buzz is softer…Sitting…In a chair. Her arms were manacled to the chair back and all of her ached. But the burning in every nerve in her body had become distant, almost like it was someone else's problem.

A male voice at her left ear repeated the question. "How'd you do it?"

Jamie was thoroughly lucid and murderously angry. *This is inoculation? That means a real enemy'll kill me, no question. So let's inoculate for that, shall we?* Eventually she found her voice. "Fuck you."

That ended the interrogation.

Within seconds, she'd been dragged by the ankles back to the buzzing room and soon hung from the ceiling again. But it didn't hurt the same way. She began to feel light, increasingly disembodied. When she checked out, it was to immerse in a hallucination that had her flying high above treetops.

But over and over, the Pirates brought her back to face their question. "How'd you do it?"

"Fuck you!" remained Jamie's sole response. She had crossed some threshold into raw, feral hostility and had come to crave the pain—proof to her of her continuing resistance.

The Pirates fulfilled her craving. Between each interrogation, she endured a long bout of hanging from the ceiling hook followed by a beating made more severe whenever she sacrificed her wrists and shoulders for an opportunity to kick a Pirate.

There were plenty of opportunities and Jamie took every one of them.

CHAPTER SIX

FEAR UP HARSH

Yep. This is it. The glare on the other side of her eyelids, the throbbing pangs of fretting flesh and muscle and joints meant just one thing. *This is awake.* Jamie knew she'd have to open her eyes. Any minute now. *Fucking A.*

Awake had taken a while, amalgamating slowly from a jumble of sensations that approached, then receded, then approached again until they connected up into dreams maybe, or memories. Of people pulling on her arms, lifting her by her arms, but her legs wouldn't stay beneath her and she couldn't raise her lolling head and around her sounded voices and clanging metal.

Jamie realized she lay on her back, her arms stretched above her head. More than anything, she wanted to curl into a tight little ball and—

Goddamn. Shackles on her wrists and ankles immobilized her. *Goddamn.*

She had to move something, anything—had to move *now*. This was what made her eyes open at last, made them squint into the glare that wouldn't go away and see a single, bare light bulb in a wire-meshed cavity in the ceiling. She would have looked around to confirm the sense she had of being engulfed by concrete walls, but before she could do anything, the light bulb started to spin.

Suddenly her head filled with a rush of white noise. She closed her eyes against the dazzle, against a tide of nausea rising from her belly into her throat. Maybe a few seconds later, maybe hours, the noise in her head abated. That's when she noticed the other sound. Could it really be that someone was snoring?

Ha! Not just anyone. Arnoldt snored distinctively. Jamie had always hated Arnoldt's snoring—until this moment. Gingerly, she turned her head and slivered open her eyes once more.

She saw Moss first. He was closer, between her and Arnoldt, and all three of them were handcuffed naked to bare metal bed frames. In a cell. Moss's eyes were shut.

"Yo," said Jamie. "Yo, Moss."

He didn't move, but Arnoldt burbled an especially long, loud snore.

"Fear up harsh."

The whisper, a woman's, came from Jamie's left. She turned too fast toward it, and for a half-second her eyes refused to focus. Then she saw Martina Rhys.

"How you doing?" Jamie whispered back, squinching her eyes to make sure what they saw was real. Rhys, too, lay naked and cuffed. Jamie's clit punched a double flip, and for a time-stretched heartbeat, then two, she let the churning surprise of Rhys's robust tawniness, Rhys's exquisite bare breasts, eclipse everything.

"Got waterboarded today," Rhys said wearily. "Moss took the worst of it. Light for Arnoldt and me." Beneath velvet-smooth skin, Rhys's abs tightened and rippled as she strained against the cuffs to turn toward Jamie. "What the hell happened to you? You look like my mother's mincemeat."

"Yeah. Well. It's what I get for playing with boys." Jamie yanked hard on the single pair of cuffs that shackled her hands above her head to the bed frame, twisting to get a better view of the thick wire netting on which she lay. The bed frame groaned metallic protest.

"Don't do that." Rhys's dark eyes flitted toward the cell door and the dank hallway beyond the bars. "Noise attracts them. Not a good idea."

"How long've you been in here?" asked Jamie, shifting leftward again, determined to keep her eyes from leaving Rhys's face.

"Couple days. This'll be the third night. I think. Hard to tell exactly. They never turn off the lights. Put hoods on us when they take us outta here to be interrogated. Tough really knowing what time it is."

"They come around a lot?"

"It'll be a while now, assuming the pattern holds. They're done with us for the day. You just missed the swill they call chow and the second trip to the head, so you'll need to hold it 'til the end of the next watch, which I figure means it's morning. You'll hear 'em playing poker any minute now, after their chow, which we get to smell just to make us a little more crazy. Last night, Arnoldt swore he could smell beer. They won't check us again 'til right after the next watch starts."

"When?"

Rhys shrugged in her cuffs. Her eyes—dejected eyes, Jamie thought—seemed to be pulled unwillingly to the ceiling light. "I'm guessing maybe four hours. Dunno. Hard to tell exactly."

"You get a look around? You know—layout, gates, guard movement?"

"Yeah." Rhys said it slowly, a question—Didn't you?—and turned her head to look at Jamie, who encouraged her with a quick, tell-me-more nod. "Uh," Rhys continued, nodding back, "when they had us digging holes and moving rocks all day."

"When'd they grab you?"

"Same time as your squad." Rhys sounded glum. "I was bringing a message to Fontana, since we were under commo silence. It's been nine god-awful days by my count. I *think*. Which means they should've let us outta here last night. But when Arnoldt said something about it, they just laughed and gut-punched him. So much for the rules of engagement."

Jeezus. Nine days. The Pirates would have to release them by the end of day ten no matter what. So just one more day of the Cock. No matter what. *Shit. One more day.* Inside Jamie's head, way inside, someone started screaming.

"Cameras and microphones?" Jamie hoped she sounded calm.

Rhys shook her head. "Maybe in the light bulb. Or a pinhole setup in the fixture or the walls somewhere. Couldn't find anything obvious from here."

Jamie squinted again at the ceiling light. *If they're playing poker, they're probably not doing surveillance, so what if—* Not likely to work, but even the thought of it eased the screaming in her head. She stretched herself out, pushing with her feet, pulling with her fingers, trying to give her shackled hands more reach as she strained to touch the edge of the bed frame, which creaked and clanked.

"Shh!" Rhys's expression shifted from disapproving frown to

confused dismay when she saw Jamie's fingers continue their scramble along the top edge of the bed's wire netting. "What're you *doing*?"

"Sorry." Jamie eased her movement, which ended the bed's complaint, but she didn't stop stretching, didn't stop reaching. Because maybe, just maybe... *Yeah, yeah, feels like baling wire.*

"What the hell're you doing?"

I'm trying, *dammit!* But Jamie decided not to say it aloud, decided not to look back at Rhys. Instead, she sent her fingers back and forth, back and forth along the top of the bed frame, which now emitted tiny irregular squeaks.

"Oh christ, that's just great." Rhys didn't disguise her anger. "Two snoring pricks and a fucking wingnut."

Jamie heard the disappointment in Rhys's hoarse whisper. *Expected more, huh? Well, this is all I've got. I don't know what else to do.* So much for even getting to be friends with Martina Rhys. Jamie squeezed her eyes shut and continued her search. *Please, just ten or eleven inches...*

"Will you settle down, dammit?" Rhys's voice darkened toward desperation and she seemed not to notice the small snap that came from the top of Jamie's bed frame. "You're driving *me* nuts now!"

For a nanosecond, Jamie ceased all movement. *Almost, almost...* When she began a small repetitive motion, she saw Rhys's eyes blink too fast. Chest heaving silently, Rhys turned away from her just as the taunting sounds of the Pirates' poker game and the tunes of an old Latin-hip fusion rock band wafted toward them.

Jamie stretched herself farther, harder, kept her hands circling rhythmically in defiance of the restraints. *Come on...come to Mama...* And then, at last, another snap. She raised her hands as much as the manacles allowed and angled her head back, back to gaze at the length of wire. *Yes, thank you, yes, yes!* Jamie clutched it in both hands and let the rest of her body relax.

But not for long. *Okay, okay, now gotta break it in two.* Jamie stretched again and pushed the wire against the concrete wall a few inches from the top of the bed frame to make the first bend. The metal resisted—a good thing, since the tools she needed to craft had to be strong, and a bad thing because hard metal would be tougher, maybe even impossible, to craft at all. Sacrificing her hands and her ankles, she kept at it.

"Ha!" Jamie exhaled when she finally felt that third snap. She craned to get a look at what were now two pieces of wire, one in each hand. They still needed a lot of work. She decided to start with the short piece. *Can't do shit without a torque wrench.* She'd work first on bending it.

"Rhys."

Rhys ignored her.

"Dammit, Rhys, talk to me."

Rhys turned and scowled but refused to meet Jamie's eyes. "What?"

"If we could undo these cuffs, and maybe get the cell door open—"

"Oh christ! Will you shut the fuck *up*? This goddamn shit ain't over yet and if I'm gonna get my ass through tomorrow I need some sleep."

"Listen to me, Rhys, okay? Indulge me for a minute." Jamie stopped all movement and stared Rhys down. "If we can get out of the cuffs and open that padlock on the cell door—*if*—can you see a way we can get out of the camp?"

Rhys snarled between clenched teeth, her slivered eyes now launching their fury at Jamie. "So you know how to pick locks or something, Gwynmorgan?"

Jamie fluttered her eyebrows and winked.

Lips slightly parted, Rhys gaped. Jamie grinned.

"My god," puffed Rhys. "My god. Let me think." She fell into silence, her eyes closing.

"No promises, understand? These pieces of wire I've liberated are a little soft, but they might just work. If I can make them into something, then we need a plan for getting the rest of the way out. And that's on you, Rhys. 'Cuz I didn't see the camp at all. Nothing."

"Okay…" Rhys murmured, her face tightening, her eyes staring through Jamie, who'd already resumed work on the torque wrench. "How to get out…"

After a while she spoke up again. "It's a long shot, you know? But what the fuck. If they're not using cameras and if they stick with the same protocols, maybe I *can* see a way. Mmm, we gotta get out of the cuffs and open the cell before the next watch. Before. We whack the four guys down there playing poker. That'll be the hardest, but we can get pretty close before they see us, since they're around a corner. No line of sight to our cell door."

Rhys paused. After an unsteady inhalation, she continued. "We wait for the next watch to arrive, take them out, too. That'll be easier. We'll have the advantage of surprise and can use this watch's stunguns. Then we use their keys to unlock, um, let's see, two other doors. And we walk out as the departing watch. It'll be about twenty-five meters to the gate. But it'll be dark. Our faces will be shadowed by boonie hats. Nearest guy will be like ten, fifteen meters away. Far as I can tell, they don't challenge the winking skull and crossbones at the gate. We just wave at them and walk right out."

Jamie craned to get a look at the shorter length of wire. The last inch or so of one end had been bent about eighty degrees. "Bingo."

"Yes!" breathed Rhys.

"Now I gotta file it down. Cross your fingers." Again Jamie sacrificed her shackled ankles and hands to reach the concrete wall and scrape the wire against it. She scraped for a long time before examining the result. Yes, the wall was hard enough, the wire soft enough. "Slow going," she said. "Need to taper this fucker down."

Sensing Rhys's eyes move slowly over her nakedness and inspect her while she worked, Jamie counted the number of times she'd feel a swath of warmth on her skin and then find Rhys's gaze on the very spot. Once, twice, four times, five…

Too many times. *Because I'm going too slow. How long 'til a Pirate shows up? How long have I got?* And then, at last— "Yesss! We're in business!"

Rhys didn't hide her tears this time. Neither did Jamie.

"We make for their barracks," Rhys said, triumph in her whisper, while Jamie began work on the longer length of wire. "It's about twenty meters beyond the gate. Should be a truck there, maybe two. If we can get a truck, we can drive around the bay and be back in our own racks sometime tonight."

Rhys stiffened, her face ominous. "But the fellas have to go along with us. Four guys in the Pirates' watch. We need four of us to pull it off. The boys might want to just wait it out."

"Plus I have to make this wire into a workable pick," Jamie added, rewarding herself with a sneak-glance at Rhys's breasts. "Needs a little forty-five-degree bend at one end and— *Fuck!*"

Like it had a life of its own, the wire had flipped out of Jamie's fingers, which chased it, fumbled with it.

"No, Jamie, *please*," Rhys gasped just as Jamie caught the precious wire and managed to hold on to it.

"Okay, it's okay. I got it." Jamie closed her eyes, swallowed against the acidic splash of fear that stung her throat. She'd almost lost the torque wrench, too. "I got it."

"Take your time, Jamie. We got time."

"Yeah." Jamie let her eyes slide open and closed and open again. "Yeah, I'll take my time. Thanks." With swollen, bloody fingers, she continued while Rhys lay still and stared at the ceiling. Rhys didn't say it, but Jamie knew: They were running out of time. "Not as smooth as it should be, but I got one end done," Jamie whispered finally. "Gonna give it a try."

She began with the handcuff lock on her left wrist, twisting and warping her hands to work the torque wrench and the pick. Seconds, then what must have been minutes ticked by, and her hands started to cramp. "Damn. I popped a pair of these in thirty-eight seconds once. Ah, wait."

The first cuff clicked open, freeing Jamie's hands.

"Yes!" Jamie and Rhys whispered in unison.

With a groan of relief, Jamie raised her arms. Then she tried to sit up, but the cell went spinning again. "Dizzy," she murmured and flattened onto her back.

"Take it slow," Rhys said. "Nice and slow. And quiet, Jamie. Real quiet."

"Yeah. We still got time, right?"

"Yeah. Plenty of time. Just lie there a minute and breathe."

Still on her back, Jamie soon got the cuff on her right wrist to open. Not long after that, she sat up and stayed up. In another couple of minutes, she had her left ankle liberated, then her right.

"Easy, easy," Rhys said when Jamie tried to stand. "One small step for womankind, okay?"

Jamie forced what she hoped was a smile; she'd need all four limbs to get to Rhys's bed frame two feet away. "How about one small crawl?"

Like it would hurt too much to watch, Rhys's eyes shut when

Jamie leaned erratically toward the handcuffs on her wrists and inserted the torque wrench and pick into the first lock.

But Jamie's feel for the lockpins was reviving, and soon Rhys was free. She eased up from the bed carefully, giving Jamie's shoulder a thankful squeeze before she moved off to survey the hallway outside the cell.

"Shit!" Rhys's face had gone crimson. "I knew it. Fucking knew it! All the other cells are empty. I bet everyone else but us is back at the squadbay."

Behind her, Jamie tottered to Arnoldt's bed to wake him. "Wanna get the hell outta here? Rhys has a plan."

Wide-eyed, Arnoldt nodded. If he was thinking about lying there naked with two naked women standing over him, he gave no hint of it.

"Good man!" Jamie patted his chest. "Gotta wake up Moss, so give me a minute. And keep snoring, Arnoldt, but not too loud."

Moss roused more slowly, but he also agreed to the escape attempt, wrath flaming his eyes. Five minutes later, the men were on their feet and Jamie worked the padlock while Rhys laid out what each of them would do.

They executed Rhys's plan with resolute precision. Moss knocked two Pirates out cold before the other two knew what was happening. By Jamie's estimation, they completed the almost noiseless takedown in less than two minutes. Once all the Pirates were stungunned, Arnoldt and Moss kept up the sounds of the poker game while Jamie and Rhys dragged the four Pirates back to the cell. One by one, Jamie and Rhys stripped them, hogtied them with the cuffs, and gagged them with their own underwear.

Then they donned Pirate uniforms, careful to place the black bandanna armbands just right to show the red winking skull-and-crossbones insignia. So far, so good. Rhys's what-the-fuck plan was actually working.

"Wish we had time to play unstrip poker, fellas," said Rhys when she and Jamie brought Pirate uniforms to Moss and Arnoldt. "I'd beat your asses."

"Like hell," objected Arnoldt, who actually held a hand of cards. "I've never once lost to a girl."

Moss did not seem amused. "Jeezus, Arnie. Put that shit down!"

They gathered intel from the Pirates with brutal, stungun-supported efficiency. Rhys zapped the one with the most attitude while the other Pirates looked on, then she and Jamie hauled the one who seemed the most nervous out of the cell for a quiet conversation about who and what was where. The ashen-faced Pirate told them everything they wanted to know. Sincerely and as fast as he could. Soon after, a second, somewhat less cooperative Pirate confirmed what the first one said.

"Okay, so we believe them, right?" Rhys asked, fingering one of the stunguns.

"Yeah, I think so," Jamie answered.

"Well, if they told us the truth, then we still got a few minutes before the next watch shows up. We need to zap them again. All of them. Five-second jolts. That'll do them for a solid fifteen minutes. Five-second jolts, okay?"

"Yeah," Jamie said. *Long time, five seconds.* "I can do that."

❖

"Don't go fast, Rhys," urged Jamie. "Not yet." She didn't say what she couldn't stop thinking. *Walking right out of the camp, creeping through the Pirates' barracks like we owned it—way too easy.*

Rhys nodded, her hands tight on the steering wheel of the Pirates' truck as she maneuvered it away from the mock POW camp area.

"Still clear," Arnoldt said again without looking away from the rearview mirror, which he'd angled so he could watch the road behind them.

They all consumed saltine crackers and bottled water taken from the Pirates' barracks like it was the last food they'd ever get.

"You said you punctured all the tires, right?" Jamie asked for the third time.

"Every frigging one," Arnoldt replied for the third time, then allowed himself a long swig of water. "And you didn't wake anyone in their barracks, right?"

"Nope," Jamie said, exchanging a quick smile with Rhys.

A kilometer down the road, driving faster now, Rhys jerked the steering wheel hard to the right.

"What the fuck are you doing?" screeched Arnoldt.

"Let's go get the black boxes. Your squad's first, since it's the closest," Rhys said, already heading toward the water tower.

Arnoldt's are-you-crazy look became a shrug. "What the fuck."

"How about you, Jamie?" Rhys asked. "Up for it?"

The water and crackers had helped Jamie stave off the sensation that her body was turning to Jell-O. She fingered the stungun she still held, a real weapon. *And I'll use it, too, if any of those Pirate bastards come near me.* "Yeah, okay. What the fuck."

Moss stuck his head in the truck's rear window, his spirits obviously buoyed by water and crackers. And freedom. "What the fuck," he said. "I got plenty of room back here."

Shortly after 2300 hours, the truck rolled to a noisy halt under the floodlights outside Class 2801's squadbay on the other side of the base.

They'd have arrived sooner, but after picking up the black boxes, they detoured to the Exchange for more water and crackers. After nine or whatever days, water and crackers was all they could handle. Except for Arnoldt, who bought Slim Jims and several beers with money they'd found in the Pirates' pockets.

"Rise and shine!" Arnoldt hollered as he stumbled out of the truck.

Private First Class Rhys's two semesters of college gave her time-in-grade that put her senior among them. Hence Rhys was in command, and she'd wanted them to assume the position of attention upon exiting the truck. But she adapted. "Okay, Arnoldt, so let's try parade rest."

"Yes, ma'am!" But Arnoldt's feet splayed too far apart and his hands, on a mission of their own, formed an unsteady cone around his mouth. "Hey, you goddamn jarheads!" he bawled. "I said rise and fucking *shine!*"

The crowd he attracted in short order included the chief instructor, whose presence inspired Arnoldt to shut up and grin at Jamie instead.

Standing at attention, Rhys cleared her throat. "Private First Class Rhys reporting," she said. "Along with Private First Class Gwynmorgan and Privates Moss and Arnoldt."

A step behind Rhys, Jamie hadn't yet achieved the position of attention because the ground now rolled like the deck of a ship in heavy seas. The scene before her started to recede, which annoyed her. She really wanted to see this part.

In what seemed to Jamie like slow motion, Rhys waved to the back of the truck. "Hey, Moss, all three."

Moss tossed out a sixty-pound black box. "Squad One," he said without emotion. "Squad Two," he said as the second box thudded into the dirt. The third box landed at the chief instructor's feet, drawing a whistle from the man. "Squad Three."

Several seconds passed. No one made a sound. Jamie had to blink a few times to keep her vision from going blurry.

Rhys cleared her throat again. "Marine Scout/Sniper Class Two-Eight-Zero-One has completed its Combat Opponent Confidence Exercise mission, Gunnery Sergeant."

A boisterous cheer erupted from the rest of the class, now bunched behind the chief instructor, who signaled for quiet. "Escape?" he said.

"Yes, Gunnery Sergeant," said Rhys. "Also—" She signaled to Moss again, who jumped out of the truck and reached back in to tug at an object clearly heavier than sixty pounds. With one massive hand, Moss pulled out a hogtied Pirate and carried him about five feet to the chief instructor.

As Moss let the man go, Rhys finished. "We've captured an enemy combatant."

The Pirate hit the dirt belly-first and grunted, inspiring another long, elated roar from Class 2801. Moss dropped cross-legged to the ground, a serene smile on his handsome face as his eyes gradually closed. And then he was gone, engulfed in blackness. Everything was gone, except for Rhys's voice.

"Drama queen," said Rhys, sounding to Jamie like she had moved to the far end of a long tunnel. And then she was gone, too.

CHAPTER SEVEN

PROMISE

H ow'd you do it?"
    Oh god, please no. How could the Pirates have gotten her back? Had the lockpick, the escape, all of it, been a dream?

Jamie's eyes flailed open to find a low-lit room and high-tech guardrails rising up on either side of her. *Hospital.* The relief was intoxicating. *Really is over.* Her eyes closed and she tried to relax into the comfort of a pillow behind her pounding head.

Yet every cell in her body shrilled. *Oh jeezus, I saw an IV line...* Pharma. It burned cold where the needle violated her left hand and it roiled up her arm in a ruthless plunder of her strength, her reason, her will. *What kind of shit are they pouring into me?*

"Shush." Rhys's voice, almost whispering. "Gwynmorgan's still out."

"Okay, okay."

Fontana? But Jamie's eyes wouldn't open again. She was dizzy, she was sinking. She wanted to run, but her body didn't work, and in her head all the thoughts and images that ever formed there brawled chaotically with each other.

"So come on, Rhys. How'd you do it?" Fontana repeated.

"Gwynmorgan can pick locks."

"No shit."

No shit no shit no shit ricocheted across Jamie's brain until it coalesced into something she could hang on to. *Gotta get that IV line out.*

"I have a question for you," said Rhys. "Why didn't the Pirates release us with the rest of the class?"

"Answer depends on who's talking. Latest version seems to be that you guys offered what they're calling 'a valuable training opportunity.'" Pause. "But—"

"But what?"

Jamie's hands had been crawling toward each other. Now her right hand grabbed for the needle in her left. *Pull it!* When she did, the effect was immediate. Everything hurt more, everything became clearer, all the world calmed down.

"Well, by some remarkable coincidence, you were the only ones who paint-blanked any of their guys. Gwynmorgan got two, so did Moss. You and Arnoldt each nailed one."

"Fuck!" Rhys's voice pitched low and venomous.

"Word is they crossed way over the line. Messed with Moss and especially Gwynmorgan really bad. Worse than you and Arnoldt."

"Fucking assafrass," Rhys said. "That explains a few things." Jamie liked the way Rhys sounded. Protective, maybe even a little possessive.

"Scuttlebutt's saying Karpinsky wilted double-time," said Fontana. "Word is he told them right off it was Gwynmorgan who gave the alert. Told them she'd been out there for a while, and right after Moss hooked up with her the two of them must've seen something."

How'd you do it? *So that's what they meant.* Jamie shuddered against the recollection, against the escalating pain. But at least the world made sense.

"And here I was worrying we might've gotten a little too stungun-happy," grumbled Rhys.

Fontana snorted. "So, ready for the good news?"

"There's good news?" Rhys's tone dripped sarcasm.

"Karpinsky's been dropped on request. And the whole Reconnaissance Field Interrogation Training Program is under formal investigation—what they do, how they do it. Officers scrambling for cover, NCOs transferred. It's one big fucking scandalous jackup."

"And nobody wants to fry our asses?"

"Hell no, Rhys." Fontana chuckled. "All four of you are in the Scout/Sniper Finish with bells on. You guys've given our brass one whomping gloat."

❖

"God, woman, you're soaked. Must've been quite the downpour," said Rhys when Jamie entered their room. Short hair wet and spiky from her shower, only a towel wrapped low around her waist, magnificent breasts glistening, Rhys stared. "The price of going last, huh?"

Jamie decided the best reply would be a minimal shrug, offered as she peeled her gaze off Rhys to lay her E112 sniper rifle in its designated position in the cabinet next to the door. She'd managed to avoid the thrall of those breasts and look right into Rhys's eyes. Even so, she couldn't figure out if Rhys knew yet.

Now she had two reasons to keep her back to Rhys: The temptation of Rhys's breasts, and she didn't want Rhys to ask about her day. Jamie started removing sodden gear and tried to ignore the trill of arousal set off by even this sidelong glimpse of Rhys unadorned. "The op order's been revised," she said to the wall. "I'm teamed with Moss next. You got Arnoldt."

"Yeah, I know," Rhys lamented. "Wish me luck."

Scout/Sniper Class 2801—now twenty-six strong—had moved to dormitory-style barracks, two to a room. So for Jamie, fourteen-hour days were punctuated by vertiginous nights in the bunk right below Martina Rhys's. Night after night, she fell asleep imagining the galvanic power of Rhys's touch, dreamed of Rhys wrapped around her, only to wake pulsing and wet and impoverished.

At least the days offered no opportunities for such inventions; the members of Class 2801 were far too busy.

Usually the pigs, as the instructors labeled all scout/sniper trainees, operated in teams of two and four, alternating as spotter and sniper. But on this day near the end of the first phase of their training, they'd each worked alone on very long distance targets in an evolution called the Known Distance Solitary Shoot. Rhys had gone second out of twenty-six and finished up hitting the black four out of five times at 1500 meters—a fine performance that Jamie, the last shooter of the day, heard about well before she got to the 1500-meter line.

Yet for all the competitiveness of Scout/Sniper School, Jamie didn't think about Rhys's shot as something to beat. Getting into the zone, into that immaculate bubble with an E112 sniper rifle served as its own reward.

One of the instructors called the electronic-firing E112 a "masterpiece" and Jamie couldn't disagree. It combined accuracy, range, durability, quick-swap barrels, and light weight with a pulsed nano-laser calc array in its smartscope.

"This weapon," the instructor said as he cradled an E112 and held up a sleek new-generation .416-caliber bullet between thumb and forefinger, "is designed to put ten of these within five inches of each other at a thousand meters. Any pig who can't do that with this baby does not belong here."

Jamie melded with her E112; together they hunted their target. The weapon relieved a snipe of all that calculating, of course, thanks to the smartscope—but, as Jamie was learning, this had always been the easy part anyway. The hard part involved stillness.

For Jamie, shooting started with the calm of that immaculate bubble, which so many other recruits at Parris Island never quite found. It enveloped her while she took aim, absorbed the calculation readouts, visualized the bullet's trajectory. She sensed a profound secret she could almost comprehend when the calm deepened into a still point between her last exhalation and her next inhalation—a still point that proclaimed its transcendent Now and nothing moved, nothing in all the world but her one finger separate from the rest of her making its one minimal flick. Then came the clap of sound, the rifle butt recoiling its satisfaction into her shoulder as she watched the wedge-shaped trace of the bullet finish its fated journey and slam down the target amidst a distant burst of dust.

Everyone else had finished the Known Distance Solitary Shoot by the time Jamie faced the target 1500 meters away, so only the instructors saw her hit black five out of five at that distance, then again at 1800 meters, and, finally, at 2100 meters. More than two kilometers. Certainly no record, but sure as hell the best *she'd* ever shot.

Even so, Jamie didn't want to talk with Rhys about that, didn't want to see the squinty resentment that Rhys wouldn't be able to mask. Better to talk about tomorrow.

And why not? The marksmanship fundamentals and observation exercises of Phase One paled next to the upcoming tests of their abilities in stalking and unknown distance shooting. Tomorrow began the make-or-break part of Scout/Sniper School. Long slogs through swamp and thicket, fistfights with gargantuan insects, sleepless nights. Crawling through underbrush carefully enough not to rouse birds or crickets.

Hunkering motionless for hours disguised as a thicket. Lying dormant for days at a time in your own urine waiting to engage a target.

So say something, dammit. But saying something would require turning around, and maybe Rhys had taken off that towel…

Jamie found Rhys's lack of self-consciousness glorious—and terrifying. Every time Rhys dressed or undressed in front of her, she struggled not to gawk. Rhys seemed oblivious when, always a nanosecond late, Jamie looked away to carefully peruse the floor, to hope the flush of embarrassment wouldn't creep above her neck to flame across her cheeks.

Then sometimes Rhys would slide by too close, too slow in the tight space. And Jamie's breath would catch and her body would cease all movement, as if immobility would keep the hum of her need from exciting the molecules of air around her like a tuning fork.

This time, though, Rhys didn't budge. "Orders got changed because of Fontana," Rhys said. "Scratched his cornea on a bush during the burn-through yesterday. Had to drop, so I end up with Arnoldt."

Jamie turned around. *Christ, Rhys, how the hell do you find out about stuff so damn fast?* "Fontana's out?" she managed to say. "Jeez, that's shit luck." She meant to say more, but she'd found Rhys staring at her and couldn't pull in a full breath because her gut had seized up.

"C'mon, Gwynmorgan, let me help you get that hydration pack off your back." Rhys stood now in front of the gear cabinets. They were inches apart; despite the distracting proximity of Rhys's breasts, Jamie noticed that Rhys's abdominals, too, had tensed.

Jamie turned away again, exhaling, swallowing against the cramp in her throat while Rhys pulled a strap over one shoulder. Rhys's fingers lingered. Did they linger on purpose? Could the heat on her neck be Rhys's breath, or just her own hysterical imagination?

A hint of honeysuckle—Marty Rhys's scent—filled Jamie's nostrils and the heat rose to caress her face. Which was probably why she never registered the clumsy clomping in the hall outside getting louder, closer—not until the door burst open and Arnoldt blurted, "Yo, girls, it's almost chowti—"

Jamie froze, but Rhys whirled to face him. "For chrissake, Arnie," she barked, "I'm *menstruating* here! How about knocking first?"

Mouth agape, Arnoldt stumbled backward out of the room,

slamming the door as he retreated. Jamie couldn't move, couldn't look at Rhys. *What did he see? Was there something to see?*

After a long pause, Arnoldt's subdued voice came tentatively from the other side of the door. "You guys ready to get chow? It's, uh, eighteen minutes and counting. Beef stew tonight, y'know! And mashed potatoes!"

The women glanced at each other and tried not to giggle. Whenever possible, Arnoldt was first in the chow line. And Arnoldt's favorite chow was beef stew.

"I need to wipe down my weapon, Arnie," Jamie called to him. "And I gotta shower. How about saving us a couple slots? We'll be there in twenty."

"Sweet! Me and Moss'll head over now." And he galumphed down the hall.

"Jeezus, Rhys, you have a real gift." Jamie shook her head, let the grin take her face before she dipped her head. "I bow before the master. I think maybe you finally got us a bit of— What?"

Rhys glared at Jamie. "Heard about your twenty-one hundred meters."

Fucking A. "Marty, I—"

"How the *hell* did you do that?" Dark eyes blazing, Rhys took the step toward Jamie that brought their bodies together, and then she claimed Jamie's mouth.

Oh. My. God. She's. Kissing. Me. Every nerve ending in Jamie's body fired at once and she plunged into the sweet lilt of Rhys's breath, the opulence of Rhys's lips, Rhys's tongue. She heard a moan—her moan, pulled out of her by the current pulsing between them. Her jittery hands clasped Rhys's hips. Her clit punched double flips and triple flips that soared into her belly, into her chest as Rhys's tongue asserted, then lured, then caressed.

"Gotta stop," Rhys murmured too soon.

"R-Raincheck…"

"Promise?"

"Oh yeah, Marty, I sure as hell do. Cross my heart."

❖

Everything was squared away at last—weapons, gear, and

uniforms cleaned and stowed, studying done, quarters inspection-ready. The barracks building had gone quiet and dark. And the gibes rippling through the chow line had made it clear that on this night, on any night henceforth, nobody would be barging in without knocking first.

Judging by Rhys's second-thoughts glance during chow, Jamie knew she should be having second thoughts, too. Straight, gay, frontside, backside, the Corps had accepted intimacy between marines—but with two notable, old-line exceptions more rigorously enforced than ever after queers became legal and cunts got the right to qualify for combat units: No fraternizing between officers and enlisted personnel, and no sex between marines in the same unit. Both were considered detrimental to unit cohesion and order, and all culprits faced inevitable reprimand, demotion, and reassignment.

I shouldn't do anything, Jamie decided as she stripped down to the Marine-issue coyote-brown tank top and mid-thigh briefs she always slept in. But she stretched herself out on her bunk, not under the blanket, and battled to remain still. The kiss had done that. The kiss had made her incapable of not blatantly staring while Rhys's sleek form emerged out of the uniform's woodland camouflage. In Rhys, Jamie beheld everything she imagined a woman should be, everything she was not.

Rhys had a kind of blond abundance. There was something sumptuous about her face, an exuberance in those unlikely brown eyes, a ripeness that showed her to be truly whole, from the inside out. When at last she tapped off the ceiling light, a moonbeam angled through the room, casting new shadows across the resplendent curves beneath her underwear.

From the lower bunk, Jamie watched, waited. Would Rhys decide that sometimes a kiss is just a kiss, promises be damned?

Like she was ready to climb into the upper rack, Rhys planted a foot on the bunk frame, then looked down. "Ever done this before?"

"No," said Jamie, who had lost the fight for stillness. Rhys was nearly three years older; now the gap felt cavernous.

Rhys shook her head and softly repeated it. "No."

"I've wanted to, though." Jamie should've stopped there, right there. Not another word. Not another twitch. She had rules about this. About caring too much, needing too much. Showing too much. *Let*

Rhys step over the line, right? Rhys is in command here, right? But Jamie grabbed Rhys's hand. And she begged. "Oh god, Marty, please touch me. Just this once. Please. I can't stand it anymore."

"Mmm." Rhys's gaze strayed the length of Jamie's restlessness. "Just this once."

Rhys descended quick, catlike, her breath bathing Jamie's face as she pumped her hip between Jamie's legs and roughly pinned Jamie's wrists. Raised up on both arms, her face ruled by a fierceness Jamie hadn't seen before, Rhys stared down and thrust her hip again.

It's said that whenever two marines are together, one is in command and the other is formed. Every muscle in Jamie's body quivered as she formed up beneath Rhys, arching into Rhys's energy. "Please touch me," she whispered.

Rhys went abruptly still, her eyes softening. "I will. Just this once." She sinuated herself along Jamie's length, and beneath the humid sweetness of her breath Jamie met her lips, startled at the new tremor of contact, and undulated into her kiss.

"Close your eyes," Rhys ordered.

Jamie obeyed. Rhys's warm fingertips danced under Jamie's tank top and played with her eager nipples. *Yes!* Jamie wanted to shout. *Yes, yes, just like that.*

But Rhys abandoned her. For an abyssal second, Rhys was gone and Jamie almost opened her eyes. Then Rhys's hand was massaging her belly in a slow, deliberate, descending circle.

"Did you know in women this is called the *mons veneris?*" Rhys ran her fingers into Jamie's pubic hair.

"Uhh...n-no—oh...*oh...god...*"

Rhys cupped her hand and continued her massage. "Mmm..." Rhys's fingers plunged and circumnavigated their prize. "Like in venerate."

And that's when Jamie discovered what ascension was; at the end of Rhys's fingers, she levitated, bounced, rollicked, like a puppet on a string. *This is gonna make me...I wanna see her, look at her when I...*

"Uh-uh..." Rhys matched the movement of her finger to the cadence of her command. "Keep...your...eyes...closed..." The rhythm of Rhys's touch accelerated, then ceased. "Unless you want me to stop."

"N-no...please..."

"Mmm," Rhys purred, fingers trilling.

Jamie shuddered, molten and helpless. In all her many anticipations of surrender, she had never quite imagined this. "Oh god oh god oh god," she heaved, bucking on the bed, her throat tensing futilely against sound as she dangled at the end of Rhys's fingers.

"Shh." Rhys slowed, her touch lightened. "Eeeeasy." She leaned in and kissed Jamie, absorbing the small sounds of Jamie's whimper.

Simmering now, Jamie defied Rhys and opened her eyes. She had to look at this woman who made her feel so... "Oh god, Marty...I...didn't...know..."

Rhys grinned. "Now you do." Her rhythm syncopated, quickened, deepened. "Almost." She bent close again, kissing Jamie's breathy moan, riding Jamie's surge. "Do you like Almost?"

"Y-yes." *Oh yes yes yes yes yes...*

Rhys's rhythm changed again, the air Jamie had just inhaled burst out of her, and Almost tipped into a spinning, spiraling, electric climax that lit every synapse.

Arching, twisting, Jamie clutched Rhys as she came, remembering their first moments together, naked and manacled in a prison cell, afraid and in pain. She was thankful for it. If they hadn't shared that torment, they'd never be allowing themselves this ecstasy. Jamie ebbed slowly, unwillingly, chasing the waves of quaking elation.

At last, she turned on her side toward Rhys. "I want to do that for you," she said in a hush, maneuvering Rhys beneath her. "Just this once."

"Yeah." Rhys's eyes sparked. "Just this once."

In exactly the way she'd always imagined initiating a kiss with a woman, Jamie kissed Rhys—lightly at first, to make sure she was really wanted, then strengthening, committing.

Mons veneris. Jamie nuzzled into the soft, resilient warmth of Rhys's breasts. Rhys didn't move, but her breathing went quick and shallow and her nipples stood at full attention, ready for inspection in the ghostly moonlight. Jamie approached them slowly, slowly, watching Rhys's breasts rise and retreat and rise again with her respiration, then shiver with the first hint of Jamie's breath upon them.

Like in venerate. Mouth lingering at Rhys's nipples, Jamie stroked

Rhys's contracting abdomen and slipped her fingers between Rhys's legs. She'd wondered so often about this First Time. Would she know what to do, recognize when she was doing it right? Should she ask?

It's said that marines are taught to think for themselves. With scrupulous care, Jamie gazed at Rhys, listened to Rhys, explored Rhys, and discovered a body eager to adhere to Newton's third law of motion: *If you press a clit with your finger, your finger is also pressed by the clit.*

And then Jamie closed her eyes and lost herself in Marty Rhys.

"Not bad for a beginner," Rhys said later before climbing into her own rack.

"Really truly?"

"Um, yes, really truly."

But Jamie couldn't shake the impression that there was something Rhys preferred not to say.

❖

"No leave after graduation." Rhys reported one day in early May as the squad took a pee break. "Just overheard the chief instructor talking about it."

"That is not funny," said Jamie. They were supposed to get ten days' leave after Scout/Sniper School. Just three weeks left and then ten days when she'd get to go home with Marty, have ten whole days with Marty.

"We're shipping out right away. No leave."

"You serious?" asked Moss.

"They already got us assigned to units," Rhys insisted. "Gonna end up in Okinawa, most of us. Then the Philippines. Another fight over the Spratly Shelf."

"Nah," said Jamie. "That's way too fucked up. You must've heard wrong."

But, as usual, Rhys had heard right. Several days later, it was official. They were all about to become part of Operation Palawan Liberation.

"What the fuck is a Palawan, anyway?" grumbled Arnoldt.

"Didn't you listen to anything they said?" Rhys grumbled back.

"Southmost major island in the Philippines, Arnie," said Moss.

"Oh yeah." But Arnoldt's tone was a question.

"Officially an Incursion," sighed Jamie. "Islamist, but Chinese backing."

"Yeah?"

Rhys rolled her eyes. "Jeezus, Arnie, were you fucking sleeping?"

"We were fucking up all night!" Arnoldt protested. "I only dozed off for a couple minutes. So what else?"

Jamie ticked off the grim details. "Bad guys took over bunches of gas and oil platforms on the Spratly Shelf, and also Palawan and, uh— oh yeah—the Calamian islands to the north and Balabac to the south. Expeditionary Unit's been deployed from Oki—amphibious assault on one of the Calamians. Place called Busuanga. Fierce resistance." Jamie tapped Arnoldt's head once, twice. "Any of this ringing a little bell up there?"

"Oh yeah. What else?"

"No leave after graduation," said Moss glumly. "Been cancelled. We go straight to Oki like thirty-six hours later."

"What?"

❖

"Hey you. Gwynmorgan."

Jamie welcomed the sound of Rhys's voice, even so hoarse and subdued. Somehow, as Jamie couldn't help but hope, Rhys had found her way to Jamie's side in the enormous plane.

After the graduation ceremony, when Jamie received the Class Top Gun award and a boost to lance corporal, she wondered if Rhys would even try to hook up with her for the long flight west.

Because Rhys had taken a tough double punch. She'd come in a humiliating third in the marksmanship scores. Worse, Class 2801's lance corporal promotions had been based on points and, according to scuttlebutt, Rhys had missed the cut by only one—a single devastating point. She'd concealed her disappointment well, but Jamie saw the tense lines locked in around her mouth, the small cleft that lingered between her eyebrows.

Yet here she was anyway. Surrounded by their gear and the reverberations of the plane's four huge engines, Jamie found real comfort in sitting shoulder to shoulder with her and hoped Rhys felt the same, even in their silence. Among the three hundred marines aboard, conversation stayed clipped, utilitarian. They were all preparing for the combat that was about to define their lives.

After they'd been airborne for about an hour, Rhys talked some, trying to tease, before reading from the duty station orders she yanked out of Jamie's right chest pocket. "You told me where you're going, but god, my mother wouldn't stop bawling, and I forgot. Let's see: Second Marine Division, Eighth Marine Regiment, Third Battalion Scout/Sniper Platoon."

"Just back from Busuanga. Word is they had it pretty rough."

"I, uh…" There was a higher frequency in Rhys's voice and she had trouble pulling in a full breath. "I didn't think my very first duty station would take me into actual combat."

"Yeah." Jamie grunted sympathetically, staring down at her knees. "Me either."

But what else could she say?

The first time she held an E19 at Parris Island, Jamie knew the Corps had given her the weapon and taught her how to use it for a reason. Sooner or later, she understood right then, she'd probably shoot at someone, and they'd probably shoot back. When she found out she could do Scout/Sniper School, she grasped that she might get shot at plenty. And she figured that, yes, she could get killed. Now, as the plane rumbled westward, she felt the odds climbing fast.

Who'd give a shit if I die? Jamie quashed a shrug, but the thought persisted. She glanced at Rhys, who gazed intently at her. What did Marty want? Solace? Hope? For herself, Jamie had neither. But, but—

"You want Marty to care if you die."

Jamie knew that voice. The white-haired woman from her dream, from some inner world that couldn't possibly be real, had whispered to her again, soft in her ear. Yet the voice sounded as real, as tangible as anything Jamie had ever heard. What's more, she had to admit, it had a point. And impeccable timing. How much should she worry about which side of the reality tracks it came from?

From her left chest pocket, Jamie retrieved a neatly folded black bandanna with a red winking skull and crossbones. She handed it to Rhys with her own wink and a small smile.

"Hey." She bumped Rhys's shoulder. "You'll be okay."

Jamie believed it, too. Marty would continue to exist; Marty would be the one who'd care about what happened to her. The only one, probably, but at least there'd be somebody.

Maybe Jamie's faith was catching, because the apprehension in Rhys's face eased as she held the now-unfolded bandanna with both hands and stared at it.

"Wait." She turned to Jamie, her eyes worried. "*You* should have this—"

Nudging Rhys's shoulder again, Jamie patted her left chest pocket. "I kept two," she lied. "That one's yours."

Rhys carefully refolded the bandanna, put it into her own left chest pocket, and after that, Jamie could tell, Rhys found it a little easier to breathe.

They slipped into silence, then into fitful sleep. They got to disembark for twenty minutes and stretch when the plane refueled on the West Coast, then once more on Oahu, but they didn't talk, merely stood beside one another, shoulder leaning into shoulder. Jamie pushed away thoughts of what would come next, sometimes having to blink back tears, and inhaled Rhys's scent while she silently counted down the hours, the minutes left to them. Rhys had been assigned to the same regiment but a different battalion, and they wouldn't see each other much. Maybe not at all. Maybe not ever again.

For a brief while after she first made love with Marty Rhys, Jamie allowed herself the illusion that some sort of intelligent hand might be at work. Hell, for the first time in her life she could actually envision being happy—after just-this-once turned into twice and then into three times and then she stopped counting.

When she stopped counting, she started dreaming, imagining. Even imagined that she and her buddy, her lover might get away with serving in a unit together, and that might turn into a life together.

Now, however, Jamie reverted to what she knew to be the implacable truth. *Alby might've been a weary river, but I'm just a grain of sand caught in the wind. And there sure as shit ain't no such thing as an intelligent hand.*

When the plane's wheels hit the Marine base tarmac on Okinawa, Rhys laced her fingers through Jamie's and held on until the plane stopped moving.

As they lugged their seabags into the Okinawan humidity, Jamie said to Rhys, "Text me so I know you're not in the brig, okay?"

"Yeah, you too, Gwynmorgan."

"Promise."

"Promise," Rhys said and managed to hold on to her smile.

CHAPTER EIGHT

CHERRY

"Gonzo! This one's yours."

Shaking his head, a square rock of a guy whose nametape read "Alonzo" inspected her like she was a dubious piece of meat.

Three meters away, Lance Corporal Gwynmorgan wanted to make a careful examination of the grass at her feet, but she forced herself to meet Alonzo's obsidian gaze while he checked her out. Abruptly, he began to walk away. As an apparent afterthought, he said over his shoulder, "On me, cherry."

Trying to ignore her roiling gut, Jamie grabbed her seabag and scrambled after him. Caprice, she decided; the platoon NCO had assigned the new replacements to the Three-Eight scout/sniper unit's depleted squads with what seemed like random indifference. If she'd been standing a few feet to the left or the right, would she be someone else's spotter now? *That's what I frigging get for chumming with Arnoldt. And why, why do I always end up in the same place as Arnoldt, anyway? Why couldn't I have ended up in Second Battalion with Rhys?* Trudging behind this grim man to whom she'd be chained indefinitely, Jamie saw Caprice as a wanton, narcissistic goddess descended from some unseen pantheon for a momentary trifle. *And now frigging look at me.*

Sooner than she expected, Alonzo halted at the entrance to a tent, clearly his tent. It stood in a sea of tents—large ones, small ones—arranged as though they comprised their own forward operating base. He swung around to face her. "Whole Three-Eight's in FOB-hooches. Don't want us getting too comfortable. Except for the ocifers, of course.

Their heinies are in air-conditioned wetbox CHUs." He squinted at her. "Regs say you're allowed to hooch up with another female, but if you want to be part of *my* snipe team, you better figure on planting your hammock here and busting hump. And I mean twenty-four seven, understand? Your call. And call it now, because I'm a busy dude."

What the fuck is this? Some kind of crude come-on? Jamie studied him for a heartbeat, assessing, deciding. "Here," she said. *But I'll fucking rip your face off if you fucking touch me.*

His head dipped a minimal acknowledgment and he ducked into the hooch they'd now share. Bigger than a traditional field-hooch, but not even close to the size of the containerized housing units that typically filled established forward operating bases. Jamie got the hint. Operation Palawan Liberation would be going down "in the rough."

"So this is the drill, boot," Alonzo said when she followed him in. "I sleep on the right. You're over there. I'll find us a sheet or something to string down the middle for when I need to scratch my balls or you need to"—he shot her a frowning glance—"do whatever it is you do. And when you're sleeping, you will keep your back to me. I don't wanna hear you goddamn breathe, got it?"

"Got it, Corporal."

He glowered his command: Stand fast. "You do exactly what I say when I say and you might see your next birthday. Your job is to watch my back and follow my tracers. You see something interesting, you point it out, short and sweet. You call the wind or calc the Coriolis effect or air density or what-the-fuck-ever if and only if I request it. You position your ass to give me corrections when I say. *I* decide where we go, how we get there. Out there, *I* decide when you piss and when you shit. *Comprende?*"

"Yes, Corporal, I do."

"Hmph." Once more, his eyes moved slowly down her body and back up again. "How goddamn old are you, anyway?"

"Seventeen, Corporal."

His wide, dark-featured face revealed nothing. "Stop calling me corporal. And *maybe* I'll stop calling you cherry...cherry. Name's Alonzo, like the nametape says." He paused for one second, two... "Medicos shoot you up yet? They're poking everyone with a fancy-ass multi-flu shot. So's we don't bring home a new pandemic. And make sure they give you that beta-defensin booster, paleface. Otherwise you'll end up with tropical ulcers and god-knows-what nasty jungle shit."

"Yes, Corp—um—" Jamie stopped. Calling him Alonzo just didn't seem right. He ignored the question in her eyes; she was on her own about that.

"You got about two hours before chow. Use that nice little pole set they gave you to erect your hammock and grab some rack time. You'll need it. Tomorrow you get the rest of your new gear and we'll have to diddle with the platoon for a while. Then I start putting you through your paces."

Jamie used some of that two hours to call Rhys, but didn't get her. So it was down to textmail, and everyone knew better than to write anything truly private in a textmail destined for sifting through a military filter server.: hope u ok .. no liberty in sight .. need some beginner's luck .. jg

❖

The new cammies felt good against the skin. Unlike what Jamie had worn at Parris Island and snipe school, this light material breathed well and its subtly redesigned camouflage pattern disappeared into the tropical forest background. Even the boonie hat's brim shaped up just right.

"The Corps ain't giving this to you just to pamper your sorry butts," explained a battalion supply NCO as she supervised distribution of the stuff. "It's a surveillance countermeasure. Wear it, get underneath it, behind it, and the enemy will not see you—not with thermal or infrared or radar. But our combat operations centers *will* see you, understand? Because it's full of nanomolecules that the geeks can automatically program using downlink signals. Cammies, tarps, everything. Understand? Means they got y'all showing up bright and shiny for our satellites and drones. So behave, boys and girls. When you're out there on an op, you're on Candid fucking Camera."

Then came the IMS wraps like what the Pirates had. Wraparound eyewear with a built-in comlink and built-in integrated multiwave sensors—thermal, infrared, and radar—that Jamie had coveted ever since the Cock. But the snicker about UFOs that rolled through the veterans of Operation Palawan Liberation's "rough landing" on Busuanga was lost on Jamie.

"Means 'unidentified fucking out-there,'" Alonzo jeered when Jamie dared to ask him about it. "When the enemy gets their hands on surveillance countermeasures—and some already have—integrated multiwave sensors are just about useless."

❖

"Three weeks, cherry." Alonzo sounded dire. "Ain't much time to make you into something. Next lesson commences once we finish this afternoon's combat conditioning march."

Three weeks. That's how long her platoon would train on Okinawa before helicoptering back into Busuanga ahead of the rest of the battalion.

From the first moment, she "belonged" to the laconic, cynical Alonzo, and he kept her on the job twenty-four seven as promised. No time for Rhys, who even came by once looking for her but ended up leaving a scribbled note on her vacant hammock. No time for anything but training. "When u around?" Rhys texted over and over.

"Wish I knew," Jamie had to reply every time.

Although Alonzo didn't talk at all unless their work required it, Jamie managed to put together some essentials from the scraps. He insisted on sharing a hooch with her only because he didn't want to end up "out there" with a raw newbie who could get him killed; she had no sense that he liked her. And certainly he didn't like officers, having recently been demoted by a whole committee of them to save some ringknocker's commission.

Over his wife's objections, he'd just started his third enlistment when everything went to shit—the demotion, the transfer to the Three-Eight, and, only four weeks later, what he referred to just once as "the inexcusable chaos" of Operation Palawan Liberation's first salvo on Busuanga. "Embrace the suck my ass," he bitched. "Nothing'll get you screwed like ambitious officers planning missions off of really shitty intel."

Like all modern Marine scout/sniper units, the one attached to the Eighth Regiment's Third Battalion Headquarters Company had long since been restructured into a classic platoon made up of three sergeant-led squads, each comprising twelve people trained to work in two- or four-man teams, led by a platoon NCO, cared for by its own corpsman, and commanded by its own officer, a first lieutenant who reported to the battalion's intelligence officer.

Forty-two souls in all.

The Three-Eight's snipe platoon had lost sixteen people in the battle for a firm foothold on Busuanga before the battalion was relieved and sent back to Okinawa. Thirteen of those lost, an entire squad worth of snipes, had gone home TUIAB—tits up in a box.

It didn't take Jamie long to figure out what Alonzo never discussed. He'd survived unscathed because he was very good at what he did. By the fourth day of training, she appreciated her incalculable good fortune—even though Alonzo used up all her free time and smoked her ferociously when her concentration slipped, forever hollering the amount of training time left to them.

"Whatsamatter with you? Seventeen days and five hours left, cherry. I want you goddamn frosty! So stop groping your goddamn dick—I mean your goddamn clit—and go again. Go. *Go!*"

About the twentieth time he said something like this to her, Jamie understood: More than self-preservation motivated Alonzo; he'd consider himself a contemptible failure if something happened to her that he might, however remotely, have prevented. He wanted to see in her the automatic, instinctive responses that would save her ass during the indiscriminate, unpredictable savagery of the Real Thing.

From Alonzo she also learned more than a few tricks of the trade. Some of it concerned techniques that hadn't yet found their way into the Corps's formal training—like how a .416-caliber round really could take down an attack helicopter if you could put even a single one into just the right place in the rear rotor housing or that particular spot on the belly of certain types of Chinese helos where a wayward hydraulic line was slightly exposed.

Occasionally it involved "just in case" workarounds: How comlinks and IMS detection gear could be taken live without the required link to the unitag ID implanted in every marine's ear cartilage—"Just in case the enemy rips your goddamn ear off." And sometimes it was about every woman for herself: How to avoid such lance coolie unpleasantries as latrine duty and field day cleanups, how to finagle the field meals of one's choice rather than whatever some supply sergeant shoved at you.

Alonzo should have been NCO of a snipe platoon, or at least a squad, but the idiots who demoted him hadn't even given him a fire team to lead. Caprice left him only Lance Corporal Gwynmorgan, on whom he focused everything—all the knowledge, experience, and instinct of a decade in the Corps.

What Jamie learned from Alonzo caused her to worry for Rhys, whose textmails hinted at a more typical journey—from by-the-numbers training into a miserable stretch of new-guy servitude without encountering a decent noncom with the time or inclination to teach you how to get out of your own way.

❖

"Hey, Arnie!"

Sixteen days on Busuanga, and Jamie had seen him only once before. Not surprising. The Three-Eight's snipes spent little time at the battalion's forward operating base and rarely did they all muster at the FOB at the same time.

Instead, they went "out there," to the forward edge of the battle area or well beyond it. Working in pairs or as fire teams or entire squads, they served as guardian angels overwatching a company while it "disinfected" the island's fields, farms, and small villages. Or they slithered unnoticed through mangrove swamp or into sweltering, dripping forest to reconnoiter territory claimed by the enemy, the self-proclaimed People's Islamist Army.

"Well. If it ain't Gwyn-fuckin'-morgan."

"Whuddup, boy?"

"Just come in." Arnoldt looked and smelled raunchy after several days prowling steep, dense-growth hillsides, but he was juiced. "Cleaned out a little fishing village called, uh— Ah shit, who knows what it's called. Anyway, I spotted a couple of their snipes. First time for me, y'know? And my shooter nailed 'em nice and neat, one shot each." He glanced around before continuing, to make sure no one else heard him. "But jeez, Gwynnie, I *hate* them fucking snakes. Almost got bit by a temple viper yesterday. Foul green thing with white stripes, a good three feet long. I can deal with the crocs, y'know? But them snakes…"

"Alonzo catches wolf snakes sometimes when we can do a fire. Says it's okay because they're invasive, like the PIA. Cuts 'em into strips and barbecues 'em. They kinda taste like—"

"Oh christ." Arnoldt's face scrunched. "Don't talk about it. Tell me what's for chow tonight. In the mess, I mean."

"You're in luck." Jamie winked. "Beef stew."

"Ooh-rah! When you gonna be there? Maybe we can catch up."

"I wish, but I'm out of here in like an hour. All of second squad's heading way up north with Lima Company. Clearing coastal caves."

"Done it twice. Last time, we didn't find anybody. The PIA sons of bitches just get in their boats and sail away. Sure as hell don't seem to want to stand and fight. Word is the puff is out of their dragon, and *we* might be out of here soon. Back to Oki. Or maybe even stateside."

When Jamie mentioned all the talk about going home to Alonzo, he shook his head. "Nah. Way too easy." He squinted at her—an order. "Don't you goddamn believe it. Once we take the coasts, we go inland, because that's where the enemy's going. Into those goddamn hills and mountains with all those caves and primeval forests. It's gonna take a while. Trust me."

"But—"

"Listen to me, kid. We're TL-ing here, understand? Which means—"

"Tee-elling?"

"Treading lightly. Being nice to the civilians, respecting where they live, to show we're on their side. Why do you think we never get any air support? Because the brass already made a goddamn mess with air support, three days after the first assault started. Took out a schoolyard full of kids. Very not cool. So now all we see, maybe, if we're lucky, is a helo or two. The high-tech fight's going on out there on the Spratly Shelf where it's all oil and gas rigs. We do this fight here with the small stuff—squad automatic weapons, rifle-propelled grenades. Rifles in the hands of riflemen. And with snipes slippy-sliding into those goddamn hills."

"But we lose all advantage, don't we?" Reading about fourth-generation conflicts was one thing. But having to actually fight that way... "The PIA have snipes and small arms, too, and they claim to have civilian support."

"Don't worry, kid. Our side has you and me. And we'll be ready when this goddamn thing pops."

"When's it gonna pop?"

Alonzo shrugged. "Right after the PIA get the supplies they need. Soon."

❖

In boot camp, recruits counted training days. Aboard ship in the Fleet Marine Force, marines counted deployment days. During Operation Palawan Liberation, they counted RT days: How many days of the Real Thing done. Nobody jinxed themselves by tallying out loud how many days they had left to go.

For the first week or so, Jamie had tried not to count, but that didn't work. Every time she sent Rhys a message, or received one, all she could do was count. And yearn. So she allowed herself to think about the count just once a day, real quick when she woke up, right before she opened her eyes.

RT thirty-one. No chance to text Marty today.

Today Kilo Company would sweep PIA from the market town of San Salvacia. Kilo's three platoons would descend from three directions—first platoon moving up the only hard-surface road from the south, second platoon coming in off Guro Bay from the west, third platoon approaching from the north through the forest via a much longer, more rugged route that began on the banks of the winding, swampy Busuanga River.

An odd assortment of Three-Eight snipes had night-inserted some twenty-seven hours earlier to scout and run overwatch for Kilo. Satellite-borne cameras scanned from afar, but there'd be no air cover. Helicopters had a way of revealing to the enemy that marines might be in the neighborhood.

Working as a two-man team, Alonzo and Jamie had spent the night a kilometer northwest of the village in a tree hide that enabled them to overwatch the arrival of both second and third platoons as dawn lit the eastern sky. Alonzo and Jamie always worked as a pair, always on the toughest assignments that put them far "out there." Most of the time they were on their own, free of the worst follies of military hierarchy. Jamie believed it was the closest the platoon leaders could get to a demotion workaround for Alonzo.

The last two missions had kept them at the edges of small hamlets where they set up hides from which they targeted PIA, especially snipers and those with rifle-propelled grenades. But this mission took them once again into Busuanga's breathtakingly exotic forests and swamps.

To Jamie, at first, the island had seemed like a dramatic and strange Magic Kingdom. Then, in a matter of days, it started coming after her.

Compared to the wetlands of the Carolinas, Busuanga was like another planet. But a month in, Jamie had begun to think of herself as acclimated. To the heavy, clouded nights that robbed the sky of stars. To the rancid humidity, to the intense, unrelieved sweating, the perpetual thirst, the immense effort required to draw in a full, satisfying breath. To the unremitting attacks by insects, some huge and bizarre, others tiny and insidious, all of them escapees from some science fiction horror flick.

She had fought it at first. Tried too fervently to get dry and clean every day or two, needed too desperately to ease the endless itching that moved from one body part to another, always preferring locations with hair. All day, every day, she envisioned armies of many-legged monsters consuming her flesh.

After a while her crotch always itched and, yes, she scratched. Until Alonzo ordered her to stop and gave her antihistamines, hydrocortisone, and a coldpack. Once she obeyed, she adapted.

Sort of. She learned how to always be thirsty, always be sore and tired and just a little breathless. And itchy.

RT thirty-one and it had gotten a bit better. She'd become accustomed to the dull dread greeting her first waking awareness, didn't let it devolve into that longing for home that ate up so many of the marines around her.

It was because of their dreams, this longing. Jamie was sure of that after hearing so many conversations drift into descriptions of dreams rife with flawless portraits of everyday moments that once seemed so mundane—riding a bus through the same familiar streets, eating a favorite kind of ice cream, watching old videos. Regular, boring day-to-day life was what they dreamed about. Then they'd wake up in a hell ruled by mosquitoes and crocodiles and snakes and sweat and weird rashes.

For the first few days on the island, Jamie dreamed about Marty Rhys. Vivid sexual dreams that kept her squirming for hours. Not anymore, though. Jamie didn't dream at all anymore, which made Busuanga a little easier to cope with.

RT thirty-one and the plan called for Jamie and Alonzo to stay put. Which was okay with Jamie. Their hide had the virtue of being well off the soggy ground and free of snakes. They'd picked it for its elevation, for its superior burn-through qualities toward the east and south, for its ability to support their hammocks, for its strong, climbable branches that meant they could shift position quickly and evade being spotted by the enemy.

By 0700, however, combat operations center chatter and downlinked satellite visuals received via the comlink in their IMS-wraps made clear that third platoon had almost immediately bogged down north of the village in river swampland made deeper than expected by heavy monsoon rains. Worse, the snipe teams assigned to the hills east of the village had gone dark—no commo, no tracking signals.

"Goddamn," said Alonzo. "That's it. We're outta here. Gear up. Weapons, ammo, water. Leave the rest."

They'd received no orders, but Jamie knew better than to question him. So she was ready when the order came moments later: Head northeast on the double to suss out a better route for third platoon and scout for PIA.

Soon legions of leeches ambushed them as they trudged in and out of black slime up to their thighs. The slime sucked them down, detaining them for the crocodiles they couldn't see, taking them way beyond merely wet and filthy. Jamie had already witnessed a man lose a leg to a croc's jaws. And the leeches were enormous and clung to their pant legs, sensing the proximity of their blood. She'd heard stories about what happened when leeches got up your nose or up your twat, about all the diseases they vectored.

Alonzo said he was watching for crocs and showed her how to remove the leeches, starting at the smaller, thinner end by breaking the seal they created, then repeating the process at the other end, and finally tossing the pernicious creature well away. Jamie mastered the technique damn fast.

Keeping count with a taut mutter, she used her combat knife to fillet every single one with fastidious efficiency, then clamped the knife between her teeth until she spotted the next predator. Alonzo let her do it as long as she didn't slow down; he seemed to understand this was the price for her sanity. And it kept her mind off crocodiles.

Could Alonzo have anticipated this? At first light that morning, while she took her turn lathering on more cloakcream, he kept watch and whispered the whole time about his arcane plot to acquire two additional pairs of boots when they returned to the FOB so their others could get a chance to really dry out.

Now, when her head dropped to scrutinize the slime for new abominations, he nudged her to stay frosty, nudged her to focus beyond the grasping, choking, greedy growth. "C'mon, kid, keep those eyeballs where they can do some good. *We* do the surprising, not them."

The thought of those dry boots helped her obey.

CHAPTER NINE

YOU KEEP ON GOING

Though they hadn't detected any sign of either civilians or PIA, the frown on Alonzo's face looked different from any Jamie had seen on him so far. He was more than frosty. He was jumpy. And that made her jumpy.

Then came the call for help from Kilo Company's other two platoons, which had moved into San Salvacia without waiting for third platoon or, it appeared, the lost snipes who should have been overwatching the town from hides on the hill to the east.

The sweep of San Salvacia had turned into a clusterfuck.

Now, according to ops center commo, an intense grenade and small arms counterattack pinned down Kilo's first and second platoons near the village center. Those not already lying dead or wounded on the dirt road had taken refuge in the only concrete structure in the village, a colonnaded marketplace near the pier.

Resupplied at last by their allies 1,300 kilometers across the South China Sea, PIA fighters had made a stand in San Salvacia. Although Jamie and Alonzo were a kilometer away when the calls for aid came, they were closer than anyone else and arrived first.

"There," Alonzo whispered, pointing to a two-story wood-and-wattle house about halfway between the blacktopped road and the bay. It was the sole two-story building east of the firefight. First platoon must have moved right by it, believing it secure. Maybe it was. Maybe not.

Alonzo and Jamie approached it from the north, through the forest. It looked empty and quiet, as did the small shack closer to them, but the second floor of the house offered a perfect place from which to ambush first platoon once it moved past.

Jamie had already learned how to think like Alonzo. *Got to assume there's PIA inside, unloading on Kilo.* An electric-hot blast shivered through her arms and legs—the Fear making a grab for her. She managed to shiver it out of her, imagined it into a dark puddle at her feet.

A nod to Alonzo, a quick look behind her to ensure all was clear, and she scurried through low brush to a corner of the shack, her E19 set to silent rock-and-roll. She looked up, swung around the corner weapon-first, and looked up again. Clear. She signaled Alonzo and a few seconds later he joined her, watching her back.

The small-arms fire she heard sounded farther away, coming from the bay to the west—not the building in front of them. She used the IMS capability built into her comlink eyewraps to conduct a quick sweep. Nothing. *Good. No civilians anyway.*

But if these PIA fighters had surveillance countermeasures, her IMS "eyes" wouldn't spot them. This building she was about to enter might be crawling with unidentified-fucking-out-there PIA. She and Alonzo moved fast to the door a few feet away, and Jamie crouched low, swiftly slipping through it. Dimly lit, but she beheld an empty room.

The effects of this commutation quivered through every muscle in her body.

Breathing harder, trying to ignore the high-frequency vibration that engulfed her, she took it in. Holes in the wattle walls, dank. Empty food cans and packaging on the floor. The dark, pungent smell of sweated fear. Not very long ago, this place had lots of people in it and they were plenty scared.

Still crouching, Jamie scooted across the space to the only other doorway and swept the rooms beyond. Alonzo followed and covered the open stairway. First floor clear and IMS indicated the space above them was clear, too. But suddenly rifle fire erupted from the building's roof. The sounds were distinctive—Chinese Type 86 sniper rifle and QBZ-96 assault rifle fire.

Jamie took the stairs carefully, silently, anxious that they'd been seen and now headed into a trap. *But why would they shoot and give themselves away? Maybe they didn't see us the same way we didn't see them.*

Halfway up, she stopped cold and flattened onto her belly, her head just above the plane of the second floor. IMS now blipped something thermal straight ahead, on the other side of a wall where a small balcony overlooked both the street and the area behind the house she and Alonzo had just traversed. Then she got another blip coming from above.

She stared in the direction of the balcony. The image there moved slightly. *Is that a frigging foot? Why didn't I pick that up before?*

Two unidentified-fucking-out-there anyway. Probably more. *And what else do they have? Detection technology that can spot a little bit of me?* She sprayed a line of muffled E19 fire through the thin wall at the balcony while hiking herself onto the second floor and then rolled on her back to pepper the steep-pitched rush roof above.

On her feet again after finishing her roll, she extended her spray of fire along the rest of the roof while she darted into the second and then the third room, chancing that somebody in the fourth room wouldn't pop her. A lone cry from above informed her she'd scored at least once.

Now Jamie edged into the fourth room low and cautious, rifle leading.

She saw their legs first. Her gaze got stuck on the mud clinging to their boots. She froze, had to think and think again about moving her eyes. Then her gaze leapt frantically from one boot to another, and she counted.

Ten boots. Ten Marine Corps-issue coyote-brown boots. *Why didn't I notice this on IMS? They're here now. IMS shows them right here on the screen.*

That's when she saw the blood. Blood covered the five contorted bodies laid out on the tarp, pooled around them on the unidentified-fucking-out-there PIA tarp. A brief flash of calm, detached lucidity took her.

Throats have all been slit. Probably right after being made to call out a false all-clear. And then first platoon passed by and ended up trapped with their backs to the bay. So. It's really true. PIA fighters don't take prisoners, only hostages. And they kill their hostages.

Jamie hadn't looked at the faces of the dead. Hadn't yet found the courage to look right at their faces. But there was something about—

No. No no no no no. She closed her eyes for a single heartbeat, hoping her fevered brain had made it all up.

When she opened her eyes again, they settled on one of those faces. It told the story of the man's terror as he died, and she felt what he felt—the choking, gasping desperation, the unwilling fade into hopelessness. She stared into lifeless eyes still shocked at the prospect of actually dying.

Arnoldt's eyes.

It was slow. She could see it in his eyes. Slow and agonizing and there had been no peace, no acceptance of the inevitable.

❖

You came down the street ahead of the platoon, didn't you? Slipped in here just like we did, thinking it was clear. But they saw you. Aw jeez, Arnie, why'd they see you and not us?

Alonzo's hand on Jamie's shoulder caused her to flinch.

"C'mon, kid. We're not done yet."

Jamie didn't move, couldn't move, so Alonzo pulled her out of the room, forcefully but not roughly. He pulled her all the way back to the balcony, then down into a crouch with him behind a knocked-over table. But all she could see was that room and those boots and Arnie's face.

Alonzo grabbed her chin. "Gwynmorgan! Look at me."

"Was our dumb fucking luck, wasn't it?" Jamie murmured, her chin still in Alonzo's grip. "If they'd posted someone out here on this balcony even a minute earlier, we'd be lying there with Arnie."

"Don't indulge yourself, kid." Alonzo's eyes demanded her attention. When he didn't get it, he put both hands on her shoulders. "Look. At. Me."

"Do it. Look at him." It was the white-haired woman's voice, firm and soothing and about an inch from her left ear. Jamie blinked, but she saw only Arnoldt's dead eyes. "You must look at Alonzo. You must look now. Now." She became aware of a rushing sound, blinked again, and saw Alonzo.

"We're not done yet, Lance Corporal."

The steadiness in Alonzo's voice helped. She nodded.

"Okay, that's better. Cover me from here. Three fast clicks means I want you topside pronto." Alonzo's eyes indicated a ladder to the roof. "Otherwise you're down here watching over front and back. Got it? Front *and* back."

"Yeah. Got it."

And she promptly bellied onto the deck, cradling her E19, grateful that Alonzo had already shoved the PIA body off the balcony. Her chosen position behind battered chair remains offered no real cover, but it gave her visual concealment and the views she needed—of the yard out back through which they'd come and of the street in front where the firefight was intensifying. There were vulnerabilities, of course. Someone cloaked could get close by moving along the edge of one of the neighboring structures and maybe even sneak unseen into the first floor. But the balcony remained her best bet for covering her snipe's back.

Jamie heard Alonzo turn and climb the ladder to the roof, but she forced her eyes toward the spaces below her. She thought she was staying frosty, thought she was keeping her mind off Arnie and doing her job. But by the time she heard the first report from Alonzo's weapon, she realized the combat operations center chatter, which should have been at least minimally audible through her comlink, had disappeared—and she hadn't noticed. Ops center visuals were gone, too.

Her eyewraps' IMS detection still seemed to work, but its comlink capability had failed, and now she was well and truly alone. She scrounged her memory for the last of the ops center commo. About the snipe teams that should long since have made it into those hills east of the village, should have been hunkered in and targeting PIA, right? *Four hundred foot elevation, distance of maybe nine hundred meters. Easy for an E112 in the hands of a decent snipe. Maybe if they'd been there when they were supposed to...*

Alonzo fired again, then once more only seconds later. That's when she thought she saw it—a slight, quick blur at the edge of her vision. She swung her weapon toward it, even though nothing showed on IMS, but it was gone. *Another UFO? Or am I freaking?* Above her, Alonzo fired yet again, and an instant later another brief blur caught her eye.

Nope, that's real. Jamie belly-crawled a few feet to the edge of the balcony, pretty sure she'd find a PIA fighter right below her. Ignoring the thrumming in her ears, she peeked over and there he was, waiting, his weapon already pointed at her because he'd guessed her location exactly. *Fuck. You're the last thing I'm ever gonna see.*

But his head was turning away from her, toward the sight of a thermobaric grenade exploding a hole in the roof of the building where the Kilo platoons were trapped, and she had time to let loose a point-blank burst from her E19.

He was not alone, however.

"Lonz!" she yelled as QBZ-96 rounds screamed past her. "They got us!" She fired at the two other PIA fighters who'd been making a move on the building, forcing them to seek cover. She knew one E19 wouldn't keep them at bay for long, and then they'd get her and Alonzo, too. She strafed the tree trunks protecting them, hoping to give Alonzo time to climb off the roof. *Where is he?*

"Lonz! Get down *now!*"

Grenades. Two of the dead marines in that fourth room still carried dual-barreled, grenade-firing E19s. *With full grenade ammo stacks, both of them.* She remembered that. She remembered everything about the fourth room and the people in it. *I need those grenades.* Jamie scrambled off the balcony, firing bursts as she went, and made for the fourth room.

By the time she descended to the first floor, she saw out the window that PIA fighters, scores of them, had begun moving from three directions toward the concrete building that sheltered Kilo, barraging the marines inside. The two PIA fighters she'd encountered earlier now approached the streetside screen door about four meters away from her.

Figured you already nailed me, huh? Jamie had a half-second jump on them and fired. They went down and she kept going, running through the doorway and into the street toward the concrete building. Toward the kill zone. She had one grenade-firing E19 slung across her back and, running an erratic zigzag, sprayed the street with another. When she popped off two grenades in rapid succession, some of the PIA fighters reacted, and soon QBZ-96 rounds whined past her and pinged the ground nearby.

She crouched lower but didn't stop, not even when she heard Alonzo behind her. "*Jee*-zus, kid!" His voice pitched high in protest. "What the fuck are you doing?"

Then he must have started firing, too—a dead marine's E19,

judging by the sound. It got the PIA to shift their fire to him just in time, because the weapon she'd been shooting was out of bullets and out of grenades. Jamie slammed into the ground belly-first about thirty meters from Kilo Company's shelter, flipped the second RPG E19 off her back, and started firing again—now taking the time to aim.

Behind her, Alonzo did the same. The near crossfire they created forced the PIA guys in the street to hesitate. Jamie took advantage of it, clambering to her feet and diving left, away from Alonzo's position. This attracted PIA fire to her again, and Alonzo exploited it. Out of the corner of her eye she saw him leap from one shack roof to the next and lay fire across the rooftops to the west and southwest, giving her the chance to duck behind a shack across the street and claw her way to its roof.

Jamie had three grenades left. She fired one, then another, and had chosen a target for the third, finger poised on the trigger, when someone said too softly, too close, "Cover your nine."

She fired the last grenade as she turned her head leftward, just before something very sharp and very hot slapped her head back and spun the world into blackness.

❖

Jamie would never have believed that a person with a really bad headache could be dead. But it must be possible, because her head hurt like hell, and there was no way she could still be alive. She decided she must be having one of those near-death experiences. *Bet they happen to everybody. You hang around for a couple minutes for one last look, then fade out. Near death becomes irretrievable death, and then...and then...*

And then she could have sworn she heard somebody say "Goddamn."

This isn't anything like I thought...

"Uhh-*uuhh*!" And Jamie was gasping, clawing, kicking, assaulted by a horrific glare.

"Easy, kid, easy." Alonzo's voice. "You stay down."

But she had developed a sudden, violent need to gulp air. "C-Can't breathe." *That was me. I said that.*

"Breathe shallow, kid. Shallow."

She tried it and found air. *So. There's air after death.* The glare became shadowed and Jamie thought she saw something form out of chaos. *If I have eyes, I can focus, look around...* And, yes, there above her loomed Alonzo. Now tears threatened her eyes. She had failed to save him.

"Aw, Lonz, you're dead too."

He grinned. "No, kid, and neither are you."

Whoa. Not dead. Jamie stared at him. *So maybe being dead doesn't hurt after all.* She always *had* thought that was its virtue.

"Sorry," she said eventually, unable to speak above a whisper. She clutched Alonzo's sleeve. "I'm sorry, Lonz. Had to leave you. More PIA...had to try and nail them...knew where we were. No cover in there...had to try 'cuz—'cuz they—"

"Yeah, well." He stopped her. "Don't sweat it, kid. You did good."

"Fucking head," she muttered when his eyes seemed to water up. "I'm seeing three of everything."

"You got a goddamn hard head, kid. Bullet bounced right off, left you with a real nice souvenir there over your left eyebrow."

Breathing more easily, Jamie smiled, thankful that he didn't seem pissed, and reached for the wound. The bandage Alonzo had put over it felt wet and tinged her fingers red.

"Think you can stand up?" he asked.

"Weapon." She tried to look around for the E19. "Need ammo."

"Don't worry about that. Fight's over. The good guys won." He grinned again. "And *you* helped, kid."

As Alonzo got her to her feet, several Kilo marines found them. One was the company's commanding officer. Not just a captain but an Annapolis captain, according to the insignia on the ring he wore that Jamie was thrilled to see just one of rather than two or three. Her vision was settling down. She focused next on his nametape and tried to organize the letters she saw there. At the third "a," she brightened. Yes, the letters made sense: Cavanaugh.

Captain Cavanaugh looked them over, eyes narrowing. "You the one who fired those grenades?" he finally asked Jamie.

"Yeah," Alonzo answered, wrapping Jamie's arm across his shoulders. "She sure as hell did."

The captain did that familiar double take Jamie had already seen plenty of in her almost eight months in the Corps. She? Irritating when it came from somebody who outranked her, since she had to swallow it without smart-assing back. But at least it distracted the captain from the corporal he had started to snarl at for, Jamie guessed, neglecting to call him sir. He relented and instead spoke without hint of any emotion. "Very glad you could make it to the party."

Alonzo and Jamie nodded back and responded simultaneously.

"Yes, sir," said Jamie.

"Knock on wood," said Alonzo, as impassive as Cavanaugh while he rapped the knuckles of his left hand on his head after staring pointedly at the captain's class ring. "Maybe there's more where she came from."

The captain's eyes flared, but he chose to walk away.

Still holding Jamie up, Alonzo moved into the street. Two corpsmen bent over wounded marines while the survivors mopped up, generating sporadic fire. Third platoon remained absent. So did the snipes who were supposed to have occupied the hill to the east.

"Lonz," said Jamie like she'd just found out, "Arnie's dead."

"I know, kid. I'm sorry. Arnie was a good guy."

"Lonz." She grabbed his cammie blouse. "Arnie's *dead*! They slit his throat, Lonz."

"C'mon, kid, let's find you a corpsman."

RT thirty-one and on this day, for the first time, she had killed—taken five human lives for sure, probably more. On this day, for the first time, she saw close up in real time what it meant for someone to no longer exist.

"Lonz, I-I don't know what to do."

"You keep on going, kid. You just keep on going."

❖

The mission was deemed a success. This was supposed to help account for why more than half of the ninety-eight marines involved in it were killed or wounded—a number that looked only slightly less horrendous when third platoon got counted in, raising the number of marines on the mission to 147 and reducing the casualty percentage to around a third.

It was a good sign, Alonzo declared, that off the record this was regarded as a jackup for which somebody needed to be held accountable. Somewhere up there lurked an officer with a functioning brain.

But his approval didn't last long.

"What crap!" he spat when he found out the blame had been ladled upon third platoon's hapless commander on the notion that if third platoon had gotten to San Salvacia sooner, the PIA would've been driven out faster and losses would've been much lower.

"Those mission planners are living in fucking fantasy land. PIA's got as good as us in countersurveillance technology. God knows what else they're catching up to. Means we're losing some of our best force multipliers. Only us snipes staving off attrition now. Until our brass figures that out, there'll be more San Salvacias."

A couple of weeks later, word came forth: Jamie would get a Purple Heart, she and Alonzo would be awarded Silver Stars. Arnoldt's family got the flag draped on his coffin, neatly folded into a triangle.

At least Alonzo was restored to his previous rank. But in name only. To Jamie's amazement, he remained frozen out of a leadership billet.

"Why, Lonz?" she asked him. "I just don't get it."

"Made some enemies a while back." He shrugged. "And we don't hurt enough yet for that not to matter. Won't be long, though. Fun's over. It's going to go down real nasty now. We'll be running out of snipes pretty goddamn quick, and pretty goddamn quick they won't be able to be so picky. I give it three months. Max."

It occurred to Jamie that she and Alonzo could be separated, that he might be transferred to a whole other snipe platoon. The prospect clenched her belly. She could not conceive of how she would survive in this nightmare without him.

Her other problem concerned the damn medals. People wanted her to talk about what went down. In truth, her recollection had blurred and garbled. What little she knew for sure she didn't want to discuss with anyone.

Jamie suspected, though, that Alonzo understood. She'd been convinced she'd die that day and dreaded past tolerance dying hard, dying excruciated like Arnoldt. So she chose not to wait, not to hope for the reprieve Arnoldt never got. She didn't want to know what would hit her. She tried to make it quick, sudden. An instantaneous snap of a death.

CHAPTER TEN

OVER THAT GODDAMN MOUNTAIN

Alonzo's E112 lay beside him, as motionless as the man. He'd taken out three PIA scouts smooth and fast, but too late Jamie's binoculars swept past the anomalous shape. Too late, she grasped what the shape meant: A fourth one. "Down!" she warned, too late.

She only imagined she saw the bullet drill into him. But she heard the splattering, crunching sound that overwhelmed her alert—the only sound, since the PIA shooter was too far away for the report of his rifle to reach them. Alonzo grunted and shivered and his head fell forward onto his rifle butt before she could pull the nocs from her eyes.

"Lonz!" She yanked him down behind the cover of a shallow limestone ledge and leaned in close to his face, unable to cease imagining the bullet boring, churning into his body. *Please*, she begged mutely as the moment replayed and she fought the way it made everything stall. She needed to move faster, faster.

He wasn't dead. He'd passed out and was bleeding prodigiously. But he wasn't dead. She squinched away tears. Not dead yet. "Stay with me, Lonz."

They were alone, of course. Just the two of them over the ridge of a small Busuangan mountain, slippy-sliding into what was about to become the next contested space—just about the island's last contested space. Her mind tear-assed. *First, stop the bleeding—or at least slow it down. Then—then— How far to where I can get him some help?*

She flipped her comlink to CEA—the automated Call for Emergency Aid. Frequency-hopping. Multi-spectrum. Active cancellation. For the first time, she wondered how much time all those commo scrambling technologies would really give her before the enemy multilaterated their position.

From her first-aid kit Jamie extracted all three packs of antibiotic coagulant powder and emptied them into the bloody, raggedly gaping wound she'd found when she tore Alonzo's blouse out of the way. Semiconscious, he groaned. She wrapped his shoulder as tightly as she could with one, then another compression bandage. He groaned again.

The comlink's distinctive warning beeped faster. *That PIA scout's trying to find us.* The enemy's range-of-search for her signal was narrowing, closing in. But still getting cancelled. They still had time. *I'll go left, retrace the way we came, use the concealment of those trees…*

Her comlink crackled reply as she finished bandaging Alonzo's shoulder. A casevac was being dispatched. Then came the mute autoscrolling reminder: "Maintain commo silence…casevac will find you." The comlink took itself dark. Now the enemy lacked a signal to multilaterate, but she had to get Alonzo back over the ridge and to a clearing large enough for the helo to land.

The clearing's coordinates took up residence in the corner of her eyewraps shadowscreen. *Half a klick up. Another half a klick on the other side of the ridge, maybe more.*

A flurry of automatic weapons fire chipped the limestone five meters to her right. Two weapons anyway: The PIA scout wasn't alone. *But they're guessing.* Relief oozed through her belly when more rounds nipped the rock farther right. *And they're guessing wrong.*

She slipped Alonzo's E112 onto her chest and, crawling, dragged him from behind the ledge into the concealment of the forest. A quick, deep breath and she lifted him, heaved him over her shoulders. And staggered. His weight almost defeated her: He was several inches shorter than Jamie but heavier—perhaps twenty pounds heavier—and his rifle added another seven pounds.

The same subtle, narrow pathway they'd spent hours carving out with their machetes loomed above her; she'd have to drag him over the really steep parts. She inhaled a couple more quick, deep breaths. *Can't think about how long this is going to take. Just go. GO!*

She adjusted his weight on her back and checked the time as she started climbing. Behind her, more bullets assailed the limestone ledge. 1451 hours, just past the peak of the sun and heat.

❖

Exhausted, trembling, and sweat-soaked, Jamie laid Alonzo down as carefully as she could just on the other side of the ridge, behind real cover at last. His breathing was shallow and choppy, but he was alive. 1532 hours.

Where's that goddamn helo? Why can't I hear it yet?

She chugged much-needed water and hoisted Alonzo onto her back again. They both groaned from the effort. Although she was still on the path they'd made earlier, she knew the descent would be even tougher than the climb.

Soon Jamie strained to stay centered under his weight, to keep them both from careening down the rough incline. Her legs, her back, her arms, her abdomen all screamed and burned their complaints, but she kept going, each step bringing her closer to the helo rendezvous point.

At last she heard it, that unmistakable thump of rotor blades, and realized the sound had been there for a while, building. It tempted her to halt, that sound, but she was nowhere near the clearing yet and Alonzo didn't have much time. So she stumbled on, stopping and laying him down only when she saw three cammie uniforms running toward her.

She knelt over Alonzo and studied him. Still breathing, color going from white to gray. 1609 hours.

❖

Jamie lingered at the field hospital while the docs pumped blood back into Alonzo and operated on his shoulder. Refusing to return to her platoon until she was sure he was okay, she silently hovered as near to him as she could get.

After two days, one of the nurses took pity on her, gave her a medical excuse to bring back to her unit, and let her stay awhile with Alonzo before he was medevacked out. She stood at his bedside for almost an hour, wordless and shuffling, waiting for his eyes to open and find her.

"Hey, kid," he mumbled at last. "I'm going to Oki. Then home."

"Yeah." Jamie nodded, smiling. "That's real good, Lonz."

"Hauled me back over that goddamn mountain, didn't ya?"

She frowned at the floor, thumbed her boonie hat. *I'm the reason you got whacked, Lonz.* She said nothing, but that's when she became aware of her back aching and his blood all over the cammies she hadn't taken off for five days.

"Got my baby?" he asked.

Jamie nodded again.

"You hang on to it. See it earns its keep."

"But—"

"They're gonna make you a snipe. Sorry I won't be here to see it." Alonzo managed to lift a hand for a high-five. Jamie slid her hand along his and held it, trying to keep the sadness out of her eyes. "You stay safe, kid."

"I will, Lonz," Jamie replied as a hospitalman began moving his stretcher. "You too." She released his hand.

Alonzo was right. Promoted to corporal, she also became leader of a fire team, which outraged her. *She*, not Lonz, got a fire team?

Then she found out that her fire team would include a transfer from Second Battalion, the newly promoted Lance Corporal Martina Rhys.

CHAPTER ELEVEN

OPERATIONAL RISK MANAGEMENT

"Heard about Arnie."

"Yeah." Rhys drawled it carefully, the same way she might countersign a sentry's challenge when she lacked confidence about the correct password.

Of course, Jamie knew Rhys had heard, but not from her. Jamie had refused to talk with anyone about what happened to Arnie, and that wouldn't be changing. Not now. Probably not ever. She needed to make sure Rhys understood that. Head lowered, hands burrowed into her pockets, Jamie waited. Rhys said nothing.

"Don't get me wrong." Jamie nodded just slightly before she lifted her eyes to glance at Rhys's breasts. "I'm sure as hell not complaining. But isn't it kinda odd that they put two women together on a snipe team?"

"God, Gwynmorgan, I worry for you." Rhys sighed in mock consternation. "Don't you ever talk to anybody?"

"Guess not."

"Haven't been eating much either, huh?" Rhys's gaze moved down and back up Jamie's length.

"They keep making beef stew." Jamie fidgeted and threw Rhys a don't-go-there glance. "Can't eat it anymore."

"We're an experiment," Rhys said quickly. "Some regimental HQ hotshot wants to try teaming us for scouting missions—you snipe, me spotter. Thinks we don't stink as much as the penis people. Some frigging thing about hormones."

A few months ago, Jamie would've laughed, but now she barely smiled. "C'mon," she said, "our humble hooch is this way."

Once inside the tent, Rhys reached for her and she responded. But all during the kiss that Jamie had wanted for so, so long, she struggled not to weep.

❖

When it came to living day-to-day through the Real Thing, Alonzo taught that the people who mattered were the grunts around you and your senior NCOs. Commissioned officers occupied another, almost abstract universe. They theorized, they coordinated, they scheduled, they planned. They stuck to themselves and expected to be cleaned up after. For the most part, they were worth avoiding.

And for the most part, Jamie didn't bother to form opinions about individual officers. That changed the first time the Three-Eight scout/sniper platoon's new commander opened his mouth as the platoon stood at attention before him.

"I am here to ensure this unit outperforms every United States Marine Corps battalion scout/sniper platoon on the planet. Squad NCOs, you will bring comprehensive, up-to-date personnel note files to the platoon leadership meeting at fourteen hundred hours."

"Uh-oh," Rhys mumbled without moving her lips or her eyes. "Another hard-ass king of esprit de crap."

"Now. As you know. The, uh, Three-Eight is now part of an Expeditionary Brigade that's, uh, eight thousand strong now," First Lieutenant Koenig droned on. "This Force has driven the PIA from Busuanga and from the islands of, uh, Culion and Linapacan farther to the south."

Koenig paused for effect. And to pace along the line of snipes so he could make sure everyone was properly eyes front. Then he stopped and pivoted to face the platoon. "Soon we go to Palawan Island itself."

"Ta-*dah*," murmured Rhys.

The first lieutenant resumed pacing. And lecturing. "Long considered 'the last Philippine frontier' and rich in both fossil-fuel and mineral resources, Palawan Island is, uh, more than six hundred klicks long but only about forty klicks across at its widest, bisected by a cave-riddled range of small but rugged mountains running its length."

Koenig paused again. He frowned as though he'd misplaced something.

"Fucking A," Jamie muttered to Rhys, "who writes this guy's speeches?"

Koenig nodded at no one in particular and pressed on. "Relentlessly exploited by illegal logging, the canopies of once-extensive forests are thinner now and cover just, uh, thirty-five percent of the island, making the steeper-sided valleys prone to flooding and mudslides. This and the devastation of the pandemic ten years ago have reduced Palawan's official population to well under five hundred thousand people." Koenig pushed out his chest. "Now. In preparation for our mission on Palawan..."

For a solid half hour, he kept the platoon standing at attention. Typical new CO. Start with an inspection, bitch about the condition of everyone's cammies because everyone's weapons and combat gear were good to go. Then order them all to get haircuts and announce that he would personally supervise a short-notice physical fitness test that would be the beginning of a complex, demanding, and mostly useless combat fitness training exercise.

"Things been going pretty good, huh?" said Rhys as she glanced around the Three-Eight's new forward operating base.

Jamie continued to pound in the last tent stake. "Mmm."

"Hell's bells." Rhys almost smacked her lips. "We scooted 'em out of El Nido in a day. A few pings and poof!—they're gone. Two weeks and we got almost the whole frigging municipality. What'd they say? Seven hundred square kilometers, right? Goes on like this and we could be finished with this tropical paradise by—"

"I'm gonna go start finagling with Supply, before the crowd," Jamie said. "We'll be needing all kinda shit for this Squeeze Play op."

She couldn't stop thinking about it. Operation Squeeze Play called for taking the northern third of Palawan in one swift sweep via an air-sea flanking move across a rugged eight-kilometer-wide isthmus some hundred and fifty kilometers south of the Three-Eight's new FOB. In a single action, the Marines would reach the northern outskirts of Puerto Princesa, the island's capital, and in the process surround and trap what the intel geeks estimated to be at least a regiment's worth of PIA.

The Three-Eight's snipes' role seemed straightforward enough.

Ahead of the infantry's thrust, they'd use a diversion to night-insert by helo right onto the isthmus. Once Squeeze Play commenced, they'd hold the high ground across the narrow stretch of land and for several hours, until infantry units relieved them, block what would be only minor PIA movement.

First squad would cover the northwest section from the highest elevation on Mount Peel down to the western oceanside cliffs, while third squad would take the middle stretch from Mount Peel to Baheli Peak. Second squad—Jamie's squad—would form a jagged line from Baheli Peak southeastward down a ridge that terminated above the only paved road across the isthmus, the main coastal artery along which significant numbers of PIA fighters would attempt to move.

The last 1,200 meters of this ridge belonged to Jamie's fire team. Jamie and her spotter had orders to make a hide at the southeast end of the ridge and from there hamper PIA attempts to travel the coastal road. The other two members of Jamie's team would locate farther up the ridge to prevent anyone from sneaking behind Jamie and her spotter. Properly placed, second squad's three fire teams would be able to cover almost five kilometers of ridge.

Assuming no PIA fighters already occupied Mount Peel or Baheli Peak or the ridge. Assuming there weren't too many PIA. Assuming they'd be "raw"—not cloaked by countersurveillance gear.

Near the bottom of the chain of command, Corporal Gwynmorgan had her doubts. Every instinct in her screeched *NO!* If the Squeeze Play intel was even a little bit wrong, they'd be screwed. The entire mission would be screwed. *And when the hell is intel ever totally right?*

RT110 and she'd started to wonder if the officers planned missions for the same conflict she fought in—the one where the PIA turned up in unexpected numbers and in unexpected places, the one where the enemy regularly had countersurveillance gear and were actually figuring out how to use it. *Where's this Squeeze Play intel coming from, anyway?*

Jamie sent Rhys off to snoop. "Not a whole lot of unit info or recon about the isthmus," Rhys reported after friending one of the battalion S-2's staff assistants. "Intel's mostly from informants and agents run by contractors—those peace-and-stability outfits like Columbia Aegis and FDL/Roque. Mercenaries and their freelance spies, you know? But the brass trusts it."

Jamie sighed. *Wish I did.*

❖

"Just make sure your people are ready, Corporal."

So much for all that hoopla about operational risk management. "Hey, Sergeant, I'm just respectfully pointing out to my squad NCO that there's some tactical residual risk and respectfully requesting the resources necessary to mitigate that risk, okay? Standard operating procedure."

"What-the-fuck-ever, Gwynmorgan. Request denied. Get your ass outta here."

At least Alonzo's buddy in Supply found a way to get Jamie three GLaC SAWs—grenade-launch-capable squad automatic weapons— and as much ammunition as she figured her crew could haul. At the end of the ridge overlooking the road, she'd use a new dual-barrel E112 sniper rifle able to fire armor-penetrating .50-caliber as well as anti-personnel .416-caliber rounds.

When Rhys found a moment to privately bitch about lugging a GLaC SAW and all that ammo up the ridge, Jamie popped like a kernel of corn.

"This is a classic clusterfuck, Marty! Koenig's been told to make it work somehow and he isn't gonna push back. Probably can't, because the big shots don't think much'll happen along the ridge. They think it'll all go down at the road. And they sure as hell don't want to believe the PIA have any surveillance countermeasures worth mentioning. Well, we're gonna find out. *Us*, not the fobbits in the ops center."

Rhys scowled, her expression eloquent: What the fuck do you know, *Corporal*?

"Think about it, Marty. We drive a wedge north of Puerto Princesa, right? And what're the PIA really gonna do?"

Skepticism jutted Rhys's chin. "Jeezus, Jamie, *I* don't know. That's what we got brass for."

"And the brass built the whole op on merc intel. What if the intel's *wrong*, Marty? The mercs work all sides—the Corps, the energy industry, defense contractors, god knows who else—and they got some damn merc agenda of their own."

"So you wanna just ignore our orders?"

"No, not ignore them. Work our bolt, you know? Adapt our orders to the real world."

"Oh yeah, General Gwynmorgan? And where's *your* intel coming from?"

"From a hundred and eighteen days of this shit, that's where. You see how it's been going. Most of the PIA have countersurveillance gear now and they're pretty good at using it. C'mon, Marty, think about it."

"Fuck, Jamie, I'm not *supposed* to think about it!"

"Dammit, don't you get it?" *Jeezus, Marty, three months in that green zone outside the Two-Eight's FOB didn't help* your *edge sharpen any.* "PIA units will converge on the isthmus when they realize we're cutting the island. Even if they're not on the ridge already and we're able to get into position up there, it won't take long for them to pile into the ravines below us. They'll try like hell to break our wedge wherever they can. Means PIA coming at us from the south *and* from the north to take the ridge, Marty. And if they take just a small slice north of us, we get cut off. And if our infantry comes up late and all we have are sniper rifles and E19s, we get overrun. And then we get our fucking throats slit like Arnie. Is that what you want?"

Rhys's eyes went wide.

Shit. Jamie hadn't intended that last thought to spill out. But at least it got Rhys's attention, made Rhys hesitate and consider. What was on Rhys's mind showed, too, as her eyes slitted and her chin pushed out farther. She wanted to know how Jamie dared to even think like this, much less act on it.

Jamie drew in a long, calming breath. *Try it again, goober. If you can't sell Rhys, this'll go uprank and then we'll be worse than screwed. We'll be impaled.*

"I know Koenig said this one should be easy. That it'll all go down right on the coast and all we have to do is occasionally nip at a few guys who light up bright and shiny on our IMS. But our own experience with cloaked PIA tells us that bit of the intel is dubious. Maybe everything's sweet—but it could all be complete shit. Way I see it, we'll be snipes for a few hours. If we're lucky. Then we'll be infantry, and while we're screaming into our comlinks for help, the four of us will be trying to keep god knows how many PIA from breaching more than a klick's worth of ridge." Jamie rested a pleading hand on Rhys's shoulder. "I've been checking out the topo maps and the imagery. Our piece of ridge has lots of cover—crevices, caves. Several places where we can move back and forth for almost thirty meters staying behind good cover.

Little fortresses. That's where we position, that's our leverage. Gives us decent odds, you know? And if I'm wrong, Rhys, you can ream me when it's all over. I'll wear my skivvies on my head for a month, okay?"

"Okay." Rhys nodded grimly. "You're the corporal, Corporal. I'll do it."

"Thank you."

"When this is over, Gwynmorgan, I want to see you draped in bright red skivvies, understand? Those ones with the naked dancing women."

"Deal," said Jamie. "Now about the GLaC SAWs…"

❖

Because of Rhys—only because of Rhys, Jamie had no doubt—the other two fire team members, Omara and Ebbers, allowed themselves to be loaded up without a squawk.

The diversion, a helo assault of identified PIA boats out on Honda Bay, went well enough that Jamie's team got to the highest part of their section of ridge on schedule before dawn. And they encountered no PIA at all.

For Jamie, it was a happy but disconcerting surprise. At least this part of the Squeeze Play intel turned out be to right on the money. *What if the rest of it's solid, too? Should I back off?*

"When the hell is intel ever totally right?" the voice whispered in Jamie's ear as the team reached a deeply creviced outcrop that rose well above the surrounding trees.

Just my luck this'll be the first time.

"Just your luck it won't."

"First hide's here," Jamie heard herself say. "It's yours, Ebbers." Then, one more time, she went through the commo protocol that would enable her to get away with what she was about to do. "No uplink communication with the ops center. Receive only. Word is some PIA have active cancellation countermeasures now, so we don't know anymore how quick they can multilaterate our signals. Means for this one all commo between us is limited to no more than five seconds, then at least a fifteen-second delay before resuming."

Jamie waited for them to confirm, then pointed to a high point on the outcrop. "Set up there, Eb. It's a good spot for your GLaC SAW, you got a clear three-sixty sweep there. Make sure your IMS detector covers all three hundred and sixty degrees, but don't rely only on IMS, because some of them will cloak. Keep your eyeballs on both sides of the ridge. And don't get too comfy. This'll be the Mexican jumping bean fixed-position defense. You'll pick up and move plenty, to, uh—" She turned slowly, pointing to other spots on the outcrop. "There, and also there. Both got sweep and good cover. Also, I'm belaying the initial order. We're now four one-man units. For this one we're *all* snipes. And we'll all be infantry before it's over, so keep your GLaC SAWs prepped and mobile. You'll be scurrying. A lot."

Omara and Ebbers exchanged an are-you-serious glance. The order to abandon protocol, to work alone without a combat buddy, was insanely dangerous, but Rhys didn't blink. Omara and Ebbers said nothing.

"We'll have three more hides along the top of this ridge and they'll each have line-of-sight one to the next. Last one'll be me." Jamie pointed southeast. "Slightly more than a thousand meters down that way."

Jamie climbed with Ebbers to the first spot she'd chosen, then the other two, and made sure he was as ready as she could make him. "Good shooting, guy," she said as she left. He nodded but couldn't smile.

Rhys occupied a similar outcrop some four hundred meters southeast of Ebbers, and Omara took up a position another three hundred meters farther along. Setting up her team took all day. By the time she approached her own position where the ridge ended above the road, daylight was ebbing fast. She came upon four cloaked PIA snipes only because one of them pulled down his pants at their latrine and her IMS picked up his bare backside.

They weren't human beings. Not yet. Jamie saw them as targets to be stalked and eliminated. When she was close enough—maybe twenty meters—she exhaled evenly to produce the almost-but-not-quite hum that soothed her racing heart and generated a band of calm between her temples, behind her eyes. This she always did while she sighted a target, refusing to think about time passing as she hummed into that instant of utter stillness between breathing in and breathing out—and squeezed off a shot, then three more before she inhaled again. One silenced pistol shot each, smooth and fast and fatal. She shoved and pulled them out of their hide without looking at their faces, avoiding the blood from their wounds, thankful for the darkness that helped keep them anonymous.

After that, she used the PIA snipers' hide to good effect. Most of the targets on the road below required shots between 1,500 and 1,800 meters. But not all. Three separate times during the windless dawn, she made a 2,600-meter killing shot. The confusion this caused—because it was impossible to hear the rifle report or determine where the shots came from—stalled the PIA for hours.

It also triggered precisely what Jamie feared: PIA fighters hastened inland—initially to find her, then, as Squeeze Play progressed and Marine infantry units cornered them, to search for a viable back door across the isthmus. Jamie's team staved off attack from both sides of the ridge, but mostly from the south, where swarms of PIA fighters poured into the ravines below and climbed up the ridge right at Omara, then shifted west toward Rhys first and finally Ebbers.

The GLaC SAWs saved their part of the mission. They benefited from a bit of luck, too. A few PIA lacked countersurveillance gear—just enough so that their tactics became evident and predictable, especially in the comparatively lower-elevation sector defended by Rhys, who managed to adjust position and keep any enemy from getting past her.

Omara and Ebbers were less fortunate. Just about all of their attackers had cloaked up, so the few blips that appeared on their IMS revealed no patterns.

"Where the fuck is Lima!" Jamie and her teammates screamed over and over.

When Lima Company at last ascended the ridge from the north, forcing back the PIA fighters who had started to push past Ebbers, no one in Jamie's team had more than a handful of rounds left. Even worse, both Omara and Ebbers had suffered go-home wounds. Yet, somehow, they were all still alive.

❖

"Hey, did you hear?" After sleeping for ten hours and then departing the hooch in search of chow, Rhys had come back sounding almost animated.

Jamie didn't look up from cleaning her E112. "Nope."

"We're getting Silver Stars."

Jamie stilled her hands and fixed her eyes on the weapon as a wave of heat wrapped around her head. *Let's see: Forty-one going in. Eighteen killed, six wounded bad. Close to sixty percent functional loss. Yep, Silver Star country. And all squared away in less than three days. Might be a record.*

"All of us in second and third squads."

Hmm, eighteen posthumous Silver Stars. Now there's *a challenge. Bet they won't be doing* that *in one afternoon.* "What?" Jamie looked up. "Not the two wounded from first squad?"

"Oh, they'll get Purple—" When she saw Jamie's hard stare, Rhys shut up and slinked into her hammock. "Sorry. It just doesn't feel real yet, I guess."

"Yeah, well, give it a while."

After a long, squirmy moment, Rhys offered up more scuttlebutt in a chastened near whisper: "Heard Koenig's claiming upchain that he issued a last-minute 'field adjustment' to our orders." She snorted. "So he's getting a commendation."

"Better than me getting a court martial." Yet a court martial and a demotion to buck private had plenty of appeal; she'd be spared responsibility for anybody but herself. She returned her eyes to her rifle so Rhys wouldn't see them.

"The medal—that's a good thing, right?" Rhys pleaded.

"Least for us it's not posthumous." But Jamie wouldn't look up again.

The next day, the entire battalion was relieved and given ten days' rest at a resort on Culion.

Just before they boarded the helicopter that would take them to the island, the NDYs—promotions for those Not Dead Yet—were dispensed. The process was informal, tattered even, conducted not by Lieutenant Koenig but by Staff Sergeant Daggett, the platoon's senior NCO. He called Rhys's name first, telling her she picked up corporal and was now a fire team leader.

"Okay, that's it," Daggett said in a glum monotone after ticking off several more promotions. "We'll do the pin-the-tail-on-the-donkey dances on Culion."

Nodding congratulations to Rhys, who couldn't suppress a satisfied smile, Jamie lifted her seabag and turned toward the helo, pleased and relieved that she and Rhys would be equals again.

"Oh yeah, one more." Jamie halted at the sound of Daggett's voice behind her. *Shit shit shit shit...* "Gwynmorgan, you're boosted to sergeant. You'll take second squad."

❖

"I heard this place used to be a leper colony once." Rhys gazed at the faded pink concrete-block building in front of them; she hadn't looked at Jamie on the helo and didn't look at Jamie now.

"All I want is a clean bed and a real hot-water shower." Yet Jamie doubted the stink of fear in her armpits would ever wash away, just as she doubted anything could ever sate her gnawing, growling hunger for— What? She didn't know. It was just another feeling that didn't matter anymore.

Jamie shrugged at the building, one of the several Culion "resorts" pretty much taken over by the Corps. This one had been constructed early in the century with a certain pre-pandemic flourish and obviously hadn't been updated since. But once inside the tired room she'd share with Rhys for the next ten days, Jamie discovered that the plumbing still worked and even the noisy, twenty-year-old air conditioner functioned, more or less.

Without a word, she stripped off cammies, then skivvies, and walked straight into the shower. Under its surprisingly energetic spray, Jamie leaned her head and elbows against the tile wall, closed her eyes, and let the wall keep her upright.

"You okay?"

She hadn't heard Rhys follow her into the bathroom and she didn't reply. She couldn't bring herself to think about finding whatever it was she'd need to reply, or even move.

Rhys stepped into the shower behind her and Jamie shivered as she felt Rhys's hands slide across her back, around her hips. Down, down slithered Rhys's hands, and Jamie moaned the implacable need that fired in her clit and jolted into her belly.

Unleashed by Rhys's touch, Jamie spun around blind and reckless.

She grabbed Rhys's hips and, pulled off balance, Rhys toppled into her, pushing her back against the shower wall.

"Hey!" protested Rhys.

But Jamie's grip didn't loosen. "*What*, Marty?" Eyes squeezed shut, she yanked Rhys off the floor and into her pounding, relentless privation. "Think I got something special?" Jamie slammed herself ferociously against Rhys's hipbone.

"Hey!" Rhys shouted this time, shoving hard enough to break Jamie's grip. "What the fuck are you doing?"

Jamie gaped at Rhys's outrage-red face. Every muscle in Jamie's body had gone rigid and she couldn't get herself to breathe in or out until— "Omigod." She yanked her hands away from Rhys. "Omigod, I'm so sorry, Marty. I didn't mean to—I-I—" Jamie's back was glued to the wall. Water sprayed into her eyes, into her open mouth.

Rhys's face had already relaxed, as if the spray of water had the power to wash away all her upset. "It's okay." Her hands palmed Jamie's face and kept it from veering away. "It's okay, Jamie." A soft kiss brushed Jamie's cheek. "C'mon, let me wash you."

"I'm sorry, Marty." Jamie lowered her head, unable to look at Rhys even when Rhys kissed her again and slowly, carefully encouraged her away from the wall to soap up her quaking body. Immersed in shame, Jamie didn't lift her head until Rhys handed her the soap.

"My turn. Now you wash me."

Jamie eased the soap over Rhys's flesh, hesitating at Rhys's breasts, between Rhys's legs.

Together they rinsed the suds away, and Rhys toweled Jamie down, kissed her jittery shoulders, then her neck, then her mouth. Unable to stop shaking, Jamie let Rhys lead her to one of the beds.

Rhys nudged her onto the mattress, lay down beside her. Without a word, Rhys kissed Jamie again, long and cajoling, and then led them into making love. Jamie shuddered once, violently, and groaned when Rhys's deft touch brought her to culmination.

Thereafter, Jamie was not allowed to move.

Instead, Rhys climbed Jamie's body. Like she was straddling a wild animal, Rhys rode, and Jamie bucked and surged beneath her, coming again, calming only after Rhys, too, was spent and exhausted. They fell asleep entwined.

When Jamie woke, she found Rhys staring at her. "What?" she asked sleepily, curling toward Rhys's shoulder.

Rhys cradled Jamie's head, bestowing on it an affectionate kiss. "You've got to tell me what's going on with you."

Jamie couldn't prevent the cringe. Rhys must have seen it but didn't give in. "Talk to me, Jamie."

Jamie tried to move away.

"Oh no you don't." Rhys laughed softly and tugged Jamie back onto her shoulder. "You stay right here."

Jamie didn't resist but didn't speak either.

"I'll ask, you answer. Okay?"

Jamie closed her eyes, tried to keep her face impassive. Maybe this would all stop hurting so much if she just didn't move.

"Okay?" Rhys asked again.

She was going to have to open her eyes. She looked up at Rhys and offered an infinitesimal nod. "Okay."

"How've you been sleeping?"

Jamie's shoulders hunched, she frowned at the battered dresser across the room.

"Uh-uh, not an answer. How've you been sleeping?"

A sigh. "Not so great."

Rhys's gesture told Jamie to elaborate.

"Bad dreams," Jamie said, allowing herself a quick glance at Rhys.

Rhys didn't seem surprised. "Same ones or different?"

"Variations on a theme." Jamie glanced up at Rhys again.

Go on, insisted Rhys's eyes.

"I'm, uh, I'm out there on a mission, y'know?"

Rhys's chin shifted up, down—a nod.

"And, uh, my spotter gets hit. Or sometimes another guy in my fire team gets hit. But I can't get him back. Something always happens—I can't pick him up, or if I get him up, I can't make any headway to the med-station. Or I get hit, or he gets hit again and his head explodes all over me." Jamie inhaled deeply and shook her head. "And now…"

"Now?" Rhys prompted.

"Couple times, y'know, recently—couple times I'm out there with a bunch of guys, maybe even a squad, that many guys, and—" Jamie couldn't let her gaze go anywhere near Rhys. "This was before they gave me second squad, Marty. *Before.*" She waited for Rhys's stiffness, for Rhys's peevish withdrawal.

"And?" Rhys sounded okay. Still warm, still holding on.

"A-And," Jamie stammered finally, "I'm the one who's put together the mission, when to go, where to go—y'know?—and they all get whacked. Everyone's KIA, including me. Me last. I watch them all get it, one by one, hearing them scream, knowing I did this to them. Last part of the dream both times, right before I wake up, I feel the rounds hitting me, tearing into me. Hurts like hell, but it doesn't take me out. Last thing I see is the knife coming for my throat—a black blade—and then I can feel my own blood on my chest. It's sticky and warm. I'm choking and getting cold and it's warm on my chest."

Jamie didn't talk about how, over the previous month, most of the dreams had been about Rhys. Rhys's throat slit. Rhys dying in her arms. She snuck a peek at Rhys. *Fuck. She knows.*

"When did it start—the dreams? After I got here?"

"First one was after San Salvacia. After Arnie." Jamie shook her head, focused her eyes on the dresser again. "They got a lot worse after Lonz was hit. I-I couldn't help him."

"You *did* help him." Rhys exhaled her relief. "You saved his ass, Jamie."

"I should've seen the guy sooner. If I'd seen him sooner, maybe he wouldn't have got that shot off and Lonz—" Jamie's eyes were hot, stinging when she looked back to Rhys. "And if I'd been smarter about where I sent you and Omara and Ebbers—Jeezus, I thought you were fucking dead, Marty! I thought I fucking killed all three of you."

"Can I tell you something?" Rhys asked.

Jamie shrugged.

"You're the best goddamn marine I've ever seen."

"Yeah." Jamie snorted contempt. "Right."

"I figure you've saved my ass at least three times since they hooked us up. And, by the way, I'm fucking glad I went along with you on Squeeze Play, 'cuz that was one of those times."

"Well, I guess I should just be grateful I don't have to wear red skivvies on my head."

"I mean it, Jamie. You're so damn good sometimes it makes me damn jealous. You got incredible instincts. And you're a scary-fine snipe."

Jamie fidgeted. Rhys rested a hand on Jamie's chest to keep her where she lay. "Dammit, I saw you on the bus to Parris Island. You were scared shitless just like the rest of us. You started out *just like the rest of us*. But you—I don't know how the hell you did it, but you've *got* something, Gwynmorgan. And I'm just trying to—"

"I'll tell you what I got. Three months in the field with a really good teacher, that's what. Plus a little luck and a lot of worrying."

Rhys flashed a brash, unbelieving smile. "I can help you with the worrying part."

"Yeah? Show me."

Rhys rolled on top of Jamie and began with a kiss.

❖

Rhys was right about the worrying part. After making love with her, Jamie slept free of nightmares. As Jamie woke the second time in the privacy of the Culion motel room, the sun had begun to sink beneath the watery horizon visible from their second-floor windows.

"Didn't even notice we had a view 'til right now," Jamie said when Rhys woke, too. "Take a look."

Nestled together, they stayed quiet and watched the sun set, their breathing gradually synchronizing, relaxing. They were, for a little while anyway, safe. *This*, Jamie thought, *in all the world I want this*.

The dense tangle in her solar plexus began to slacken when she reminded herself that she had the evening and nine more days after that. It seemed like a lot. "Guess what," Jamie said soon after the sun disappeared.

"What?"

"Today's my birthday." Jamie gazed at Rhys, smiling her thanks. "I'm eighteen as of right now. And tomorrow we'll have been in the Marine Corps for exactly one year."

"Well then, Sergeant Gwynmorgan, we gotta celebrate."

CHAPTER TWELVE

ATTRITION

"And remember, a barangay is a town or village that's part of a larger municipality," Jamie reminded her gathered squad the day before they left Culion. "Word is we're gonna be moving into the barangays of Puerto Princesa, which the PIA won't give up easily."

But their orders changed an hour before they climbed into the helo. "Short detour, boys and girls," said Daggett. "We're going to Panay for a while. Three-Six needs some help with cleanup."

It was one of the larger Philippine islands, about 250 kilometers east-southeast of Culion, where too many of the PIA cut off during Squeeze Play had ended up, and it was easy duty because the PIA elements there were exhausted and demoralized and just as resented by the Panay locals as they were by the people of Busuanga and northern Palawan.

Jamie called it the Real Thing Lite and regarded it as a gift. More than once, her squad's virgins survived newbie mistakes that would've been fatal during the Real Thing Heavy. After two months, all thirteen squaddies helicoptered out of Panay healthy and wiser.

"Tell me why the fuck we're *here* again?" griped the large, blunt-featured Corporal Ramirez, one of Jamie's fire team leaders, when the helo touched down on Palawan.

"They're ba-ack," mocked Rhys, winking at Jamie. "Sneaking around Baheli Peak through that sieve Ninth Regiment calls a forward edge. And coming this way. Welcome to picking-up-right-where-we-fucking-left-off."

The Three-Eight had been ordered to saturate the area around the same coastal road at the eastern end of the Palawan isthmus where

Jamie had made what Rhys proudly called "those three Squeeze Play sweet shots." On the high ground prowled the Three-Eight's snipes. Again.

Together with the platoon's two other squads on their right, second squad—now Sergeant Gwynmorgan's squad—skulked across the higher southeastern slopes of Baheli Peak to plug holes in the still-porous battle area some thirteen kilometers north of the Puerto Princesa peninsula.

Jamie's squad and third squad did fine. But one of first squad's fire teams, along with the squad's sergeant and Staff Sergeant Daggett, got slammed. First squad's sergeant suffered a go-home wound, and only days after the newly arrived Expeditionary Brigade commander had pinned one of those Squeeze Play Silver Stars on his chest, Daggett died.

So on February thirteenth, the Corps promoted Jamie again, this time to staff sergeant and Three-Eight scout/sniper platoon NCO. Rhys made sergeant and got second squad. "Least these days when they give us the billet, we actually get the rank, too," she said. "Must be diddling all kinds of rules so they can jack the hell out of our composite scores. Or something."

"Yeah." Jamie forced a smile. Rhys had a right to be excited. Maybe Rhys was even ready for a squad. As for herself, Jamie knew damn well she had far to go before being solidly good at leading a dozen people, and now she had a whole platoon and a first lieutenant to deal with. Forty plus one. Her attempt at steady calm was all bluster. Hell, maybe Rhys's bouncing excitement was all bluster, too.

They both understood why the Corps had forsaken its usual practice of having marines do a job long before being awarded the job's rank—indeed, too often without ever being awarded the job's rank. But they scrupulously avoided the A-word. Seven months into Operation Palawan Liberation, the match-up of billet and rank helped morale from tanking further in the face of a grave command vacuum that virgin leaders couldn't seem to fill, no matter how thorough their formal training or experience elsewhere. The A-word hovered over all.

Once Jamie even heard it said by Captain Pinsof, the battalion's intelligence officer who was Koenig's boss. Well, overheard it. But she heard it, no question: Attrition.

She didn't tell Rhys about what she heard, but Rhys's sources had also been whispering essentially the same thing. Because this war of attrition featured enemy sniper attacks on officers and even senior NCOs, whom PIA fighters had learned to recognize despite hard-to-see rank insignia.

"The PIA're reading deference, not rank insignia," Jamie kept saying to anyone who'd listen. "Just watch. It's not an accident that the guys who demand the most deference get whacked the quickest."

So by default, because nothing else worked, most replacement leaders were culled from within a Palawan unit's own lower ranks or from other units in the Palawan. Unit strength then underwent a "virgin resurrection" from the bottom up, since pulling newbies into the lowest possible ranks gave them a chance to learn from the NDYs.

Of course, it was all quite ad hoc and unofficial. So were the extended deployments.

Snipers were the first ones locked into their units and told they were staying. Then everyone got an additional six months in the Palawan. For those doing the fighting, home seemed to be receding further and further, but Staff Sergeant Gwynmorgan didn't give that any thought. Instead, she counted days as a platoon leader, just once each morning.

And she cogitated about how to do the platoon's missions sufficiently well that no mission had to be done twice. "Hard enough to get everyone back alive the first time," she'd say.

Jamie had lost two snipes and one spotter to go-home wounds in the barangays at the edge of Puerto Princesa. But no KIAs. Twenty-three days as platoon staff sergeant and no KIAs.

Then the battle for the little city ruptured into climax. Along the edges of Third Battalion's push, its snipe platoon worked Puerto Princesa's narrow streets toward the capitol building. Jamie had just hooked up with second squad, which now tentacled out from the Three-Eight's right flank, traversing narrow alleys and closely packed rooftops.

The damage to civilian structures in the immediate area surprised her. Until this final, desperate fight for Puerto Princesa, the PIA had adhered to a key rule of engagement in this conflict—as little harm as possible to civilians or civilian property. Now, as Eighth Regiment claimed the town building by building, street by street, PIA snipers and grenade launch teams targeted Marine infantry and military vehicles without care for the fate of nearby civilians.

This made the combat especially vicious, but after six hours, none of Jamie's people had been wounded, none killed. She harbored a cautious optimism she was trying not to think about when, up ahead on a rooftop, Rhys signaled.

Trouble. Jamie made it to Rhys's position, listened to the exploding grenades and small-weapons fire, then told Rhys she'd take one of second squad's fire teams with her toward the ruckus.

"I'll let you know when to move up."

Rhys nodded and Jamie crawled and ducked with four others toward the intensifying din. Soon they came upon an intersection where guys from Second Battalion had gotten themselves lost and then trapped. They were pinned down and several were lying exposed in the street, probably dead. PIA fire had created a large, fierce kill zone. Moving into it was a death sentence.

Jamie picked a couple of rooftops from which the two snipes with her could return effective fire and deployed them with their spotters. Then she comlinked Rhys. "Come in cautious, Marty. And bring Doc with you." *We're all going to be walking out of here today. No body bags today.*

In her peripheral vision, she saw one of the marines in the street move. The man floundered, unable to save himself but in too much pain to lie still so he wouldn't attract more enemy fire.

That's when she heard the sound—like a piece of cloth being torn so slowly she could discern every one of its threads exploding. She stared at the marine, frantic for the sound to stop. But it didn't, and she knew if one more thread snapped he'd be dead. And in a body bag.

She dropped from the low roof, ran to the man, dragged him off the street and out of the kill zone. When she noticed a civilian, hurt but not dead, she ran into the kill zone again. Around her she saw more wounded and helped them, thinking only, *No body bags today.*

Afterward, a fog shrouded the whole experience. The enemy must have fired at her—the sounds of weapons fire surrounded her, windows shattered, wood snapped, small chunks of the street blew away at aberrant angles—but none of that concerned her. No, all that was background, like a video she scarcely noticed. She didn't remember the bullet scraping her arm or the orders they said she gave.

But she recalled the relief of risking for the sake of saving a life, not ending one. Jamie wouldn't let Rhys talk about it in her presence and brushed away the passing comments about a citation, which in her view required an officer with either a hard-on or something to hide. No doubt the brass at the assorted combat operations centers had more important events to focus on.

Three days later, she found out that plenty of officers had seen the whole thing. They'd watched enthralled from the regimental FOB's combat operations center—meticulously referred to as "the FOB Cee-Oh-Cee" by the brass but called "the fobcock" by the grunts. Here, for the first time, ops center technicians used a new communications upgrade to track the trajectories of every high-velocity projectile within range of the lenses of the recently launched Trajsat satellite. Now during a mission even the bullets got to be on Candid fucking Camera.

One of the ops center techs added up the number of F3Os—fatally fast-flying objects—that had zipped through the kill zone around Jamie during what turned out to be seven runs into the street to rescue the wounded. The tech made big bucks off the betting pool set up to guess how many times Gwynmorgan dodged a bullet that afternoon.

Jamie refused to let anyone tell her the number. Just as she refused to count how many sniper kills she had. It was much easier not to think about what you didn't know. Then Rhys brought back the scuttlebutt that she'd been put in for a Navy Cross and another Purple Heart.

"Oh great," Jamie grumbled. "More fruit salad for the neatly ironed service uniform I've worn three fucking times since I joined up. I don't like it, Marty. And I sure as hell don't want it."

"Why not? You damn well earned it."

"Yeah, and so did plenty of other people who never got anything 'cuz there were no fucking officers to fucking see it 'cuz their commissioned fucking heads were way too far up their commissioned fucking asses."

"I buy that," Rhys said. "But it's not just about you and all those guys who got nothing. It's also about the guys in the platoon. They had your back the whole time. And they're damn proud of you. Some of that Navy Cross is theirs, staff sergeant."

"They can have all of it." Jamie hurled her boonie hat across the hooch. "They can have all my rotten fruit salad and every one of these shitty little stripes." She clawed at the stubborn supervelcro bonding her rank insignia to the collar of her cammie blouse and had it ripped halfway off before Rhys stepped in front of her and stilled her hand.

Their eyes locked. Perhaps Rhys would've said something. Perhaps Rhys would've dared the illicit kiss Jamie yearned for. But before she had a chance, Jamie stomped out of the hooch.

❖

The Three-Eight's new FOB in Puerto Princesa occupied a dreary space at the airport north of the sole runway. Enclosed by the usual sandbag and razor-wire perimeter, it included a few key support containers—the battalion FOBCOC, a dining facility, several sanny boxes with long lines of filthy marines waiting to shit, shower, and shave—as well as a sea of closely packed hooches and too many grunts who needed some liberty but weren't going to be getting any for a while yet.

The FOB also had a recycling unit, already surrounded by a pile of junk and debris four meters high. Here Jamie finally came to a halt before a battered fifty-five-gallon steel drum. "Fuck!" She swung the toe of her boot into it. Hard. Its small metallic thunder echoed back at her, an invitation. She kicked it again. "Ow!" And stumbled. "Fuck!"

Her bruised foot landed on a three-foot length of copper pipe. She kicked it, too, and it clamored against the steel drum. The sound of metal on metal became another invitation. Jamie picked up the pipe and raised it high before whacking the drum with it. "Fuck!" She swung again. "Fuck!" And again. "Fuck!"

She moved to a neighboring drum and used the pipe on it. A different sound bounced back at her, lower but harmonious with the earlier one. Worth comparing. In quick succession, she pounded the pipe on the first drum, then the other, and liked the effect—a high-low "Fuck you!" clang.

A second length of copper pipe made producing the two tones easier. More variety, she thought, and stepped through the junk, rapping on various pieces of debris to hear what sounds they offered up. When she approved, she dragged the piece nearer the two drums. She arranged, then rearranged a dozen objects and began to drum on them in earnest, producing a rattletrap, melodic percussion.

Jamie released herself to the sound of it, the beat of it, the effort of it. She began to dance as she drummed, she yelled and squealed as she tried new combinations of clangs, new rhythms.

"Hey, Gwynnie. Hey! How about this?" A grinning Ramirez stood nearby holding a crumpled chunk of water heater. He hammered it with his own piece of pipe.

"Yeah!" Jamie shouted without stopping. "Why the fuck not? Try over there." She tilted her head. "Bet it'll work fine near that humvee door panel."

More snipes appeared and added "instruments" to the mélange. As the sun set, someone hollered something about a bonfire, and soon a wooden pyre flared into the night while a dozen snipes drummed. A hooting, cheering audience formed around them, and Jamie became a conductor of sorts, still dancing, leaping on and off what had evolved into two rows of percussive trash.

When she started to weary, a lithe, caramel-complexioned woman stepped up. "I can do it, Gwynnie."

"It's all yours, Avery. Get everyone as tired as I am." They danced side by side for a bit so the drummers would grasp that Jamie was handing over the lead, and then she edged away.

"Feeling better?"

Jamie inhaled Rhys's scent and turned slowly toward it. Reflections of the bonfire cavorted in Rhys's eyes, but Jamie saw another flame there, too. She shook her head and walked away from the crowd, from Rhys.

After a couple minutes, Rhys caught up with her. "Jamie."

"I'd give it to you if I could," Jamie said without slowing down or turning to face Rhys. "But it just doesn't work that way."

"Maybe it does. For me."

"Yeah? Some kind of contagious magic?"

"Who knows?"

Jamie stopped, her back to Rhys. "And my orgasm makes you what? A better snipe?" Jamie's voice descended to a hoarse whisper. "What if I'm in love with you, Marty?"

"Well, maybe I'm in love with you."

"You're not." Jamie resumed walking. "Don't fuck with me."

Rhys stepped alongside her. "I *want to* fuck with you. Being in love with you sounds okay, too."

"Why? Because you think you'll—?"

"Because you're a turn-on, Gwynmorgan."

They had reached their hooch. Jamie stood next to it and peered at Rhys. "So are you, goddammit."

❖

Jeeeezus…

"Shh!"

Whereupon Rhys recommenced nibbling, sucking, while two of her fingers went spelunking.

Sprawled sideways on her hammock, Jamie lost sight of Rhys's head between her legs as she convexed into Rhys's mouth. Rhys kept her there until her orgasm burst out—one crest, then another and another and another…

Will you touch me like this when you nail a target twenty-six hundred meters away? When, god help you, some general pins a Navy Cross on your chest? When you outrank me?

CHAPTER THIRTEEN

NO LONGER A SCOUT/SNIPER

The explosion rocked the ground, causing Jamie and the people around her to seek cover. "Shit," Rhys said, "fifth time today. This is getting downright disagreeable."

Now that it had been moved out of Puerto Princesa to the other side of Caramuran Bay, the Three-Eight's FOB made an especially easy target for mortar shells fired from the Beaufort Range foothills above it to the west. The overstretched Marines had become far too vulnerable to PIA ping-and-run attacks.

But not for long.

"On me, Staff Sergeant," Lieutenant Koenig said once the dust cleared. "And prepare to take detailed notes."

Lieutenant Koenig commanded by notes. And checklists. In the beginning, Jamie hated it, and Squad Leader Gwynmorgan got lambasted more than once for what Koenig called "inadequate leadership accountability." Her view changed the day Koenig said, "Staff Sergeant, there's more to warfighting than instinct. Instinct won't make sure you've got ammo when you need it or teach your people how to call for fire."

He was right, of course, and after that Jamie paid more attention to admin and logistics. Koenig responded by eliciting her input about missions and then claiming her ideas—those "detailed notes"—as his own.

This latest mission, Koenig informed Jamie, would ultimately involve moving all three of the Eighth Regiment's infantry battalions inland; they would inch into every ravine, over every ridge, onto every summit to push out an enemy now virtually invisible to Marine surveillance technology.

The highest mountain in the area—the 1,300-meter Thumb Peak—needed to be secured early on. And that was where some mission planners urged a momentous change in the rules of engagement: Air support and plenty of it—including use of rockets and missiles launched from attack helos as well as fixed-wing aircraft.

Which was why the Brigade's new commanding officer—a major general named Embry who had a reputation for being astute and rambunctious—was taking to the field. Any decision he'd make to uptick the conflict must, he insisted, be made "out there."

And from rather high ground, too. Embry wanted to go to the top of Thumb Peak. On foot. And the Three-Eight's scout/snipers would get him there. Elements of Second Battalion, simultaneously approaching Thumb Peak from the opposite direction, would help keep Embry up there for as long as he wanted.

"It's a frigging cloud forest," groused Ramirez, now first squad's sergeant, upon learning his people would be Embry's escorts. "What's he think he'll see? That using rockets and missiles on the PIA is a no-brainer? Du-uh!"

Jamie suspected the general had an itch. *Embry commanded snipes once, and he's famous for getting down and dirty with the grunts. He's been here long enough to want to know what "out there" is really like.* However, she said only, "Mmm, dunno, Ram."

That's because more recent news had thoroughly rattled her. Koenig, too, would go to Thumb Peak. In truth, he had little choice: The first lieutenant's job was tactical. Theoretically, he had to be in the field, "out there," at least once in a while—and now theory had careened headlong into practice. If he fobbited this one, his career would be shot to hell. So for the first time in his five months as platoon CO, Koenig would lead a mission "in the frigging flesh," as Jamie bitched to Rhys.

Koenig had been a solid guy once, according to the scuttlebutt Rhys dug up—willing to face down the scary stuff. What happened to him? The stories shared only something about a shrapnel wound and the Three-Eight snipes being his comeback.

Initially, he embraced Jamie's suggestion that first squad carve its way up to Thumb Peak along the highest of several ridges extending southeast from the summit nearly down to the coast. Then he spent anxious hours making changes and changing his changes before coming full circle. So Jamie's plan stood. Two fire teams would scout along the ridge slopes—one on each side of the ridge. A third fire team would accompany the big shots, First Lieutenant Koenig, and a corpsman. Jamie and Ramirez would roam, trading off tip and tail.

To reach the top of Thumb Peak before Eighth Regiment widely engaged the enemy, first squad and the big shots would need to begin their journey two days ahead of Eighth Regiment's movement. A unit from Second Battalion would likewise depart ahead of the main force, approaching from the northwest to meet them on the summit.

Koenig's excuse for a final briefing didn't take long, so Jamie and Rhys had one more chance to huddle. Over maps and topographic animations and the latest intel, they reviewed again how the platoon's second and third squads would ply various ravines and ridges in support of the Three-Eight's push inland.

"You gotta hit the rack," Rhys said finally.

"Yeah." But Jamie continued to frown at the Three-Eight sector topo animation.

"Your work here is done, kemo sabe." Rhys reached for Jamie's shoulders and steered her out of the FOBCOC. "Time to sleep now."

The usual nightmares plagued what little sleep Jamie got. Rhys woke her well before dawn and helped her gear up while she tried to figure out why this mission had her so spooked.

"Gotta go," Jamie said finally, reluctant to take her eyes off Rhys's face. "But I'll—"

"Yeah." Rhys winked. "You'll be watching." Rhys turned her eyes skyward, smiling. "We'll do a real nice dance for you."

Jamie smiled back. "Good hunting," she said, holding on to the high-five Rhys offered, wishing she could hold on to it forever.

❖

The mission had been dubbed TOP, so First Lieutenant Koenig's operational risk management worksheet showed those three letters and a date.

Jamie glanced at the list of identified mission hazards. She

worried most about two: The weather could bite them, and so could
PIA scouts, who were bound to be invisible behind state-of-the-art
countersurveillance measures.

Full fucking circle. Once more, as long ago, success depended
on fighters' honed instincts, on knowing how to hide, on what the
unaided but experienced human eye could see. First squad had to
exploit maneuverability and surprise. Remain undiscovered by the
enemy while moving as quickly as possible through tangled tropical
forest ahead of the erratic shift from the dry season into "the hanging
habagat"—the annual southwest monsoon.

The change from dry to wet could quickly make their climb of the
rugged, mudslide-prone slopes not only uncomfortable but dangerous,
too. Heavy monsoon rains and cloud forest fog also often confounded
satellite infrared detection systems, which messed up their ability to
track and coordinate the activities of deployed units. So everyone hoped
to complete the mission before the monsoon gained real momentum.

Shortly before they embarked, the major general showed up in
full kit with three others—a light colonel named Zachary, who was his
intelligence chief, and a couple of very protective, well-armed senior
NCOs.

The way the major general nodded too politely at the antsy Koenig
nipped at Jamie's intuition. *Embry dislikes him.* As, perhaps, did
Zachary, a plain, lean, no-nonsense woman in her late thirties whose
reputation as Embry's trusted G-2 was widespread.

"Staff Sergeant Gwynmorgan," the major general rumbled in his
burly baritone when he spotted Jamie, "glad to see you're along on
this."

"Sir." Officers were not Jamie's favorite species, but she respected
this man who'd pinned a second Silver Star on her chest and written her
Navy Cross citation himself. Especially if he didn't much like Koenig.

Major General Embry's smile briefly lit his attentive eyes before
they shifted back to the mission commander. "Okay, Lieutenant, tell me
how we're getting up to Thumb Peak and where you want us."

"Of course, sir," Koenig said and ushered Embry and his entourage
to a minutely detailed virtual-three-dimension topo display, thirty
inches square. Jamie followed them and watched Embry. *An in-fighter*,
she decided, *willing and able to risk a punch to win.* "We'll move up
from Iwahig along the highest ridge, sir." Koenig pointed. "Here. It'll

be pretty strenuous at first, but it'll get us to the most advantageous elevation the fastest. By the morning of day three we should be just below the summit..."

❖

Within minutes of their departure the rain started, slowing their climb. To maintain absolute stealth—to be invisible—they avoided the most-traveled mountain trails. Instead, they stuck to little-used tracks, and at times first squad carved minimal paths through the forest. Nine hours and almost eight klicks later, to Jamie's surprise, they'd seen no PIA. She dared to hope no PIA had seen them.

The second day began cloudy but rainless, and the major general appeared tired. He was in ace condition but in his mid-forties and out of practice. He continued, however, to hold his own. In the afternoon, the rain returned heavier than before. Still, they encountered no PIA, even though the end of the day put them perhaps an hour from the summit.

Nine months battling these people and I'm still confounded by where and when they don't show up. And where and when they do...

Before they broke camp on day three, Jamie downlinked, decrypted, and displayed the Eighth Regiment FOBCOC's satellite mission-monitor imagery, which she kept at the corner of her eyewraps' shadowscreen so she could watch as Rhys and second and third squads began their op.

Despite intermittent rain, which at times made their detection gear unusable and occasionally obscured the FOBCOC downlinks, they'd stayed a titch ahead of schedule. Now the noise of temperamental precip provided audio cover, so they moved a bit faster than expected. Then a classic cloud forest fog supplanted the rain; its density interfered with detection and commo gear, forcing them to inch along with such caution that it seemed they hardly moved at all. When the fog finally abated and they could pick up the FOBCOC downlink again, it showed a Second Battalion unit approaching the summit from the northwest only a bit late.

Still no sign of PIA, though, and this perplexed Jamie. She expected to see nothing on the detection gear, but by now some hint of nearby PIA should have manifested. An unnatural silence ahead of them, a twig twisted out of place. Something. Yet no one in the squad had spotted anything, heard anything, and the Second Battalion guys were proceeding apace.

Maybe they're pulling back. Maybe this one's gonna go down easy...

A minute later, or perhaps two, all hell broke loose on the other, northwest side of Thumb Peak's summit. Jamie had just taken point, and instantly her left hand sprang up in a fist, signaling the squad to freeze.

So much for easy. She put the distance at less than three hundred meters. The FOBCOC downlink displayed on her shadowscreen confirmed her guess. Twenty-eight tiny Second Battalion figures on the display huddled about two hundred meters north of the summit. Pinned there, they only sporadically returned fire. A spritely tangle of fine red Trajsat filaments converged on an area just north of the summit itself, defining the enemy's location.

First squad had halted about sixty meters southeast of the summit and some twenty-five meters below it. A glance at the map animations on her shadowscreen showed Jamie their disadvantage. Judging by the FOBCOC downlink, the PIA position had the benefit of higher elevation and good cover.

Right behind her, she knew, Lieutenant Koenig saw the same thing on his eyewraps. She turned to him, waiting for orders, but he gaped at her wide-eyed as though he'd never seen her before. *Okay, fine, I take that to mean: Carry on.* Jamie nodded to him like he'd given her an order to scout.

She signaled Avery, who was smart, feline agile, and a damn good shot. Crouching low, Jamie led Avery toward the weapons fire, then sent Avery northwest while she headed north.

"How many are we dealing with?" Koenig demanded when they returned.

"We saw six on the summit, more farther north—" Jamie began.

"How fucking many altogether, Staff Sergeant?" Koenig only barely controlled his voice.

Jamie stared at him. *Oh christ, he's starting to lose it.* "I'd say a platoon, more or less," she responded carefully. "We couldn't see all the way up the slope without giving ourselves away, so—"

"So you don't know," Koenig snarled.

Before Jamie could reply, Koenig whirled to face Embry and, a little breathless, proposed calling in air support—actually said "And plenty of it," clearly expecting the major general to like the idea.

Embry listened, glanced at Zachary—and then, abandoning protocol, he spoke to Jamie. "Suggestions, Staff Sergeant?"

Their eyes met and Jamie understood: He didn't want to use air support at all, much less before the main thrust of the mission got under way.

"Uh," Jamie stuttered, "uh, yessir. I don't believe they know we're here, and their surveillance doesn't see us, which means we can get very close to their position, because we can use the concealment of the forest until we—"

"But we don't know how many there are," Koenig interrupted with edgy impatience.

"No, Lieutenant, not reliably," Jamie replied, "but maybe we can find out more—"

"We gotta keep commo silence, Staff Sergeant. So how the hell do you propose we do *that*?" Koenig croaked angrily. This second outburst had plainly pissed off Zachary, but Embry's hand on her forearm kept her quiet.

"Watch." Jamie waved over five squaddies, then whispered briefly to them. They moved six or seven meters downslope, behind an outcrop that kept them safely out of sight of the summit.

Two of them assumed lookout positions. The other three began a slow-motion stop-start dance that lasted about two minutes.

"What the fuck are they doing, Staff Sergeant?" Desperation now laced Koenig's high-pitched whisper.

"Watch your fobcock display," she told the officers, forgetting her pronunciation, deciding to ignore Embry's eyebrow perking in apparent amusement. A minute later, their eyewraps' shadowscreens showed some of the tiny figures on the other side of Thumb Peak forming into a series of patterns. "Aw-*right*," Jamie said.

Embry smiled broadly. "That new high-tech signaling technique your idea, staff sergeant?"

Jamie grinned back. "I wish, sir. Sergeant Rhys thought it up. This is our beta test."

"Translate," Embry said.

"Fifty PIA, give or take. Most of them north of the summit, about seven meters down, a handful right at the top where there's less cover, some of their main force starting to flank. The Two-Eight guys figure it's because they've interrupted the PIA supply route," Jamie said. "Could mean more PIA coming up behind the Two-Eight guys. But if so, they haven't been encountered yet. Also means, in my opinion, that the PIA don't know we're here. I believe they'll hyperfocus on Two-Eight and neglect their back, at least for a while. So if we move our asses before they realize their oversight, we can do it, sir. We can take them without air support."

"Let's hear your plan," said Embry.

The major general, his intelligence officer, Koenig, Ramirez, and Avery squatted around Jamie. "We split up," she said. "Ramirez and one fire team head east. They're Alpha team. Avery takes a fire team west—Bravo team. Lieutenant Koenig and I move with Charlie team onto the rock formation right there just south of the summit." Jamie pointed. "See it just beyond those trees?"

Everyone except Koenig nodded.

"Sir, I'm hoping you and your staff and the corpsman can take up position farther downslope beneath that ledge there and cover our backsides."

"Yeah, Staff Sergeant, I think we can manage that." Embry smiled while he thumbed the assault rifle he'd lugged up the mountain.

"Fog's not impeding commo at the moment, so we passive-signal the Two-Eight guys pronto and tell them to open up at, let's see, eleven forty," Jamie said. "That'll give us time to get our teams in place. Alpha and Bravo will have minimal cover, but adequate, and an almost even elevation with the main PIA position. Two-Eight lays on suppressive fire aimed right up the middle between them, but below the summit itself. At the same time, Alpha and Bravo open up from both sides, creating crossfire and a diversion so Charlie team can come over the formation from behind and bag the PIA on the summit. Then Charlie targets the main PIA force from the summit while Two-Eight moves up and Alpha and Bravo squeeze from the sides."

Koenig looked pale. Even though his head moved up and down, Jamie had no confidence that he really comprehended what she'd said. Embry studied her, his craggy face scrunched around narrowed black eyes.

"That's it, sir," Jamie said, uncomfortable under the major general's matter-of-fact scrutiny. "That's the plan."

Have I made a complete idiot of myself?
"Sounds solid," said Embry. "Let's do it."

❖

Alpha and Bravo teams moved out first, since they had more distance to cover. Three times while Charlie team slinked into position, Jamie asked the ashen first lieutenant if he felt okay and suggested he might want to join the major general. Three times he declined.

Shit. He should be back there with Embry, sucking up, pretending to provide cover. Stupid, stupid, stupid mistake—and christ, we're gonna pay for it. Don't have much time before he wilts.

No time at all, in fact. As Charlie team clustered beneath the rock, Koenig's sudden gasping about air support escalated into shouts for them to stop. He was loud enough to attract PIA attention, but then the Two-Eight guys and first squad's other two teams started shooting. Even though Koenig had probably given them away, they had to stick with the plan and move up and over the rock formation. It was Koenig's order to give, but he didn't.

"Go *go GO!*" Jamie rasped after waiting an extra second for the order, and they went. All except Koenig. In the corner of her vision, Jamie saw him curl against the rock. She left him there.

They found eight PIA on the summit. The four snipes with Jamie took six from behind with ease. Two other PIA had turned toward them, perhaps reacting to Koenig's shout. Jamie nailed one but missed the other and scrambled up the last few feet to the summit after him. He fired at her twice, blowing the E19 she carried out of her hands with the first shot.

When his second shot whisked off her boonie hat, the world slid into slow motion, giving her time to consider the decision before her.

Dive for cover while reaching for the pistol strapped to her thigh and shoot it out with him? Or stay up and lunge one more fast, long step to grab his weapon and wrench it from him?

The odds, she concluded, favored grabbing his weapon. As she did it, he twisted slightly to one side but held on. So did she, and they tumbled, skidding across the rock formation and landing resoundingly about two meters from the quailing first lieutenant.

Jamie and the PIA fighter rolled across the uneven slab of rock wrestling for control of the weapon. At last, on her feet again, Jamie gained just enough leverage to bash the butt of the rifle into the PIA fighter's larynx.

The blow's crunchy-squishy sound formed a memory she knew she'd never be able to forget. Adrenaline-drenched, clutching the man's QBZ-96, she saw his life ebb from his eyes as he choked. Before his deflating body met the ground, she turned away to face the first lieutenant.

Still hunched against the rock formation, Koenig had extracted his pistol from its holster. Now he shakily pointed it at her.

"Lieutenant!" Jamie exclaimed in astonishment.

His eyes dilated and, staring at her, he angled the barrel of the pistol to his temple. *Shit. I don't have time for this.*

Putting the odds of Koenig doing it at about three to one, Jamie spun around toward the summit, figuring her life would be better without him in it.

But then, growling "Ah hell," she swung the QBZ-96 back at Koenig and squeezed off a single shot that nipped his outer thigh inches above his knee. He screamed, dropped the pistol. She glanced downslope and bellowed, "Corpsman!"

Both Embry and Zachary stared back at her—witnesses.

Jamie had no idea why she did it. She did not plan to do it.

No matter.

Soon she'd be marched off in manacles. The Corps did not excuse someone shooting an officer. Ever. *Guess handcuffs and leg irons and convict scrubs* are *gonna be my fate.* First, though, she'd do everything she could to keep her guys alive. She turned and scrambled back up to the summit toward the commotion of automatic-weapons fire.

An hour after it ended, Jamie remained atop Thumb Peak, sitting cross-legged, watching the sun descend toward the sea far to the west. The sky had cleared of clouds; at least she'd see stars tonight.

There'd been sixty-three PIA—more than they'd thought—but her plan had worked almost perfectly. Four from first squad wounded, but no KIAs, plus all but one of the Two-Eight guys still alive, too. Before dark, any minute now, a medical helo would arrive and drop a mobile trauma unit to treat the wounded. Dawn would bring a Second Battalion company to relieve them and evacuate the wounded. So far, the rest of the Three-Eight snipe platoon had also done well, according to Rhys: No KIAs, only two go-home wounds.

This outcome accorded Jamie such overwhelming relief that she wasn't really sure she could stand up. After all, this had become her last mission. Ahead was only— She banned the thought. No point in thinking.

A klick and a half to the west rose another peak nearly as high as the one on which she perched, and she wondered if a PIA sniper lurked there. She knew a good snipe with a decent weapon could make the shot that would kill her. She had, more times than she cared to contemplate.

Sure would solve a lot of problems. But no one fired. The fight hadn't gotten there yet. When she saw Ramirez approach, she nodded at him but said nothing. Ramirez sat next to her and, without a word, put her boonie hat on her knee. Late-afternoon sunlight shone through the holes where the PIA round had drilled it.

"Thanks," she said but didn't keep her eyes on him. In the waning light, he looked too much like a dark-haired Arnoldt.

After a long minute, he spoke. "The general wants to see you." He angled his head toward Embry's location.

Exhaling, she took the hat off her knee, put it on her head, and rose stiffly. "Perimeter all set up?"

"Yeah, and scouts patrolling three-sixty 'round the summit."

"Good work. And, Ram, see that everyone up here's under wraps." She inclined her head westward. "No doubt that peak over there makes a great sniper's hide."

Jamie climbed down the rock formation that had sheltered Koenig and was startled to find him still there, his bloody right pant leg ripped up to his hip, his blouse off and balled behind his head. The corpsman hovered above his leg while talking quietly into her comlink.

Koenig was unquestionably in pain, but his eyes were clearer than they'd been all day. When he looked up, Jamie thought she saw a faint smile. She wanted to pass on by but knew she ought to say something to this man, so she paused, searching for words.

The first lieutenant eased the burden of the moment with unlikely dignity. "Gwynmorgan," he said. "Nice shot."

She noticed that he didn't refer to her by her rank and understood this meant something. Jamie opened her mouth to respond, but was interrupted by Lieutenant Colonel Zachary, who barely glanced at Koenig. "Miz Gwynmorgan, the general would like a moment," Zachary said. "I'm sure Mr. Koenig won't mind."

Koenig's head went up and down slightly and his face relaxed into an undeniable smile as he closed his eyes and eased back his head. *Miz? Mister? What the fuck? I thought that went out with c-rations.* Jamie fended off a wave of dizziness. *Oh. I get it. They're being polite 'til they disarm me. After which I'll get dragged away in chains.* She laid down the Chinese rifle, then pulled her pistol from its holster and put it on the ground.

"Yes, ma'am," Jamie said. Turning to face Embry, she caught Zachary's smile. A small, satisfied smile. *What the fuck?*

"...And our momentum," Embry was saying into his comlink, "depends on having reliable leadership *now* in those key units." Embry listened, then shook his head. "In my judgment, sir, we have no other option...Mmm, let's just say several...Yes, sir, I'll make damn sure they stay below the media radar."

Having induced the air to leave her lungs, Jamie found inhaling difficult. She managed only a strained, wheezy, "Sir!" when the major general terminated the link. *Oh god, here it comes.*

"Mr. Koenig has been relieved," Embry said as soon as he steered her out of the corpsman's earshot. "I'd like you to take his command. And his rank. Right now, so this platoon remains mission-ready."

Jamie gaped at him. "What?"

"It's a combat appointment—what civilians call a battlefield commission," Zachary said, her tone congenial despite Jamie's lapse in military decorum. "Will you accept it?"

Zachary held out Koenig's rank insignia in the palm of her hand. Jamie stared at them, blinked, and gaped once more at the major general.

"You want to make me a *first lieutenant?*" she asked, heretofore unaware that such a thing was even possible. "You can do that? After I—? Sir, you saw what I—"

"Yeah, I saw. In my judgment, you made the best possible move. And yes, I damn well *can* kick your ass into a commission. Only one person can stop me now: You."

"But—"

"Look, Jamie." Embry's hand claimed her shoulder. "I know you'll see some flak. The Pentagon likes to pretend there hasn't been any need for combat appointments since the Viet Nam Conflict back in the nineteen sixties and seventies. But even the Joint Chiefs admit to a leadership problem that business-as-usual promotion rules have made worse. So they've developed some legal workarounds to keep this brigade at required force levels. Fact is, you're not the first we've boosted this way, and you sure as hell won't be the last. We need to leverage the experience of people like you who know their way around here, know what works and what doesn't. Because for this one we've always got to occupy the moral high ground. We absolutely must keep the population of Palawan on our side. And that takes skill."

"Iron fist in a velvet glove."

"Exactly." Embry's eyes flashed with a man-do-I-know-how-to-pick-them delight that Jamie could see but couldn't quite believe. "We'll win faster and our win will stick if we can avoid significant uptick for as long as possible. Maybe even avoid it altogether. So we need leaders in the right positions who grasp that, who work hard, work smart, and can keep marines alive and effective without beating the crap out of this place. I had you figured for this after what you did in Puerto Princesa."

For a second, just a second, the light in Embry's eyes changed. Jamie could have sworn his eyes twinkled. *No! This is insane!*

"I just didn't figure it'd happen this soon. But I learned a long time ago to take opportunity where I find it." Embry's hand, still on her shoulder, firmed its grip and kept rhythm with his words. "You made a difference today. Proved you can do a one-lite's job. And the Three-Eight needs a one-lite—not a two-lite, not an NCO—running its snipe platoon."

"Sir, I don't think I'm suited for—"

The index finger of Embry's other hand pressed lightly against her lips and she stopped breathing. "I saw you there," he almost whispered, "that night at the airport, thumping and pounding away. I saw you give your people exactly what they needed exactly when they needed it. Real leadership."

Are you crazy? I wasn't leading anyone. I was fighting with my girlfriend. I stubbed my damn toe...

"And I need that leadership, Jamie. The Three-Eight needs that leadership. Don't stop now. Not now."

His eyes drilled into hers while his finger slowly retreated from her lips. Released, she gulped for air. *Oh god. Marty.* Jamie ripped her gaze away from Embry and let it float upward. The sky had deepened into a rich, soothing blue. *Oh god.* She ached to escape into the calm, the freedom of so much blue.

On her shoulder, Embry's hand twitched. Reluctantly, Jamie brought her eyes back to him and exhaled. "Okay. I'll accept the appointment, sir."

"Good girl," Embry said and proffered his right hand. His grip was strong but had no need to dominate; he didn't release Jamie's hand until he finished speaking.

"Your appointment is permanent. Already approved upchain. Takes effect today. Right now. Means your enlistment has ended and you're no longer a scout/sniper, since commissioned officers are not permitted that honor. But you *will* have the honor of commanding scout/snipers."

"Yes, sir." Jamie couldn't pull her eyes away from the man. She had plunged and now she was falling and falling and everything was upside down. She had no idea what to do next.

Perhaps it showed, because Embry returned his hand to her shoulder in a way that struck her as fatherly. "When you get off this mountain, go straight over to Eighth Regiment HQ to sign on those dotted lines and pick up your certificate of commission. It'll be ready by the time you get there. Zach's informing your battalion commander of your appointment as we speak. He'll approve whomever you recommend to replace you, and he'll be instructed to run interference with the desk jockeys to get it done ay-sap. Especially if you promote from within your platoon, which I encourage you to do."

"Yes, sir, I certainly will."

"After that, I want you to just keep on doing what you've been doing. Your S-Two—Pinsof, right?—will help you with the admin bullshit. And good luck, First Lieutenant."

"Thank you, sir."

A smile, a final pat on her shoulder, and the major general walked off, already talking into his comlink again. *Wait!* she wanted to call to him. *I'm not ready yet.*

CHAPTER FOURTEEN

MA'AM

*C*hrist all-fucking mighty. Propped on a stool, elbows splayed on the rough wooden bar, Jamie put her hands to her face and rubbed. *I can't fucking believe I fucking said yes.* She kept her eyes closed. Otherwise she'd look at Rhys again. That had been hard enough the first time, after she'd returned from the regimental FOB. Because of course, Rhys already knew. Rhys even knew where to find her and when.

"So is there anything you *don't* know?" Jamie had joked when she came upon Rhys standing just outside the Three-Eight's FOBCOC.

"Oh yeah." Rhys didn't smile. "Plenty. Ma'am."

Ma'am. Jamie's stomach had turned at the sound. She wanted to halt on the spot and plead with Rhys to have some pity, try to understand; she wanted to yell at Rhys to never, ever call her that. But she said only, "Wait for me, okay?"

When she came out of the FOBCOC, she carried the papers that made Rhys's promotion official. This time Rhys didn't look at her at all. The ground had become much more interesting. So Jamie had slapped the papers against Rhys's chest, against those breasts she tried so damn hard not to think about, and walked on without a word. She'd wanted to go back to their hooch, that tiny movable space they'd shared for six months which was almost like a home—but she figured Rhys wouldn't follow, so there she'd be, all alone, engulfed in the misery of her lieutenantness.

Better to head for neutral territory: The makeshift, rank-blind joint just inside the Three-Eight FOB's outer perimeter where everyone went for "light refreshment" whenever they'd been told there'd be no mission the next day. By the time the bartender plunked down the seltzer water Jamie ordered, Staff Sergeant Rhys, the new Three-Eight scout/sniper platoon senior NCO, had taken the seat next to her.

Jamie picked up the seltzer water and drank half of it in one throat-stinging gulp before she glanced over to see how Rhys was doing.

Rhys stared, no longer bothering to camouflage her surprise and anger.

"Buy you a drink?" Jamie said, hoping to find a crack in Rhys's slitty-eyed façade.

"Thanks." Rhys blinked. "A beer."

Jamie ordered it, paid for it, and the two of them sat hunched over the bar in silence. Too soon, the place filled with marines whose conversations remained uncharacteristically low-key.

"...nah, takes six months of The Basic School just to make second louie..."

"...I'm telling ya, there *is* such a thing as a battlefield commission..."

"...doesn't even have any business being an E-six, and she came back a frigging *one-lite*..."

"...right over there at the end of the bar—"

Jamie shoved back the bar stool. "I gotta go," she said to Rhys and slipped out the back door.

"Christ, you're hard to track down."

Jamie startled at the sound of Rhys's voice behind her. She'd picked this spot among the sandbags to lie low and feel sorry for herself. Count on Rhys to come along and make her feel like even worse shit. "Nobody's supposed to find me here."

"Yes, ma'am." Rhys turned on her heel.

"No, Marty, wait. I'm sorry."

Rhys halted. "Ma'am?"

"Oh god, please don't do that. Please, *please* don't ever fucking call me that."

For one of those infinities in an instant, Rhys remained statue-still. And then her shoulders relaxed. "Damn," she said, shaking her head as she turned back around, and Jamie saw a smile tease her mouth. Like she couldn't quite help herself, Jamie thought as Rhys sat pretty close, close enough for Jamie to be grateful.

Rhys placed two bottles in the space between them. A peace offering perhaps. Or an offering of condolence. *Okay. Maybe this'll be okay.* Jamie eyed the bottles. "What're those?"

Rhys tapped one, then the other. "Scotch. Bourbon. What's your poison…ma'am?" She shoved her shoulder into Jamie's while she drawled the form of address reserved for officers, DIs, and female royalty.

"Oh christ," Jamie groaned. "You're gonna really make me pay for this."

Rhys nodded an impish challenge. "Big time…ma'am."

"Fuck. I'm doomed."

"That's true, you are. So, what'll it be, Lieutenant ma'am? Scotch or bourbon? Or both?"

"Uh, well, I don't really know." Jamie squinted warily at the bottles.

"You…don't…know," repeated Rhys, a crease forming above her nose. Suddenly her eyebrows lifted into her forehead. "Shit, Gwynmorgan! You've never had either scotch or bourbon? Not even on Culion?"

Jamie shook her head, provoking a giggle from Rhys.

"Ever had a drink of anything? Beer? Wine? *Anything*?"

Jamie shook her head again. "I like a good lemonade…"

"This is gonna be exceedingly interesting." Rhys twisted the tops off both bottles and handed one to Jamie with an order. "Small sip."

Without hesitation, Jamie violated Living-with-Alby Rule Number One—never inebriate—and obeyed. And promptly gagged. "Omi*god*, that stuff's fucking awful!"

Rhys handed her the other bottle. "Of course, Lieutenant, by rights you should clear your palate before you—"

"Yeah. Sure." Jamie took a swig—*"Aaaghh!"*—and sprayed it all over the ground in front of her.

Chuckling, arms folded over her chest, Rhys settled into the sandbags while Jamie tried to stop coughing. "Hmm, maybe I can find you some lemonade."

Jamie raised her head from between her knees and looked over at Rhys through watery eyes. "Give me that," she said, grabbing the first bottle and taking a hearty gulp from it. She recoiled into a turbulent flinch and tears streaked her cheeks, but she kept down what she swallowed. Finally she gasped for air, opened her eyes. "Whoa. Really does taste like crap, huh? But the way it goes down your throat and makes your belly all warm—sure can see why they call it firewater."

Another savage cough sent her to her knees, then onto her backside so she ended up facing Rhys, legs askew. "Fuck," she moaned and emitted a loud belch.

"Scare-*ee*." Rhys giggled before she bleated like a sheep. "Ma-a-a'a-a-am."

Jamie stuck out her tongue. "Fung-goo you, stiff sergeant." Then she reached for one of the bottles. "Lemme try that again." It went down easier this time and she merely snorted. "Want some?" She offered the bottle to Rhys.

"Nah, I'll work on this one."

"Marty?"

"Mmm?"

"Doesn't mean shit, y'know."

"Sure it does."

"No." Jamie took a large swallow from her bottle, then coughed and wheezed. "Just a piece of paper. 'S all bullshit."

"The whole fucking regiment's buzzing about you."

"So what? Now I'm sullied or something?"

"You crossed the Rubicon, Jamie."

"Marty, please."

"Well, it wasn't my idea. Lieutenant."

"You think I *wanted* this? You think I *like* it?"

"You're a goddamn officer. Ma'am."

"Jeezus, Marty, I only went along with it to save us from another Koenig." Jamie thumped the bottle she held onto the ground between her knees. "It's your dream, not mine. Well, you can have it, okay?"

Rhys's eyes filled with tears. "Just doesn't work that way, remember?"

"What about your contagious magic?"

Rhys shrugged and looked away.

Jamie raised the bottle to her mouth and belted down more of its contents. After she did it twice more, Rhys took the bottle from her.

"How'd you get all the way up there?" she asked when she realized Rhys stood over her.

"Come on." Rhys reached down a hand. "Time to hit the rack."

Jamie didn't move. "Think we can keep sharing the same hooch? Y'know, unit responsiveness and all that?"

"Don't know, Lieutenant. How about we talk about it in the morning, okay?"

❖

Jamie woke nauseous and aching and remembering her question. Even before she opened her eyes, she knew Rhys's answer, could feel Rhys's answer in the sparse almost-echo of unoccupied space around her. Rhys had packed up and moved out.

She waited for the tears to stop trickling down her temples into her ears, tried to steady her breathing and accept the inevitability of it. Rhys was just a few feet away, only a couple sheets of thin cloth and mosquito netting between them. All forty-one of the people in the Three-Eight scout/sniper platoon—*her* scout/sniper platoon—were right there. If she shouted, every one of them would come running. But knowing this didn't help her feel less alone.

Chapter Fifteen

Coyote

We got a bunch of civilians here wanting help," Ramirez reported over his comlink.

Cleanup duty. For the third day in a row, one of Jamie's squads had encountered—and successfully terminated—rogue PIA snipers. Ramirez and his people had been scouting ten kilometers upstream from Iwahig, inching along the river's steepening southern bank, while second and third squads had dispersed into the ridges above the north side of the river.

And now civilians. This news surprised Jamie, who prowled the high ground with third squad. The citizens of Palawan had been skilled at getting out of the way of the conflict. Except for Puerto Princesa, rarely were they caught in any crossfire. Jamie's surprise deepened when Ramirez said there'd been no skirmish, just ten souls on the run, hoping to find safety downriver.

"Christ, Ram. Ten? Where from?"

"Well, we're mostly communicating with our hands, you know? Seems to be south of here. Called, uh, Apur—Uh, Apur-some-damn-thing."

"Apurauan?"

"Yeah. Apur-uh-whatever."

"So they've come over the Anepahan Peaks. That's a haul. At least thirty klicks. Jungle klicks. How they look?"

"Hungry thirsty tired terrified."

A chill tingled along Jamie's spine. Her gut tensed, too, because she hadn't been visited by that chill in quite a while. Certainly not in her thirty-five days of lieutenantness, thirty-five days of scouting and cleanup missions that dinged three of her people, one seriously. But nobody killed. No chill, no KIAs. Maybe a coincidence, maybe not.

"Okay, Ram, back at you shortly about how to bring them down to Iwahig for debriefing."

Over the next several days, even before Ramirez got back to the FOB with his ten souls, the chill skittered up and down Jamie's back more and more often, reigniting her belief that saying yes to Embry had been a calamitous mistake. *I am so out of my league. Officers are supposed to know what the hell is going on, but I don't have a clue.* All she had was a prickly spine and the unceasing fear that any minute now she'd get someone killed.

If the Three-Eight's officers met to talk about what was percolating, they didn't invite "Embry's bastard child." She'd heard the insult twice in those first couple of weeks after she returned to the Three-Eight's FOB with a one-lite's black bar on her cammie collar—even though her boss, Captain Pinsof, had introduced her around as Lieutenant Gwynmorgan, like she was for real.

Pinsof had seemed okay that day—the day she now thought of as EBC6, her sixth day as Embry's Bastard Child. Yet since then she'd spent little time with the rushed, harried Pinsof—at briefings and debriefings mostly. And yes, he asked her how she was doing, but she figured he wanted to hear she was doing fine, so that's what she said, even though she was— *I'm lost, that's what. Fucking lost.*

"It's because you're hardly ever in the goddamn FOB, much less in the officers' mess," Rhys said from her side of the Rubicon, exasperation showing. "If you want to find out what's really going on, you have to hang around and shoot the shit."

So Jamie had tried to do what Marty suggested: Go to the officers' mess.

She'd tried just once—on EBC24—and she ate alone, meticulously ignored by the other officers, who talked with each other in clarion tones about how the Pentagon wouldn't publicly admit to the existence of combat appointments. And someone said, "Hey, I'm all for mustangs, but these fucking coyotes…"

She stood then, picking up her food dishes because she saw that the officers in the mess just left their dishes for some lance coolie to clean up, and she sure as hell wasn't going to let any enlisted person do servitude for her. Dishes in hand, she turned toward the word. Coyote:

Combat-boosted from mid-level NCO all the way to one-lite. Coyote: Breaking in line and fucking up promotions for "real" lieutenants.

The word had come from Captain Cavanaugh, commander of Kilo Company, the guy Alonzo didn't salute at San Salvacia. "Oh," she'd said that first and only time in the officers' mess. "So a coyote's like a mustang, only smarter and faster. Good to know. Sir."

She stood there long enough to return Cavanaugh's frigid stare, then walked away—only to spend days haunted by one shoulda after another: *Shoulda told them the Marines could use more coyotes and a whole lot less of this feudal crap from the days when only aristocrats could be officers and the enlisted were slaves. Shoulda told them what they can do with their damn commission. Shoulda kicked that asshole's balls into his throat...*

So on EBC37, Jamie had only Marty Rhys to talk to about Ram's civilians. Rhys had just returned to the FOB with second squad, which gave Jamie a few moments to watch her from a distance, to yearn for what used to be, before Thumb Peak, before Marty lost her lust for contagious magic.

It was the same memory, always, and one more time Jamie savored it, their last time together. They'd been on an easy mission, a couple of days and nights cleaning up the high ground north of Puerto Princesa. Easy enough to actually relax in the magnificent limestone cave they'd found. That night, away from the rest of Rhys's squad, hidden in the unconditional darkness, their sounds masked by a small waterfall nearby, everything she'd hoped for with Marty seemed possible.

For a little while that night, touching Marty, kissing Marty, bringing Marty to fierce, breathy consummation, she believed Marty might be in love with *her*. Not her combat instincts or the way she could nail a distant target. Just her, for her own sake. She made love to Marty that night from deep within; she turned herself inside out. "I want you to care if I die," she said. "I'm in love with you," she said. "I would die for you," she said. That night, she gave Marty everything she had the power to give and wanted to give more, more.

Jamie remembered as though remembering was a sacred act. Rhys saying, "I know, I know." Rhys saying, "Shush now." Rhys holding her, kissing the top of her head while she took refuge in Rhys's bewitching breasts, her clit sated but throbbing anyway.

Flashes of it all crossed her consciousness every time she saw Rhys, talked with Rhys. And at night, too, when she was alone in her hooch, hoping Rhys would come to her again, just once, just this once, seeking magic.

EBC37 and Jamie had only the yearning; she wanted the yearning to beat in her clit and twist in her belly and claw its way up through her chest until it grabbed her throat. Better than nothing. Just before Rhys noticed her, she pushed it down, into its prison, to keep it from showing.

"Hey, Rhys," Jamie called out.

Rhys nodded, but her eyes stayed veiled.

Still the same. Before Thumb Peak, the way Rhys used to get edgy, the way she couldn't hide how pissed she was at being stuck, still, a rank behind—it had galled Jamie. After Thumb Peak, that edginess disappeared, and now Jamie yearned for it, too.

EBC37 and she still hadn't been able to get back across that Rubicon. Not for lack of trying, though. Jamie started trying even before her firewater hangover had worn off.

"Please, Marty," she'd said. "Tell them to talk to me like always. Jamie, Gwynnie, Gwynmorgan, whatever."

"Okay, Lieutenant Whatever. It's a deal."

And Rhys had mostly made it happen. Except Jamie had to let newbies start out with "LT," which remained a semi-scandalous breach of Corps etiquette, but not as dastardly as "Gwynnie." Plus, of course, she had to suffer her crew's ma'am crap whenever other officers came around.

EBC37 and as Jamie approached her, at least Rhys was willing to use the greeting that had become their private joke, delivered with her usual arched, that's-all-you-get eyebrow. "Hey, Lieutenant Whatever." But her smile evaporated when she saw Jamie's face.

"Hear about those folks Ram brought in?" Jamie asked.

"Please don't tell me they're refugees."

"Wish I didn't have to."

"Ah shit. Zhong? Confirmed?"

"Yep. Chinese regular army soldiers in the frigging flesh."

❖

When Jamie spotted her boss, he'd almost reached the last place in the FOB she ever wanted to go, but she couldn't allow that to stop her. Not this time.

By chance and maybe because of those chills needling up her spine, her ignorance hadn't killed anybody—yet. At EBC65, though, Jamie sensed the looming limits of dumb luck and instinct. She needed to find out what all the other officers knew. Those scraps of gossip and banter she heard at briefings had to be hiding *something*. The time had come to chase down her commander, the battalion's intelligence officer. *But please, please, not in there.*

She'd missed him at the FOBCOC; even so, if she moved fast enough, she could intercept him, might persuade him into a u-turn. "Captain Pinsof!"

"Hey, Gwynmorgan." A smile creased Pinsof's broad, pleasant face—a genuine enough smile that it reached his eyes and helped Jamie resist a knee-jerk urge to bolt. She stepped in front of him, hoping he'd have to stop.

"Want some coffee?" he asked, his thick, sandy-colored eyebrows elevating slightly while he waved an oversized mug. Jamie realized his question was rhetorical, and he wasn't even slowing down.

"Uh…" She stepped sideways. Any excuse to decline and retreat would do, but before Jamie found one, Pinsof planted a massive hand on her shoulder and nudged her toward the entry to the officers' mess.

"I owe you an apology," he said. "We should be getting together regularly so we can pick each other's brains. But it's been crazy as hell ever since Thumb Peak. Price of progress, I guess."

"Yes, sir." *Jeez, that sounds okay. Now if we could just turn around and go back to the fobcock…*

"Come on." Pinsof's smile made her suspect he'd read her thoughts. "It's being automatically deducted from your pay. Might as well get a meal out of it once in a while."

None of the half dozen officers in the mess outranked her, but every one of them looked her over as though Pinsof had walked in with an especially mangy dog.

"Have breakfast with me." Pinsof said. "I gotta eat something, and I hate eating alone."

Keeping an eye on the other officers, Jamie nodded. Pinsof led her through the well-stocked food line, ordered scrambled eggs, double bacon, and home fries from the cook, then got her to do the same. He introduced her to the mess clerk—"Make sure you always take real good care of Lieutenant Gwynmorgan, Peter"—and ambled to a solitary table while casually letting her know the hours when the officers' mess was mostly empty.

"Peter can fix you up with a decent meal that you can pick up at the kitchen entrance and take back to your hooch. I do it all the time. By the way, have you heard?"

As Jamie shook her head, she saw that smile again. *Okay, you know perfectly well I haven't heard.* She suspected nobody'd heard. Maybe that was his plan: He'd talk while she chowed down. Jamie started with the eggs, wondering if Pinsof had guessed this was her first hot meal in six weeks.

"Just got word from Brigade HQ." Pinsof spoke a little too loudly. "They're saying the Three-Eight's got the only snipe platoon without any KIAs. Not a single one since you took over as platoon NCO. No go-home wounds for a month, either. Same month in which everyone else has put in for replacements, by the way."

"Dumb luck, sir," Jamie mumbled around a mouthful of home fries. "We're getting the easy assignments, that's all."

"Nah, I don't think so, Lieutenant. I know everybody's assignments, and I'd say yours've been as tough as any—tougher."

Jamie shrugged without missing a bite. "Got a good team."

"Yeah, you do. And I notice you pretty much built it yourself."

"Had lots of help, sir," she replied between swallows. "Rhys is a much better platoon NCO than I ever was. Probably be a much better officer too, if she ever gets the chance. And our squad leaders—Ramirez, Elliott, and Avery—are primo."

She scanned the mess again. At a table four meters away, three second lieutenants clearly unimpressed by Pinsof's remarks were attempting to scowl her out of their presence. She shifted in her chair slightly to keep them beyond her peripheral vision.

"Amazing how ill-behaved some people get," Pinsof said resoundingly after following her glance, "when they can't control their envy." Then he glared at the two-lites until they abandoned their table.

Jamie stopped eating and examined Pinsof. "Thanks for that." *Maybe with this guy I can shortcut around the usual bullshit.* "Sir, I need to get my people prepared for what's coming next—" She halted at the sight of Pinsof's forming frown. *Oops*. She'd just hijacked the conversation from her commanding officer. "Sorry, sir."

But his expression seemed to relax into curiosity. "Please go on, Lieutenant."

"Well…" Jamie stalled. What was it about talking to Pinsof that wound her up like this? It reminded her too much of those last hours before a mission, after the planning and packing, when you contemplated—or not. Whatever it took to keep The Fear from ruling you. Rhys, who traveled around before joining the Corps but hated airplanes, once compared it to flying: You figure there's nasty odds you'll crash and burn, but you say okay, I can deal with it if it comes to that, I'm ready—and then you get on the damn plane and try like hell to keep your fists unclenched.

This was even worse. This time, Jamie found herself in the pilot's seat, and the flight had forty-one other souls aboard, and the corporal in the pilot's seat had been faking everything for sixty-five interminable days. Jamie flexed her hands. "I want to talk about the rules of engagement, sir."

"Okay. What about them?"

"Well, they're about to change, aren't they? I want to know when. And how. I need to know what everyone else knows."

"I'm not following you, Lieutenant."

Oh christ, I thought he'd be straight up. I can't let him *keep me out, too.* "You guys all talk, right? You got a line all the way up to Embry, to the Pentagon even. So you know what's coming. But—" *Shit, shit, just say it!* "But nobody's talking to me, Captain, so my people are hanging out there, unprepared."

"I'm afraid that's my fault. But I gotta tell you, Gwynmorgan, nobody around here is anywhere near as connected or as omniscient as all that." Pinsof's smile had developed a gallows look to it. "Nice thought, though."

"But you talk, right?"

"Sure." Pinsof took a gulp of coffee. "For instance, I'd ask you why you think the rules of engagement will be changing."

Jamie said nothing.

Pinsof twirled his free hand toward her. "And you'd say…"

"Uh, well, I'd say that it seems to me we're heading for either truce or uptick, and I'm betting uptick."

"Why?"

"Counterinsurgency against the PIA has worked so far because people in the north don't like PIA. That's changing as we go farther south. The Chinese Muslim PIA's home is the Muslim barangays south of Narra and Quezon. Plus we're dealing with Chinese regular army more and more now. The Zhong fight much better than the PIA, and they'll want to hold on to the southern part of the island. So as we get closer to Narra, we're approaching stalemate."

"Hmm." Pinsof leaned his chair back. "Tell me why you think the rules of engagement will be affected."

"Because politically, we can't afford a stalemate and neither can the Zhong, but neither side's wasted enough for truce. So it's going to uptick. Way I see it, major uptick would amount to conventional ops—a devastating, indiscriminate air war over the whole island. Nobody'll win hearts and minds doing that. But the Zhong want a limit to the conflict, and so do we. I think that adds up to more intense attritional engagements. A moderate uptick with changes in who we hit, maybe, or how hard. I want to know what and when and where and how so I can get my people ready."

Pinsof stared at her. *Fucking A, is he setting me up?* Jamie bent over her home fries and finished eating them before Pinsof spoke again. The one time she glanced up from her plate, he was still staring at her. *Oh shit, he is, he's setting me up.* But then she thought she heard him sigh, so she glanced up again.

"Wish I could tell you," he said, catching her eye. "Wish I knew." He eased his barely disturbed plate of food toward her and gestured that she should take what she wanted.

Now Jamie stared. At Pinsof, at the breakfast he obviously had no interest in eating, at the sudden informality of the moment. She didn't realize she'd picked up a piece of bacon from Pinsof's plate until it was in her mouth. "Christ, isn't anybody talking about this?" she asked.

"Not to me." He shrugged. "Not officially."

She leaned forward slightly. "What about unofficially?"

Pinsof studied the hands folded in front of him on the table as if they belonged to someone else, then looked up at her. "Tell me your thinking."

Jamie almost balked. But maybe Pinsof didn't have permission to say what he knew. If she could guess, however, he might nod or…

"Well, my thinking starts with China, where lack of water has caused the old coastal alliances to break down. Now, instead of coast versus interior, it's north versus south. Southern China has water, northern China has encroaching desert. But the northerners control the central government, and the central government's after the south's water, and that's making for lots of internal conflict. Raising hell on the Spratly Shelf and Palawan distracts the restive masses by pushing patriotism buttons with old territorial claims. Helps relieve Muslim discontent in the northwest, too. But you know, ever since Thumb Peak I keep thinking the Zhong are trying to fool us with one whomping diversion."

Pinsof's eyes flared. "Do you? So what do you think they're diverting us from?"

"From their real goal, which is a thin tentacle of territory down to and including the Balabac Strait. High strategic value for a bunch of reasons."

"And those reasons are?"

"Oh." *A test, like in school.* Jamie sat upright. "Legitimization of claims to the southeast Spratly Shelf and those new fossil fuel discoveries. China would get control of the southern entrance to the Sulu Sea, too. Also gives their central government a great excuse for a defensive naval presence that could be used to blockade key southern ports like Hong Kong, Macau, Guangzhou—should the north-controlled central government ever perceive the need."

"So why'd you say the Chinese would want to keep southern Palawan for 'a while yet'? What do you mean?"

"Well, sir, since the Zhong already have Balabac and the airstrip on Bugsuk, I figure they're making those islands into a garrison. For ten years they've resettled bunches of Chinese Muslims to Balabac and southern Palawan, right?"

"Yep. Taking over fishing, agriculture, businesses, just about everything."

"And now the Zhong say they're protecting threatened ethnic Chinese interests. That's their excuse for backing the PIA, for a military presence on Palawan as well as Balabac and Bugsuk, and for attacking Philippine oil platforms on the Spratly Shelf. But I think they're planning very long-term and anticipating reversals."

"Two steps forward, one step back," said Pinsof. "Overall gain of one step."

"Yeah, exactly." Jamie picked up another piece of Pinsof's bacon. "Taking the Spratly platforms as well as Palawan, Balabac, and Bugsuk—that's two steps forward. Relinquishing most of the platforms and retreating from Palawan is one step back. A very slow step, so we won't realize that they expect to give up Palawan and will sacrifice their Muslim emigrants. All so they end with a couple of important Spratly sites and Balabac and Bugsuk. A territorial claim to Balabac that's widely regarded as legitimate will change the whole balance of power in the South China Sea, including the Spratly Islands and the Sunda Shelf all the way to the Java Sea."

"So as we move farther south, the Chinese will send more troops, and those troops will get more aggressive. For a while." Pinsof smiled. "And during that while, you think the rules of engagement will go all to hell."

"Yeah, I do." A tightness around Jamie's head let go at last with the relief of being able to like Pinsof. "And if that's happening, then by now the PIA and the Zhong're making life a bitch for the indigenous populations down there. Which would mean refugees. Probably more than we've seen so far."

Slowly, Pinsof's head moved down, then up. "Last week, a boat with a couple dozen animists fleeing from Balabac made it to Puerto Princesa. Two more showed up there yesterday."

Jamie nodded while her stomach corkscrewed and the familiar chill prickled up her spine. "Kind of like circumstantial evidence, huh?"

"So, Gwynmorgan, where did your intel for all this ruminating come from?"

"Everywhere. Pieces here, bits there—like a KIMS game—from watching how the Zhong fight, from thinking about their next moves, from reading about them to suss out what the fuck they want and why the fuck they want it. From worrying. Lots of worrying."

"Well." Pinsof flashed his gallows grin again. "You ought to know that the stuff you brought up pretty much mirrors the major conclusions of a Pentagon report—classified, by the way—that I got about twenty-four hours ago."

"No shit, sir?"

"No shit, Lieutenant." Pinsof winked. "No shit. For a minute there, I wondered if you hacked into my comlink."

"Sorry. All I can hack are mechanical locks." Jamie straightened her back against the assault of a new chill. "Captain, does that report say anything about Borneo?"

Pinsof squinted at her. "What do *you* think about Borneo, Gwynmorgan?"

"That maybe the Chinese would like to control both sides of the Balabac Strait, and to do it they might exploit their close ties to Malaysia and move military units into Malaysian Borneo."

"No." Frowning, Pinsof shook his head and stood. "That's not in any report I've seen."

"Well, it's just my ill-considered opinion." Jamie stood too and stretched her taut hands. She had so hoped Pinsof would show her how screwed up she'd been about all of it—the uptick, Balabac, all of it. Now, doomed to the wrong side of the Rubicon, all she wanted to do was curl up and go to sleep. "Thank you for breakfast, sir, and for handing over your bacon."

"You got my bacon because I like the way you think, Lieutenant."

"Out of the mouths of coyotes, sir."

Jamie left the officers' mess with a couple of bottles of lemonade, an appointed time to meet again with Pinsof, and a malicious headache.

CHAPTER SIXTEEN

MERCY

Jeezus, not again!" Rhys's voice crackled through Jamie's comlink. "Elliott, snipers up on the double!" And then Rhys ticked off the coordinates and directions that two teams from third squad would need to create crossfire.

Jamie checked her shadowscreen grid. *Yeah, Marty, just right. Thank god you're so wicked good.*

EBC148 and marines were moving through an especially viscous August heat toward Narra on Palawan's southeast coast some sixty-five kilometers below Puerto Princesa. They'd have to fight for every building, every street. Ahead of the Three-Eight's infantry companies, its snipe platoon crept into the town to scout and report.

Almost immediately, Gwynmorgan's ghosts, as everyone called them now, discovered that the PIA had pretty much disappeared; mostly Narra was occupied by Chinese Army soldiers. And the town was full of way too many civilians. Why hadn't they evacuated, the surprised officers in the Brigade FOBCOC asked. The snipes quickly discovered the answer: Chinese Army units were corralling groups of civilians and executing them. Rhys had just come upon another roundup.

As third squad's drama played out, Jamie had to relegate it to a corner of her shadowscreen and focus instead on traversing several rooftops with first squad. By the time she hunkered next to Ramirez and again centered her shadowscreen on Rhys and third squad, it was over. The Zhong execution squad commander and two of his soldiers had been shot dead; civilians unharmed. Rhys reported the encounter, finishing with the words Jamie always wanted to hear: "Zero-zero." Nobody in the platoon wounded, nobody killed.

On several rooftops to Jamie's left, first squad fanned out. She cringed as she watched them. They were getting sloppy. She wagged a finger at Ramirez and clicked up the platoon's NCO frequency. "Gotta keep your people frosty," she barked to her sergeants and fire team leaders. "And hydrated. We're not done yet."

They'd been at it for nearly eighteen intense hours, approaching from the northeast through Aborlan. Now, as they slipped deeper into Narra itself, they were dog-tired. But they had hours to go; sloppy wasn't an option. Sloppy caused real numbers to replace the hallowed zero-zero.

Jamie took a moment to upsize the Narra grid on her shadowscreen so she could study the distribution of forty-two bright green dots, one for each member of the platoon, including her. Second and third squads were moving precisely where she thought they should. Soon first squad would be, too.

"Whaddaya say, Ram?" she asked.

Ramirez pointed to a low concrete block structure about three hundred meters in front of them—a school, according to their shadowscreen overlays.

When Jamie gave him a thumbs-up, he comlinked instructions to his squaddies. Two four-person teams would approach the school on the ground. The third team would split into two two-person units and, along with Jamie and Ramirez, provide overwatch from the nearby rooftops.

A hundred meters later, Jamie saw it—the sixth one of the day, but the first time it was happening right in front of her: Some fifteen civilians, adults and children, huddled against a playground wall while four Chinese soldiers belligerently pointed assault weapons at them. Two already bloodied bodies lay between the civilians and the soldiers.

By rights, somebody else should've taken the shot. But the civilians had little time left, and only Jamie had an unequivocally clear line of sight. It wasn't a challenging shot—no more than a hundred meters. She lifted her E112 to aim at the Zhong leader just as his mouth opened to order the civilians executed.

Worried he'd utter the fatal command, Jamie squeezed off a round even though she knew she'd be firing low, at the target's gut rather than his head. At the very same instant, the man swung left out of her smartscope's field of view. And suddenly the scope filled with a red spray. She thought she glimpsed a child's profile.

"Oh dear god."

Ramirez, who'd arrived just in time to see the whole thing, also reacted. "Shit!"

The high-pitched horror in his voice told her: She'd glimpsed right. Jamie didn't need to scope in to know the kid was dead.

"Oh dear god," she whispered again. Her head had become too heavy to hold up; her forehead met her rifle butt as a wave of nausea watered her mouth and made her sweat.

"Enemy's dispersed," Ramirez said shakily. "All taking off like scared rabbits. Haven't fired another shot."

Jamie couldn't move. She squinched her eyes shut against the red spray, but it stayed there, staining the inside of her eyelids, forcing her to breathe in desperate, huffing lunges—in, out, in, out…

"Gwynnie?" Ramirez asked from the other end of a very long tunnel.

She had no hope of being able to answer him.

"Gwynnie," he said more urgently this time, "It wasn't your fault. If you hadn't squeezed it off when you did, they'd *all* be toast now."

She wanted to agree with him. She tried to speak. But the sound she heard from herself was a strange, garbled "Unnhh." In slow motion, she managed to open her eyes, lift her head, but her eyes wouldn't focus. She couldn't swallow.

"Sometimes shit happens."

Coughing out a breathy "Yeah," Jamie stared at her rifle, at her hands, but kept her gaze from the scene a hundred meters in front of her. "Call it in, okay, Ram?" she rasped. "No editing."

"Sure, Gwynnie."

She listened to Ramirez tell the ops center that she'd just killed a little kid. He finished with her favorite words—"Zero-zero"—but they just didn't sound the same this time.

Still looking at her hands, Jamie asked, "One of your teams there yet?"

"Yeah, moving in right now."

"Ask them to find out who the kid is. Was."

❖

Just don't think about it, okay? Just close your eyes and don't think about it.

But her eyes didn't close. Dim light ruffled at the top of her hooch, quickly pursued by a new burst of cheerful commotion. The bonfire next to the FOB's recycling unit had been lit. In her hammock in the dark, Jamie waited for the metallic clangs and bangs, the heavy thumps and guttural whoops of her snipes' celebration.

Ever since that first time at the Puerto Princesa airport—which Jamie still occasionally blamed for turning her into Embry's Bastard Child—her snipes had made a ritual of beating up on junk metal and burning up junk wood once everyone convened at the Three-Eight's FOB after a major, all-platoon mission. Somehow, Jamie couldn't remember how, leading the celebration had become the platoon NCO's job. Rhys's job now, and this time at the new FOB site in Narra, Rhys had inverted the order of events. This time the bonfire started things—Rhys used it like a call to prayer—and the madcap drumming and dancing would follow.

For the first time, Jamie wondered if any of them comprehended what they were really celebrating: The second zero. No KIAs. For 202 days, Gwynmorgan's ghosts had suffered no KIAs, but on this night, Jamie would not join them. Nor would she click up her comlink to do admin chores or attempt another Mandarin language lesson or pick a video or a flashgame or a book or some music to relax with—that would require an energy, a strength, that had bled out of her with the last shot she fired.

If the night sky had been filled with stars, Jamie might have left her hooch and found an isolated place to sit and just look at them, like she used to when she was a kid. She needed the refuge of stars. Especially tonight. But, confined yet again beneath the Palawan's glutinous cloud cover, she had only the idea of stars, the idea of a tiny point of light where she stashed the good stuff—memories of who Alby might have been, dreams of a life with Marty, the hopes she dared to harbor for herself. On a starry night, she'd pick out one tiny point of light and be able to believe in the good stuff.

When did the light go out? Jamie couldn't remember. It was still there after Culion—wasn't it?—when the nightmares would chase her awake and Marty would be next to her in their hooch and for just a moment she'd gaze at Marty still asleep and feel almost safe.

EBC153 and the clouded Palawan night tolerated no stars and, still, no sleep. Jamie blinked at the obliterating blackness that engulfed her now. It had materiality. It had intent. It had been waiting to separate her from the flickers of the bonfire, from the sounds of raucous snipes, from all the world. *Maybe if they'd have just let me be Corporal Gwynmorgan like I'm supposed to, I'd have been with second squad and that kid would be alive and I'd be out there drumming and dancing with Marty, with all the guys, and that kid would be home in bed. Sleeping.*

The blackness pressed against her chest as she lay in her hammock. It stole her breath, wrenched her already aching belly, choked the hope out of her. Hope that maybe someday she and Marty might touch each other again. That maybe the Corps would send her to school and she'd find a nice little place to come home to and—and…

At least everyone in the platoon's alive.

This was the only thing she'd ever done right. But it had been trumped. Killing a little kid trumped everything.

What'd I expect, anyway? If I was good *for something, Alby wouldn't have needed the pharma, wouldn't have been driving to Provincetown that day. And Alby'd be alive, too, and I'd have a decent life where I don't have to kill people.*

She closed her eyes. As if on cue, a huge metallic jangle sounded— the snipes had begun their drumming—and behind Jamie's eyelids crimson spurted ferociously at her out of the blackness. She flinched, expecting to feel body-heated blood slap her face, but it didn't.

Jamie ripped her eyes open. She would try to keep her eyes open forever.

❖

"I want you to come with me." Jamie knew better than to make it an outright command.

"This isn't a very good idea," Rhys said. But after a glance at Jamie's face, she stiffened into the position of attention, eyes front, attitude visibly adamant. "Sorry, ma'am."

"Oh christ, Marty, please stop that. *Please.*"

Rhys continued to stand at attention, but her eyes swung left to meet Jamie's. Beneath Rhys's sideways glare, Jamie finally looked away in defeat.

"I can't stop my commanding officer." Rhys stepped in front of Jamie. "But I can try to stop my friend."

"Your friend needs your help," Jamie replied hoarsely. "I have to do this. I'm *asking* my friend to come with me."

"When was the last time you had something to eat?"

"I'm not hungry." Jamie started to pace in a tight, tense circle.

"How long since you slept?"

Jamie answered with a small shrug.

Stepping in front of her again, Rhys forced her to stop pacing and grabbed her shoulders. "Jamie. Why?"

They were alone in a corner of the Three-Eight's FOB, their privacy endowed by a pile of sandbags and a couple of supply tents.

"I have to do this. I *have* to." But Jamie lowered her head to avoid Rhys's steady gaze.

"And you want me to do what exactly?"

Jamie shrugged again.

"For god's sake, you've been cleared," Rhys said. "That means you didn't do anything wrong."

"According to the Corps. After what? A five-minute review of a few ops center videos?"

"According to the Filipinos, too, dammit."

"What if it was *your* kid, Marty?"

"Shit." Rhys kicked a sandbag.

"Okay. Never mind. Just forget about it." Jamie began walking toward the FOB's main gate.

"Christ, I can't let you leave the base by yourself, Gwynmorgan. You're fucking dangerous." So Rhys followed several steps behind her.

Half an hour later, Rhys still a pace behind, Jamie knocked on the door of a modest concrete-block house in a well-manicured Narra neighborhood.

A woman in her late twenties answered. A head shorter than Rhys, her delicately featured face was shadowed and puffy, and her red-rimmed eyes flared as they swept down and back up Jamie's cammies, pausing at the pistol on Jamie's thigh, the rifle cradled in Jamie's arm. Even so, she asked with preternatural calm in perfect Aussie-accented English, "May I help you?"

"My name is Jamie Gwynmorgan, and this is Marty Rhys."

Jamie's voice quivered and she had to struggle not to avert her eyes. "We're looking for Angara Bulanadi."

"I am Angara Bulanadi."

"We'd like to speak with you, ma'am." Jamie tried to steady her voice but couldn't prevent her eyes from blinking. "Perhaps we can talk in your garden, in back?"

For a long moment, Angara Bulanadi said nothing. "All right," she said finally, and led them along the side of the house and through a gate to a small, very green garden. She closed the gate and turned to face Jamie. "Please tell me what this is about."

Jamie handed her E112 to Rhys, looked again into Angara Bulanadi's tormented eyes, and tried to get her contracting diaphragm to allow a full breath.

"Ma'am, I'm the one who—"

"It was *you?*" Angara Bulanadi asked, immediately winded. "Oh my god, *you* killed my daughter?"

"Yes," Jamie said, looking away, then dragging her eyes back to this woman's shocked face. "I did. I-I've come to tell you that I'm sorry for— For what I did. I was aiming at someone else." Withering under Angara Bulanadi's stare, Jamie broke off to attempt another breath. "But th-that doesn't m-matter. Your daughter is dead, a-and my life is forfeit to you."

With a trembling hand, Jamie unholstered the pistol strapped to her thigh. "I'll end my life now if you wish, or you can do it."

Next to her, Marty said nothing, didn't move a muscle. Jamie gulped a breath, gripped the pistol hard to steady her hand, and offered the weapon to Angara Bulanadi, whose face was now savaged by rage and grief.

"My friend Marty will remove my body and see that you're not in any way involved if there's an investigation of my death." Jamie paused, lifting her jaw to help her breathe while she glanced at Rhys, who seemed to have been stunned into a kind of blank bewilderment. She continued when Rhys didn't budge. "This is the safety." Jamie flicked the small lever on the pistol. "And now it's off. All you have to do is point this at me and squeeze back this trigger."

Angara Bulanadi took the pistol from Jamie, who dropped to her knees, clasped her hands behind her back, bowed her head, shut her eyes. And waited. She shuddered once but didn't move again. Her mind offered up no words, no images—just the deep blood red behind her eyelids as the last seconds of her life stretched into an infinity of guilt and regret.

She thought she sensed the barrel of the weapon at her right temple. *Please. Just do it.* And then Jamie heard the sound of the pistol's safety pushed back on.

"No," said a hushed voice. Angara Bulanadi's consummately gentle voice. "I don't want your life to end. Thank you for showing me that."

Jamie's eyes fluttered open to see the woman hand the pistol to Rhys, then walk serene and unhurried through the garden to her house and cross its threshold. Before closing the door, Angara Bulanadi turned around, her lovely face now at peace. She peered down at Jamie, who still kneeled, still sought release from a world bathed in blood.

"My daughter's name was Awa." Angara Bulanadi's voice lilted through the eerie quiet. "It means 'mercy.'"

CHAPTER SEVENTEEN

DARK AND SILENT

A waning moon still mostly full outlined the mountains rising before her and set off a wave of apprehension. How would she get there without a comlink? No comlink meant no satellite downlinks of close-up real-time imagery, no topographical details, no precision info about where she was or whether her path was the most optimal or how far she had yet to go.

Nervous about her visibility in the moonlight, Jamie crouched low and listened. Yes, she heard running water—a creek, maybe even a small river ahead of her, between her and the mountains she needed to reach.

Sooner than she expected, she found a river larger than she expected. She stepped nearer its bank, and without warning she was falling, her feet somehow flailing above her head, her back and shoulders colliding with a series of saplings that cracked under her weight until her body encountered one that resisted her. She rebounded off it, tumbling now, her hands unable to grasp anything to slow her down, and then blackness took her.

Jamie roused to dappled sunlight twinkling through trees that loomed over her. She lay on a moderate slope, one leg twisted under the other, her arms tossed lopsidedly above her head. Against the light, a shadow rustled, shifted—and uttered a small gasp.

"Oh." A child's voice. Then the shadow moved and Jamie saw a little girl's face, her dark eyes aglow with amazement.

"Awa?" Jamie asked.

The child scampered down the riverbank without reply.

"Awa! Wait!" By the time Jamie got herself up, the child had begun to wade into the river. "No, Awa, don't."

On the opposite bank, someone waved at the child and shouted encouragement—someone dressed like a marine in cammies. Jamie gaped.

"Marty?"

Jamie ran into the water, which was deep, too deep, and it pulled her down. She fought to keep her head above the churning black water that had started turning red. *"Marty!"*

"Ow!"

Jamie lurched. Someone had grabbed her arms.

"Jamie, wake up."

Marty?

"Come on, Jamie, wake up."

Jamie's eyes opened to Rhys's bemused face and Rhys's hands grasping her wrists. "Unhh—w-what?"

Rhys let go of Jamie and backed away from her hammock. "You okay?"

"Uh, yeah." Jamie blinked, glanced around her hooch. EBC193. "Weird dream. What's up?"

"Looks like some of us are gonna get a shooting mission again."

❖

Rhys just wouldn't give up. "Jamie, I should do it," she said for the third time.

"No. I'm taking it."

"But—"

"No, dammit!" Jamie glowered. "Don't make me pull officer shit, okay? I'm going. Me. Not you."

Rhys was undeterred. "Jeezus, Jamie, you're a goddamn mess. You shouldn't be going anywhere, and sure as hell not into the Mantalingajan Range—"

"I'm fine," Jamie snapped. She didn't want Rhys bugging her yet again with that taking-too-many-risks crap. "Fifty-nine goddamn days from now we get on a plane home, Marty. Operation Repo will swallow more than half of that. It's our last major gig, and I'm gonna damn well make sure Avery's people don't get pushed around by that recon commander."

It wasn't a Three-Eight mission, this effort to rescue some seventy or eighty American and Filipino prisoners of war from a site on the outskirts of Malihud, a Muslim fishing village deep in Chinese-occupied southern Palawan. Instead, elements of a Marine Reconnaissance Force company would spearhead it. Most of the recon guys would approach from the southwest across the Sulu Sea via several stealth helicopters deployed from Navy vessels many miles offshore.

But the mission planners also decided to send a second unit trekking down the spine of the island to pounce from the north. Together, the recon units would break into the camp and lead the POWs back to the helicopter transports and out.

Because of their six weeks of scouting deep into the mountains southwest of Narra, Gwynmorgan's ghosts had been drafted as guides to get that second recon unit into position, then provide overwatch during the rescue before withdrawing into the mountains and back to Narra. They'd have just twelve days to traverse 110 kilometers of the island's highest, most challenging terrain. To do it, the chosen squad would need the aid of their contacts among indigenous groups of Pala'wan, Tau't Daram, and the Tau't Batu, those cave-dwelling, swidden-cultivating "people of the rock" who spent part of the year high in the same mountains through which the snipes had to travel.

Hindering the snipes was the remainder of the annual southwest monsoon, which had only just begun to slowly recede. Yet it was only during the monsoon that the helpful Tau't Batu traditionally occupied their cliffside limestone caves. For the dry season, they tended to move down into the valleys. On this mission, like so many, timing would be everything.

The whole thing had an eleventh-hour quality to it that made Jamie's spine twitch. Although she had little chance to think through what might go wrong and devise contingency plans, she tried. Chief among her worries: Unlike the recon guys, who'd depart Malihud by helo with the POWs, her snipes would be staying on the ground, which would certainly attract Zhong attention. To get back to the Three-Eight's FOB west-southwest of Narra, they'd have to evade the Zhong for a hundred and ten mountainous klicks.

"Want to be a pack mule?" Jamie asked Rhys two days before departing with Avery and second squad.

"Huh?"

"I'll feel better about this if we go with an alpha strategy and stash some food and gear in a few of those caves along the way," Jamie said. "I'd like you to pick a couple teams and follow us into the mountains. You'll carry extra kits—you know, weapons and ammo, neutralized comlinks. Also MREs, hammocks, tarps, first-aid kits. Even some cammies—those new non-electronic passive-identifier kind our satellites can see without them emitting signals the enemy can track. I want you to hide the stuff in empty caves. You'll stay a day behind us and I'll let you know as we go about which caves to supply."

Rhys nodded eagerly. "Right And then we can catch up with you and—"

Jamie shook her head. "Uh-uh. Then you hightail it back to the FOB and keep your damn heads down. Do not volunteer for anything. This isn't over 'til everyone's on the plane going home."

"But—"

EBC204 and Jamie placed a finger over Rhys's lips, then enveloped her in a tight hug. "It'll be all right, Marty," Jamie said, not letting go. "Let's just figure out the details on this and wish each other luck, okay?"

Rhys returned the hug with a suddenly fervent grip. "Okay, Jamie. Okay."

❖

Some of the indigenous groups Gwynmorgan's ghosts met with only a week earlier had already departed the mountains for the lower valleys. But others provided shelter, showed the squad paths that saved hours of trailblazing, and reported sightings of Chinese patrols in the lower valleys.

Rhys, Ramirez, and eight snipes followed. Jamie conveyed intel about the enemy and told them which caves to supply via a new short-burst splinter-noise commo technique that made anything picked up by enemy electronic signal detectors sound like random environmental noise.

The first two cave sites—one just north of Mount Calibugon,

the other west of Mount Landargun—were uninhabited. The last, a Tau't Batu site already vacated for the season, lay south of Mount Mantalingajan and about twelve kilometers from the position where Gwynmorgan's ghosts would cover the recon units during the rescue mission.

When she showed her people the locations of the three stashes of extra kits and ordered them to memorize the coordinates, Jamie said, "Except for the weapons, ammo, and comlinks, we'll leave whatever we don't use for our local friends." Then, aware of the distinctive chill stippling her spine, she added, "But if we gotta split up on the way back, or if anyone's unaccounted for, then we leave everything in place that we don't need. Just in case."

Operation Repo commenced on schedule at dawn on November sixth, EBC219, roughly an hour after a diversionary attack on Brooke's Point up the coast got under way. Despite low clouds and rain, the nine helicopters—three Shark transports and six Barracuda stealth attack helos—showed up as planned, the muffled sounds of their arrival reaching Jamie's ears only as they appeared out of the quickly evaporating sea fog above a field next to the POW camp.

Using thermal imaging to help them pick off tower guards, second squad's teams opened fire on cue from hides in the foothills north of Malihud. Within thirteen minutes, according to the readout in a corner of her shadowscreen, Jamie saw prisoners scrambling to the transports. She attempted to keep a rough tally—fifteen here, twelve there, another fourteen. Right on schedule, one of the transports took off, escorted by a Barracuda.

Then the mission clogged up. The strongest, healthiest prisoners had gotten to the helo first, and many of those who remained needed help making it to the other two transports. Comlink chatter told Jamie the recon force had found more prisoners than anticipated and required extra time to get them out. Meanwhile, the enemy had begun to fight back.

"Three lavvies this side of the river," Avery reported from the hills east of the Malihud River. "We'll be able to snuff 'em before they get to the bridge."

But Zhong soldiers with rifle grenades were closer to the POW camp than the armored personnel carriers Avery had spotted, as well as more numerous and much harder to see. From their elevated hides, Jamie and the four snipes with her managed to take out three Zhong teams before they could launch, but she worried about others.

"RichBitch, RichBitch, Zhong attack helos on your high ten coming in fast," one of the Barracuda pilots yelled to another. "Count three—belay that—count five enemy birds. Five enemy birds. Cover your ten, RichBitch!"

Then one of the two Shark transports still on the ground exploded. A Zhong grenade had hit its mark. With fire erupting in the cockpit, the helo's occupants poured out and stumbled toward the remaining Shark.

Over her comlink, Jamie heard marines screaming. Operation Repo had gotten dicey fast. *So much for the mission schedule on this one.*

While enemy helos engaged the Barracudas in an air battle overhead, the snipes on both sides of the river didn't withdraw as planned—instead they started picking off enemy targets at greater and greater distances. This gave the recon units time to evacuate everyone out of the disabled helo and into the third transport, which finally lifted off and moved out to sea.

Although all the POWs had extracted, the last Shark departed minus some of the recon guys, who had but one option: Retreat toward the snipes' hides. The snipes did what they could to slow the enemy's pursuit of them.

"Our strays'll get to my position first," Jamie told Avery, then instructed her to immediately pull back into the mountains. "We'll pick them up and follow you. Figure join-up at zero-six-hundred at gridpoint September niner three niner four. But don't wait past zero-seven-hundred. The boogey men'll be chasing you."

"Roger," crackled the comlink. "Join-up at zero-six-hundred at gridpoint September niner three niner four. See you there."

Above Malihud, a dozen helicopters battled while six stray recon marines scrambled to Jamie's hide. "We're outta here right now," she said to them as soon as they arrived. "Splinter-noise commo from now on. I'll take point and—"

A menacing new sound made her look up. The rotors of two

helicopters—one of the enemy's and a Barracuda—had collided and both aircraft careened wildly.

The enemy helo smashed into one of the POW camp towers, detonating timed explosives placed there by the recon guys. As a conflagration claimed the camp, the crippled Barracuda tilted into an erratic spiral that brought it toward Jamie's position. It finally clattered and grated into the forest only thirty meters away and just a meter or two above her elevation, flipping over as it came to rest without exploding.

Jamie and the recon leader looked at each other. They'd have to check the Barracuda for survivors and retrieve them quickly. "We'll get 'em, ma'am," said the recon leader.

Minutes later he signaled Jamie: A finger pointed up once, twice— both crewmen alive. Then, a moment later, his fingers mimicked two pair of walking legs. *Yes. Both ambulatory.*

But they'd lost precious escape time. The mission plan would have to change again.

Within minutes, ten of them were out of Jamie's sight, already climbing along the west bank of the Malihud River into the forested hills. If all went well, they'd be able to follow it for about five kilometers to an elevation of nearly three hundred meters, then cross it and start the strenuous northeast trek toward the two-thousand-meter Mount Mantalingajan, where they'd join up with Avery.

Meanwhile, Jamie and two snipes diverted the enemy. Jamie began by firing a grenade into the Barracuda wreckage, which triggered a sizeable explosion she hoped would destroy any still-functional equipment and preoccupy the Zhong long enough to provide the margin the three of them needed to evade and escape.

"Leave just enough of a trail for the first hundred meters," she told her snipes. "We want the Zhong coming after us, not the others."

The three of them headed east to cross the Malihud River, as though they were making a desperate run up the coast, trying to get past Brooke's Point and out of enemy territory. Once well across the river, they picked out enemy targets as they went.

It worked for a while, for more than a kilometer. Then the enemy started to get wise.

"Okay, guys," Jamie said, holding out her hand to be scanned, "secure me into your eyewraps and give them to me for a minute." Quickly she marked a pathway on each of their shadowscreen maps that would take them to the rendezvous with Avery. "You're getting off here. Start in that crevice right over there." She tilted her head toward the cliff-like rock face behind her. "See it?"

The two snipes nodded.

"Steep as shit, but great for hiding your trail from the Zhong. You'll be able to climb it all the way to the top of this ledge, then head due north for maybe an hour to reach the track I marked. Got it?"

They nodded again.

"Good. Keep absolute stealth. Your goal is to avoid detection and hook up with Avery. Do not engage unless you're positive you've been spotted and there's no other choice, understand? Take my water and MREs and give me half your four-sixteen rounds."

"You sure, Gwynnie?"

"I'm going east for another half a klick, see what else I can nail. Then I'll cut north, too. But you remind the sergeant that she waits for no one past zero-seven-hundred. *No one.* I'll fucking nail her to a cross if she delays one fucking second. And you be sure to quote me on that if necessary. Good climbing. See you back at the ranch. Now go."

"Soon," each one said, offering a departing dap.

Jamie didn't watch them leave. She moved east as fast as the terrain allowed. The first time she found a natural hide and fired from it, she popped three targets and managed to skip out before the enemy determined her position. She pulled that off twice more, but the fourth time they found her after only one shot.

Soon her mental processes shifted from tactical planning to surviving second by second. Jamie survived and evaded and occasionally attacked for almost three more hours. With her very last .416 round, she even nicked a Zhong helicopter that was heading north, flying too low and too close to where she figured her people were.

Wounding the helo came at a price, however. It gave the enemy an accurate fix on her position. Within a minute, an enemy bullet almost took her head off, instead ripping her comlink eyewraps from her face and out of sight. She had little time to retrieve them; they'd self-destruct in less than a minute if she didn't she initiated proper shutdown or re-established physical contact with them. Without them, she'd be stranded a hundred and ten klicks beyond the Marines' forward edge, lost to the ops center.

Jamie could feel the countdown...Six...five...four...three...

Another enemy bullet whined past her nose. "Jeezus fucking christ," she wheezed, "what's it fucking take?"

Now she had only her pistol to slow down the enemy just feet away. Bereft of options, she decided to use her last bullet on herself. But as she pointed the pistol at her temple, it saved her life by blocking a Chinese bullet. It also banged hard into her cheek, knocking her down. She reached for her combat knife, but it, too, had vanished.

Weaponless, on all fours, trapped at the brink of a gully muddied from the recent rain, Jamie dove, hoping the thin brush below might hide her, and somewhere on the way down, her rolling world went dark and silent.

CHAPTER EIGHTEEN

NO WAY OUT

"Shih shen?"

Splayed on her belly in thick, sucking mud, Jamie didn't move while she thought about the voice. *I know what he said: Dead body...a question...in Mandarin.* But had the voice been real, or was she dreaming?

A harsh blow struck her shoulder blade. Too harsh, too real. The malice in its lightning-flash sting revved her heartbeat and cleared her head. *Oh god...don't move, don't move, don't breathe...*

"Sho bu ding."

They're not sure. Maybe they'd just go. A long, hopeful moment passed, and then she heard the squishy, gurgly suction of feet laboring through the muck toward her. Soon she felt a finger on her neck, searching for her pulse. Her stomach twisted, her heart slammed its dire warning against her chest: *doom-DOOMED...doom-DOOMED...*

The hand departed. "Hu-aw zhe."

That one she knew, too: "Alive." *Oh god oh god oh god...*

A boot asserted itself roughly against her belly and shoved hard. Then a ruthless kick missed her ribs but drove the air out of her lungs. She grunted as the muck acquiesced with a wet *pop!* and she flipped onto her back—the day's catch.

The right side of her face was slathered with so much mud it sealed her eye shut. But her left eye opened to find six Chinese soldiers standing over her, six QBZ-96s pointed at her. Their blurry images shimmied and swayed. She willed herself to jump up and attack, force them to shoot her. But her body didn't budge. Not her arms. Not her legs.

"May-ee," declared one of them. "Jin."

Despite The Fear's dissonant wailing in her head, Jamie

remembered the meaning: "American military"—and she flashed on the stories she'd heard about how Chinese soldiers didn't much like United States marines. Stories from *before* Operation Repo.

Without removing their eyes from her, the soldiers began arguing. She couldn't understand their words, but their rancor and repugnance were unmistakable. Based on the flush she saw in their faces, the way the veins in their necks protruded, how close the QBZ-96 rifle barrels came to her nose, Jamie assumed they were bickering about which of them would be granted the honor of pumping her full of bullets.

"Gway paw," jeered one of them. She'd heard that before, too. It meant "white bitch." But not just white. Ghost white. The white of the dead.

Not dead yet, though. The resentful accusation in his tone told her. *They're not gonna do it. Jeezus, they're not gonna kill me.* She exhaled the breath she'd been holding, but she knew their decision to let her live had nothing to do with international humanitarian law.

The squabble continued, but now it seemed to be about who'd get stuck having to lay hands on her. *At least they don't seem interested in rape.* Eventually, two of them grabbed her cammie blouse and yanked her upright and forward onto her knees. The sudden movement sent the world spinning. She staved off dizziness while the soldiers bound her hands behind her back, but when they jerked her to her feet, she sank to her knees again and vomited.

After her retching devolved into dry heaves, they pulled her to her feet once more. Two of them held her up while two others removed much of her gear—the pistol holster, the load-bearing vest, the canteen, the first-aid pouch. They searched her pockets, repeating "Yeh-un jing"—eyeglasses. She responded with a blank stare; this was her first chance to play dumb.

Mud still caked her right eye, but her left eye perceived daylight's fade. The Palawan's primeval night would soon be upon them. EBC219 was almost over.

They shoved her out of the soggy bottom of the gully, kicking and berating her every time she staggered or fell. She fell often. The coast road running through Malihud was perhaps two and a half klicks away, and her frequent stumbling impeded their progress, created opportunities for the unexpected… A lot could happen in the Palawan dark…

"Bah-ee chih!" yelled one of the Chinese soldiers when she

skidded sideways down a slope and attempted to turn an accidental stumble into an escape.

Jamie doubled over to protect her belly from his kicks. Profoundly regretting that she hadn't tried harder to get them to shoot her right after they found her, she stayed curled up beneath the blows, unable to prevent the moan that oozed out of her as her strength waned.

It threatened to rule her, this moan. It wanted to tear her open, this moan, so the frenzied panic she'd been holding at bay could flood in, drown her. She began to lose all ability to reason, to hope. Her mind registered only the pain of the beating and the pulsing rhythm of her rampant terror. *Oh god oh god oh god…*

Never in her life had she felt so helpless. She couldn't even cover her head while they kicked her, couldn't squirm out of the way of their blows, couldn't stop yelping her body's protest. There had to be something she could do, something…

Maybe I should just wilt. If she was unreservedly servile, they might ease off and she could get through it, she could survive. "Please," she said, struggling onto her knees when the kicks ceased. She looked up, beseeching the nearest Chinese soldier not to hurt her anymore. "Please…ching-*ng?*"

He growled something she didn't understand and whacked her flat with the butt of his rifle.

doom-DOOMED…doom-DOOMED… Drifting at the fringe of consciousness, Jamie grasped the message in her heart's urgent pounding: *No way out.*

The beating renewed until a shout from one of the others stopped it, and the soldiers turned away from her. She watched them fade in and out as blackness dappled the margins of her vision, she heard them berated by a voice that sounded choppy and angry and strange. *Gotta try, gotta…* When she lifted her head, no one noticed. The deepening dusk might claim her if she could just roll down the slope, just a couple feet to the tall grass at the edge of the path and then roll—

She had a half-second lead on them, but her legs couldn't help her. The nearest soldier slammed his rifle butt into her stomach, and she passed out.

By the time they slapped her back to groggy awareness, dusk had given way to darkness. Two of the soldiers lifted her up and another put a container to her lips: Water. She needed water, craved water, and she gulped as much as she could. The soldier issuing orders peeled the mud off her face; from here on, she'd see the unconditionally murky night with both eyes.

"La dao!" he said, as though he believed she'd understand him if she could see out of both eyes. Jamie did understand—he'd told her to forget about it—but she gave nothing, no hint of comprehension.

❖

"All coercive techniques are designed to induce regression."

Ever since she first read those words back in scout/sniper school, she'd tried to honestly appraise what she was capable of enduring. When Operation Repo began, she still hoped that maybe, just maybe she'd be able to leave the Palawan without having to find out. She'd clung to that hope right up to the moment she sent her last two snipes north into the hills and pushed on alone.

What would the Zhong try to find out from her? Stuff about the battalion, future ops, Operation Repo— *They'll want to know which way Avery's taking everyone through the mountains…*

Jamie had no doubt about how it would go down. *Pain, relief, threat of more pain.* It had already started: The burden of the journey into Malihud had shifted from Jamie to the six Chinese soldiers. They kept her upright and moving, her first taste of the seduction of relief. And then— *'Round and 'round 'til I break. Because everybody breaks.*

She had to find a way to stall, to keep herself from giving up and giving in at least until Avery got second squad back to the FOB. *At least twelve days.* Even then, she could get somebody killed if she told the Zhong too much about her crew—where they were based, how they worked. *No, no, it's gotta be the whole thirty-nine days.* The whole thirty-nine days until her snipes were on that plane home.

Jamie's mind, as helpless as her body, flailed. *"In the darkest hour—" How the hell does that go? Something about light and hope, right? In the darkest hour, light and hope. Oh christ, what a fucking fiction!*

One of the soldiers holding her up tripped her when the guy in charge wasn't looking, and she hit the raggedly inclined ground with a brutal thud just as she thought she might've heard somebody say, "Fiction's good."

Fiction? A chill scurried alone her vertebrae as the soldiers picked her up again. *Of course. All warfare is based on deception.*

Her mind quieted and within minutes, she saw it—the perfect diversion. *I could tell them we're gonna invade Borneo. That'd screw 'em up good, because we're never really gonna invade Borneo. And after a while, when I recant, they won't know what the fuck to believe.* She'd have to concoct all kinds of details, remember as much as possible from the mapping imagery about the terrain of the northern tip of Borneo. And to make it believable, she'd have to hold out for a long time. *Thirty-nine days…*

For the next hour, Jamie invented plans for a five-pronged amphibious assault on both sides of East Malaysia's Marudu Bay as well as three islands to the north of it. *Three islands, right? Yeah, yeah, three. I remember three.* Her Marines would be changing the rules of engagement. Her Marines would beat the crap out of northern Borneo, southern Palawan, Balabac, Bugsuk, all of it all over the Balabac Strait—and unless the PIA and the Zhong withdrew, they'd be trapped and annihilated. *Yeah, fuck 'em. Fuck 'em all.*

While the Zhong soldiers pushed her, dragged her, but mostly carried her, Jamie reeled trancelike through images of an initial briefing with Pinsof about the kinds of training exercises needed to prepare her people. In the gloom, she could see the expression on his face, taste her own nervous anticipation as he laid out the plan's preliminaries.

By the time her captors delivered her to their commanding officer, she'd decided the Invasion of Borneo was a damn fine idea and she was glad she hadn't been told more about it. Because she couldn't reveal to the enemy what she didn't know.

❖

First came the Zhong commanding officer's surreal politeness, his curiosity about her gender and her rank while he ordered her hands unbound and fastidiously examined the filthy cammie blouse he'd asked her to remove. Next came his jumbled, euphemistic warning about "me-an chah-ng"—forceful exhortation—while her wrists were bound again after she declined to tell him anything other than her name, rank, military identification number, and date of birth.

Then Jamie found herself in a faintly lit concrete-block structure that probably had once been a Christian church but now was stripped of pews and altar. The two rows of four-inch-thick lally columns supporting the building's roof seemed forlorn, abandoned.

Soon a sirenic thirtysomething woman in a white lab coat, like a physician's, appeared and leaned against one of the lally columns. The fingers of her right hand fondled the column like a lover.

"Well, you're a right mess," she declared in posh-British-school English after Jamie was forced to kneel before her.

In any other circumstance, her sleek, unblemished beauty would have been intriguing. But she was the Special Chief Interrogator—Shoo Juh Gwah-un Yen, or something like that. The Zhong commandant had warned Jamie about her, and the glacial disdain inflecting her voice made Jamie shiver, *Shoo Juh, or something like that.* A bad omen, the way that sounded. *Like fuck you backwards.*

When Jamie returned the interrogator's gaze, the woman slapped her hard and snarled in what Jamie realized was the Cantonese of Hong Kong: "Beh moot loon yeh ar?"—What the fuck are you staring at? After issuing several commands that Jamie couldn't understand, the woman left.

Jamie quickly discovered what Shoo Juh ordered: A lengthy and invasive strip search. Afterward, two soldiers shoved her face-first to the floor, grabbed her ankles, and dragged her to one of the lally columns. They positioned her knees on either side of the column before shackling her ankles, then untied her wrists and wrenched her arms behind her, forcing her back into a cruel arch and her crotch into an inexorable collision with the column. Finally, they manacled her wrists the same way as her ankles—on the other side of the column.

Stifling a cry, aware of an ominous shadow lowering over her, Jamie strained to get her legs beneath her. Eventually she found a way to ratchet herself onto her knees and ease the pressure on her arms by flattening her back against one side of the column while her fettered wrists and ankles snugged against the opposite side.

But when the dead-eyed deputy interrogator ordered her hosed down, the position became impossible to maintain. Jamie battled, mostly unsuccessfully, to keep the pressure off her wrists and crotch and the water out of her airway. The interrogators' exhortation had begun.

CHAPTER NINETEEN

SHING

How many times do I breathe in and out in a minute?
After November sixth, the first thing Jamie lost was any sense of the passage of time, despite trying to count using the only measure she had: Her breathing.

From the start, they asked her questions. The first ones came from the deputy interrogator and they were incessant. "How did you get to Malihud?" "To which unit are you assigned?" "Where are the others?"

A Zhong soldier did the interrogator's dirty work, slapping her whenever she began her single response, "I am authorized to inform you of my name, my rank—"

She was kept chained to the lally column and not permitted to sleep. When she nodded off, someone thumped her awake again.

Maybe this is just one long, really uncomfortable day. Or night? Maybe they've figured out how to make every second feel like a month.

At some point the deputy interrogator announced in his grating monotone that Jamie's reticence would now elicit shing. He repeated his questions. Guessing what shing was, she repeated her sole reply anyway. The deputy interrogator stepped back and nodded to several soldiers, who released Jamie from the lally column, dragged her to a heavy wooden chair nearby, and quickly bound her hands to its arms and her feet to its legs.

"Perhaps when I ask you questions next time, you will be more interested in answering them," the deputy interrogator said before leaving the building.

Despite being bound to it, Jamie found sitting in a chair to be an improvement over the lally column. What's more, the only soldiers in sight were the door sentries. Did she miss something? Maybe she'd guessed wrong about shing, maybe this was actually the relief part of—?

The sound came from right behind her. A boot scruffing on the floor? Even before she swung her head toward it, her body snapped like a huge, overstretched rubber band. Every muscle contracted into a fiery convulsion. Flashes and spots ricocheted in front of her and millions of tiny needles attacked her. Violent, dissonant ringing drowned out all other sound. She gasped for air.

A stone-faced soldier waved an electric baton in front of her, then pulled it out of sight as he murmured briefly to someone else. Before the effects dissipated, she was shocked again without warning or further comment. After a few more times of this, she passed out. They poured water over her and resumed. None of them touched her. No one spoke.

Sometime later, Jamie roused to find herself chained again to the lally column and face-to-face with the special chief interrogator, who bent over her and casually said, "Tell me which regiment you're in."

Tag team, huh, Shoo Juh? Jamie shook her lolling head. *No way's it been thirty-nine days yet.*

This round of questioning seemed to last longer than before. So did the shing that followed. The only variation lay in the interrogators' arrangement of Jamie's punishments: Electric shock now mixed with aerial suspension and plain old beatings with leather straps and rubber batons.

As her world imploded, Jamie floundered for distractions from her turmoiling body and the dense, dimensionless blackness deepening around her. She clung to two words: *Not…yet…*

And then… A moment came—a black pearl of a moment, lustrous and beautiful—when the pain ebbed. The interrogators had to back off, seduce her with sleep and water and food and being left alone before what they did could hurt again.

Jamie came to desire the pain, pursue it. Her mind swerved into a realm without words, without thought; she abetted her tormenters, prodded her shuddering, thrashing body toward the euphoric instant when the pain spun her around, launched her into the pearl black—and she was at last beyond anyone's reach.

❖

The slight sounds had repeated many times, but Jamie didn't believe they were real. Abandoned by all energy, abandoned by life itself, she waited to slip away into nothingness. But the sounds persisted. Something was wrong.

Then, at last, she perceived a pattern. So maybe the three new prisoners she thought she saw when she opened her eyes were *not* a mirage.

The taps and scratches came from the prisoner tethered to the lally column closest to her. Jamie lifted her head and looked up at him. Naked, bruised, vaguely familiar. He glanced toward the nearest Zhong soldier, then shook his head, an almost imperceptible warning. She understood: The prisoners were not allowed to talk to each other.

The man tapped and scratched again.

Morse code?

He did it once more: "·-- ···· --- ··-"

Jamie muddled through her misery to her knees, then to a dim scout/sniper school memory of, yes, Morse code—and deciphered w, h, o, u. *Oh, right: who u?*

After a time, she recalled enough to sound a response—"--· ·--"
—but stopped when a soldier approached to examine her.

"Gwun mo garn!" he sneered and kicked her twice, knocking her knees out from under her.

"Gwynmorgan," she corrected, exerting to angle her head so she could meet his eyes.

"Dee-oo lay lo mo!" he cursed and kicked her again—in her gut, to elicit that grunt-groan the Zhong soldiers seemed to so enjoy. She considered staying there—her back perniciously arched, her hands already going numb from the pressure on her wrists, her crotch martyred against the column.

It wouldn't have been difficult to just fade out. Easier than doing anything else. But she wasn't alone anymore. Jamie turned her wavering gaze to the man trying to communicate with her.

"· ·--- · ···" Eyes. He blinked it out twice before she understood and struggled to her knees again. Kilo38, he blinked, then signaled a name she recognized: Cavanaugh, the captain who didn't like coyotes.

Jamie blinked her request. "Date"

Cavanaugh blinked back. "29 11"

Twenty-three days. She shook her head, disbelieving.

"29 nov" his eyes assured her.

"3 8 ss ok?" Jamie asked.

"repo rtb ok no ss kia at 26 11"

Her eyes closed and she let her head sink with the relief of it. *They got back. They're all still alive.* Jamie counted... *Thirty-nine minus twenty-three. That's—come on, goober, thirty-nine minus twenty-three is, is—sixteen. Sixteen more days and what I say won't matter. Just sixteen more days...*

She had many questions for Cavanaugh, but no chance to ask any of them. The Zhong soldiers had figured out that their prisoners were communicating. Shoo Juh responded by segregating Jamie and personally supervising both shorter interrogations and the longer punishments that followed. Soon the woman's arrogant, suggestive smile haunted Jamie's jumbled consciousness and filled her fractured nightmares.

With what little lucidity she had left, Jamie surmised that she'd become Shoo Juh's experiment or toy or both. She could not distinguish day or night, truth or lie, reality or imagination. But she knew the passing of each moment brought her one moment closer to the end of those sixteen days.

❖

Crumpled into a humid, gritty corner, unable to guess where she was, Jamie achieved awareness gradually, blurrily. *Jeezus, still alive... Still naked.*

The heavy, stale air stifled her breathing. All of her hurt, a tumult of burning, screeching muscles and nerves—but she tried anyway to get up like a normal person.

And whacked her head so hard she landed on her ass again, dizzy and throbbing.

They had locked her in a grotesquely small space; the ceiling couldn't have been more than five feet above the floor. Five feet by five feet by five feet, slimy concrete-block walls, a solid metal door with a kind of hatch at the bottom, illuminated only by a dim sliver of unchanging light visible through a small air vent near the low ceiling.

Jamie had no clue how long she'd been wherever this was. Her struggle for coherent recollection failed entirely. There was only the fiery, thudding pain, the utter debilitation.

And nothing hurt more than her hands. She couldn't move them without swooning. Squinting through the gloom at them, she gagged. Her hands were gone, replaced by two freakishly swollen and discolored globs of tissue with deep, bloody, insect-infested lesions. And she had no idea how it had happened.

She tried to brush the insects off the wounds, hyperventilating into horror when the futility of the effort became obvious. The wounds bled then, which slightly eased their throbbing and, improbably, soothed her.

The blood didn't look red in the murk of the cell. Her hands oozed black and she watched them, fascinated. *I bet this could kill me. Infection, blood poisoning, gangrene. That'd do it. Just lay here. Don't fucking budge. And it'll happen. Just lay here...just lay here...just... lay...here...*

Maybe Jamie slept, maybe she fainted. When she woke, she had to pee desperately. And, alongside an underlying stench of human waste, she could smell... *What is that?*

In the dimness, she spotted two bowls near the small hatch at the bottom of the cell door. The bowls contained the usual tasteless rice concoction and fetid water, and they tempted her. She was thirsty, she was hungry. If she just leaned forward, or turned and rolled sideways, she could reach them...

No! No food!

Because she couldn't remember any chants from boot camp or the FOB bonfires, she invented a new one—her favorite Cantonese insult, learned in Narra. "Seek zee gay. Seek zee gay." Eat yourself.

Okay, okay. No food. But I gotta pee. I don't wanna die in a puddle of my own pee, for chrissake.

Being sorta picky, aren't we? Nothing wrong with a little pee. Some people use it as a disinfectant, y'know.

No. I'm not gonna pee here. Not here where I'm gonna die, dammit.

Fine! Pick a spot, any spot.

Slowly, Jamie crawled. The corner she'd picked, diagonally opposite "her" corner, already stank. For a reason, she discovered: There resided the shithole. She attempted to squat over it, lost her balance, and the backs of her wretched hands were sprayed with her urine.

Disinfectant? She toppled onto her knees and put her palms under the stream emanating from her.

What the fuck are you doing?

Learned this during the Cock, remember? In the Survival part of Survival-Evasion-Resistance-Escape, remember?

The Cock?

Survival. Worth a fucking try, right?

It hurts.

Yeah. Dying hurts, too. When Jamie finished peeing, she crawled to the door and consumed the paltry contents of both bowls.

CHAPTER TWENTY

OUT OF THE NIGHT THAT COVERS ME

The first time Jamie saw the scorpion, she freaked and tried to kill it, but it escaped through a crevice near the cell door. Consumed by a frenzy of envy and claustrophobia, she retreated to her corner and slammed her head against the wall. But she kept herself from screaming. If she screamed, she would lose her mind and never find it again.

The next time the scorpion appeared, Jamie warily let it be. It wasn't interested in her; instead it chased—and caught—a two-inch cockroach. After that, Jamie decided to catch cockroaches but couldn't. Her hands didn't work well enough to catch cockroaches, not even the ones she encountered in her food bowl.

Finally, she squished one with her heel, deposited it near the scorpion's crevice, and waited. "Hey," she said when the scorpion appeared. "Got something for you." But the scorpion rejected her cockroach and soon found one of its own. "Oh. So you like 'em live. You'd be up the creek without those pincers of yours, huh?"

Jamie stared at her own aching, nearly useless hands and shook her head. She continued to place them beneath her when she peed, which helped. She did other things she remembered from the Cock, too: Drain the pus from the wounds and clear away the dead tissue, enlist the aid of maggots if necessary.

It was, indeed, necessary.

She didn't even have to attract flies with morsels of food. The flies preferred her hands. Three times, she let maggots grow and feed on her wounds, watching them devour the rotting flesh, waiting for the blood to flow, for those brighter slices of pain, sign the maggots had reached live tissue. Then she brushed the maggots off her hands into a wriggling clump near the scorpion's crevice and put her hands in a flow of urine.

Bit by bit, the appalling wounds improved enough that she could use her fingers to explore every centimeter of the dark cell, learning the texture of the concrete blocks and the crumbly mortar between them. No microphones, no pinhole cameras that she could discern, but she discovered thick tie-downs embedded deep into each of the corners near the cell's low ceiling. Tie-downs to which the Zhong could chain her whenever they wanted.

How long did she have before they wanted?

"Gotta get stronger," she explained to the scorpion the first time she lay on her back, arms across her chest, knees pointing upward. "Whaddaya think? Twenty crunches? Fifty?"

Once she could weakly wiggle her fingers, she practiced picking up the bowls not with the heels of her hands but with fingers that actually moved some. When at last she could fully bend her wrists, she tried pushups. It was a close fit; her feet crowded into one corner and her head nearly touched the walls at the diagonal corner, but she defied the pain in her hands and eked out one, two, six, ten. Each time she did them, she did a few more. Because each one might be the last one. They could come anytime with their shackles. Anytime...

Jamie worried a lot about time. All efforts to measure it proved fruitless. The minimal light never varied. Beyond a low, remorseless buzzing and the intermittent whine of mosquitoes, she heard nothing except when someone slid the scanty ration of food through the door hatch. Nor were the scorpion's irregular visits any help.

Using her accelerating exercise regimen, she attempted to test the tempo of mealtimes. Sometimes food and water arrived only several hundred carefully paced crunches and pushups later than the last time. But often the span was much longer and she felt the effects of dehydration.

"At least they're still bothering to screw with me," she told the scorpion as it sucked the innards out of a cockroach. "Guess maybe I *didn't* say much."

❖

"Guess maybe I didn't say *much*."

Scorpion had been gone for a while, but upon her return the conversation picked right up where Jamie left off. "Why dump me in here all this time—unless they've already got what they wanted? But if they got what they wanted, why keep fucking with me?"

Ignoring Jamie, Scorpion scurried after a spider. Yellow and black, like the poisonous ones in the mountain forests. Scorpion took no chances and stung the spider with its tail.

"Mmm. Nice work."

Scorpion settled in for a leisurely meal and Jamie tried to remember. "Dee lee-yee. Shoo Juh kept saying something like that. I used to know what it means. If I could just re— Hey, that's it: Means 'the inside scoop.' Right, and they kept calling me 'gwun mo garn' like it's some kind of insult. You were probably there, huh? Watching while they pounded on me 'til I said what they wanted. But god, I don't know what it was. What'd I tell 'em, Scorpion?"

❖

Okay, try it. Jamie opened her eyes, surveyed the cell, closed her eyes again, and sighed. "You're not coming back anymore, huh?"

She was sure now: Scorpion had disappeared for good.

"C'mon, time for pushups." But she didn't move from her corner.

Without Scorpion, it was tougher to talk herself out of believing the ceiling was sinking, slowly claiming the sepulchral compartment until at last its vast weight would crush her. When she glanced up, she saw glowing red droplets form above her on the descending blackness.

Finally the moment arrived when she couldn't look at the ceiling at all, because doing so provoked in her an intractable dread. If she looked up, she'd see blood showering down upon her. And then she'd scream, she was quite sure of it. And once she started screaming, she'd never stop. *I will die screaming.*

Without Scorpion, this thought began to rule her. It acquired a life of its own and found ways to embellish itself, making her say it all out loud, in bits and pieces, until it crescendoed.

"Everyone else has been freed, and they're home now, safe with people who love them. But not me, because nobody on this whole fucking planet knows I exist. Not even Marty Rhys. Oh god, not even Marty. Only person who gives a shit about me is that interrogator.

And the only reason she gives a shit is because she wants me to die screaming. She's keeping me here even though the goddamn war's over so she can gloat and laugh while she watches me die screaming and squirming and—and—"

Tightening into a fetal clench, eyes squeezed shut, Jamie rocked herself back and forth, half humming, half grunting. To push away the implacable sameness. To keep from screaming. Then she heard— *What's that?*

Adrenaline gushing, she listened for her only human contact—the scrape of bowls of food and water nudged by a Zhong soldier through the door hatch. But no—there was only the menacing black and its relentless blood threat—an immutable hell made just for her. Not that quick snap of a death—no, no, never the relief of a bullet bursting in to her brain, a final, exuberant blast of light and sound and then the everlasting relief of nothing.

"Oh god, oh god, I'm the only one still here."

"No, you're not."

Jamie sprang to her feet so fast she smacked her head on the low ceiling but didn't notice as she whirled in a full circle searching for the owner of the voice.

The cell was empty, of course. "Great." She slumped back to the floor. "Now I'm hallucinating."

"Oh, you've been doing that for a while."

Her head swung around once more to catch the woman whose voice nuzzled in her ear. But she found no one.

"It's only your fear, you know."

Jamie didn't respond. But something—*someone*—was waiting. Palpably waiting. "Okay, I'll bite," she grumbled finally. "What's only my fear?"

"Getting you to believe that all the others have been freed. They haven't. They're still here. They're worried about you."

"How the fuck would you know?"

"You won't die if you scream."

"Leave me alone."

"Screaming won't kill you—won't make you crazy. Try it."

In the cell's perpetual dusk, where mere moments protracted into forever, it didn't take long for the idea to rule her completely. Screaming won't kill you.

What the fuck. Jamie threw her head back and screamed as loud as she could, deep and throaty at first, then high-pitched and piercing. After she emptied her lungs, she filled them with the cell's foul air and did it again. Then again and again and again until she exhausted herself.

❖

For once she hadn't dreamed at all. No Shoo Juh supervising a beating. No little girls getting their heads blown off. No Marty Rhys baring exquisite breasts.

Jamie opened her eyes to the sight of a small bundle just inside the door hatch. For a while, she stayed curled up and stared at it, waiting for it to evaporate. When it didn't, she poked it with her foot, cautiously.

Omigod, omigod—it's real. She crawled to it—and found a hammock. A hammock!

Was this a new kind of relief? The latest mindfuck by Shoo Juh? Jamie didn't care. Defying the limits of her clumsy hands, she suspended this treasure from the tie-downs, stretching it diagonally across the cell. At just the right angle, keeping her feet together, she could fully extend herself in it. Soon she slipped into another deep, restorative sleep.

Sometime later, she heard scratching, tapping near the air vent. Morse code? Hoping it, too, was real, she ransacked her memory to translate it. First came three dashes. *That's an o!* The scratches and taps continued.

"Out of the night that covers me,
black as the pit from pole to pole,
I thank whatever gods may be
for my unconquerable soul"

The first verse of *Invictus*—every letter, even the commas, scratched and tapped in full. Then, "d04 m04." A pause was followed by "h09".

Who had risked shing to send her hope and tell her she'd made it to 0900 on the fourth of April? And should she signal back?

Hell yes. "- ···· −·− ···-"—thku.

"−−− −−− ···· ·−· ·− ····"—oohrah.

Jamie cried first, then she giggled, then she pumped out a hundred pushups.

CHAPTER TWENTY-ONE

BREATH ON THE WIND

A sultry whiff of the coming habagat at last reached Jamie's cell and strengthened into meaning. *Could be May by now.* What seemed like soon after, the door to the cell creaked open to a ferocious glare.

"Suh!" ordered a pair of intensely backlit legs. Whenever had arrived. Jamie sheltered her eyes and crawled toward the cell door, trying to stave off The Fear with the hope that all those pushups and crunches would somehow help her.

Before she could attempt to stand, her hands were manacled behind her back, but for once the Zhong soldiers left her ankles unfettered. They had to lead her, and slowly. She was blind and nauseous; the insides of her head clamored to escape her skull, her legs faltered. Eyes squeezed shut against the blazing light, she tried to count the steps she walked. Perhaps a hundred, perhaps more. And then people she couldn't see sat her on a stool beneath a dazzling spotlight and hosed her down with deliciously cold water.

"Now that you have a better understanding of your options, are you ready to continue our conversation in a civil manner?" The special chief interrogator's words triggered too many memories. Shoo Juh always began with that same chilly veneer of civility.

Oh god, I can't do this again. Jamie kept her head bowed, unwilling this time to look into the woman's always-animated eyes and suffer the inevitable punishment for such insolence—a merciless slap across her face.

"You're not quite done yet…" The familiar voice was barely more than breath on the wind. Jamie knew better than to seek its source or doubt its sagacity, but she begged for reprieve. *No, please…*

"She prefers to believe you. But he's here again to get you to recant and then find a way to kill you so you don't say anything else that's inconvenient."

What? I don't get it. Panic gnarled Jamie's belly. *Please. I don't get it! What am I supposed to—?* Then Jamie heard a voice—her own voice, steady and calm—saying, "You don't care what I know or what I say."

The special chief interrogator's shadow loomed. "Oh, but I *do* care."

Jamie couldn't see the sparse, cruel smile teasing the interrogator's delicate lips, but memory told her it was there. She shook her head. "You care about having an excuse to hurt me, about watching me try to jump out of my own skin." Squinting now, Jamie looked up into that icy gaze and finally understood what she'd seen there all along: Shoo Juh was turned on.

Eyes sparking wildly, the interrogator slapped Jamie so hard she fell to the floor. "You are punished because you do not respect your superiors, hong mao."

This deeply derogatory term for non-Asians meant "red fur," to denote they were less than human. It was the interrogator's favorite insult, and it worked. After the soldiers picked her up and returned her to the stool, Jamie bowed her head and didn't look up again.

"Tell me about Banggi, hong mao."

Ignoring the taste of her own blood seeping from her lacerated lower lip, Jamie risked an attempt to stall. "Please, may I have some water?"

After a minute, one of the four soldiers guarding her put a canteen to her lips and she swallowed as much as she could as fast as she could, leaning forward to get the last of it as the guard withdrew the canteen.

And that's when she realized someone else was there, too. Jamie tried to sneak a look, but saw only a civilian's hiking boots and blue jeans. A wave of acidic terror shuddered through her. *This is him. The one who wants to kill me.*

"Gwun mo garn," he said then, oozing contempt. "'The soldier in endless hell.'"

Jamie couldn't identify his accent. Certainly it wasn't any sort of Chinese, but it paralyzed her. She'd heard that accent, that voice before.

"Cantonese is so useful," he said, "for exposing darker truths like yours, cunt. Gwun mo garn, the sniper who shoots innocent children and—"

"Zhu zhuay!" Shoo Juh barked. "You've had more than your share, lee-eh huaw."

She just told him to shut up, didn't she? And I think she called him a bastard.

The interrogator turned to Jamie. "Tell me about Banggi, hong mao."

But Jamie could find no words. This Bastard who knew too much about her had robbed her of words.

"I will not wait much longer." Shoo Juh came close enough for Jamie to glimpse her eyes churning with impatience.

The threat in those eyes stutter-started Jamie's brain. *Banggi... Banggi... Oh shit! Borneo!* She stared at the floor. *Invasion of Borneo.* And heard a tremulous echo. *There was only...only...*

Jamie imitated the echo as it faded. "There was only one briefing b-before, before I was...I-I can't remember—"

"All right." Shoo Juh paused behind a façade of near amiability. "We will review what you've told us about this briefing. Who was present and what was discussed?"

Jamie said nothing until Shoo Juh bent closer with her wordless threat.

Our training...training... "Our training was discussed."

"Yes, yes. Training for what, hong mao?"

Jamie was close to panic. Somewhere beyond the spotlight, the Bastard watched, waiting for his chance. *Just a preliminary briefing...*

"It was just a preliminary briefing. Just the scout/sniper platoon leaders, so we'd know how to train our people for the invasion."

"The invasion." Shoo Juh prompted expectantly.

"Of—of Borneo," Jamie mumbled.

"You know I need certain specifics, hong mao. Who briefed you?"

"The battalion's intelligence officer."

Shoo Juh came closer, seeking something else. "And—"

No names, no names. "Th-there were some other people, too," Jamie said, forcing herself to glance at the interrogator's face for hints about what to say next.

Shoo Juh seemed not to notice the glance; she came closer still. "Who were they?"

Jamie played for more hints. "Don't know. We weren't introduced."

The slap across Jamie's face stung as it resounded. But it didn't knock her off the stool.

"Were they civilians?" Shoo Juh asked too avidly.

Civilians? Damn! This is about the mercs! Jamie drew in a slow breath. *You want mercs, you got mercs.* "They weren't in uniform," she said. "When I came in I saw one of them waving around some kind of contractor ID."

"Which contractor?"

Jamie shrugged. "I didn't get a good look."

The interrogator gazed into the dark beyond the spotlight where the Bastard stood. Then she leaned over Jamie. "Tell me what you know about how the invasion will proceed. All of it, hong mao."

But Jamie had little to tell. *Amphibious assault…Marudu Bay…* In a stuttering hush, trying to hide a high-frequency shudder, Jamie stumbled through what little she now recalled of the fiction she'd concocted months ago.

From his corner, The Bastard snorted loudly and stepped nearer to the spotlight. "That's ridiculous! Why would—"

Without taking her eyes from Jamie, Shoo Juh held up a hand to silence him. "We already know of the American interest in Banggi and Balambangan," Shoo Juh growled at Jamie. "Now you talk only of entering Marudu Bay. Not even Americans can be that stupid."

"That's right!" the Bastard shouted. "She fabricated the whole thing."

"I have cooperated," Jamie said softly, seeking time to think, time to recall the topo maps of northern Borneo.

The interrogator's eyes glowed. "You have lied to your superiors, hong mao."

Too late, Jamie recollected more. *Islands! Banggi and Balambangan are frigging islands off the northern tip of Borneo!* "I-I coulda got it wrong," she said. *Shit. Shit. I just blew it.* "There was only the one briefing—a-and yeah, I think I must've got it wrong. Pulau Banggi first, and Balambangan, then into Marudu Bay…I-I'm sorry, I get confused. I have trouble remembering."

"You see?" the Bastard said. "She lies. It's all a lie."

Shoo Juh's sculpted face, impermeable as glazed porcelain, filled Jamie's vision. "You said before that five places would be attacked simultaneously, but nothing about entering Marudu Bay."

"After," Jamie said, blinking to keep her eyes from closing out the sight of Shoo Juh. "Into the bay after we take the three islands and either side of—"

"No!" the Bastard screeched. "There will be no invasion of Borneo by the Americans or anyone else. I will prove it. Just let me have this lying cunt again for a—"

Shoo Juh wheeled to face him. "Your organization serves many masters. Perhaps some of its loyalties are in conflict with others."

"No," the Bastard said. "*She* is deceiving you, not us."

"Perhaps." Anticipatory excitement sparking in Shoo Juh's eyes.

If she asks me more questions, I'll fuck up again...What the hell, I'm screwed anyway... Jamie ran her gaze over Shoo Juh's body, halting at the woman's crotch. "Already creaming, fah kao yee-un chuh?" she taunted. "Only way you get gao chao, isn't it?"

Through the glare, Jamie saw shock overtake the interrogator's fine features. The guards gawked in amazement. Jamie's attempt to use Mandarin terms for sadist and female orgasm was jumbled but comprehensible, and it detonated Shoo Juh like a bomb.

The Bastard laughed—an odd, abrasive sound that Jamie realized she'd heard before—while Shoo Juh howled orders that the guards scrambled to obey. Frozen at the center of the tumult, Jamie peered with new understanding into the dark where the Bastard's darkened form lurked. *You. You're the one who did this to my hands.*

Then the guards yanked Jamie from the stool and began obeying their orders. Shoo Juh still shouted. For a brief while, Jamie managed to translate some of her words. "Bian"—whip. "Shung"—rope. "Ko kuh"—thirst. "Chee-ih tao"—beg.

"Go now," a voice in Jamie's ear soothed as the beating intensified under the chief interrogator's ardent surveillance. "I'll show you the way."

CHAPTER TWENTY-TWO

SAINT EH MO'S

This is Gwynmorgan?"

Male voice, tinged with relief and far, far away. Though it nearly whispered, Jamie heard it quite clearly.

"Yes, sir. Not ready to wake up yet."

Female voice—gentle, concerned. *From North Carolina...Nah, not that lucky. Smells too much like the Palawan...*

"So that's everyone. Twenty-two of ours, eight Filipinos."

"Yes, sir. We got everybody now."

Jamie's hands hurt—the same ceaseless throbbing that made it so hard to move her fingers for so long. *Yep. Still here. But I like this dream...* She drifted away from the conversation, wishing only that the woman from North Carolina would touch her. *Soft, on my cheek first, then down my neck and—*

A gush of pain splashing white-hot across her back and buttocks ended Jamie's reverie. She tried to find relief by moving but could only jerk and squirm. Her eyes sprang open but refused to focus. "Aahh fuh-*uuh*..."

"Lieutenant Gwynmorgan? Ma'am?"

Her eyes had to close. "Please. Don't," Jamie muttered through clamped teeth. "Call me that."

"Try to relax, ma'am—uh, Lieutenant," soothed North Carolina. "I got something here that'll help."

Uh-oh. Jamie made her eyes open again and blinked through most of the blurriness. Hammock. And cammies. Not naked anymore. And North Carolina looking really young and pale, holding a med injector. "Morphine?"

North Carolina nodded solemnly, bringing the injector closer.

"No. No ph-pharma. Makes me nuts. M-More nuts."

Jamie tried to wave the injector away but her hand hardly moved. The pain flamed through her in waves. *Aw jeez, gotta get outta here.* The next wave made her gasp.

"But, Lieutenant—"

"C-Corpsman, right?"

North Carolina nodded again, her round, genial face creased with worry.

"'Kay, Doc, need you to help me get off my sorry ass."

North Carolina's touch was just as Jamie imagined it. Gentle, firm, confident. A gift. Soon she'd been eased onto her left side and the pain began ebbing into something less incendiary.

"Thanks, North Carolina." Jamie let herself fade toward sleep. *Wow. Not dead yet. How'd that ever happen?*

❖

"Good to finally meet you, Lieutenant," said a tired-looking man in oversized Marine Corps cammies as soon as she woke. "I'm Donato."

A major, according to the brown oakleaf on his collar, whose somber Mediterranean features were eased by an earnest smile. Jamie pegged him as a regimental fobbit. He didn't have to bother telling her he was the senior POW officer and therefore her acting CO. He started a handshake but stopped when he saw her wounds and gripped the edge of her hammock instead. "How're you feeling?"

"Stronger, I think, sir." Jamie glanced at the hand the major decided not to shake. "Sorta."

"It'll get better. We figured you for all kinds of infections and ulcers. But the corpsman says you're in pretty good shape. That beta-defensin booster really works. You just need some antibiotics, which we finally have."

With effort that left her breathless, Jamie shifted her weight in the hammock, waving off the major's offer to help. When she got herself hiked up on her left elbow, she divulged the obvious. "I'm, uh—Guess I'm a little disoriented."

The major's smile warped into a grimace. "I'm not surprised. It's the eighteenth of May. Saturday."

Jamie looked around. She lay in a hammock strung across a dreary cell constructed in the same Malihud church to which the Zhong had brought her months ago. Tight rows of gray-black bars comprised two of the cell's four walls; a door of bars had been swung open to a hallway. Beyond it she saw other cells, but no Zhong. "I'm real glad to be here."

Donato raised an eyebrow.

"I mean with you and everybody instead of, you know..."

"Yeah. We're real glad to have you, Lieutenant."

"I didn't think I'd ever, uh—Why'd they stop, sir?"

"Same reason we now have soap and a fighting chance against dysentery," he said, his smile restored. "Truce talks. The Red Cross is supposed to be here by the end of the month. First step toward an exchange of POWs. With a little luck we'll all be out of here a month after that."

"That mean I can get a toothbrush, sir?"

"Lieutenant, take it easy," North Carolina said, grabbing Jamie's arm just in time to keep her from toppling out of her hammock.

"Aw, come on, North Carolina, where's your spirit of adventure?" Jamie winked back, subduing a flinch. "Gotta check out all the changes to this palace. I hardly recognize it. So I'm getting out to that grand foyer there with you or without you. And how about calling me something easier to pronounce?"

North Carolina appeared puzzled.

"Like Gwynnie. Or LT if you really, really have to."

Jamie reveled in not being hungry or thirsty, in breathing air that didn't smell like a sewer, in wearing her cammies again—even if they seemed a size larger than the last time she had them on. No bones had been broken, no organs ruptured, no tropical ulcers had devoured her flesh and tendons and bones. Except for what the Bastard did to her hands, the interrogators had been fiendishly careful to maximize pain and minimize impairment. *Like it's not over yet.*

Yet maybe it *was* over. Ever since news of the truce talks, life in the small POW camp had improved markedly, according to North Carolina. Not just the end of interrogations and more and better food but also iodine to purify the water, toothpaste and medicines, no forced labor, no one in the isolation cells, the return of their uniforms. Best of all, the doors to the dozen cells were left open all day, permitting everyone access to the common hallway and even a yard outside.

So now that she could stand up and shuffle around, nothing would prevent Jamie from walking every possible inch of the camp. And the sooner the better. But why should her shuffle toward the cell doorway attract so much attention from the other prisoners?

"What's up, North Carolina?" she asked, angling her head lightly in the direction of a group of POWs. "Do I look that bad?"

North Carolina grinned. "It's not about that, ma'am—um, LT. It's because you're, uh, kind of a legend. When I got here, some people said you were dead. But Captain Cavanaugh didn't believe it. He was sure you were still alive—like a faith he had. Then last month we made contact."

"Yeah." Jamie lowered her head and blinked back tears. "I remember. I'll never forget it."

Before Jamie had a chance to ask who had scratched and tapped Morse code that day, other POWs began coming up to introduce themselves. Jamie engaged each one, moved by the mix of concern and exultation in their eyes and pleased that word had spread about not calling her ma'am. She repeated every name she heard, determined to memorize all of them.

But where was Cavanaugh? Leaning on North Carolina's arm, Jamie walked out of the church to the adjoining yard and looked around.

A bit more than thirty meters by maybe twenty meters. Concrete-block walls roughly three meters high, razor-wire on top. Razor-wire dead man zone inside of, say, three meters. A few floodlights, no obvious cameras. One tower, small—bet it's frigging uncomfortable, hardly any shade—and it's got, let's see, one blind spot for sure and maybe another where that heavy door is. Hmm, where might that door lead? And how come I don't see him?

"Where is he?"

"Ma'am?"

"Captain Cavanaugh."

North Carolina's face clouded. "Dead," she murmured. "Escaped with two others about a month ago. Shot when they got caught a couple days later. The Zhong brought 'em back here, laid 'em out right there in the yard—" North Carolina's hand indicated the spot. "Made us all come out for a good look. They said 'escape results in death.'"

Jamie stared at the spot where North Carolina pointed. "I see why you call this place Saint Eh Mo's."

She tried to lean a little less on North Carolina while they walked 'round and 'round the yard, indifferent to the light rain that portended the coming monsoon.

"Okay," Jamie said when she'd spent herself. "Guess I'm done."

North Carolina nearly carried her back to her hammock. When they got there, Jamie held up her hands. "Can you help me with these, Doc? They're about useless and sore as hell. Feel like a couple of ham hocks. Think massaging them, moving around my fingers some might help them hurt less? I'd like to be able to work a button, you know?"

Gently, the corpsman took Jamie's hands in her own. "Sorry," she said when her exploratory contact made Jamie flinch. "Punctures through your palms, right? Nails or spikes? When'd this happen?"

An electric dread slithered down Jamie's spine. "Don't know." Her heart pounded as she tried to duck the shards of memory hurdling toward her. "Remember who, but not how or when."

"I don't have much experience with this kind of thing," North Carolina said without raising her eyes from Jamie's hands. "But I'll give it a try." She gently stroked the edge of one hand, then the other, until Jamie's pulse decelerated. "It's going to be painful though, LT. And we'll have to do it over and over. As much as you can stand."

"Then we should start now."

After a couple of minutes, they found their pace.

"How's that? Want me to keep going?"

"Yes." It hurt plenty, but Jamie wasn't ready to relax. Not as long as she remained in Saint Eh Mo's, in the place where Shoo Juh or the Bastard could come for her anytime they wanted. "Do you—" Her eyes closed while she coped with a new slash of pain. Exhaling carefully when it diminished, Jamie opened her eyes and gave the corpsman a please-continue nod. "Do you mind me calling you North Carolina?"

"No, ma'am!" North Carolina blushed at her mistake, but Jamie gestured it away with a smile. "I like it," North Carolina said shyly, continuing to work on Jamie's hands. "Nobody ever gave me a nickname before."

"What's your real name?"

"Cordelia Jones, Hospital Corpsman Third Class. But, LT, ma'am?"

"Yes, Doc?"

"May I request that you keep calling me North Carolina?"

"I'd be honored to, North Carolina."

❖

Don't scream. Don't. Give 'em. That.

Maintaining unblemished silence made them hit her harder and took so much strength and effort that the fadeout came sooner. Sometimes soon enough.

But this time Shoo Juh was on to her: The blows had been moderated so she'd last longer. The next one was carefully timed. She'd just inhaled, and now the pain streaking across her backside coerced an unwilling moan into her tremulous release of breath.

Jamie was stretched out hard and naked, like Da Vinci's Vitruvian man. Her feet, spread wide apart, scarcely reached the floor. Her hands clasped the ropes snaking from an invisible ceiling to encircle her wrists. She tried to comprehend how the interrogator signaled the men pummeling her, for she knew Shoo Juh ordered the when and what of each hit. But she could see only the woman's insatiate want, her tormentor's thrill in knowing no one could stop the beating, certainly not her.

The next strike, across her shoulder blades, came like all the others—unexpectedly—and it interrupted her attempt to take a breath, causing her to choke as her diaphragm spasmed.

"You have lied to me, hong mao."

Oh god oh god. It's starting.

With the next carefully modulated stroke, its first igneous pulse grabbed her. Jamie screamed then, deep and raw and angry, full of fear and objection. But there was no way out. Accompanied by the interrogator's pernicious laughter, the blackness spewed its cruel crimson reminder that this was and always would be her righteous punishment.

No please…

"LT ma'am, wake up."

North Carolina? What're you doing here?

"Wake up, LT."

Someone jostled Jamie's shoulder and her eyes opened to a dim, echoey space with rough makeshift walls of concrete block and heavy metals bars. *Oh yeah. Shoo Juh threw me back, like a fish not worth eating.* Jamie rubbed her face to be sure.

"You okay, LT ma'am?" North Carolina looked worried.

"I was, uh, yelling and stuff, huh?"

"Nightmare?" North Carolina glanced into the shoulder bag she always carried. "I can give you someth—"

"No. No thanks. Only cure for me'll be to get the hell out of here." *And far, far away from that woman and her Bastard.* "But if I'm, you know, agitated in my sleep, you wake me up soon as you see it, okay? I want you to wake me up."

"Yes, ma'am."

"I'm no ma'am, Doc." Jamie edged her legs out of her hammock. "God, I gotta get outta here."

"Soon, LT. Once there's a truce."

Jamie stood and paced the narrow space between her hammock and North Carolina's. She stretched, reaching her arms up high, standing on her toes, lifting her chin to crane her neck. But it didn't help. "Ever think about escaping, North Carolina?"

"I did, but…" North Carolina shrugged.

"Cavanaugh."

"And now the truce talks."

"I don't know, Doc. You really think the talks are for real?"

North Carolina frowned. "The major thinks so, ma'am. He got official word from the Zhong commandant, and they've eased up on security a lot. A whole lot. The Zhong wouldn't do that if the talks weren't real. And they let you out, LT ma'am, didn't they? You bet it's real. You just take it easy and get some sleep, okay?"

"Yeah, okay, North Carolina."

But Jamie didn't sleep—not until she decided to prepare for escape. Just in case.

CHAPTER TWENTY-THREE

SHE VOLUNTEERS

The instant she strode into the yard with the rest of the Red Cross team, Jamie noticed her, and noticed that she seemed to be a study in contradiction.

The clothes she wore—undyed linen bush shirt with its sleeves rolled up to her elbows, rumpled linen pants, well-worn light hikers— all belied her erect, formal bearing. A graceful, made-for-primetime sweep of her hand whisked both sunglasses and a wide-brimmed hat from her head—only to expose the no-nonsense of bob-cropped hair, once a dirty blond, now abundantly streaked with white.

And her eyes—Jamie watched her eyes comprehend her surroundings even while she appeared to devote all her attention to the Zhong commandant who walked next to her. She positioned herself so she could both engage the commandant and direct an evanescent nod to the prisoners clumped at the far end of the yard. By the time she and the other Red Cross people disappeared into the old church building to inspect where the prisoners were locked up at night—part of the Red Cross visiting procedure—the Zhong commandant seemed almost eagerly deferential.

Could she possibly be who Jamie thought she was?

No. No, dammit, it's got to be just an eerie resemblance. Or I'm hallucinating again. Hell, it's only been nineteen days since Shoo Juh regurgitated me. I still wake up thinking I'm in that tomb, looking for Scorpion. No, no way. How could somebody like Lynn Hillinger ever even get to a place like Saint Eh Mo's?

But Jamie had to be sure. Several folding tables had already been set up in the yard for the next stage of the visit: Prisoner registration and interviews. Heavy habagat clouds threatened rain that could cut the interviewing short, but Jamie went straight to the back of the line that formed in front of the table where she-can't-really-be-Lynn-Hillinger sat. By the time Jamie stood before her, the clouds had thickened and her shoulders sagged a little. Jamie waited for her to look up from a small comlink screen, waited to see her face-to-face and make sure.

Just when she began to lift her eyes, a whiff of premonitory monsoonal wind danced filaments of almost-white hair across her forehead. Unadorned lips parted slightly, hinting the familiar smile.

In the same instant Jamie was sure, Lynn Hillinger's gray eyes flared and bucked, and Jamie saw what they saw, like looking at herself in a mirror: The malevolent red craters on the backs of her hands, the streaks of cruel bruises and scars circling her wrists. And thin. Way too thin. The sight caused Jamie to flinch.

But those gray eyes didn't flinch. Instead, they peered right through Jamie's wordless what-the-fuck endurance, right to the urgent, indigent yearning that no one was ever supposed to notice but that Jamie wanted noticed more than she wanted just about anything.

And then Jamie saw Lynn Hillinger's vehement ache to nourish, the rush of protective anger. The force of it made Jamie's eyes close; a humming warmth vibrated through her chest and a moan oozed up, up from some abyssal place inside her. *Oh god.*

Not far away, a couple of guards laughed. "Kong zhong," one said.

Jamie didn't know what the words meant, but she'd heard them before. During shing. She snapped open her eyes and glared at the woman seated before her. *What are you doing here? Are you fucking crazy?*

Lynn Hillinger's eyes flared again, then dove back down to her comlink screen.

Breathless, chest cramping, Jamie also looked down, overcome with an intense need to study her boots.

"Please, have a seat." A gentle voice, quite different than the last time Jamie heard it on TV more than two years ago.

"Yes, ma'am. Thank you." Jamie pulled her eyes from her boots, sat, and ticked off name, rank, military identification number, date of birth, date of capture.

"You said thirty-one October of what year?" Gray eyes glanced at the comlink screen before them. "So you're, uh, *nineteen?*"

"Jeez, Senator, it *is* that bad, huh?"

Senator Hillinger rubbed the edge of a finger across her lips and the faint smile forming there; her head shifted back and forth almost imperceptibly. "I, um, did have the impression you were older."

"So how does a United States senator become a member of an International Red Cross delegation that's visiting prisoners in enemy territory?"

"She volunteers."

Jamie remembered the Hillinger senate run, remembered enjoying the blunt, take-no-shit independent candidate, an unabashed lesbian who relished tweaking standard-fare politicians' tails. She was a master of the spontaneous sound bite, an entrepreneurial big shot too clean to browbeat or blackmail, and attractive, too—trim, energetic, a spirited smile the cartoonists loved to caricature. By the time she won the election and became Massachusetts's newest senator, Jamie had been carried off by the aftermath of Alby's death. But for a few seconds that Tuesday night in November, Jamie watched her on TV surrounded by her cheering family and thought, *What would it be like to have a mother like you?*

"Why? Why the hell would you volunteer?" But Jamie retreated when one of Senator Hillinger's eyebrows arched. "Uh, ma'am."

"Well, Lieutenant, somebody had to." The famous smile played at the corners of her mouth. "I pushed hard for an arrangement whereby each side has a representative on the Red Cross team visiting its prisoners of war. Seemed kind of gutless not to be willing to do the actual heavy lifting. Which is to make sure we bring home as many of you as we can as soon as we can."

"We're grateful, ma'am. But isn't that why we have a State Department?"

"Indeed, and they're working quite diligently between martinis. However, as a rule they prefer consulates to POW camps."

Undeflected, Jamie leaned forward. "This is a dangerous place. Your life is at risk here. We call it Saint Eh Mo's—that means 'evil demon'—for a reason."

"Yes." Senator Hillinger almost seemed to blink back tears. "A reason that shows all over you. I'm hoping our presence has mitigated the worst of it."

Jamie could not sustain this woman's gaze. She looked down at her battered hands, perplexed to find them stiffly compressed into fists. "Yes, ma'am, it has. More th-than you can imagine."

Jamie had noticed the Zhong official hovering a few feet away. He'd shadowed her ever since she'd stepped into line. Now he came closer, warning in his squinted eyes. He offered the senator a cursory bow and with excessive politeness pointed skyward, where looming monsoonal clouds darkened. This "private" interview would be shorter than most.

Senator Hillinger acknowledged his demand with a dip of her head, then looked despairingly at Jamie. "I'm so sorry. I should've—" She flipped her hands palms up, gesturing frustration and failure. "Are you okay?"

"Yes, ma'am, I am. Thanks to you."

Senator Hillinger stood and Jamie rose, too. "Stay strong," she said, leaning closer to Jamie and proffering her hand.

Her warm hand trembled. Jamie didn't want to let it go. *Forgive me. I didn't mean to be rude or frighten you.* "Please, ma'am," Jamie whispered, staring into gray eyes that seemed sad now, helpless. "Get out of here as fast as you can. Please."

The next afternoon, torrential rains swooped in from the southwest to inundate all of lower Palawan. The habagat's opening salvo triggered so many landslides and floods that Saint Eh Mo's prisoners heard about it because the Zhong guards bitched even to them.

Most of the Red Cross team members departed just ahead of the inundation, having acquired what they came for: An authoritative list of the POWs in Malihud, an accounting of their condition, an inspection of the camp, and brief prisoner interviews. But four Red Cross people remained behind for a few more days to provide additional medical aid to the POWs and the citizens of Malihud.

To Jamie's dismay, Senator Hillinger was one of them.

CHAPTER TWENTY-FOUR

I WANT TO SAY GOOD-BYE

Saint Eh Mo's sodden yard had filled with POWs using the day's monsoon torrent like a shower to clean themselves and their clothing, applying soap to skin and cammies alike, then rinsing in the rain.

"Sir." Jamie stepped alongside Major Donato as he walked the yard's perimeter. "I request permission to attempt an escape."

His head swiveled. "You saw her, too?"

"Oh yeah. Staring right at me from the tower with that look, that ice-smile."

"And you think it means…"

"The negotiations are in trouble and she knows it. Why else would she bother climbing into that god-awful oven of a tower? She was picking out her playthings. And I've been picked." Jamie sucked air in an effort to soothe her agitated gut and resumed working her hands, alternately fisting and stretching them.

Until that morning, no one had seen Shoo Juh in the three weeks since news of the truce talks broke. The prisoners regarded her absence as a sure sign that the talks were for real. Now, two days after the Red Cross interviews, Shoo Juh had returned. *And that smile. Not good. Not good at all.*

A glance at Donato told Jamie he remained skeptical. She tried again. "Sir, if Shoo Juh's back, then there can't be much time left before everything goes to shit."

"We don't know that," Donato said. "You need to calm down, Lieutenant. You need to act like a leader and calm down and help everyone else calm down. Understand?"

"No, sir, I don't understand. I don't think we should calm down. Not now. Not ever 'til we get our asses outta here and back to our own people."

Donato stopped walking. "Dammit, Gwynmorgan."

"Sir, once the last of the Red Cross people go, I'm toast. We've all got our shots now. Our supplies of antibiotics and antifungals. They're finishing up today, right? Leaving tomorrow morning."

Donato shrugged an affirmative.

"I can't—" Jamie worked her hands faster now, kept her face away from Donato. "I can't do it again. I-I'd rather be killed escaping."

"Lieutenant, I don't want to hear this. *Nothing* has happened."

"That's exactly right. We're still here. Shoo Juh's still here. They'll still shoot us like Cavanaugh if we try to leave."

"You'll attempt it no matter what I say, won't you?"

Jamie didn't reply.

"How many want to go with you?" Donato asked.

"Haven't talked to anybody about it. Probably a lot more today than yesterday."

It took Donato a while to speak. "I'm a mistake, you know."

"Sir?"

"I didn't just get captured. The Zhong kidnapped me. Very daring. But I was the wrong guy. They wanted the brigade G-Two, but the damn fools couldn't figure out the difference between a man wearing a brown oak leaf and a woman wearing a black one. Hell, I'm not even intel. I'm the world's original fobbit screenwiz. Supply all the way. I'd been on this hellhole island about six hours when it happened. Couldn't even tell the Zhong where the latrines were, much less anything about intel ops."

"Guess that's the good news."

"All I want to do is get the hell home so I can resign my commission and go to work for my father-in-law like I should have four years ago. I think our best bet is to wait out the truce talks. But Shoo Juh interrogated me, too. And I don't want to ever be in the same room with that woman again."

"You and me both, sir." *Okay, so he hasn't actually denied me permission. That'll do.*

Nobody knew it, but Jamie had acquired the first tool of escape the day the Red Cross showed up in the yard. As one of three POW officers, second behind Donato, Jamie'd been ordered to select a crew of prisoners to do the actual work of erecting the tables for the Red Cross people to use during prisoner interviews. When the Zhong guard standing next to her pulled out a handkerchief to wipe sweat off his face, she glimpsed a pen fall unseen from his pocket.

She worried, even then, about Shoo Juh lying in wait, setting her up. But she placed her boot over the pen anyway, kneeled down anyway to retie her bootlaces, retrieve the pen, and hide it. Bent to eighty degrees, the metal clip on the pen's cap would suffice as a torque wrench.

Of course, Jamie still needed a pick. *Can't practice without a pick.* And god knew she needed the practice. Almost three weeks of North Carolina's ministrations had helped her hands regain some dexterity, but would she still have anything like the subtle sensitivity so essential to coaxing open a lock? *A paperclip, a paperclip, my kingdom for a paperclip.*

❖

"LT ma'am, wake up."

"Come on, North Carolina, that ma'am stuff has gotta go." Then Jamie opened her eyes. *Sun hasn't risen yet.* "What's up? What time is it?"

"Zero-five-thirty." North Carolina's face kaleidoscoped from uneasiness to excitement to fear. "The major just found out the Zhong commandant's coming to make an announcement."

"Coming? You mean here, to the cells?"

North Carolina nodded. "Before first muster. Before they unlock the doors."

Oh shit. "When?"

"Fifteen minutes. Zero-five-forty-five. Whaddaya think it means, LT?"

"Dunno, North Carolina."

❖

"Only temporary." Thus did the Zhong commandant's announcement begin—and end. He sprinkled "only temporary" into the middle a couple of times, too, but it didn't make his news any easier to hear: The truce talks had been "recessed."

He offered no specifics; worse, he said the four remaining Red Cross people would be required to stay in Malihud "to protect their safety." For how long? "Jin chee," came the ambiguous reply—soon.

The POWs whispered about hostages. Yet because of the Red Cross presence, and perhaps especially because of the senator's presence, the Zhong behaved as if successful negotiations were inevitable and imminent—beginning shortly after the commandant's announcement, when the cell doors were opened only a half hour later than usual.

"Yeah, sure," muttered Jamie. "They gotta pretend, don't they? Otherwise they've brazenly kidnapped an International Red Cross–affiliated United States senator who's supposed to be safe here. Safe and free to leave when she damn well wants." Donato nodded. Others nodded. But by day's end, only Jamie wanted to talk about it anymore.

"Bao?" she spouted. "That means protect, defend. What do the Red Cross people need to be protected from? What does Senator Hillinger need to be protected from? The PIA maybe? Does that mean the Zhong can't control the PIA? Or are they using the senator to—"

"Hey," Donato said. "Maybe it's just about the mudslides and washed-out roads."

"Except that—"

"Enough, Gwynmorgan." Donato glanced around the cells. The last of the POWs were returning and behind them the guards had started the lockdown ritual. "Don't push it."

Jamie understood. Nobody wanted to preserve Saint Eh Mo's truce talks regimen more than she did. The cells unlocked during the day, the POWs enjoying unrestricted access to the yard. Food and medicine still coming. The Red Cross team continuing its work unhindered out of its small office in the camp's administration wing just on the other side of that heavy door in the yard's wall. The guards pretending to smile. And the interrogation chambers still vacant.

Hardly more than twenty-four hours after hearing that the truce negotiations had been suspended, the POWs' fears eased and they'd reached consensus: The breakdown truly must be temporary—or else the old draconian security would already have been imposed again. The brief spike of interest in escape waned once more.

But not for Jamie. *It's all about time. If the talks don't get back on track, they'll let the Red Cross people go, they'll nasty up camp security, and the rest of us could be stuck here for years. Goddamn, there's so much I don't know, so much I can't even begin to guess. How long before it all goes to shit? And where the fuck am I going to find a paperclip?*

❖

"Think I could melt down a toothbrush handle with a lighter?" Jamie asked North Carolina during their usual afternoon perambulation of the yard.

"Ma'am?"

"Some of the Zhong have lighters, and if I could—" Jamie shut up as two guards approached.

When they politely asked her to accompany them to the administration wing, she hoped maybe Senator Hillinger had asked for her. After the guards indicated that North Carolina must stay behind, Jamie's spine prickled. But she had no interest in upsetting the precarious status quo, and, god, she wanted to see Senator Hillinger again.

"I'll be fine, North Carolina." She patted the nervous corpsman's arm and walked off alone with the guards just as huge raindrops announced the day's cascade.

On the way to the door to the administration wing, Jamie spoke to the guard who she'd seen more than once with a lighter. She knew with certainty he spoke some English. Not on this day, however. He said only, "Gahn mahng"—hurry. A hazy, half-formed instinct alerted her. *What if this isn't the senator's summons?* But she brushed it off.

Once in the administration wing courtyard, once the heavy, solid door locked resoundingly behind her, the guard she tried to speak with brandished manacles.

"*NO!*" Jamie roared as the guards grabbed her arms. "*NO FUCKING WAY!*"

She yanked herself free of their grip and pivoted away from them into a feral crouch, ready to fight. Jamie knew now where they intended to take her, who they were taking her to, and she couldn't let it happen. Not ever again. She wouldn't see freedom after all. She would die right here, right now. Maybe she could even make it quick, sudden. An instantaneous snap of a death.

"NO!" Jamie howled again as the guards shouted at her and several bursts of automatic-weapon fire from the tower bit the ground inches from her feet without persuading her to surrender.

That's when, at the periphery of her vision, she saw Senator Hillinger appear in a doorway some twenty meters away.

"Stop! Tee-ing hwah-aw!" The senator's shout mixed outrage and fear and was tinged with the steadfast expectation that she'd be obeyed.

"Omigod," Jamie gasped when she saw Senator Hillinger running toward her, toward the bullets. She dropped to her knees and clasped her hands around the back of her head, which halted the shooting just in time.

The guards had backed well away from the bullets, so Senator Hillinger reached Jamie first and put out a hand to forestall them. As they vacillated, she tried to talk them out of using manacles.

"It's all right, ma'am," Jamie said from her knees. "They're just following orders." She looked up at the English-speaking guard. "Ming ling. Yes?"

"Shih," he agreed, obviously relieved.

"Duh-way boo chih," Jamie pleaded, eyeing each of the guards in turn as she tried to say "forgive me." Then she bowed her head before carefully, slowly drawing away her hands, reclasping them behind her back, and rising to her feet.

Every muscle in Jamie's body went rigid as the manacles clutched her wrists. A vibration quivered through her; she felt like she was about to explode. Somehow she managed to turn her head and get a last glimpse of Senator Hillinger, now drenched by the monsoonal downpour, looking small and hopeless. And then the Zhong guards spun her around and marched her off to the interrogation chambers.

❖

Leaning lightly against a table in the nearly empty room, Shoo Juh greeted Jamie with a tranquil smile and gestured toward two four-legged stools. "Have a seat." In almost any other circumstance, her tone might have seemed solicitous.

Obeying, Jamie watched her, seeking motive. This time, for the first time, she didn't wear a lab coat; she stood before Jamie dressed in classic black silk tunic and pants, dry and elegant and cool. Shoo Juh dismissed the guards once Jamie sat on a stool, dripping and still manacled.

This was also the first time Jamie could recall they'd ever been entirely alone. For a long moment, Jamie stared at Shoo Juh and Shoo Juh stared back. Jamie girded for the usual heavy slap across her face—punishment for looking the interrogator in the eye—and she shivered, liberating droplets of water that clung to her. The last time she'd seen Shoo Juh, the Bastard was there, too, and she was beaten unconscious. Repeatedly.

"Thirsty? Want some water?" Shoo Juh asked at last.

No slap? Jamie's shiver ceased abruptly. She tried to remain impassive but felt her eyes widen in surprise. "Yes, thank you, I'd like some water." *My god, I sound so normal.* She wondered if Shoo Juh would release her hands so she could drink the water.

Shoo Juh reached to the table behind her for a bottle of European-branded spring water and twirled off the cap. When her gaze returned to Jamie and their eyes engaged again, Jamie froze, every muscle unconsciously commanded to stillness. Just one lithe movement brought Shoo Juh to Jamie's side; her left hand petted Jamie's jaw as her other hand deftly positioned the bottle at Jamie's lips.

Her own lips nestled into Jamie's hair. She cajoled in a near whisper, "Here, it's cold. Drink."

Splendidly chilled, the water trickled out of Jamie's mouth and down her neck. She couldn't swallow it. Shoo Juh's fingers, still gentle, played suggestively, electrically along Jamie's jaw from her chin to her ear.

No...please... But Shoo Juh's fingers slithered onto Jamie's neck and menaced her head back, igniting a thin, irresistible flame under her skin. The flame snaked from her throat into her chest, into her belly, and seared her tense, pulsing clit before it coiled deep into the adamant need for punishment that Shoo Juh had discovered and cultivated with such skill, the need Jamie hated and couldn't escape—not now, maybe not ever. Legs quaking, pelvis heaving, Jamie squirmed in her helplessness; one more time, the interrogator had taken everything.

Shoo Juh laughed softly, the heat of her breath alarming the nerves around Jamie's right ear. "Relax, hong mao. There will be no questions for you today."

The water bottle returned to Jamie's mouth; Shoo Juh's body undulated along Jamie's manacled right arm and shuddering shoulder. Somehow able to believe the interrogator's words, Jamie swallowed once, again. Then, without warning, Shoo Juh grabbed the manacles and yanked ferociously.

The momentum shoved Jamie off the stool and onto her knees, and then she was dangling. Shoo Juh's practiced hands had attached a rope to the manacles and pulled. A rope Jamie didn't see, so rattled was she by this woman's gaze, this woman's power over her. A rope that must already have been tied to some hook in the ceiling, which Jamie also didn't see because all she could see was this woman's looming threat.

"What?"

Arms jacked up behind her, feet barely reaching the floor, the cruel fire stinging her, burning her, writhing her, Jamie squinched away any sound of complaint and contorted toward Shoo Juh's coldly fascinated eyes. "What...do...you...want?"

"Startling, isn't it, how pleasure merges into pain and pain into pleasure," Shoo Juh said, transfixed, her eyes gulping in the sight before her. "Like truth and beauty."

Jamie's *NO!* exploded into a shriek. *"What do you want?"*

Then she was thrashing on the end of the rope, wrenching her arms mindlessly, kicking, swinging. Anything to provoke her pain to hurry, hurry and overwhelm all other sensation—anything to keep Shoo Juh from lowering the blackness over her, from inciting it to burst into a spray of blood.

"WHAT DO YOU WANT?" Jamie screamed it, wailed it over and over. Shoo Juh stepped away from her flailing legs and watched her for a few minutes with untroubled detachment, like a scientist observing a lab rat. Then, evincing a minute frown, Shoo Juh released the rope and she hit the floor head first with a vicious, silencing thud.

Staring up at Shoo Juh, she wheezed her question yet again. "What...do you want?"

Shoo Juh came nearer, an expression remarkably like regret on her face. Jamie tried in vain to wriggle away from her.

"I want to say good-bye." She sighed, seizing Jamie's shoulders and lifting with improbable strength until Jamie sat on the stool.

Breathing heavily, bleeding from her forehead, Jamie doubled over. Her head, her throat, her shoulders, her arms, her wrists, her hands, her genitals burned and throbbed. She wept without sound, debilitated into numbness. Into defeat.

How long did the interrogator ponder this sight? Jamie didn't know; Jamie was no longer witness to anything. Eventually, Shoo Juh leaned over her and kissed her neck with audacious sensuality while unlocking and removing the manacles.

Moaning at her release, Jamie cradled herself tightly, fetally, rocking back and forth on the stool. Shoo Juh kissed her again and then sat facing her on the second stool. "The PIA will be arriving in ten days to take over this facility."

What? What did she say?

"The PIA?" Jamie raised her head to look at her tormenter.

"Yes." The interrogator's eyes, patient now, probed Jamie's face for comprehension. "And as far as they're concerned, all of you are hostages. Including your senator."

Jamie sat suddenly erect, alert, awash in adrenaline. "And the PIA generally kill their hostages."

"Yes, they do." Shoo Juh stood, called in the guards, and ordered them to escort the hong mao to the Red Cross office for medical aid.

CHAPTER TWENTY-FIVE

WHETHER TO LAUGH OR CRY

O w!"
"Sorry." Leonard, the Red Cross physician, placed a sympathetic hand on Jamie's shoulder. "But we don't want this to get infected."

Restless for him to finish, Jamie squiggled on the stretcher that served as an examination table while he irrigated the gouge in her forehead. She was only now beginning to be able to think again. *If the PIA are coming, we're in big trouble. If. If. How big an If?*

A few feet away, Senator Hillinger had propped herself against a table like it was the only thing holding her up. "Lieutenant, you look like a sodden six-year-old. God, I don't know whether to laugh or cry."

Jamie smiled; she liked the way that sounded.

"I'm sorry." The senator looked distinctly penitent. "I should've— But I might've made it worse—I just—I didn't know what to do." Clearly she was someone who found indecision unsettling, someone who probably couldn't remember the last time an analysis of all the alternatives, even with just seconds to run through them, hadn't produced a clearly preferable choice, an actionable item. But not this time.

"Yeah, well, it's usually like that with Shoo Juh."

"Who?"

"The Zhong special chief interrogator. She's, uh…"

"Responsible for your present condition." The frowning senator pushed herself away from the table while Leonard dabbed Jamie's wound.

"No doubt the official Zhong version will deny that, ma'am."

"How about the unofficial version? What happened?"

Leonard now closed in with a small brown bottle. "Iodine," he said. "This'll sting some." Sting it did. But soon he was affixing a bandage.

"What happened?" Senator Hillinger pressed.

Jamie gazed resolutely at her—*Not yet*—and got a nod in return. She and Leonard exchanged a brief look, and Jamie sensed beneath their pretense of normalcy an edgy but thus far frustrated quest for a way to end their predicament.

Now catapulted out of numbness, Jamie bounced from question to question. *Does that electric fan over there near the door have a higher speed that'd be loud enough to mask our voices? What'd give us hints one way or the other about whether Shoo Juh lied or told the truth? Jeez, do physicians ever use paperclips?*

Jamie turned to Leonard. "I can't leave yet." Her words were mouthed more than spoken. "I need you to pretend to keep treating me."

The doctor didn't skip a beat. "Well now, Lieutenant," he said rather loudly, "I don't like the look of *this* one bit. I'm going to run a quick test." He picked up a mouth swab and a skinny, three-inch-wide white rectangle. "Open sesame." In seconds, his deft hands had swept the swab across the inside of Jamie's cheek and inserted it into the rectangle. "Stick around. We'll have results in ten or twenty minutes."

"Yes, sir." Jamie lifted off the stretcher and hoped she appeared casual as she walked over to the fan. "Do you mind if I cool off some while I wait?"

The senator understood first. "Good idea," she said and stepped next to Jamie to boost the fan's speed.

Starved for lubricating oil, the fan emitted a metallic screech and clanked erratically. Jamie removed her cammie blouse, stood in her soaked T-shirt in front of it. "Much better. Thank you, ma'am." She turned around so the fan blew at her back and she faced Leonard. "Sir," she whispered, "can you check outside real offhandedly and tell me how close the guards are?"

Leonard obliged, adroitly moving his slight runner's frame to the door. Seconds later, he reported in a hush, "They're on the other side of the yard trying to stay dry. Closest one is at least eighty, a hundred feet away. Want me to stay here and keep watch?"

"Yes, sir. Thanks."

He was close enough that he, too, could hear Jamie's murmured account of what Shoo Juh said, Jamie's comment that she was inclined to believe it but wanted some sort of confirmation, since she couldn't fathom the interrogator's motives. She did not need to explain what the arrival of the PIA meant. Everyone knew the fate of those unfortunate enough to become PIA hostages. For a long moment, the two civilians stood in frozen silence, their faces tense.

"Any chance this interrogator comes from southern China?" Senator Hillinger finally asked.

"She could," said Jamie. "Hong Kong maybe. She speaks Cantonese. And the King's English."

"Damn." A new frown formed on the senator's face. "This is mutating much faster than I expected. We're in a four-way fight now. With four-way brinksmanship."

Jamie was confused. "*Four*-way?"

"Two sides—us and the Chinese." Senator Hillinger squinted at the floor as if she could find a secret there to be deciphered. "And two factions on each side. On both sides, one faction wants to keep fighting, the other wants a truce. And on both sides, neither faction quite has the upper hand." Her eyes rose to find Jamie's. "What's scary is that the center of gravity is probably shifting. And, covertly, some of the players are realigning. It's a fair guess that the factions on each side with a stake in continuing the conflict have opened a new back channel or two. And the factions on each side that want a truce—"

"You're not suggesting Shoo Juh wants a truce?"

"Maybe she does. *If* she told you the truth."

Jamie thought a mindfuck was likelier. Certainly it felt like a mindfuck. *How could that woman ever want anything I want?* The next thought made Jamie lightheaded. *What if Shoo Juh did all that to me so she could offer up intel to help persuade her side toward truce?*

"It doesn't matter," Jamie said as much to herself as anyone. *What matters is the PIA. We need to know if they're really coming.* Maybe these civilians could help find out one way or the other. After all, they weren't quite prisoners. Not yet. And what they were and were not capable of might determine the future of everyone in Saint Eh Mo's. *Okay.* Not a lot left to lose anymore. *So okay.* "Where're they housing you?" she asked them.

"In the officers' quarters," Senator Hillinger said. "Access is across the yard from the interrogation area."

"Can you move between here and there at will, no questions?"

"So far," said Leonard.

"Hmm. I'd like to try a small experiment," Jamie said. "It entails one of you going over to your quarters to get something you need to bring back here. While you're there, stall a little, check out everything you can without being obvious. Look for any signs of people leaving or getting ready to leave. You know, gear getting packed or already gone. Like that."

"I'll go," Leonard said. "I get less attention than you do, Senator. And I need more iodine anyway. Besides, it's my turn to get wet."

"And, sir, if you spot a paperclip along the way and can grab it without being seen…"

Leonard's eyebrows hiked before he winked comprehension. "Ah. Interesting hobby, Lieutenant. I'll see what I can do."

"Don't push it, sir," Jamie said. "They'll be watching you."

The doctor shuffled around for a second, then boomed, "Excuse me for a few minutes. I need to get some more iodine," and departed.

Next to Jamie, Senator Hillinger sighed. "God, I'm such a damn fool. I've been trying for these last two days not to feel like a prisoner, but that's exactly what it amounts to. So much for being part of the solution. I really thought I could make a difference."

"You did, ma'am. Make a difference, I mean."

Senator Hillinger lowered her shaking head, and Jamie thought maybe she trembled. "Talk about being outflanked. We haven't been able to contact anyone—not the Red Cross people, not anyone in our government or our families—since just before the Chinese recessed the talks." Her shoulders hunched. "We keep trying and they keep telling us it's just a communications glitch and it'll be fixed jin chee, jin chee. I guess I've wanted to believe that. Figured it was probably just as well that I couldn't get through to Rebecca and the girls for a few days. What would I say, anyway?" She glanced up at Jamie. "How would I have explained it to them? I acted on impulse, I admit it. I knew there were risks to staying on here instead of leaving with the others, but I saw the chance for a game-changer and jumped without asking them or even telling them. I thought if I—" She grabbed fistfuls of her own hair and growled her frustration through gritted teeth. "God, I don't even know anymore what I thought. Except I sure as hell thought wrong."

"For what it's worth, you *have* made a difference, ma'am. At least for all of us here." Jamie wanted to scoop up Lynn Hillinger, hold her, hug her, thank her. "Especially me. I think you're the reason Shoo Juh had to stop. I don't think I had much time left…"

Lynn Hillinger curled her hands into her pants pockets and turned her head to look up at Jamie. For a moment she said nothing while she looked, and Jamie wondered what she was trying to see.

"Why did you become a marine, Lieutenant?"

Jamie snorted. "Seemed like a good idea at the time."

Senator Hillinger nodded with a wry, I-know-the-feeling pucker. "ROTC? Finish college early?"

"No, ma'am. No college," Jamie inspected a small rip in her pant leg. "Didn't even finish high school."

"Really?"

"Boarded the bus for Parris Island the day after I turned seventeen," Jamie said. "Turned out to be a good marksman, so they sent me to Scout/Sniper School. And then here, to the Palawan."

"And how'd you end up—?"

"Oh, the black bar? A demented major general. Combat appointment from staff sergeant right smack to one-lite." Jamie was able to stiffly snap the fingers of one hand and smiled grimly at the victory. "Just like that. Still haven't recovered."

"Ben Embry, right?" Senator Hillinger's handsome face carried sign of recognition. "Sounds like something he's nervy enough to do."

"Yes, ma'am." *Small world up there at the top of the food chain, I guess.* "You know him?"

"Oh, indeed. Ben and I go way back." A pause. "Your family must be proud."

Jamie's head dropped. "No, ma'am. No family. Not anymore."

"None, Lieutenant? None at all?"

"Not a single living soul."

"So how long were you in foster care?"

"Uh…" Jamie began, then stopped because her breathing had become unsteady. No one had ever asked her real details about where she'd come from. Not even Marty Rhys ever did that. Not even Marty Rhys wanted to look inside her. "I, uh…foster care was fifty-five weeks.

Before that, there was only ever my mother. Died when I was fifteen. Trying to get some smack, best I can figure."

Senator Hillinger nodded slowly, telling her to go on.

"Foster care was…It was, uh…Got raped once by the husband. My own damn fault in a way. I knew he wanted to do it. But I didn't realize how much, you know? He waited for me to make a mistake, and I did finally. Thought he'd left the house, but he hadn't, he was waiting. And, uh, he jumped me."

The memory flooded in. Bob Baines's hand squeezing her throat… his fist pounding on the side of her head…her powerlessness as her own hands couldn't break his grip. "After he did that, I-I came so close to—"

There had been a moment—while she anguished for air, while she thought he'd murder her as well as rape her—when she was terrified. Afterward, moment by moment, day by day, the terror evolved into a single obsession: Kill Bob Baines.

She planned everything—when to sneak up on him, how to get away, where to go. There he was in her mind's eye, waking thrashing and helpless as she thrust one of his own kitchen knives down again and again to rip him open, the inverse of his thrusts into her.

This, Jamie had told herself, only this, would free her from the void engulfing her. And once he was dead, maybe she'd be able to sleep again. She got as close as standing over his loudly snoring form late one night with a ten-inch blade clutched in her hands, raised high and ready to plunge. She gazed at him, then at the knife, and for the first time imagined all the blood. His blood.

That was when she understood with absolute certainty that she wouldn't get away with it. She'd spend her life as property of the Commonwealth of Massachusetts in Day-Glo orange convict scrubs, locked away in a five- by seven-foot cage, drowning in the raucous desolation of imprisonment. Worse than those thirteen endless days and nights she'd endured in the county jail after she stole that car and drove it to the bluff overlooking Provincetown where Alby crashed and died. Worse because they'd never let her out. Except maybe to strap her to a gurney, force her to watch the fatal pharma flow down the tubes and into her, paralyzing her lungs, then her heart while she struggled in vain to live.

Standing over Bob Baines, knife raised high, she answered the question before her—*Is this prick worth that?*—by returning the unused knife to its drawer in the kitchen.

Jamie shook off the memory; her voice shrank to a whisper. "Joined the Corps soon as I could so I wouldn't change my mind and go through with it, you know? Now I kill strangers instead." Jamie looked down, rolled her shoulders to slough off the taunt of irony. "Get raped by strangers instead, too."

That's when Senator Hillinger reached across the small distance to anoint Jamie's cheek with a tenderness Jamie had longed for all her life.

Jamie tilted her head dreamily, instinctively into the touch, into its compassion. Tears filled her eyes. She didn't look away, not even when Senator Hillinger stepped up to her and delicately embraced her. Her breath caught, but after a moment she let her hesitant hands wrap around the senator's back, and their embrace strengthened.

Never before had Jamie experienced anything like this. Something loosened in her gut, a stranglehold released. Her breath escaped. It was almost a moan, and the force of it would have frightened her but for the way everything glowed, the way this woman's touch succored and strengthened her even while it invited her surrender. Jamie closed her eyes, submitted, and the feeling filled her, trembled her.

Senator Hillinger must have understood because she didn't let go. Jamie clung to her and tried, tried not to cry.

"Thank you, ma'am, for asking," Jamie mumbled at last, her words muffled in the delicate balm of the senator's shoulder, her tremble ebbing slowly. "A-And for listening."

Senator Hillinger relinquished the embrace to cradle Jamie's face in her hands and peer up intently into Jamie's eyes. "Can I ask a favor, Lieutenant?"

"Anything, ma'am," Jamie said, her back straightening, the marine in her returning to duty. "Anything."

"I'd like you to call me Lynn. Can you do that?"

"Oh." Jamie felt her eyes widen. "Y-Yes, I can do that. And you call me Jamie, okay?"

It seemed to Jamie that Lynn Hillinger's smile lit the room. "I'd like that very much, Jamie."

And right then Leonard entered the small office, the color drained from his rain-soaked face.

"What?" asked Jamie and Lynn simultaneously.

"I think they're going," he whispered breathlessly, winded from tension rather than effort. "I heard one guy saying beh-un lay-ee. I know that means something like 'home fort' and I got peeks of duffels getting packed. One room's already vacated. They didn't really seem to care what I might pick up on. Nobody got pissy. Nobody ordered me away. It's like they don't have any explicit instructions about us—what to let us see and hear, or not see and hear."

Leonard pulled in a long breath, then blew it out before he said loudly, "Okay, Lieutenant, let's check your test results. Come take a look at the readout. Stand right here so you can see for yourself." He put a hand on her back and let it slip around her waist, where it lingered a bit too long. "Ah. See that? Good news." He stared at her left-hand pants pocket. "Results are normal."

"Thank you, sir." *Could it be?* Jamie buried her hands in her pockets and suddenly shivered from the adrenaline coursing through her, from the new sense of possibility. In her left pocket were two large-size paperclips. She grinned, then asked Leonard in a whisper, "Think you would've noticed what they're doing if I hadn't asked you to look for it?"

"No, probably not. Not yet. But I sure as hell would've noticed that the other two people on our team have left."

"What?" Lynn said, her fear betrayed by the ascending pitch of her whisper. "That wasn't the deal. We're supposed to stick together. Are you sure? Their stuff was here this morning. It was here this morning when they left to go into Malihud center to do the clinic again."

"Well," Leonard said, "it sure as hell is all packed up and gone now."

SOPHIA KELL HAGIN

CHAPTER TWENTY-SIX

I'M SORRY IT HAS TO BE LIKE THIS

The staccato of automatic weapons fire coming from the
administration wing courtyard—and maybe North Carolina
screaming that the Zhong had shot Lieutenant Gwynmorgan—changed
everything. When Jamie reported on her "meeting" with Shoo Juh,
there was no discussion, only Donato's announcement that everyone,
including the two civilians, should vote on what to do. Pretending a
stomach ailment, Donato himself took the news to the Red Cross office
and returned with their votes.

The decision was unanimous: Escape. It was up to the three
officers—Donato, Jamie, and an Annapolis two-lite distantly related to
and named after William Tecumseh Sherman—to figure out how.

Jamie suggested exploiting the freedom granted Hillinger and
Leonard to track the Chinese force reduction. "We move when most of
the Zhong've split. Take down the last bunch fast and quiet, then use
their food and weapons to get the hell out of here before the PIA show
up."

"And use their transport," Sherman said.

"Well," Jamie replied, "sort of." Thus began surreptitious hours of
debate about the best way to get back to friendly territory.

Sherman favored a straight northeast run some sixty kilometers up
the coast past Brooke's Point to Caramay Bay. "We've held that area
since early February. We can stay on the back roads at the edge of the
foothills, away from the coastal village centers. If we can commandeer
even one moderate-size truck, we can all ride most of the way."

"I figure the back roads you want to use are exactly where the

Zhong'll look for us," Jamie countered. "Besides, Vargas and a couple of the Filipinos say the Zhong have been crawling all over the roads above Brooke's Point for months because they don't want to relinquish the nickel mines in that area."

"So what do *you* suggest?" retorted Sherman.

"We know our people took Eran Bay on the north coast in early March and that we've controlled the interior all the way to Gantung since April. So I suggest we send a small team going northeast on those back roads you talked about—as a diversion. We have them leave enough bread crumbs along the way to get the enemy to chase them. The rest of us head north into the mountains and make for Gantung."

Safety was only fifty klicks away—if they could've flown. It was a lot more on foot. Still, with a decent head start, they'd be much harder to follow over the mountain route. And much harder to catch. Jamie laid out details.

"But two weeks?" Sherman said, scowling his contempt.

Jamie scowled right back at him. She'd wondered why he'd never talked to her much; now she guessed that Second Lieutenant Sherman resented coyotes. He was a big guy who used his size to intimidate whenever he could get away with it, but he retreated under her withering stare, finishing his question with overblown formality. "Uh, ma'am."

She kept on staring at him until he looked away from her. For the first time since becoming an officer, Jamie *wanted* someone to call her ma'am.

"Two weeks is worst-case," Jamie said to Donato, the person who'd make the decision about what they'd do. "The good news is we can use existing paths most of the way. That'll keep down the macheteing. I know some of the Tau't Batu caves and a few of their shortcuts. Plus we might find some supplies in one of the caves near Mantalingajan. *If* we average about eight klicks a day, *if* we can contact our people and they meet us part way, *if* nothing fucks up when they come for us, then we could be safe in a FOB in as little as four or five days. But—"

Sherman shifted his legs impatiently, his thoughts plain: A keyboard major and some damn poser.

"You got a problem, Lieutenant?" Jamie growled.

"No." Sherman crossed his arms over his chest. "Ma'am."

Jamie returned her attention to the major. "Sir, in my admittedly limited experience, planning a mission in which success depends on nothing going wrong is sure as hell the best way to guarantee that plenty will go wrong."

Donato grunted assent and Jamie continued. "Our biggest problem, besides being physically weaker than normal, is visibility. We have to assume our cammies are compromised."

Sherman fidgeted again, briefly, and Jamie knew he thought she was paranoid. Staring at him yet again, she resisted an urge to confront him, to demand he tell her how much time *he* spent with Shoo Juh.

"Even if we're out there buck naked, they'll be able to spot us with just about any of their surveillance scanners," Jamie said. "So we can hump only when the weather screws up surveillance technology, particularly infrared. At lower elevations, that means rain—the heavier the better. But heavy rain creates the worst possible conditions for the kind of foot travel we need to do. The habagat is our very treacherous best friend."

She leaned toward the major, who, she suspected, believed he'd die escaping and would have voted to risk staying—had he voted first. He voted last, however, and had the courage to make the prisoners' decision a true concord. It couldn't have been easy for him.

"It'll be slow and dangerous going, interspersed with stretches when we have to get underground—literally—because we don't have rain or fog or sufficiently high air temperatures to obscure our bodies' heat signatures. Like I said, we *might* do it in four or five days. But there may be no supplies on Mantalingajan. Somebody—like our forty-five-year-old senator—may get hurt or be weaker than we expect. There may be landslides, flooding. We may have to lay low because there are PIA all over the mountains. So we have to be prepared for it to take longer. And we've got too many people to be able to live off the land. We can pick up water as we go, but we need to bring as much food as we can scrounge. Because we damn well are not going to lose *anyone*."

Thirty-two people. Get all of them out alive and intact. Get all of them back alive and intact. Donato opted for Jamie's plan and put her in charge of leading the mission, beginning with the escape from Saint Eh Mo's.

Thirty-two people, all assigned to teams, each team assigned a responsibility. The push team would handle weapons and supplies for the journey, making sure everyone had what they'd need. The civvie team would help and protect the senator and the doctor and double as the medical team. The diversion team would journey northeast up the coast. The scout team would lead the way, the perimeter team would protect their flanks, and the cover team would do everything possible to disguise their trail.

Thirty-two people clandestinely coalesced, prepared, and waited for the best moment to make their move. If Shoo Juh told the truth, they had nine days before they'd become PIA hostages. It was a big if.

❖

"We need the moonlight," Jamie argued when Sherman railed about waiting too long. "And on June eighteen, the moon'll be highest between midnight and zero-four-hundred. So we go after lockdown on the seventeenth."

That the sky remained only partly cloudy when the sun set around 1830 hours was a bonus. By 1930, Jamie had raked open all the locks in the church building and teams were stealthing into the yard's blindspots. By 2040, the tower, the administration yard, and the room the Red Cross team used as its medical office—with Hillinger and Leonard in it—had been secured.

At 2120, Saint Eh Mo's had been taken by its prisoners—no alarm raised, no shots fired, none of the few remaining Zhong able to escape. And no time to waste.

❖

"Bring him in here," Jamie said.

She stood outside the same interrogation chamber where she had last seen Shoo Juh. The commandant, the special chief interrogator, and the Bastard were all, of course, long gone. The gagged and blindfolded Zhong commander that Sherman and two of the larger POWs dragged through the doorway was only a junior officer.

Jamie followed them in and was about to close the door when Lynn appeared. "What are you doing?"

"I'm sorry it has to be like this," Jamie said, using her body to block any view of the room and inch Lynn out of the doorway. "We need to know some things. We've got an officer who can tell us and not much time to persuade him."

"Jamie, what are you going to do?"

"Whatever it takes." Jamie's hands beseeched. "I'm sorry."

Lynn stared at Jamie's hands, apparently stilled by the sight of the wounds in the center of each of Jamie's palms. She pulled her eyes from Jamie's hands and glanced toward the interrogation chamber, a sense of recognition evident on her grimacing features.

Yeah, Lynn, they might've done it to me right in there. Maybe. I can't remember. "I'm sorry," Jamie said again. "I don't know what else to do. So far, this has been too easy. Like they want us to make the moves we're making. We've got to learn all we can about what they're up to. If we don't get this right, we'll be killed way before we reach our own people."

Lynn blinked, then gulped. After a second or two, she nodded, her face betraying that her sense of control over her world had slipped from her grasp. "Yes, Lieutenant, I understand." And then she walked away.

Jamie watched Lynn's departing back and swallowed the sob that cramped her throat. "I'm sorry," she whispered too softly for Lynn to hear, her fingers brushing her cheek where Lynn had touched her.

One touch would have to be enough—because certainly Lynn's corrosive disappointment in her would turn to disgust, loathing, repudiation. But Jamie knew Lynn Hillinger would live long enough to despise her only if the right information could be extracted quickly from the Chinese officer waiting in the room behind her.

God help me, I'll torture him if I have to. I'll kill him if I have to.

❖

The Chinese officer turned out to be a man of conviction. Among his unshakable beliefs: The world's most dangerous wild beast is an unleashed hong mao.

Lieutenant Sherman unwittingly played the role to perfection, even landing a couple of punches before being restrained. Once the Chinese officer appreciated that cooperating could save him from the savage hong mao, his interrogation was over in twenty minutes.

In addition to a few rifles, pistols, and machetes, he delivered up a pair of infrared eyewraps and a multiwave scanner—both passive, both with tracking chips that Donato speedily figured out how to remove. The Chinese officer also divulged that the POWs' boots were clean but their uniforms were compromised, just as Jamie suspected. His scanner confirmed it: Not only had their uniforms' detection countermeasures been neutralized, the hems of their pant legs had been embedded with enemy nanoscale tracking devices.

After Sherman's second punch, they learned about a good-sized, fully fueled truck—transport that would get the diversion team well up the coast by morning. And the Zhong officer told them about a small trove of plastic explosive and detonators intended for the PIA; they'd put these to good use, too.

Maybe there was even more to get. Sherman thought so.

"What about when the PIA're coming?" he yelled. "From where. What about stuff that son of a bitch in there can tell us about Zhong units—"

"Asked and answered. We go north as planned, into the mountains," Jamie said, her voice low. "You are dismissed, Lieutenant Sherman."

"But—"

"You don't have much time, Lieutenant. Move."

Sherman knew explosives, and soon he'd placed claylike C-Six in several spots around the base. He also rigged up the truck, which would transport them all to the banks of the Malihud River where it descended out of the foothills. After driving it toward Brooke's Point for another fifteen kilometers or so, four Filipino volunteers would blow it up, then head north on foot toward Mount Mantalingajan to rendezvous with the main group.

By 2250 hours, the Zhong prisoners had been stripped naked, gagged, hogtied, and locked in the church cells. Saint Eh Mo's commo systems had been disabled, the bottom couple of inches were cut off the marines' trouser legs, weapons and what food they could find were packed up, and all thirty-two veterans of Saint Eh Mo's had begun piling into the truck.

As they drove away, Jamie noted the time on the Chinese officer's scanner: 2309. By 2352, twenty-seven people were following Jamie into the foothills above the Malihud River.

Almost immediately, Jamie found herself battling one surge of panic after another. What she felt so sure of back in Saint Eh Mo's—the near-eidetic recollection of Operation Repo topographical maps, the knowledge of which paths through the forest would take them to their own people—now wavered and dimmed in the dense blackness ahead of her.

She'd been counting on her recall to get twenty-seven souls well into the high forest on this first night. To build enough of a lead that by the time the Zhong focused radar and infrared detectors in their direction, they'd be invisible, hidden under thick forest canopy or tucked into a cave.

And, she now realized, she'd been counting too much on the moon. The cloud cover had thickened; when fits of rain interrupted the ashen moonlight, so little ambient light remained that the Chinese officer's passive infrared eyewraps didn't help much.

Nor did Jamie dare illuminate the path onto which she'd led these people—the path she thought, she hoped was the right one. The one she was supposed to have taken last November sixth. She moved slowly, too slowly, feeling her way, careful to keep the meager lights of Malihud behind her, clenching the muscles in her gut to stop her hyperventilating. *Oh god oh god, it's so frigging dark.*

You just keep on going, Alonzo told her once. Each tenuous step became a supplication to the deities of light and bodily equilibrium and rhumb lines. *Please*, Jamie beseeched them. *Please...Please...*

Later—somewhere between 0100 and 0200 hours—the moon emerged from a larger break in the clouds, casting a silvery glow into the forest's shadows. It was enough that they could pick up their pace. Enough to resurrect Jamie's hope.

They climbed to an elevation of close to eight hundred meters before early hints of light on the eastern horizon forced them to shelter in a large cave southwest of Mount Maliz.

It wasn't the cave Jamie wanted them to reach. By her reckoning, they'd traveled only six kilometers. But dawn was less than an hour away and they were all exhausted.

If their escape hadn't been discovered yet, the explosives Sherman laid around Saint Eh Mo's would detonate any time now. Would she hear them? Jamie lingered near the cave entrance, listening. Sherman joined her a few seconds before the barely audible sounds of explosion rumbled toward them from the south.

"Yes!" His malevolent grin reminded her of the Bastard, even though she had no memory of the Bastard's face.

"Got the watches set up, everybody good and dark?" Jamie asked, trying not to think about the people in Saint Eh Mo's. She'd ordered the church building full of Zhong prisoners spared, but the explosions nearby probably damaged it. *Them or us. Them or us.*

"Yes, ma'am. All squared away. Pricks won't see us."

"Excellent. Go get some chow, Lieutenant."

"Ma'am," he acknowledged crisply.

"And Sherman," Jamie said, "make sure you get some rack time, too. We're gonna use this afternoon's rain to make Mount Mantalingajan, come hell or high water. So to speak."

He nodded. "Yes, ma'am." But his face refused to disguise his skepticism about her forecasting skills.

Jamie watched him walk away, wishing he didn't require so much energy. She shook her head to cast off the weight of his animosity, to ease the discomfort that had been part of every waking moment for seven months and now escalated too quickly into pain—a sign that she, too, needed rest.

Rotating her shoulder blades, she forestalled a fatigue she could almost taste. *Not yet.* As mission commander, first she must make sure these twenty-seven souls were secure. It would take a while.

She exhaled. *Well, Corporal Gwynmorgan, not dead yet.* The odds were still against them, but a bit less so. After this night, just a bit less so.

Nearly an hour passed before Jamie finally had a chance to whisper to North Carolina, "How's she doing?" A few meters away, half under mosquito netting, Lynn Hillinger cautiously experimented with a hammock.

North Carolina nodded. "Okay, LT. Holding her own. She's pretty strong for a civvie."

"Good. You keep her that way, Doc. We've got a long way to go." Jamie gave the corpsman a slow nod, reminder of her special assignment, the most important job of all: Get the senator back safe to our people.

North Carolina answered Jamie's nod by straightening almost to attention. "Yes, ma'am!"

"And what about you, North Carolina?" Jamie asked.

"I'm good. Feels fi-*ine* to be able to really move around again." North Carolina inspected Jamie in that way only corpsmen get away with. "C'mon, LT ma'am, I got some chow for you over here. And I set up your hammock right next to me and the senator."

"Yeah? Thanks, North Carolina."

Jamie glanced over at Lynn, now perched precariously in the center of the hammock, clutching its edges. Amazed that Lynn would allow her hammock to be placed so close to a torturer's, Jamie approached hesitantly, ready to retreat if Lynn's eyes, Lynn's demeanor revealed repugnance or discomfiture or even just too much politeness.

"Don't tell me you've never been in a hammock before."

Lynn looked up, gauzy under the mosquito netting, and shook her head. "Uh-uh, not this kind. Sort of wiggly, aren't they?"

Hmm, that seems okay. Jamie slipped under the netting of a neighboring hammock and sat in it. "It's more stable than you think. Try lying back like this—"

Lynn complied, lumping into the middle of the hammock.

"That's it. Now straighten out and shift your legs slightly left—good—and shift your shoulders slightly right. See how you're angled just a little off-center and can lie pretty much flat?"

Lynn beamed enthusiastically. "I think I've got it!" Whereupon she spun horizontally—"Oh!"—right out of the hammock. Jamie whirled to slide underneath her just in time to catch her before she hit the ground.

"Generally," Jamie deadpanned, "we do that feet first." She wondered if the woman wrapped in her arms could sense her pounding pulse, her desire to not let go.

"Yeah," Lynn said, an appreciative grin creasing fine-chiseled features only inches from Jamie's face. "I can certainly see why."

Lynn's look, Lynn's words, Lynn's touch felt like forgiveness.

Chapter Twenty-seven

A real chance

Nobody slept much or for long.
They were all uneasy—worried that they'd been tracked, worried that every passing minute brought the enemy closer. Jamie urged them to rest, reminded them that the Chinese officer's scanner showed nothing, that they heard no helos. "We wait 'til the heat and humidity crank up enough," Jamie said. "We need the habagat, people. So sit tight."

As the cave filled with stifled foreboding, Sherman lost it. "What if there's no rain today at all?" Angry and too loud, he was only marginally in control himself. "We should go *now*, dammit!"

Jamie looked at him, incredulous at first, then with concern. He wasn't an insubordinate kind of guy, not even to a coyote one-lite, and certainly not to any kind of major. But he'd disobeyed orders when he punched the Chinese officer, and now his loss of control threatened the group's cohesion.

"Sit the fuck down, Sherman," Donato said, "and shut the fuck up."

Sherman complied, staring forlornly at the cave floor.

"On me, Lieutenant," Jamie murmured to him after a few minutes, then turned away from the others toward the darker recesses of the cave, where the bats lived. Sherman followed, his eyes hopping skittishly over the rough rock that arced above them.

"How many missions did you complete in the Palawan before you were captured, Mr. Sherman?"

He stood several inches taller and was at least forty pounds heavier than Jamie, who belligerently shoved her face upward into his. He leaned back, away from her, but his defiant jaw jutted, his eyes dared her, his huge hands formed fists.

Jamie stepped even closer, glaring up at him an inch from his nose. "I asked you a question, Lieutenant!"

For a long moment, he glared back.

Jamie didn't move, and finally he stepped away. His shoulders curled and his eyes fell. "I-I haven't completed any missions here. Got grabbed the first time out."

"Well, Mr. Sherman, I've been here for almost two years. More than fifteen months of that in combat. Don't know how many missions. Lost count a long fucking time ago. But there's one thing I have counted with great care: *Nobody* I've been responsible for has been toasted. Nobody. And I'm not about to start letting it happen now because you get claustrophobic. So you get your fucking Annapolis act together right the fuck now and do what I goddamn tell you when I goddamn tell you. No more, no less. If you do not, mister, you will be the first person I lose, because I will blow your fucking brains out myself."

Sherman gaped at her.

"Do you read me, Lieutenant Sherman?" Jamie said, a band of heat clamping around her head. She stared at him hard. *If you even breathe any of your shit at me, I will take you out right now, you fucker.* She moved her hand to the Chinese officer's pistol strapped to her belt.

"Yes, ma'am."

"Yes ma'am the fuck *what*?" Jamie spit.

Sherman blinked and brought himself to attention, his eyes focused straight ahead. "Yes, ma'am, I read the lieutenant loud and clear, ma'am!"

Jamie stepped back. "Good. You're dismissed, Lieutenant Sherman."

Just as Jamie returned from the back of the cave, a light rain began. She looked at the noonday sky to find it filling fast with ominously dark clouds. Very soon, the rain would be a downpour.

"Okay, people, gather it up," she called out. "We move in ten."

By Jamie's reckoning, the cave just south of Mount Mantalingajan where months ago Marty Rhys had left supplies stood about nine hundred meters higher and seven klicks away. Getting there meant skirting three mountains, each requiring an arduous uphill climb followed by a knee-wrecking descent.

Their path continued to retrace the one Jamie had taken the previous autumn during Operation Repo. Soon they moved along a much narrower, far more rugged track than the previous night's more traveled trail. Barely visible to an inexperienced eye, it was entirely invisible from above without the ground-penetrating radar now hindered by wet ground.

As she led the way, Jamie had plenty to worry about. Thermal detectors would spot them unless they stayed under heavy vegetation. In anything but rainy weather, they were easily detectable with lookdown infrared and radar surveillance systems. Enemy satellites and maybe aircraft, too, might already be searching for their anomalously large group.

But splitting up was not an option. So they needed the rain.

Would it continue long enough for them to get all the way to Mount Mantalingajan? Would it become so torrential that it completely washed out the steep ravine-side paths or the exquisitely woven Tau't Batu ladders and bridges they'd be relying on? Would somebody slip and fall, maybe even tumble dozens of meters into oblivion? Had the diversion team—four immensely courageous Filipinos wearing Chinese Army uniforms—gotten away? Or would they be grabbed and coerced into revealing which way the Saint Eh Mo's escapees went? Were the supplies Marty deposited still there? Had Avery needed them? Or were they already claimed by the Tau't Batu family that occupied the cave during the habagat?

Jamie's past echoed, and she actually heard her mother's voice, tinny and distant. "From too much love of living, from hope and fear set free..." Always the same apology by poetry for the debacle du jour. *Because you could never set yourself free, could you, Alby? Is this what you'd do? Get seduced by the hope, then drown in wave after wave of fear?*

Once, after a particularly degrading episode, Alby had gone to an AA meeting, and now Jamie recalled the well-known motto—one day at a time—which her mother had managed to live by for maybe a week. *One hope at a time. One fear at a time.*

One step at a time. Times twenty-seven people. *Better make damn sure they're stepping fast enough.*

The three people on her scout team were, thank god, experienced snipes. Trained to be ghosts who moved through the terrain leaving no sign that they'd been there. Trained to find their way with nothing more than a primitive map and a compass. Jamie had laid out for them the paths to the Mantalingajan cave, and at the first high point in the day's trek, she showed the ghosts the crook in the profile of the second mountain rising up ahead—a mere hint of a shadow visible for just seconds between billows of fog—and ordered them to take the lead in getting there.

During the afternoon, for a while at least, Jamie decided to fall back and push from behind, one step at a time.

She saw two weak links in her chain of escapees: Sherman, who was among the strongest physically but seemed unstable—*and a damn officer to boot, so he can do real damage*; and the civilians, who were unaccustomed to the sustained physical demands of forced trekking day after day over mountains in torrential rain.

Sherman first. Jamie found him on their right flank, hanging back but staying appropriately ahead of the cover team. A good sign. He'd decided to obey her order to be especially frosty on the right flank, where they were likeliest to first encounter any approaching enemy ground force.

"How's it swinging, Lieutenant?" she asked in a low voice as he turned around to face the subtle sound of her approach.

Excellent. Very alert, not too jumpy. He had, she knew, already checked in three times with all members of the widely dispersed perimeter team, an arduous effort that didn't show in his demeanor or readiness.

"Clicking fast," he responded good-naturedly, apparently able to leave what happened between them in the last cave. "Scanner's clean, for what that's worth in this weather. And nobody's seen or heard anything."

"Your people keeping up okay?"

The marines on the perimeter team moved singly through the thick tropical forest just far enough apart to maintain either visual or audio contact with each other and the main band on the trail. It was damn hard work.

"Oh yeah," Sherman said. "They're all strong."

"Think they can handle it if we pick up the pace some?"

"Yes. I believe they can."

Jamie nodded and stealthed back onto the narrow path, this time out ahead of the main group, because she thought she remembered... *Yep, there it is.*

In front of her, just coming into view through the sheets of rain, was a Tau't Batu bridge, the first they'd encountered, spanning a narrow but very deep ravine. If they used it, they'd avoid having to machete a new path around the perilously slippery top of the ravine. Crossing the bridge would save them at least two hours—the difference between making the Mantalingajan cave and getting caught out in the open, exposed to enemy surveillance.

But the bridge—a light lattice of saplings lashed together and anchored fast to rock now threatened by cascading water—had lost some of its anchors and looked raggedy. Ahead of her, one of the scout team ghosts had stopped to assess it. She signaled Donato, who led the main group, to halt some fifteen meters before the bridge.

The group bottlenecked behind Donato on the primitive track. Jamie noticed that it took him a full minute to stop gawking at the ravine and make sure everyone found concealment while she checked the condition of the bridge. *Christ, now I got a freaked-out major. Can't give him a chance to wilt. Everyone else'll wilt, too.*

She hurried to examine the bridge's anchors and concluded the bridge would hold. Just. *Okay. Let's find out.* She stepped onto it, walked to the middle of its ten-meter span, and tested it with pulls and jumps. When she glanced back to see how her performance was received, she registered Lynn first, mouth agape.

Gotta keep this moving. Jamie ordered the scout team to cross the bridge one at a time, then returned to the main group. "Major, we don't have enough rope to rig a safety line, but it's stronger than it looks," she said. "The trick is to go over one at a time."

Donato stared at the bridge. Despite having seen three people cross it safely, he didn't budge or speak.

"I'll give it a try, Lieutenant," Lynn said just loudly enough to be heard by the half dozen people behind her on the path. At the sound of her voice, Donato swung around to look at her but remained mute.

Thank you, Jamie tried to say with her eyes. "All right, ma'am. Let's get a couple of people over there ahead of you, okay? But please hydrate first, before you go."

Lynn nodded and reached for her canteen.

"LT ma'am." North Carolina edged around Lynn and Donato. "I should be there ahead of the senator."

Two more marines came up behind the corpsman. "We got weapons, LT," one said. "Permission to go first so we can provide cover."

"Yeah. Good idea." Jamie couldn't help smiling her relief. "Everybody hydrate before crossing. Pass the word."

The three of them crossed the Tau't Batu bridge one after the other, followed by Lynn, who gave Jamie a parting look filled with both terror and triumph. All the rest bravely followed. Jamie crossed last, then helped the cover team destroy the bridge.

"I'm so sorry," she said to the unseen Tau't Batu who would suffer from this loss. "Please forgive me. I'll try to make up for it."

Soon after, they heard but couldn't see helos overhead—at least three, perhaps more. Most of the marines recognized the idiosyncratic rhythm of Chinese WZ-12 attack helicopters—the older models used by the PIA.

Everyone took cover and froze, hoping that their immobility, the rain, and an air temperature hovering at ninety-nine degrees Fahrenheit would help them remain undiscovered. No one moved for nearly an hour, until the sounds of the helos subsided completely.

Several more hours and two Tau't Batu bridges later, Jamie spotted the cave just south of Palawan's highest peak. She took the ghosts with her to check it out and found it empty—no Tau't Batu yet.

But she had no time to enjoy the relief oozing through her. The rain had begun to ease and the day was ebbing fast. Jamie ordered two of the ghosts to scout the area and sent the third ghost back to hurry the two dozen others into the large cave, a cathedralesque product of eons of water eroding limestone with plenty of room for everyone.

She stayed to search for the supplies left by Rhys, scurrying into two tunnel-like crevices, reaching for memories jumbled by months of pain and disorientation and nightmares, returning each time to the main cavern with only her mounting dismay. *Maybe I'm in the wrong cave. Maybe there's nothing here, never been anything here.*

She tried a third cavity. Nothing. And then a fourth. Nothing.

But as she was about to withdraw, she saw a small opening leading to another chamber. And then she remembered the short-burst splinter-noise communication with Rhys. *Here. Told Rhys here because the Tau't Batu left with us, so they wouldn't be back before this habagat. Please, let it be here still. Please...*

And it was. Exactly where Rhys had placed it some eight months earlier, almost invisible beneath a couple of camouflage tarps. Jamie sank cross-legged to the cave floor, her legs too shaky to hold her up anymore. She wept, furtive, unable to stop, but unwilling to reveal to the others how overwhelmed she was.

This was their deliverance.

"My god, Jamie! Are you okay?"

Lynn. Jamie looked up and quickly nodded, giddy with thanks that of all the twenty-seven other souls in the cave, only this one had divined how to find her in its shadowy, almost labyrinthine limestone recesses.

"Yeah. Yeah. I-I—" Jamie tried to rise but slumped back onto the ground, her legs splayed out in front of her. She couldn't contain the small, nervous laugh that bubbled up from her chest, high and dissonant, prelude to her weeping.

Lynn came nearer, descended to her knees. "Jamie, what's wrong?" She wiped tears from Jamie's face with a soft sweep of her hand.

"I-I'm okay," Jamie managed at last, gulping back the rush of delirium. "God, Lynn, it's here. All of it." And she wept, grabbing Lynn's shirt, lowering her head onto Lynn's chest. She held on to Lynn, to the feel and scent of Lynn, and breathed deep and slow. She couldn't remember the last time it had been this easy to inhale a full, clean breath of air.

Cradling her, Lynn stroked her head, her back, and finally asked, "What's here, Jamie?"

Giggling through her tears, Jamie raised her head and pointed to the tarp-covered pile of packs about two meters from her toes.

"What? I don't see anything."

"There." Jamie pointed again. "It's right there."

"Oh!" Lynn tipped off her knees and plunked clumsily next to Jamie. "You didn't mention this."

"Didn't know if it'd really be here after all this time. But it is. And look, it's not even wet."

Jamie exhaled, wondrous, then shuffled onto her knees and stretched forward hands-first to pull one of the packs from its hiding place.

"Had Rhys and a couple of teams drag this stuff all the way here for Operation Repo," she said as she opened the pack. "Figured if we were gonna need it, we'd need it here. But they must have done okay, because none of this has been touched. Hmm, looks like cammies, comlink wraps, couple of IMS binoculars."

Lynn seemed puzzled. "IMS?"

"Integrated multiwave surveillance. Does radar, infrared, thermal all at once. Nice zoom capability, too."

"I've heard about those."

Jamie handed her a still-dormant pair before setting the pack aside and grabbing another one. "Ah, ammo. Lots of it. Good. Weapons gotta be right here…"

Lynn helped Jamie count it up. "North Carolina and Leonard will like this," she said when she found a well-stocked medical kit and a several bottles of iodine. "Hey, look, canteens and—what do you call these?"

Jamie glanced up from the collection of weapons, communications equipment, and cloakcream she'd gathered. "Those are hydropacks. And those packages next to them are MREs."

"Meals Ready to Eat. Right." Next, Lynn found a fat bundle of hammocks and mosquito netting. "Good. Now we have enough water containers and hammocks and mosquito nets for everyone."

"Mmm." Jamie was distracted by a pair of IMS comlink eyewraps. She tweaked the frame before shaking them back and forth.

"What're you doing?"

"Waking 'em up. Hardly any light in here, so motion'll have to do." Jamie examined the wraps again, then put them on. "So far so good. Now, let's see." She placed her hands a foot or so in front of her and typed on an invisible keyboard. "Gotta jump through all kinds of hoops to—yep, I've gotten them to bypass requesting a unitag. Limited functionality, but better than nothing."

"You-nee tag? What's that?"

"And—yeah, there it goes, it's activated." Jamie pulled off the wraps and gazed at Lynn. "You still on the Armed Services Committee?"

"I am. How the hell do you know that?"

"I read a lot. Well, I used to read a lot. It *is* public information. How come nobody told you about our unitags?"

Lynn replied with a vacant stare.

"You're scaring me now, Senator. Those little nano ID things they stick in our ear cartilage? That the Zhong take such joy in ripping out?"

"Oh, of course. The nano-polymer unique-identifier devices— NPUIDs."

"Mmm, makes them sound like a birth control device, don't you think?" Jamie got to her feet. "Guess that's why we call them unitags."

Lynn accepted the hand Jamie offered and stood, too. For a long moment, Jamie held on to Lynn's hand, frowning at it and caressing it with resolute gentleness, in terrible need of the strength this contact somehow conveyed.

Blinking back new tears, Jamie took in and then quickly exhaled a deep breath. "We've got a real chance now," she said before squaring her shoulders. "A real chance." She wanted to offer Lynn the promise—*I will get you back to your Rebecca and your daughters*—but all she could offer was the trying, so she said nothing else.

Lynn's eyes widened for a nanosecond before she nodded, and Jamie felt a tremor in her hand. *Oh. So you didn't quite realize.* Lynn squeezed Jamie's hand, and Jamie knew that for the first time Lynn understood she faced greater odds of dying in the Palawan than surviving it.

CHAPTER TWENTY-EIGHT

HOW WE KEEP EACH OTHER ALIVE

Perched on a small boulder in the dark cavern, Jamie waited for those not on watch to settle in before her. Almost all of them carried something—a weapon, a comlink, binoculars—with which their hands made small repetitive motions.

"You know the drill," she said, swinging the comlink wraps she held in a tight circle. "Keep those cranksets moving 'til you power up whatever you're working on. We won't get any help from daylight for a while yet, and we need everything we got ay-sap."

"How long's this usually take?" asked Vargas.

"Depends on how much elbow grease you use, Sergeant." Then Jamie changed her tone—low and stern, it gave warning: Do not fuck up. "The weapons and scanners with juice left in their power packs are out there now with the people on first watch. By next watch, we need the rest of this gear powered up. While we're doing that, we're also going to review the dangers of active signaling."

Despite the moonlight, she couldn't see their faces and knew they couldn't see hers because several of Rhys's tarps had been draped across the wide cave entrance. Slivers of pallid light offered the only illumination. But at least they didn't have to huddle in damp, bat-infested corners to avoid being spotted by less obvious surveillance tools, like low-inclination Zhong satellites or swooping Zhong drones.

"The gear we found today gives us some solid leverage," Jamie said. "We can see at least a little bit now, thanks to a few pairs of IMS binoculars and the IMS capabilities in the comlink eyewraps. Plus we have some passive-identifier cammies and some cloakcream, so now we can run patrols as well as post sentries without exposing ourselves to the enemy. Most important, these cammies are visible to our ops satellites, so we can use them to do a three-person passive-signal routine that our ops center will spot eventually and recognize. Our first signal went out about twenty minutes ago and we'll repeat it every half hour 'til we get a response."

Jamie paused, wanting her words to sink in.

"Once our people see us and confirm our identity, we'll get the rest of the comlink activation stuff we need so we can receive all ops center downlinks. That means weather maps and temperature data, which'll give us precise feedback on what levels of rain and temperatures keep us hidden from the enemy. So we'll know reliably when to get out of sight."

Jamie jumped to her feet to emphasize what she'd say next.

"But even after we make contact, we *must* stay passive, people. Anything we do that's active—uplinks to ops satellites, any kind of weapons fire or active IMS scanning or even comlink-to-comlink chatter—exposes us. The enemy *will* see it. This discipline must be absolute. Our lives depend on absolute stealth."

She halted again, squinting across the dark space where each of the marines and the four Filipinos sat. "I don't care how tempted you are. *Our stealth must be absolute.* Those of you on watch tonight will carry E-nineteens, but your orders are to use these weapons only as a last resort. Because if you do use them, the whole frigging PIA will be on our doorstep. If you encounter the enemy and cannot avoid him, or if you determine that he'll discover this location, then you are to remove the threat using your combat knives or machetes or some other stealth means."

"Like throttling him," growled a marine.

"Yeah, that'll work," Jamie said. "We've got seven out there now—three doing sentry, three on patrol, and a watch commander doubling as skywatcher to monitor for acknowledgment of our messages. Those of you on the next watch will wear the cammies and IMS comlink eyewraps we found today, and you'll cloakcream up before moving out from under these tarps here. Ditto with the watches after that. Remember, guys: Stealth in everything. We're phantoms and we're gonna stay that way. So repeat after me: *No* satellite uplinks, *no* active IMS scanning, *no* comlink-to-comlink chatter, and *no* goddamn weapons fire."

They chanted it back word for word in a low whisper, like a mantra—all but Sherman, who remained silent.

"Questions?"

There were none. With whispers and murmurs, the group dispersed to their hammocks, except for three men—Donato and two of the snipes—who huddled with Jamie.

"Still awake, Senator?" Jamie asked a few minutes later, settling into the hammock just inches from Lynn's.

"Mmm, just finishing my first MRE," Lynn said through her final mouthful. "These are pretty good. Reminds me of Thanksgiving."

Jamie laughed. "Hey, North Carolina, what'd you put in those baby dicks?"

"Well, LT ma'am, we did acquire some packs of pepper from the less enlightened," North Carolina said cheerily as she added Lynn's MRE packaging to the pile that would be hidden in the morning. "Have to admit, pepper makes 'em a whole lot better than I ever remember."

"Baby dicks?" asked Lynn.

Jamie laughed again. "The little hot dogs that remind you of turkey and all the trimmings."

"I think it has more to do with the company I'm keeping," said Lynn.

"Yeah." Jamie spoke in a hush. "These are real good people." *Let me be strong enough, smart enough, not to get them killed.*

Lynn said nothing. Like North Carolina, she had swung into her hammock, and Jamie figured she'd already nodded off. Then she heard Lynn move.

"Jamie, just so you know…" Lynn paused. "I understand about the Chinese officer."

Jamie shifted in her hammock to look toward Lynn, but the cave had gone too dark to see anything without the aid of passive IMS. A second later, someone jostled her hammock—a hand feeling its way.

Lynn whispered now, her hand firm on Jamie's bicep. "And we're lucky to have you as our leader."

Jamie didn't dare speak; any sound at all might jinx Lynn's words, Lynn's hope. She placed her hand over Lynn's, pressed down, and fell asleep entreating the stars she couldn't see for the luck Lynn believed they already had.

❖

Accompanied by gusty winds, rain came well before dawn. The first sounds of it against the tarps woke Jamie, who managed to exit her hammock without waking Lynn or North Carolina. She donned IMS comlink eyewraps to find her way and crept toward the front of the cave.

"Anything?" she asked Donato, who sat just inside the tarps. *Fucking A, why aren't you outside where you'll get the best signal reception?*

He shook his head. "You still got more than half an hour before your watch."

"It's okay. Go bag some sleep."

Donato handed her the only one of their four comlinks set up to receive and acknowledge an ops center response to their signaling. Then he stripped down to his skivvies; so did Jamie. She wanted to scream at Donato, but she wriggled into the soaked passive-identifier cammies he'd been wearing, applied cloakcream, and scrunched on the boonie hat—all in silence.

Jamie checked the E19 more carefully than she might had the rifle spent the last few hours in the hands of a grunt, then slipped between the tarps and outside into the eerie almost-light created by a three-quarter moon high in the sky behind a heavy cloud cover.

Seven or eight meters from the cave entrance skulked the close sentry, with whom Jamie exchanged the agreed hail-reply gestures before checking her comlink. Fifteen times already, a three-person crew had executed the routine that should have been noticed hours ago by an operations center tech somewhere.

A response would come through first as static, white noise, while the tech broadcast-scanned for possible receiving comlinks. Then the receiving comlink—the one Jamie had now—would send a brief splinter-noise acknowledgment. Or maybe two or three or god knew how many, depending on how much the ops center people worried about functional comlinks falling into enemy hands and on the extent of the ID confirmation and cryptography they deemed necessary.

These splinter-noise signals from the comlink posed real danger.

The enemy had to be hyperalert for anything anomalous and might well detect the signals' white-noise effect in such a remote place as Mount Mantalingajan. Yet such signals were also essential. Only after they were transmitted would the receiving comlink be able to pick up the usual downlink broadcasts that meant an ops center communications link had been established.

But why, after fifteen passive-signal displays, had there been no response? The weather? Then Jamie's stomached clenched into nausea. *Oh god, oh god, what if we're not receiving the response they're sending? Did I fuck up that first comlink initialization?*

If a response had been sent by an ops center but not acknowledged by their comlink, the ops center would likely conclude the enemy had been able to grab a working comlink and... And what? *This far away, we'd probably be ignored, we'd be lost, doomed.* A new wave of panic crashed over her, and for agonizing seconds she was paralyzed. *Shit shit shit shit shit shit—*

A bright green lump moved at the corner of her eyewraps. Infrared. *Somebody's there!* Jamie crouched, rifle poised. The lump took more obvious human shape, and an arm appeared. It signaled. Jamie went weak-kneed as one of the marines on patrol approached.

"All clear north, LT," he reported in a whisper.

The sound of his voice cleared Jamie's head, and she started to run through the unitag bypass procedure she'd used on the comlink. But troubleshooting it would have to wait. First they'd stick to the schedule and do the signal routine a sixteenth time.

Jamie moved farther from the cave entrance to act as sentry while three of the marines on watch positioned themselves above the cave entrance and began signaling. *Please see us.*

After the routine had been completed, Jamie stayed out there to pee. Squatting in the dark, urine splashing between her legs, she heard it: Static.

❖

"Can I give you a hand?"

Lynn turned, reached for Jamie's arm, and smiled. "Good morning."

Jamie smiled back in shy astonishment that, of all the women on earth, this one greeted her, touched her, with such warmth. "North Carolina's briefed you?" she asked as she helped pack Lynn's hammock.

"Yep." Lynn's smile broadened, her relief evident. "Sounds like the home stretch."

"Yeah. We're heading for a pickup."

"Is it true about the diversion team?"

"Two volunteers—Vargas and Tibay—will stay here and hook up with them, then catch up with us," Jamie said while she studied Lynn, trying to decide what to do. "They'll have a comlink, so we'll be able to stay in contact."

Lynn caught the examining glance. "What?"

"Just checking in. We'll be shoving off in about ten minutes."

Lynn touched Jamie's arm again. "What? Tell me."

Their eyes locked briefly, no more than a second, and then Jamie looked down, opened her mouth to speak, but thought better of it.

"Okay, then let me guess." Lynn's hands now firmly grasped Jamie's forearms. "You need to push today, don't you? To get us closer to the pickup. But you're afraid I can't hack it."

Several seconds passed before Jamie responded. "Lynn, I'm not engaging in that conversation until you tell *me* something. Honestly."

"Tell you what—honestly?"

"How you're doing. How depleted you are. How strong you feel."

"On a scale of one to ten?"

Jamie wasn't distracted by the feeble tease. "Yes. Exactly. And honestly."

Lynn sighed as she released Jamie's arms; her shoulders slouched a little. "Fair enough, fair enough." She looked up into Jamie's eyes and shrugged. "Truth is, my knees hurt. Not as much as after the first night, but I'm sore. And I'm tired. I work out, you know, I'm not a sloth. But I'm not used to these hills or being wet all the damn time."

Jamie nodded as if the conversation had ended. "I underst—"

"Wait a minute. I'm not done yet."

Like an errant child, Jamie looked at the ground and pushed the dirt with the toe of her boot.

"It's true, isn't it?" asked Lynn. "We need to really hump today, right?"

"Yes." Jamie drilled her gaze into Lynn's. "But only if you can handle it. And I don't think you can. I think you're wasted."

"More wasted than you?" Lynn said. "You've been running on empty since way before *I* came along."

"I'm a marine. It's supposed to hurt."

"I'm okay, Jamie. I can do it."

Jamie shook her head, frowned her reluctance. "No," she said softly, but found herself unable to leave until Lynn accepted her decision.

Lynn's eyes glowed with a ferocity Jamie hadn't seen before, but her voice stayed calm. "How far would you like to get today?"

"Roughly ten klicks. Ten kilometers." *Why am I even talking to you about this?* Jamie half turned away, but Lynn's hand on her arm again stopped her. *Okay, then, here it is.*

"The scouts are out there now making our trail, but it's minimal, Lynn, because we don't want the enemy to be able to see it—or us. You'll be going single file on a rough track, and part of the time you'll have to hold a tarp above your head so the enemy can't spot you, since the weather'll be just passable enough just often enough for them to get a glimpse of us if we let them. And that's not all. Downlink indicates we're on the edge of a typhoon that'll be intensifying—lots of rain, higher winds as the day progresses. That's why we're getting under way now. If we can beat a klick an hour, we'll be damn lucky. So ten klicks will take at least eight hours—very likely a good deal longer, because we'll be in downpours pretty much the whole time. Sometimes quite blustery downpours. It'll be very, very strenuous. Best scenario is it'll be really brutal."

"I understand, Jamie."

"Do you?"

"Please let me try."

Slowly, Jamie's frown relented. She grasped that Lynn was, in effect, joining up and volunteering for a mission. "Okay. But you gotta promise me: Before you crash and burn, you'll ask for assistance. Means you have to pay attention to yourself, anticipate your breaking point."

Lynn said nothing.

"Lynn," Jamie said. "That's the deal for all of us. That's how we keep each other alive. You *gotta* promise me."

"Yes, Jamie." Lynn's determination inflected her voice. "I promise you."

❖

For twelve hours they trudged, hoisting each other over ledges, lifting each other out of the mud, unsnagging the billowing tarps from branches and jutting rocks, saving each other from sliding down mountainsides. They detoured around once-tiny streams now swollen into class-six rapids. They dodged trees collapsing before the predatory wind.

During the worst of it, squall lines bristling with lightning attacked them and they cowered under shallow rock ledges, holding on to each other as thunder exploded around them like a well-aimed artillery barrage.

And when they reached their goal—a cave about halfway between Mantalingajan and Mount Landargun—Jamie watched Lynn Hillinger enter it on her own two feet, without aid, North Carolina close behind.

❖

"North Carolina tells me you're refusing pain meds," Jamie said, swinging into the hammock next to Lynn's.

"Not exactly. I just don't want to max them out. I'll be too groggy tomorrow."

"Mmm, well, don't worry about that. We're gonna sit tight until at least tomorrow afternoon."

Lynn twisted in her hammock, a too-sudden movement that induced a flinch. "Not because of me."

"I suppose it *is* because of you, in a way." Jamie's reassuring grin belied the words, and Lynn shook her head at the razzing. "Today we averaged better than three-quarters of a kilometer an hour—despite the weather and the horrible ground conditions. We're going to put the margin you gave us today to good use. You kept quite a pace. Damn impressive."

"Me?" Lynn asked blankly. "I don't get it."

"You set the pace today, Lynn. We made sure you got support, but it was you who set the pace. And you never let up."

"God, all I was trying to do was keep up."

Jamie swung her legs out of the hammock and leaned toward Lynn, two small pills resting atop the scar in the middle of her extended palm. "Take these, okay? They'll make it easier to sleep."

"Yes, all right." Lynn washed them down with a long swig of water from her hydropack and relaxed into her hammock.

Next to Lynn, Jamie relaxed, too. The wind and rain howled outside the cave, and occasionally a light spray whirled into its depths and cooled their faces.

Sleep came for Jamie softly, gently. She snugged toward it, knowing that for a few hours, until her turn on watch, she'd be able to truly rest.

"Jamie?" Lynn's voice lilted toward her from far, far away.

"Mmm?"

"What happened to your hands?"

"Mmm...can't...'mem..."

CHAPTER TWENTY-NINE

THIS IS A GIFT

Lieutenant Sherman's vehement objections didn't change Jamie's mind. "We're staying put so everyone has a chance to rest."

Everyone except Jamie and two others, who donned passive-identifier cammies and ventured into the storm to hook up with the diversion team and its escorts, Vargas and Tibay.

"Why do you have to go?" Lynn asked as Jamie put on the cammies.

"I know the paths better than anyone else."

"Christ, Jamie, you need rest, too. Why not just wait here for them? They'll find us, won't they?"

North Carolina came to the rescue. "We have to reel in our guys today, ma'am. Ay-sap. But don't worry. It shouldn't take long. And since LT might have to use splinter-noise commo to make contact, this way any splinters the enemy picks up are far enough away from here that they'll be misdirected."

Lynn didn't give up her frown, but she acquiesced with a small dip of her head.

By early afternoon, Jamie had returned with Vargas, Tibay, and the diversion team. As best anyone could tell, they hadn't been spotted, hadn't been tracked.

A day later—on the twenty-first of June—they used the remains of the retreating typhoon as cover and made it to another cave where Rhys had stashed supplies. This cave west of Mount Landargun would be their last. They had reached the pickup point. Here they found additional MREs and a couple more comlinks as well as another sniper rifle, two squad automatic weapons, and a trove of ammunition.

"Ooh-rah! SAWs!" Sherman rooted as he picked up one of the squad automatic weapons. About thirty seconds later, he began lobbying for a SAW nest with himself manning it. As he talked too fast, too loud, Jamie scowled at him on principle.

But she agreed with the idea and had already mapped out how the escapees would execute their part of the pickup plan. Her goal was to get everybody out before any weapons needed to be fired, although the odds of pulling it off weren't good.

Now that the weather had cleared, the enemy searched for them in force. Soon after they took shelter in this last cave, the mountains around them reverberated with the nearly continuous thumping of enemy helicopter rotors—not just small, two-crew attack helos, but also at least one older MI-19 support aircraft capable of carrying thirty people.

Ops center detected nothing, of course. The PIA and their helos had long since been stealthed up. But the sounds suggested PIA fighters were being ferried into the mountains south of them—close and moving north, coming closer—some as close as six or seven klicks away.

Jamie deployed shifts of marines outside the northeast-facing cave in a perimeter extending to the craggy ridge just above it. At least they wouldn't be taken by surprise, and so could choose whether or not to be taken alive.

The pickup, which would begin just before dawn, couldn't come soon enough. All thirty-one prisoners from Saint Eh Mo's listened diligently to Jamie's description of the plan.

"Ladies and gentleman, ops center has given us a new name. We are Prancer, and the spot where we will climb aboard a Shark helicopter tomorrow morning has been named Prancer X-Ray. It's a clearing about two hundred meters north of here. At zero-five-hundred, we begin our move to Prancer X-Ray."

Their Shark helo would be escorted and covered by two Barracuda attack helos. While they boarded the Shark, the enemy would be distracted and diverted by a small team of marines—dubbed Rubyfish—which would helo-drop onto a plateau about five hundred meters southwest of the ridge that loomed over the cave entrance.

Supported by two other Barracudas, Rubyfish would intercept any PIA approaching from the south and then move north over the ridge to Prancer X-Ray for a second, later pickup.

Jamie called out eleven names, the eleven strongest people she had, and took them aside. "To get everyone to the Prancer X-Ray pickup site, we need three overwatch teams. Prancer-Dog One will overwatch the Prancer X-Ray clearing. That'll be three people. I want six people on Prancer-Dog Two to maintain a mobile perimeter during our move from the cave to Prancer X-Ray. And I'm asking for two volunteers for Prancer-Dog Three. You'll be overwatching from the high point on the ridge above the cave, and you may have to stay and extract later with Rubyfish."

Four people volunteered for Prancer-Dog Three. Jamie chose Vargas and Tibay. She didn't mention to them or anyone else what she worried about most, what she'd tried most to change about the pickup plan: The number of helos. Four Barracudas wouldn't be nearly enough unless they got very lucky. However, for reasons that were beyond Lieutenant Gwynmorgan's need-to-know, four would be all they'd get.

❖

"Ready?"

After gearing up on the other side of the cave with the people in the overwatch teams, Jamie had checked on everyone except Lynn. She saved Lynn for last.

At the sound of Jamie's voice, Lynn looked up and gaped. A long moment passed before she said anything. "Do you really need—" Lynn stopped her words, but her eyes kept going, from the sniper rifle cradled in Jamie's arm to the assault rifle slung across Jamie's back to the vest laden with ammunition stacks. Clutching her hydropack, Lynn blinked. "Uh…" Her voice jittered. "Have you got water, Jamie?"

"Oh yeah." Jamie patted the two containers attached to her vest. She pulled off her boonie hat and her eyewraps and gazed intently at Lynn, but the words she'd wanted to say got stuck somewhere and she said nothing.

Lynn's eyes filled with tears.

"No," Jamie said, words now flowing, "don't, don't. You'll be fine, Lynn. North Carolina will be with you every step of the way. Just do what she tells you and you'll be safe, you'll be home real soon."

"But you—*you*—"

Jamie reached for Lynn's forearm and gave it a gentle squeeze. "Oh, don't you worry about me," she said, smiling, allowing herself one last look at Lynn Hillinger.

So she'd remember. *This is a gift. Getting these people out, getting Lynn out—it's a payment on what I owe. If I can just make it work...*

"You ready, Senator?"

Lynn grabbed Jamie's arm and squeezed back, nodding, her face tense, her difficulty swallowing apparent.

"Then let's crank it."

Jamie winked at Lynn and turned away, signaling North Carolina as she walked quickly toward the cave entrance. At the edge of her vision, she saw North Carolina step in alongside Lynn, saw Lynn watching her as she put on her eyewraps and then her boonie hat. She looked over her shoulder one final time and smiled again—to make sure the last Lynn Hillinger saw of her was that smile.

CHAPTER THIRTY

PRANCER ACTUAL

This is Rubyfish Actual. We are taking fire from the south and will engage."

Oh christ, already a clusterfuck. So much for stealth.

Rubyfish had dropped onto the plateau almost an hour earlier than scheduled because previously undetected PIA had been eyeballed little more than a kilometer south of the cave. Jamie and the five others with comlinks flipped on active signaling just as the last of the escapees emerged from the cave.

At least the chaos somewhat impeded the enemy's ability to track their comlinks' active signals, but Jamie didn't find this consoling. She would much rather have traded easy commo and real-time ops center chatter for the chance to get everyone on the helo before the enemy found anything to shoot at.

Now all that was moot and Jamie worried about her cover teams. Not Prancer-Dog One and Prancer-Dog Two. *They should be okay unless the pickup itself goes all to hell.*

But only Vargas and Tibay held Prancer-Dog Three, that high, fortress-like spot on the rocky ridge above the cave entrance. They had both SAWs, an E19 assault rifle, an E112 sniper rifle, and sweeping views of Rubyfish's position to the southwest as well as the escapee pickup point, Prancer X-Ray, to the north. *Shit. Prancer-Dog Three is the crux of this. If Vargas and Tibay can't hold long enough, the pickup'll turn into a turkey shoot. Should've risked putting more people up there.*

"Prancer Actual," a familiar voice called through Jamie's comlink, "this is Bravo Overlord confirming commo up."

"Prancer Actual rogers commo up," Jamie answered. *Hey, that's Embry. So the old man's commanding this one himself.*

"How's the senator?" crackled Embry's voice.

"Cool beans, sir. She'll be first on the boat."

"Roger, Prancer Actual." Embry's voice relaxed some. "Thanks."

Because of the scout team's earlier clearing efforts, Donato and Sherman had little trouble moving everyone as planned along the rough slope. They progressed well despite steep, jagged ground and the effort of keeping themselves camouflaged under tarps as they went. Soon they'd be crossing the coulee.

A broad, shallow scoop-out of the land, the coulee's eroded limestone floor was already mostly dry and free of mud. Scattered with boulders and outcrops of darker, crystalline rocks, the coulee began as a narrow dip in the ridge above the cave and widened to the northwest, then due north around a wooded knoll to a wide, flat area that had been selected as Prancer X-Ray.

"Make sure they're under the tarps, sir," Jamie had reminded Donato, who did better when reminded. "And once you get to that knoll, stay near it along the east side of the coulee where there's concealment. Use that concealment 'til you reach Prancer X-Ray."

Now, as she prowled the knoll watching over the line of escapees, mini versions of the ops center's screens appeared near the bottom of Jamie's comlink's shadowscreen; she took a moment to eyeball one of them, and a second later a semitransparent version of it zoomed larger. It showed the pickup drama playing out from a satellite point-of-view, complete with precise topographical grid overlays and real-time helo movements. *Yes!* The helos were right where they should be. Jamie dared to allow herself some optimism.

Positioned finally above the southeastern edge of Prancer X-Ray, Jamie saw Lynn crossing the coulee. The only weapons fire remained on the other side of the ridge, south of Rubyfish. Much closer than she'd have liked, but still far enough away. *Just thirty minutes, that's all we need...*

Then everything popped at once.

"Prancer-Dog Three reports PIA in multiple positions approaching fast," rasped Vargas. "Shit! Some are trying to move between us and Rubyfish. Count maybe thirty at OC grid November-Niner-Six moving northwest. Count five—make that eight, nine, more, there's more—at November-Niner-Seven, moving north."

PIA fighters—too many of them—now threatened to cut off Rubyfish and trap it in crossfire. The good news was that the Rubyfish commander didn't have to be told what to do.

"Rubyfish Actual copies," declared a steady male voice. "Rubyfish moving northeast toward Prancer-Dog Three and will engage additional enemy at November-Niner-Six and Niner-Seven."

But Vargas hadn't finished, and this time fear pitched his voice higher, tighter. "Oh christ, there's a whole other crew east-southeast of us, heading for the dip in the ridge. Prancer Actual, they'll be coming into the coulee straight at you. At the rate they're going, estimate twenty minutes before they have line of sight to Prancer X-Ray."

Ops center surveillance was useless, of course. The PIA fighters wore countermeasures that made them invisible to radar, infrared, or thermal detection. Now came Jamie's turn to stay steady. "Prancer-Dog Three, report number and location."

"Twenty-plus at November-Niner-Niner moving west-northwest."

"Prancer-Dog Three, priority target those heading for the dip in the ridge," Jamie ordered.

Shit. Shit. Hardly any margin. The PIA fighters approaching from the east-southeast were a mere three hundred meters from the escapees, maybe less. Time slid into slow motion as Jamie snapped off a series of orders while she scrambled to intercept the enemy. *Not enough helo support. Not enough.*

Jamie requested more, although she knew help would arrive too late. But at least she managed to get Rubyfish's Barracudas diverted, so now two attack helos targeted the PIA approaching Prancer X-Ray while two others protected the escapees' Shark transport helo. And she ordered the Shark to leave without Prancer-Dog Three or Prancer Actual.

"We will extract with Rubyfish," Jamie yelled over her comlink. "I say again: Do *not* wait for Prancer-Dog Three or Prancer Actual."

But before the Barracudas had a chance to pounce, before the Shark got close enough for the escapees to scramble aboard, someone very close to Prancer X-Ray initiated fire. A second later, Jamie heard

Donato shouting at the escapees to find cover. Then he screamed at Sherman to come back.

The lieutenant, covering the rear of the line of escapees, had abandoned his concealment to return up the coulee toward the ridge, climbing to his best guess about the source of PIA fire and shooting blind. Immediately, a PIA fighter with a Chinese Type 86 sniper rifle returned fire.

Probably a scout out ahead of the rest of them, already in the coulee. Bastard should never have fired at Sherman and given away his position, but maybe he figures it doesn't matter, because now, right now, he's reporting the location of Prancer X-Ray.

Which meant the enemy wouldn't need line-of-sight to Prancer X-Ray. *All they need is a decent grenade launcher.* If a single well-aimed smart grenade exploded a few meters in the air above them, it could kill or maim every one of the escapees. And once over the dip in the ridge, the enemy would be plenty close enough to try. Hollering orders as she went, Jamie humped, hoping to close in on the PIA scout first and then get around the knoll in time to cut off the rest of the PIA fighters as they came over the dip in the ridge.

"Some're getting past us!" yelled Vargas.

Jamie pumped her burning legs, forgoing stealth for speed, and made it back to the coulee with seconds to spare before a PIA crew appeared ahead of her. She took out three of them before they realized she was there, hardly noticing the effect on her hands of aiming the weapon, squeezing the trigger. Another ten or twelve PIA quickly turned their attention to her, exactly as she'd hoped they would.

But the PIA scout had gotten past her. "Prancer X-Ray." Jamie worked to keep her voice even and sure. "PIA snipe to your—"

Three shots popped off behind her, between her and Prancer X-Ray. "Got him!" screeched Sherman. "I fucking nailed him!"

"Good, Sherman," Jamie told him via comlink. "Glad you're a better shot than he was. Did he clip you?"

"Negative. I'm okay."

Jamie hesitated for a nanosecond while she decided: Send Sherman back north to Prancer X-Ray and out on the Shark, or let him stay and fight. She could use the help. And she wondered if he'd even obey an order to withdraw. *Okay, boy, you asked for it.* "New orders,

Lieutenant. I want you to cross the coulee and make your way up the bluff to Prancer-Dog Three."

"Roger," huffed Sherman. "Where?"

"Prancer-Dog Three. You will ascend the bluff and join Vargas and Tibay at Prancer-Dog Three. But first you have to cross the coulee."

Jamie got no reply but could see Sherman on her shadowscreen. He wasn't moving. "Move to your one o'clock. My count, Sherman, move on three." She paused for not even a whole second. "One... two..." She began firing. "Three! *Go!* Go go *go GO!*"

At last, Sherman moved. While he ran, a Barracuda swooped in low above Jamie, drawing PIA rifle fire before its autocannon shells erupted in a fiery line farther up the coulee toward the enemy. Jamie's comlink told her the escapees were boarding the Shark, and amidst a bedlam of voices, she glanced up to see a line of four PIA WZ-12 attack helicopters swinging in from the southeast. They'd be over her head in minutes.

Out of the cacophony she determined that the escapees needed another few minutes to board the Shark transport helo, that the fast-approaching WZ-12s would be able to target the escapees' helo before any of the Barracudas had time to loop around and intervene, and on the other side of the ridge, Rubyfish was firing in three directions and reporting the appearance of yet another three WZ-12s low on the southwest horizon.

Jamie hoped the Barracuda's shells had taken out the PIA fighters shooting at her moments earlier. Because any remaining PIA were about to get a clear shot at her. She rose from behind the huge boulder that had protected her from enemy fire to stabilize her sniper rifle on it and aim at the lead WZ-12.

Come on, goober, don't let them shoot first. She aimed at the rear rotor housing, pulled the trigger once, twice, again. The helicopter sputtered and tilted violently into the WZ-12 close behind it. The two aircraft arced downward, rotors mangling, pulled inexorably into a mountainside northeast of Prancer X-Ray. Jamie shifted slightly right to aim at the third helo. Four .416-cal rounds later, it bucked, did a high, slow back flip, and exploded as it slammed into the slopes of Mount Landargun to the east.

The fourth WZ-12 sprayed heavy machine-gun fire and autocannon shells down the coulee toward her. Jamie huddled against the boulder just before a shell detonated somewhere on the other side of it, its blast wave sending up dust and debris and bouncing several large rocks like basketballs. Somehow the blast wave spared her. From a low crouch, ears ringing, she twisted to follow the helo through the rising smoke of the explosion and emptied the sniper rifle's ammo stack into it—to no avail.

But a Barracuda rocket caught the helo and it skewed into a line of trees well to the west just as a chunk of rock chipped and whined an inch away from Jamie's arm. She tried to swing her weapon toward where she thought a shooter must lurk, but her left arm had gone heavy and numb and her fingers didn't want to move.

Fuck, I've been hit!

Sliding down behind the boulder, she watched swaths of blood spread along her sleeve—and her cammie blouse. *Oh, christ, a chest wound. Why am I still conscious? Why am I still alive?*

She yanked open her blouse and checked beneath her blood-drenched T-shirt to find several holes. Something small and sleek had plowed through her upper left arm and drilled through both breasts.

Must've missed the bone...that's why it doesn't hurt so much. She pulled out strips of quick-bandage from a pouch on her left leg and slapped them across her breasts and her left bicep, which did hurt. *Come on, goober, gotta focus. At least one PIA near the top of the coulee, more coming through the dip in the ridge. Sherman somewhere out there rampaging for America. Leaves just Prancer-Dog Three and me to keep them from Prancer X-Ray...*

And Vargas and Tibay now had to sustain fire in several nearly opposite directions. Jamie found herself wishing again, wishing she'd put more people up on the ridge at Prancer-Dog Three.

Wishing in combat means you fucked up. Two mistakes, goddammit!

On her eyewraps shadowscreen, she found her first mistake, Sherman, still moving toward the bluff. He stopped, and she hoped he'd merely fallen but figured he'd probably been hit, an easy target for the enemy because he wasn't wearing passive-identifier cammies. Or maybe he'd been injured by the PIA shell's blast wave.

And finally, like a spark igniting one of those old internal combustion engines, Jamie understood. He'd seen Cavanaugh bloodied and dead in front of him. Cavanaugh was his Arnie. *Shit. I'm gonna lose him.* She faltered then as hope oozed out of her. The escapees were still boarding their helo, still on the ground. And she was helpless. *I'm gonna lose them, too.*

The kickass voice out of her past startled her. *"Faster, Gwyn-moron! This ain't the freaking Magic Kingdom!"* She reacted instinctively, scurrying for its own sake, not quite aware of where she was going.

Her left arm burned and pounded and seeped blood. It hung at her side, unwilling to participate as she clambered to a small, rocky promontory in the middle of the coulee. It was an accidental choice, but a good one: She had an unobstructed view of anyone coming over the dip in the ridge—and anyone coming down the coulee toward Prancer X-Ray had to get by that spot.

"Yes. Here." Here she might, just might, hold them long enough for the Shark to get everyone aboard and get the hell out. As fast as she could, Jamie laid out both weapons, piled several ammo stacks within easy reach, and hunkered into position using her good right arm to position her nearly useless left one.

By the time she got her finger on a trigger, a dozen PIA fighters were coming right at her. She opened fire and they all went down in a few seconds. But plenty more followed close behind them. Worse still, the enemy had already identified her location.

Diving to avoid their fire, she watched the fine, wisping red lines of their bullets' trajectories on her comlink screen and called again for air support. It would be a while coming.

Mistake three: We've underestimated how much they want us and how many people they're willing to sacrifice to get us.

Jamie registered where her comlink screen trajectories indicated the closest PIA fighters were. *Right. Gotta go right.* So she shifted right, her adrenaline pumping so fiercely that even her left arm did her bidding. Five meters from her earlier position, she swung out from behind the rock formation, sprayed the area before her, and ran toward another outcrop.

Jamie was retreating but taking out her pursuers as she went. Just before she reached the shelter of the second outcrop, a spear of fire impaled her left shoulder near her neck. She staggered, breathless and battling to stay conscious as she fell.

"Shit!" she wheezed, trying to keep herself sentient. "Shit!"

Then, at last, over the comlink she heard it. The Shark was airborne with twenty-eight undamaged "packages," and, escorted by the Barracudas, would be in safe airspace in minutes.

"Prancer Actual," shouted Vargas, "PIA above you, at your three on the ledge above you!"

Without something very like a miracle, Jamie knew, the shooter on the ledge would nail her in a few seconds and she'd be dead. She stared up at the firmament's uninterrupted blueness backlighting the trees that clung to the sides of the coulee, inexplicably pleased that she'd die beneath a cloudless sky.

"This is Bravo Overlord." Embry's voice came from another universe. "We're sending in the cavalry. ETA fifteen minutes."

Jamie knew she had nowhere near as long as fifteen minutes, and she didn't want to hear Embry's description of what he'd sent to help them. She was so tired, and the sky was so blue, so, so magnificent.

But why hasn't that bastard up their started shooting yet?

"Prancer Actual, PIA above you," Vargas shouted again. "C'mon, LT, get up and go right. Go right. Go go *GO*!"

Jamie found herself on her feet, running, shoved by "go go go" to the other end of the outcrop ten meters away. Aimed at her from a ledge halfway up the bluff, a spray of shots surrounded her.

Wow. Bastard missed. Gives me...one...more...chance...

Then she heard Embry's voice over her comlink. "Don't shoot, Prancer Actual, don't shoot. PIA do traj tracking now."

Jamie growled at the thought of him watching her, at the very sound of him. "Fucker." *Why the hell didn't you give us what I asked for? Then I wouldn't need your pathetic goddamn coaching!* "Aah-aagh!" she raged. "Fucker!"

A second later she got hit again. She yelped at the pain in her left calf, her vision red-rimmed with fury as she stumbled and fell. But her rage drove her to her feet again and she scuttled limping across the rest of the coulee under fire from two directions. She made it all the way to the base of the bluff, at last protected by a shallow overhang from the PIA shooter on the ledge above.

"*Aaahh! Jeee-zus!*" Jamie gasped just as a Barracuda swung in low and close to detonate rockets up the coulee while its gunner sprayed rounds at the PIA shooter on the ledge above her.

"Hey hey there, Prancer," whooped one of the Barracuda crew. "Got some for ya!"

"Yesss!" Jamie hissed. The Barracuda had delivered her reprieve just in time.

"Prancer Actual," Vargas called. "Prancer-Dog Three reports the high road is clear. I say again: The high road is clear. Come on up, Prancer Actual. Join the fucking party."

Jamie could see the path to take up the side of the rocky bluff—steep, forbidding even. But doable. *Come on, it's doable.* She stared at it but didn't move, swooning involuntarily away from the pain.

"Jamie!" another voice shouted, rousing her. "Jamie!" it demanded again, sounding remarkably like Lynn Hillinger.

"Lynn?" Alert now, Jamie looked around. *No, no, she's on the helo…on the helo…*

"Climb, Jamie!" yelled the voice. "Climb!"

So, somehow, Jamie climbed.

Her chosen track angled between forty-five and sixty degrees straight up the face of the craggy bluff, and just one side of her body had to do most of the work. Her right arm pulled, her right leg pushed, then she flattened against a ragged cleft, wedging her nearly helpless left arm and leg for stability and leverage, groaning reflexively with the effort. She waited a few seconds—it seemed like only a few seconds—for the light-headedness to pass, for the pain to be less addling, for her breathlessness to be less desperate, and she did it again. And again.

All her awareness narrowed to this minute time and place—the protrusion just over her head that her hand could grasp, the spur from which her foot could push, the tenuous balance threatened by the pain so eager to steal what was left of her sweet reason. Finally, panting, twitching, Jamie crawled onto the level ground of the ledge and collapsed, unable to answer the imploring voices on her comlink. There she remained until yet another round whizzing too close rallied her. She dragged herself to shelter behind a worn limestone boulder and looked up.

SOPHIA KELL HAGIN

"Oh god." Jamie had known all along that this precipice was much higher than the last. She needed to climb at least twenty meters this time. *How?* Her head flopped back against the rock. She let her eyes close. *Just for a minute, that's all.* They startled open again when somebody touched her.

Sherman. Smiling like she'd never seen him smile before.

She grinned. "Could use a lift. Think you're up for it? So to speak."

"Hell, yes. All aboard."

His impressive strength amplified by adrenaline or delirium or both, Sherman belly-crawled up the steep switchback path with Jamie on top of him, using her body and the passive-identifier cammies she wore to obscure his visibility to the enemy.

It was an invaluable, strength-restoring respite. From it she got a chance to gulp some water and figure out that although they were painful, her wounds hadn't damaged anything vital. She could still think, probably still shoot. From the ops center she learned that a new horde of PIA now pushed toward them from the south. Aerial visuals also showed PIA activity to the east on Mount Landargun, just eight hundred meters away and nearly four hundred meters higher at its peak than Prancer-Dog Three.

The low-key pickup Jamie hoped for had blossomed into a major battle, the first significant exchange in two months, perhaps the most decisive of the entire Palawan conflict. And at its epicenter hunkered Prancer-Dog Three, no longer much of a fortress as its defenders, who already faced fire from enemy helicopters, anticipated new fire from enemy weapons on Mount Landargun.

Embry had deployed the better part of two regiments. Marine helos now attacked PIA positions from the air, and soon infantry would land at several spots to the north and move toward Prancer-Dog Three as fast as possible. The four POWs there and the sixteen guys on the Rubyfish team would be extracted as soon as prudence allowed. The new extraction site—Ruby X-ray—was a barely helo-accessible spot on the ridge about fifty meters southwest of Prancer-Dog Three, to which Rubyfish would withdraw.

Meanwhile, Jamie, Sherman, Vargas, and Tibay would have to hold the high ground at Prancer-Dog Three. Somehow.

❖

Prancer-Dog Three reminded Jamie of the positions her fire team had used those many months ago during Operation Squeeze Play: An irregular encirclement of boulders and jagged outcrops and shallow cavelets. A zion of natural cover.

Once the guys plugged the holes in her, she found her spot—high enough, protected enough, the right fields of view. So she functioned pretty well, in spite of bouts of light-headedness and lack of decent mobility.

Jamie didn't understand why the PIA wanted the ridge, but want it they did. Maybe they thought they'd cornered the senator and the POWs there. Maybe they saw it as a chance to keep the truce talks from resuming. So many maybes…

For the first hour after Jamie reached Prancer-Dog Three, helos parried above them, keeping each other busy. So Jamie and the others at Prancer-Dog Three got no help from the Barracudas while they staved off PIA attacks coming mostly from the south and southeast. PIA poured in from the southwest, too, but the sixteen Rubyfish guys managed to cope with that as they withdrew up the backside of the ridge to Ruby X-ray.

Everyone at Prancer-Dog Three spent their ammo carefully and well, using Trajsat downlinks to follow the sleek red filaments back to the PIA fighters who fired at them. Even so, they had to keep scrambling, keep shifting position. And, of course, the enemy knew exactly where they were.

Then, as Marine infantry approached from the north, more PIA contingents arrived, too, and the fight escalated.

"Vargas, cover your nine!" Jamie yelled. "Enemy's on Landargun, eye-to-eye with us!"

Worse, the PIA started firing long-range rocket grenades.

"Thank god they can't aim worth shit," snarled Sherman, his finger rubbing the trigger of one of the SAWs.

"Find your target, Lieutenant," Jamie warned him. "Not much ammo left."

"Incoming!" shouted Tibay.

A Barracuda attack helo exploded against the ridge a few seconds later, shaking the ground; the two-man crew never had a chance. Next came a PIA rocket grenade. It detonated just beyond the largest of the east-facing Prancer-Dog Three outcrops, but shrapnel from it sprayed around them. Vargas screamed when chunks of metal peppered his right arm. The PIA on the slopes of Landargun were finding their targets.

Here we go—the endgame. Sherman helped Vargas while Jamie and Tibay did what they could to slow down the PIA. As she fired her sniper rifle, Jamie called in helo support for what she knew would be the last time. "It's now or never, boys and girls."

She had Sherman move with his SAW to slightly higher ground a few feet from her and point the weapon eastward. "There. Eleven o'clock, fifteen degrees up."

Vargas picked up an E19. He had to prop his right arm into position with his left hand to use it. "Might as well spray 'em while I can, right, LT?"

She would've answered, but before she had a chance, Tibay thudded to the ground and rolled, clutching his left side.

"Tib!" screamed Vargas. "Tib!"

Tibay lay still for only a few seconds and then, incredibly, rolled onto his hands and knees, blood seeping across his left buttock and down his leg. "I'm okay," he said like he'd stubbed a toe. Then he crawled to his SAW, aimed it, and kept firing the last of his fifty-cal ammo.

"Hey!" crowed Sherman, pointing north. "About frigging time!"

Jamie counted nine Barracuda attack helicopters coming in fast, then spotted more following those. They had already started to fan out. Soon a small fleet of Barracudas would surround Prancer-Dog Three, soon a Shark transport would hover just fifty meters away to extract them.

My god, we're gonna make it.

Beside her, Sherman grunted hard and dropped, his chest already bathed in blood. Jamie yanked him away from a spray of fire that chipped the rock around them. *How the hell?*

Then she knew. "They're at the top of Landar—" A red-hot poker drilled through her right thigh, stealing her breath.

"LT, I'm outta ammo," called Tibay.

Jamie gulped for air as she clutched her leg. "Ahh shit!" she screamed. "Shit!"

Tibay got to her and Sherman first.

"Get me up," Jamie said. "Hurry." She pointed to the SAW. "There."

"LT," Tibay said, "I think—"

"C'mon, Tib," she insisted, "help me get to the SAW."

Vargas leaned over Sherman. "He's alive."

"You guys take Sherman and go now," Jamie ordered as Tibay propped her behind the SAW. "Fifty meters to the pickup. Grab E-nineteens and go. Rubyfish, do you copy? We need covering fire pronto for three coming at you from Prancer-Dog Three."

"Roger. Rubyfish copies and will cover."

Vargas shook his head. "LT—"

"*Now*, dammit! You're the only chance Sherman's got."

Vargas and Tibay glanced at each other, then at Sherman. "Yes, ma'am," they said in unison.

"Double-time, guys," Jamie called to them as loud as she could, then took up the SAW and started shooting.

It wasn't easy. It hurt, and her aim— Well, she couldn't aim. Not anymore. But she might be able to suppress enough PIA fire that Vargas and Tibay could get Sherman to the Rubyfish corpsman. *Only fifty meters.*

The first of the Barracudas were above her and she thought she heard the heavier thwack-thwack of a Shark transport helicopter, though she couldn't see it. Her vision had tunneled too much. But the SAW still had some rounds in it. She pulled, pulled on the trigger, felt the ferocious recoil—

And then somebody gut-punched her, an invisible fist that plowed all the way through her twice over. Jamie fell gasping, robbed of air, robbed of everything. The dissonant tumult of destruction faded as she fell, and Jamie heard her mother's voice, soft and calm:

> *From too much love of living,*
> *From hope and fear set free,*
> *We thank with brief thanksgiving*
> *Whatever gods may be*
> *That no life lives forever;*
> *That dead men rise up never;*
> *That even the weariest river*

Winds somewhere safe to sea.

Jamie recognized the epitaph she'd tried to remember but never quite could, and she knew it was the last of her emptying out.

The ground took her without cruelty—she was aware that it could have been so very cruel—and she was shown a blue, blue sky. That deep, pure blue she'd seen only in a dream once. All she had to do now to be Safe was get rid of the shadowscreen between her and the blue.

She willed her right hand to crawl across her chest and up, up to her face. Her fingers found the eyewraps that trapped her and clawed them away.

The blue came for her then, and Jamie went to it...

CHAPTER THIRTY-ONE

STILL HERE

She didn't want them to disturb the motionless, crimsoned creature sprawled below her. She hovered over it, at once imperturbable and protective, marveling at this body so familiar and yet so strange, so consummately still, so exquisitely tranquil.

Having leapt energetically toward her, they suddenly seemed to hesitate, as if adhering to her wishes, and she dared to look away, allowing herself to be riveted by the dazzling, infinite blueness above her.

Oh yes, that's where I'm supposed to be.

And she slid further into the blue. Safe was there, in the blue.

"No, no, not yet."

The sound surprised her. She didn't expect sound.

"It's not time yet."

Time? No such thing anymore. I'll just keep looking at the blue, falling toward the blue, and... She convulsed when the loudest noise she'd ever heard boomed through her body, pounding on every cell, vaulting her back off the blood-soaked ground as her heart was forced to resume beating and her lungs heaved and grated, reluctantly resuming their quest for air.

She moaned her immeasurable disappointment and faded away from the din of shouts and machines into another kind of oblivion.

❖

"My god, my god, this is the second time."

There's that word again—time.

The misery in the voice attracted Jamie's attention, but it seemed so far away, and through the window she could see a sliver of blue sky.

She didn't look toward the voice, or at the body on the bed, or at the green-clad people trying to torture it back to life. She wanted only the blue and wondered what she must do to get beyond the window.

"Please, Jamie. Oh god, please come back."

Who could possibly care that much whether I'm around or not? Jamie yearned for the blue, but she had to know. So she turned toward the lament. It came from a figure hunched on a chair in a corner of the room. *I'll be damned...*

She turned back to the window, but the blue had gone, replaced by a sallow, claustral light. She was trapped, barred now from the blue, a prisoner again.

The prisoner tumbled then and kept on tumbling. Helpless, she stood witness to the current that sparked her heart to beat, the caustic oxygen that scourged her lungs, the numerous stitched incisions still raw and angry, the myriad tubes and patches and needles and probes— all the gathered forces that cornered life back into the body on the bed.

This second return was soundless for her and mercifully painless. Yet she felt tears slide out of her closed eyes and trickle down the sides of her face.

Jamie Gwynmorgan had missed her chance again.

❖

She liked the view from this corner, high up and away from everyone. When she wanted to, she could dip down just a bit—all it took was a thought—and look out the window. Sometimes she'd see a blue sky, and the sight of it provoked a yearning so profound that she forgot everything else and didn't remember again until the pain tugged on the tether now binding her remorselessly, inescapably to the body on the bed.

Her body, ripped up by chunks of enemy metal, racked by injury and infection and malnutrition and exhaustion. Her body, unwilling to give up but incapable of sustaining wakefulness for more than a few minutes at a time.

"Jamie."

The sound of her name emerged out of soft, soothing murmurs and a delicate stroking of her cheek that brushed away images of Arnoldt lying dead in a pool of blood. She wanted to respond and managed to open her eyes. But the world had become too white, too glaring. Her eyes closed again.

"Hey, Jamie, welcome to Okinawa."

She heard the cautious elation in the voice and persuaded her eyes toward the sound, trying to focus. Eventually, Lynn Hillinger's face floated into view, tearful and smiling and so, so worried.

Jamie attempted to smile too through the escalating discomfort. "Sti' here?"

"Sure am."

"Mmm," Jamie gnashed, her eyes closing against the scald throbbing larger, faster, growing more and more shrill. She didn't want to succumb to it yet. Not yet. "Mmm. Swamp's got gators, y'know." She open her eyes again but slid away from Lynn's face, away from Lynn's soft, sweet scent, into the clemency of unconsciousness.

❖

"No, the docs haven't decided…In a day or two probably… What?…Absolutely not. If I see even one reporter, Springer, you are dead meat."

Though it was muffled, Jamie recognized who was speaking. And then the pain returned, but maybe not so much as— *As before? When I saw— Nah, must've dreamed it. Might still be dreaming.*

"Uh-huh. Mid-air refueling, so we'll do the straight nine-thousand-whatever miles to the East Coast…No, I'll stay in DC for a bit to make sure everything's okay…Yeah, Rebecca said she'll meet the plane."

Sounds so real. Opening her eyes, Jamie gingerly shifted her head toward the sound. *Looks real, too.* A woman stood turned away from her, facing a bed that exhibited the rumpled signs of occupation. Jamie blinked at the bed, trying to understand what it meant while she contemplated the woman. *It's true. That's Lynn!*

"Yes, good," Lynn told the comlink with a concluding tone. "Thank you, Springer. I'll talk to you in a couple hours. Bye."

And then Lynn's shoulders slumped slightly as she tossed the comlink onto the other bed. *Oh. Oh wow. She's been staying in here. With me.* Jamie could almost taste the abiding comfort of it.

"Sti' hanging wi' us jarhezz, huh?"

"Jamie!" Lynn spun around, her face in a broad grin, and stepped quickly to the bedrail. "How do you feel?"

"'Kay. Dunn hur' so mush." But the pain circled back toward her, taking aim. Jamie's eyes shut. Trying to kick and squirm out of her body made it worse, so she forced herself to lie motionless, to think only about breathing. *Wait! Why is Lynn here?* "You…" Jamie battled to get her eyes open, to find out. "Wha' 'bou' you? You 'kay?"

"Shh. Don't worry. I'm fine. Not a scratch." The way Lynn stroked her head was so familiar, made her feel so safe. "You just rest now, Jamie. I'll be here when you wake up."

❖

"Fuckih pharma."

Jamie would have screamed if she could have screamed. Every cell in her body roiled and shrieked. She was nauseous, dizzy, caught upside down in a vast, surreal spider web of images and impressions, able to form one thought only: *Gotta try again.*

She sent the fingers of her left hand crawling toward the needle in her right forearm. It was difficult work. The wound in her left arm was all wrapped up, and her fingers were thick and stiff.

"Fuckih pharma."

They were shooting it into her right arm on purpose, no doubt. Because getting her left hand over there to pull out the goddamn needle was really hard. But she was making progress this time. Her left hand had shinnied all the way to the middle of her belly. Now came the tough part, where she had to stretch and reach…

"At it again, Jamie?"

The wavering image of an older woman with curly red hair loomed. The woman gently placed Jamie's left arm at her side, then held her wrist, taking her pulse.

Wearing civvies. Not a nurse—maybe a doc. Jamie decided to complain. "Fuckih pharma."

"Yeah, yeah. This fucking pharma's the only reason you didn't have to be scraped off the ceiling."

"Doe nee yih."

"Yes. You. Do. Now behave. You promised Lynn you wouldn't make the nurses put you in restraints again, remember?"

Jamie tried to pull her arm from the woman's grip. The woman held on.

"Come on, Jamie. You remember."

"Lynn."

"That's right, and she's due back any minute."

"Plane?"

"No, she's just down the road at the Capitol."

"Plane," Jamie repeated, closing her eyes, trying to shuffle a jumble of faintly remembered sights and sounds into meaning. It seemed to make sense for a moment before she slipped into sleep.

❖

"Hey there," Lynn said the next time Jamie's eyes managed to open.

"Lynn." Jamie smiled, a surge of warmth filling her chest and spreading across her shoulders. "Still here."

"Of course I'm still here." Lynn leaned over her and kissed her forehead, then stroked her cheek. "You look a lot better. Not so pale. Rebecca says you're a fast healer."

Jamie exhaled with a small, delicious tremor at Lynn's gentle kiss, always on her forehead, followed by the salving touch that began with Lynn's fingers combing back her hair, then the palm of Lynn's hand slipping smooth and soft along her cheek and jaw. This greeting had become a ritual her body craved, though it was almost entirely lost to her memory. Just as Jamie concluded this, she registered the name Lynn had spoken: Rebecca.

"Your Rebecca?"

"Yep. She said you still seemed a little disoriented and thought your pain meds should be adjusted." Lynn pulled a chair closer to Jamie's bed. "Seems to have helped—"

"She's seen me?"

"Several times. I would've introduced you yesterday, but you were asleep when I got here."

"The woman with the red hair."

"That's her."

Jamie felt her face heat with embarrassment. "I thought she was a doc."

"She is." Lynn shifted her weight in the chair and suppressed a smile. "I couldn't bring you to her, so I had to get her to come to you, which wasn't hard. She wants to thank you."

"Me? Why?"

"For showing up the Pentagon's best intel wonks, who were convinced that I'd been grabbed by the PIA. They told Rebecca it was all over but the gruesome execution video and the crying. Now she's made me promise to never travel alone again."

"She didn't want you to go to the Palawan, huh?"

"No, she sure didn't."

"Reamed you when you came back."

"Oh my yes. She reamed me. Our daughters reamed me. My chief of staff reamed me. Ben Embry reamed me. Even Rebecca's unflappable mother reamed me." Lynn laughed softly. "And it all felt wonderful."

"In that case, I'd join in. If I wasn't so zonked." Jamie eyed the IV bag dangling above her with suspicion. "Fucking pharma."

"The docs have had a tough time figuring out dosage for you that didn't send you into la-la land. Rebecca says you're hypersensitive. But I'm not sure you would've gotten through the trip home without—"

"Home?"

"Well, almost."

"I don't actually have a—" Jamie tried to push herself up. "Where am I?"

Lynn's hand on Jamie's right shoulder, one of the few places that didn't hurt, stopped her. "This is the Eisenhower National Military Medical Center. Just outside Washington. I'm sorry. You seemed pretty aware. I thought you remembered."

Jamie's eyes closed. "Yeah, I-I do remember." When she opened her eyes, she didn't try to stop the tears in them from rolling down her cheeks. "You. You came back on the hospital plane with me. You held my hand."

Lynn leaned closer and took Jamie's hand again. "Yes. I did."

❖

Jamie began to sweat with the effort of lifting her head and shoulders off the pillow. She hadn't expected to wake up to the sight of a major general just standing there next to her bed all by himself like a regular person.

"Easy does it, Jamie," said Ben Embry.

"Sir," she managed finally, trying not to hyperventilate.

"The docs say you're doing better now. You've got only a couple of surgeries left to go, they tell me."

"Yessir."

"I just wanted to come by and thank you for what you did out there, Lieutenant. And I, uh, want to say that I'm sorry for not giving you what you asked me for. I should have."

"Yessir."

"I've recommended you for the Medal of Honor for getting all those people out of that prison camp. You've also been awarded the Navy Cross for your contribution to Operation Repo last November. There at the end, when you bailed out the guys from the recon unit who couldn't make it onto the helos."

Jamie's pulse had elevated as Embry spoke. By the time he finished, the machines monitoring her had started beeping and tooting.

"Sir," she wheezed. "I respectfully decline the awards." That seemed to get the machines to calm down some. Certainly it made breathing easier. A nurse came in anyway to check things out, but left as fast as she could after seeing the two stars on Embry's uniform.

"May I ask why?" Embry asked when the nurse closed the door behind her.

"For personal reasons, sir."

"Is it because of Lieutenant Sherman? I'm told you'd never lost anyone until he was—"

"Please, sir." Jamie felt her eyes heat up before she shut them. "It's personal. I-I can't…"

Jamie meant to open her eyes again in a second or two, once the whirling in her head subsided. Just a few breaths, just a few seconds, and she'd be able to deal with him again. When her eyes opened, though, the light had changed and Embry was gone. Lynn Hillinger stood next to the bedrail gazing at her.

"What happened? Where'd he go? Oh jeezus, what time is it?"

"You faded." Lynn touched Jamie's cheek reassuringly. "God, Ben can be so damn bullheaded. I asked him to wait 'til I got here before he talked to you, but obviously he had other ideas."

"Christ, he'll hang me by my toes now."

"Oh no, he won't. He's as humbled as I've ever seen him. And I met him in high school." Lynn sat and rested her arms on the bedrail. "He said you turned down the Navy Cross."

Jamie nodded, shifting her eyes away from Lynn. "I, uh—I don't believe in medals."

"You asked Major Donato to put in for all sorts of medals for the Saint Eh Mo's people."

"I don't believe in medals for me." Jamie returned her eyes to Lynn. "I'd like to give back the ones I've got. Can I do that?"

Lynn reached across the bedrail for Jamie's hand; she so obviously wanted to ask why, but she didn't. "I don't know," she said instead, and then had the grace to change the subject. "But I do know there's someone else who'd—" Lynn turned around in response to a subdued knock. "Ah, here she is now."

"Come in, North Carolina," Jamie said when she saw the corpsman hesitating in the doorway. "How're you doing?"

"I'm real good, ma'am. How about you? I looked in on you a few times, but you were sleeping. We've all been real worried."

"I'm doing okay," Jamie said. "Getting better every day. Sorry I was out of it when you came by."

North Carolina shuffled bashfully. "I'm being released today. I-I just wanted to say I'm real proud to have served with you, LT ma'am."

Jamie smiled. "You did a fine job, Cordelia. You're one of the best."

A blush rose to North Carolina's cheeks.

"Going home, right?"

North Carolina nodded.

"Anybody special there?"

Grinning, she nodded again. "James Edward Barr, Junior. We're gonna get married and make babies—" North Carolina put her hand to her mouth apologetically. "Uh—"

"It's okay." Jamie kept her own hand from touching the bandage over the four-inch incision low on her belly, kept her mind from thinking about the justice meted out by that fifth wound. "Still got the oves. And if I want babies, I can always adopt some of your extras."

North Carolina giggled. "I'm—I'm gonna miss you, LT ma'am."

"Better to miss me than miss James Edward Barr, Junior, huh?"

"Yeah, guess so."

"I won't forget you, North Carolina." Jamie raised her right hand and offered a high-five. "Good luck."

North Carolina gave Jamie's hand a dainty pat. "You too, LT ma'am."

CHAPTER THIRTY-TWO

I DON'T WANT YOUR LIFE TO END

Thursday, July 25, and for the eighth day in a row Jamie managed to get out of bed unaided. Just six days left. *Hey, I'm counting. Must be feeling better.* Time to push a little; she wanted to finish before Lynn showed up.

Almost every weekday, Lynn visited her. It was the way Jamie secretly measured time. *How many days left 'til it's just me and my shadow again.*

Jamie didn't understand why Lynn still came by, but didn't ask. Asking might jinx it. Besides, it'd be over soon enough, once the Corps shipped her off to one of those rehab places for loners like her. Just six days. How strong would it be by then, this hollow, ethereal stutter between her and the world she inhabited? Like she was always a half-step late. *Like I'm not really supposed to be here.*

But she *was* here. Stuck with herself.

Pressing the incision in her belly with one hand to contain the ache there, relying on a cane to ease the pain in her right thigh, she hobbled from her bed all the way to the far end of the long hallway outside her room and then back. For a few seconds at the end of her journey, she felt almost free of the stutter, so she repeated the effort before she cautiously inched herself into bed and dropped into depleted sleep.

On Friday, Jamie took to the hallway again. *Four laps today. Maybe five.*

On the fourth perambulation, roughly three hundred paces from her room, she turned around and found herself face-to-face with Martina Rhys.

"Marty!" she called when she realized Rhys didn't recognize her and was about to walk right on by.

Rhys halted, her expression veering from surprise to shock. "Jamie!" Her voice softened to a hush. "Hi."

Jamie limped into Rhys's gentle grasp, let her head lower onto Rhys's shoulder.

"You okay?" Rhys asked after a long moment. "Need to sit down?"

"Nah," Jamie exhaled, lifting her head. "I'm just a little tired." She gestured toward the silver bar gracing the collar of Rhys's service uniform and grinned. "Nice going, *First* Lieutenant."

"Got coyoted after you, uh—" Rhys scrunched her shoulders apologetically.

"You sure as hell earned that. Come on, walk me to my room and tell me how you're doing." After she'd broken free of the pharma, Jamie had asked around about the Three-Eight snipe platoon and heard Marty had gotten the coyote promotion. At last Marty, too, had crossed the Rubicon and they were equals. Jamie waited for the old fantasy of a life with her first love to percolate, waited for her clit to punch that double flip.

But it never happened. Something had changed.

Now Jamie glanced at Rhys and tried to understand what was different. In her service greens, silver bar on her collar, ribbons on her chest, a tan making her hair blonder than ever, Rhys looked magnificent. *No wonder I was in love with you.*

When had Rhys become past tense? Where was the Instant, the still point that defined this Before and After? Jamie recalled Way Before—so easy to see now in the Undeniable After—and as the flashes of their moments together played across her mind's eye, she recognized the slow, doomed descent of a failed flight she had tried to save from its inevitable crash. Yet she had missed the actual impact, the end of hope. Where had she been? Shooting an innocent child? Mewling in Shoo Juh's concrete tomb? Maybe it was earlier, at the top of Thumb Peak when Embry's hand gripped her shoulder and she knew she'd give in and let him make her a one-lite. Or earlier yet, much earlier, when Rhys's face, Rhys's voice couldn't hide how much it hurt to be outshot by Jamie Gwynmorgan.

For a disorienting moment, the stutter caught her; Jamie gaped into its immense empty chasm and faltered. *Each instant bears a still point, dimensionless in one plane and infinite in another, surrounded by arcs of before and after. And where am I? What world is this now?* If she hadn't been holding on to Rhys's arm, she would have toppled over.

Rhys didn't notice. While they slowly progressed down the hall, Rhys talked—about how the Three-Eight snipes ended up in the Palawan until February but managed to come home without any KIAs, about what it felt like to be an officer, about how she'd be going to The Basic School next, then to college and intel school. Her chatter became a sort of fixed point on which Jamie focused to keep the vertigo at bay, like an ice skater coming out of a scratch spin.

Listen. Leaning into Rhys, Jamie heard disquiet and couldn't figure out which of them it came from. Jamie waited. Did Rhys want to say something else, something more? It spilled out, finally, after she helped Jamie into bed.

"I'm getting married." Rhys gave Jamie a sideways glance.

Did she just say—? "What? You're—?"

"Getting married." Rhys smiled, her face an artless, fitful mix of euphoria and guilt.

"Getting married," Jamie echoed. "Who?"

"I'm gonna marry Angara Bulanadi."

Jamie gaped; she could not speak. Her head had become heavy, too heavy to hold up anymore, and she yielded it to the pillow, unable to cease staring at Rhys.

Venturing into Jamie's stillness, Rhys tried to explain. "That day— That day when Angara—When she didn't shoot you…"

Rhys's voice trailed off for a moment while she repositioned herself, planting her feet as though she stood at parade rest. "You were out of your mind, you know. Only reason I went with you was so I could keep you from—from doing what you did. I don't know why I didn't just step up and grab the pistol out of Angara's hand." Rhys sighed. "There was something about her. The rage. She looked like a monster out of a horror movie. When she put that muzzle right to your head, I was sure she was gonna zap you."

"I remember," Jamie said, letting her eyes close as the ache in her gut deepened.

"But I couldn't fucking move. I just couldn't think, couldn't act. Everything froze and—and I just stared at her, you know? Stuck. And then I saw her—god, Jamie, she became someone else. It happened right in front of me. Sadness first, and acceptance—and then I saw her forgive you." Rhys's voice cracked, and when Jamie looked, tears had filled Rhys's eyes.

"I remember."

"I'd have killed you, Jamie, if I'd been her. And when she didn't, when she said that to you—remember? 'I don't want your life to end.' You didn't see her face, Jamie. She looked at you with such compassion." Rhys's eyes swept down to the floor. "My god, I couldn't believe what I saw. It changed everything for me. Everything I used to care about, everything I ever thought—about who I should be, you know? I had to get closer to that—to comprehend it. And she let me, she actually let me. And then—"

"And then you fell in love with her."

Rhys looked up and nodded.

"Does she love you, Marty?"

"Yes." Rhys exuded quiet confidence. "She does. Unreservedly."

Jamie reached out to Rhys for what she knew would be the last time. Because Marty had gone where she could never go, not even for an instant: To the mother of the child she murdered.

Rhys took Jamie's hand, frowned at its scars. "The Corps can be a small world, you know? I wanted you to hear it from me."

"I'm gonna miss you, Marty. Miss what we had."

Rhys averted her eyes then. And Jamie understood. *No, you don't miss what you had with me. You're relieved to be rid of it. Maybe that's why you can't sit down.*

"I gotta thank you, Jamie. You showed me a lot. Not just about being a good snipe and a good leader. You were so frigging strong." Rhys rolled her shoulders like they needed respite from carrying too much, and then she finally sat. "Remember that bandanna you gave me on the plane to Oki—the red winking skull and crossbones?"

"Sure do." Jamie offered Rhys a wan smile. "My pathetic way of hoping you loved me."

"It became my—what do you call it? My talisman. And when we hooked up again later, *you*, making love to you, became my talisman. But more, too. I kept thinking making love to you would—"

"Keep you strong. Keep you alive." Jamie snorted. "We all have our superstitions."

"Yeah, well." Rhys lowered her head. "Truth is, it was way more crude than that. I wanted your skill, your instincts, your rank even. And when I couldn't keep up, when I started to hear the snarky gossip about how many times you got me a promotion— Shit, I admit it. I was fucking humiliated. But you, Jamie, you were able to be pure of heart. I'm sorry I couldn't do better by you."

"Pure?" Jamie shook her head. "But I sure as hell was horny of heart." *And god, oh god, how I wanted to love you.* "Whatever else went down, Marty, you always had my back. You kept me from suicide by PIA and Zhong more times than I can count." Jamie tried to make her smile look strong. "And you know how I like to count. We both did the best we could."

CHAPTER THIRTY-THREE

TRUST ME

"What're you doing here?" Jamie asked when Lynn approached her in the hospital hallway. "It's Sunday, isn't it?"

"It is. I stayed this weekend because the August recess starts this coming Tuesday. I have a lot to get done before we gavel out."

Jamie halted as the realization sank in. Like Rhys, Lynn had come to say good-bye. She thought she had a day or two left, a couple more chances to gaze at, talk with Lynn Hillinger. But the moment, dreaded and inevitable, had already arrived.

"I guess, uh, I won't be seeing you anymore, so I—" Jamie propped the cane against her leg and proffered her right hand. "I want to thank you, Lynn. You saved my life by coming to Saint Eh Mo's, by sticking around when the other Red Cross people left. And you've been really kind to me...all this time. I-I'll miss you."

Lynn took the hand she'd been offered in both of hers. "You don't have to do it this way, Jamie."

"Do what?"

"Go from here to the rehab facility down at Quantico when they release you next week."

"You know about that?"

"Come home with me on Wednesday. I've talked to everyone and it's unanimous: They're waiting for both of us. I've cleared it on this end, too. You've got six months of convalescence leave."

"Go with you?" Jamie gawked. *This can't be right.* "You mean—? To your—?" *But there's that slow, you-better-damn-well-believe-it nod of hers.*

"Yes. Come home with me."

"I don't know. I-I'm really fucked up."

"I know it'll be a long road back for you—"

"You don't understand. I mean I'm *really* fucked up." Jamie took a half-step away from Lynn. "I've done things you don't know anything about, awful things... You don't understand."

"I *do* understand."

"How can you possibly understand?" Jamie backed up another step. "If I told you, you'd be horrified, you'd—"

"No, I wouldn't—"

"Christ, Lynn, what I've done would be criminal if I was a civilian."

"Stop, Jamie." Lynn stepped closer. "You're not a criminal."

"I am, actually. I can give you references if you like."

"Angara Bulanadi?"

Jamie lost her balance and needed Lynn's help to make it to a nearby chair. Gulping for air that refused to enter her lungs, she stared her question at Lynn. *How do you know?*

"I met her last Friday, downstairs in the main lobby." Lynn ran the palm of her hand lightly across Jamie's back. "Marty, too. I heard them asking at reception for directions to your room, so I introduced myself."

"I-I didn't realize...Angara came with her..." Jamie rasped as the periphery of her vision went dark, like someone she couldn't see was pouring heavy black ink onto a watery surface. Her own words echoed thin and tenuous in her ears. "So you know...about...what I did?"

"I know it wasn't your fault," Lynn replied quietly. "I know if you'd done anything differently, if you'd waited even one extra nanosecond, they'd *all* be dead now, not just one of them."

This generosity gave Jamie no solace. "Awa was only six years old."

"Which is why she can never be blamed for the terrible, tragic mistake she made when she panicked and ran in front of—"

"Shoulda targeted his head. She'd have been all right if I'd just given it one extra nanosecond and—"

"There was no time. You had to take the quickest shot," Lynn reminded her. "Angara knows this. She's the one who told me."

Jamie's eyes snapped to Lynn's face. "She did?"

Lynn nodded. "While Marty went up to see you. We talked for

quite a while. Seeing you would've been too painful, so she decided to stay downstairs. But Angara doesn't blame you, Jamie. It was a horrible moment. She said she thought she and the girls were already dead, that they'd be executed *right then*. She believes she and her other two daughters are alive only because of you. She also said you gave her back her soul when you offered her your life. And, of course, you brought her Marty."

Jamie stared at the floor. *A still point, dimensionless in one plane and infinite in another.* "There's more, Lynn."

Lynn didn't hesitate. "I have no doubt there's a great deal more. And you sure as hell shouldn't face it all by yourself. Come home with me on Wednesday."

Lagging a stutter step behind, Jamie searched Lynn's face. "Why are you doing this?"

"Because while you were saving my life—"

"No." Jamie closed her eyes and shook her head. "No."

"Don't waste your breath with that 'it's supposed to hurt' crap, kiddo. My point is that I got to see *you*, Jamie." A tiny wobble inflected Lynn's voice as she finished. "Just like you got to see me."

Jamie looked over at her. "I did, didn't I?"

"Oh yes. And it creates a bond when you see another human being that way. Unveiled. We share something now. Something important."

"I don't want to talk about the Palawan."

"Yeah, well, it's not my favorite subject either." Lynn's eyes swept away from Jamie and she slumped a little. "I screwed up badly. I'm still finding out how badly." She sighed and shook her head. Then she straightened, her gaze returning to Jamie. "But if I just walk away, go on with my life like nothing happened, I dishonor what you did. I dishonor our bond."

"Better off to leave the past behind, to forget about it."

"So why'd you say you'll miss me?"

"I—Because—"

Lynn gave Jamie's forearm an affectionate squeeze. "Maybe because we've become friends, even though you're a kid and I have crow's feet?"

"Even though I'm a fucked-up gimpy stray and you have issues with wishful thinking?"

"Okay, I'll deal with that. Terms of friendship accepted."

"What about Rebecca? What's she think about you wanting to bring home a fucked-up gimpy stray?"

Lynn's hand formed a thumbs-up. "Rebecca's quite convinced you can come back one hundred percent from—" Lynn faltered for a heartbeat. "From your wounds, Saint Eh Mo's, all of it. She says it'll be easier to monitor your medical progress if you're under the same roof. And give her a chance to pick up some tricks from the only person who's ever persuaded me to go camping."

Jamie managed a wan smile, but her chest ached. "Lynn—" *You make it sound so easy.* "What if you—Or if I—" *Oh god oh god...*

Lynn leaned toward Jamie and gentled a kiss onto her forehead. "I know it's not easy. Believe me, I do know." Then Lynn's fingers combed back her hair and the palm of Lynn's hand caressed her cheek. "Trust me, Jamie, like I trusted you. Trust me and say yes."

About the Author

Born and raised in the Midwest, Sophia Kell Hagin escaped to Massachusetts and eventually got a job in IT market research and publishing. For the last twenty-five years, Sophia has earned a living as a self-employed IT market analyst and writer.

Although she has been writing fiction for a number of years, *Whatever Gods May Be* is Sophia's first published novel. A selection of her other writings can be found at her Web site, www.callithump.com. Sophia lives on outer Cape Cod with her longtime life, love, and business partner.

Books Available From Bold Strokes Books

Whatever Gods May Be by Sophia Kell Hagin. Army sniper Jamie Gwynmorgan expects to fight hard for her country and her future. What she never expects is to find love. (978-1-60282-183-5)

nevermore by Nell Stark and Trinity Tam. In this sequel to everafter, Vampire Valentine Darrow and Were Alexa Newland confront a mysterious disease that ravages the shifter population of New York City. (978-1-60282-184-2)

Playing the Player by Lea Santos. Grace Obregon is beautiful, vulnerable, and exactly the kind of woman Madeira Pacias usually avoids, but when Madeira rescues Grace from a traffic accident, escape is impossible. (978-1-60282-185-9)

Midnight Whispers: The Blake Danzig Chronicles by Curtis Christopher Comer. Paranormal investigator Blake Danzig, star of the syndicated show Haunted California and owner of Danzig Paranormal Investigations, has been able to see and talk to the dead since he was a small boy, but when he gets too close to a psychotic spirit, all hell breaks loose. (978-1-60282-186-6)

The Long Way Home by Rachel Spangler. They say you can't go home again, but Raine St. James doesn't know why anyone would want to. When she is forced to accept a job in the town she's been publicly bashing for the last decade, she has to face down old hurts and the woman she left behind. (978-1-60282-178-1)

Water Mark by J.M. Redmann. PI Micky Knight's professional and personal lives are torn asunder by Katrina and its aftermath. She needs to solve a murder and recapture the woman she lost—while struggling to simply survive in a world gone mad. (978-1-60282-179-8)

Picture Imperfect by Lea Santos. Young love doesn't always stand the test of time, but Deanne is determined to get her marriage to childhood sweetheart Paloma back on the road to happily ever after, by way of Memory Lane-and Lover's Lane. (978-1-60282-180-4)